THE FOURTH LARGEST IN LATVIA

✶✶✶✶

Mike Collier

First published (in Latvian) 2014 by Apgads Mansards, Riga.
This English edition published 2017 by Baltic Features.

© Michael John Collier 2014, 2017

Contact for rights and republishing queries:
mikskoljers@inbox.lv

For Eva

CONTENTS

I	The Capital Of Estonia	1
II	Breakfast Bacon	4
III	An Early Mistake	11
IV	A Memorable Address	17
V	The Capital Of Latvia	21
VI	A Train From Tornakalns	24
VII	North By Northeast	36
VIII	The Non-Guest House	45
IX	A Thrashing	58
X	Life At The Summit	65
XI	A Hero Of Our Time	75
XII	An Inspector Departs	82
XIII	Deep In The Woods	87
XIV	Gretel's Cottage	92
XV	The Patriot	106
XVI	A Stiff Upper Lip	120
XVII	The Stags	131
XVIII	The Helpful Mr. Smith	141
XIX	An Expert Again	147
XX	The Third Largest Rock	156
XXI	The Second Largest Rock	163
XXII	Sea Salt	167
XXIII	A Plan	176
XXIV	A New Dawn In V---	182
XXV	Two Birds With One Stone	190
XXVI	The Leaving Of Latvia	195

I   THE CAPITAL OF ESTONIA

Certainly he was in pain, though probably not quite as much pain as his grimace suggested. His cheeks were red and puffed out, his brow furrowed, with a light coating of perspiration and his lips disappeared inwards to be lost in the undergrowth of his beard. His face collapsed in a second contortion, such as might be seen in some depiction of an unfortunate pagan being persuaded into the Christian fold by crusading knights with the aid of red-hot pincers and a large wooden mallet.

Then the moment of relief – Viktor Draaks' bleary eyes opened wide, the lips re-emerged from the tangled forest of facial hair and the brow became becalmed. He let out a long, beatific sigh, the end of which was drowned out by the unexpected flushing of the chain courtesy of what must have been a sensor somewhere in the toilet bowl. Such are the features that win a hotel five stars. The rush of water gave Viktor a nasty surprise and he staggered to his feet in Simian pose, legs slightly bent and arms reaching down to pull up his shorts.

As hotel bathrooms went, this was not a bad one, Viktor acknowledged as he peered into the mirror. The bath looked large enough even for his considerable girth, the floor was warm beneath his feet and the complimentary toiletries had such tiny labels on them that they must be expensive. There was even a make-up mirror on a flexible stalk, in which the central glass was surrounded by a circular corona of bright light, like a miniature version of the array in an operating theatre. He leaned toward it, gaining a magnified vision of his luxuriant nose hair in the process. He pulled at a couple of the pioneering follicles but when he realised how painful they were to remove this way, quickly abandoned the stratagem and faced himself, naked in the full length mirror.

At least his flesh still looked elastic, even if that very quality was being tested by a fair amount of excess flab. Viktor had been born with a clumsy but robust frame. He looked stronger than he was, as if somewhere deep within him he should possess the earthy strength of peasant forebears. But years of study and an academic career had seen that seed of vigour slowly dry and shrink while the husk looked unchanged. Perhaps it was not yet dead, but it seemed unlikely it would ever emerge again now that he was into the middle of middle age. Nevertheless there remained something distinctly bearish about Viktor's appearance – an irony, as others had noted – and the impression was reinforced as he emitted a low-pitched growl and scowled briefly.

The growl was a subconscious phenomenon of which he remained unaware, though it certainly had not escaped the notice of others. The scowl was to check his complexion. The wrinkles around his eyes and the corners of his mouth were quite distinguished, he noted with satisfaction. He felt himself to be a "character" and characters needed a characterful face and a characterful presence. Viktor certainly had both, though like the bearish growl, perhaps his idea of his character did not always tally with the one his acquaintances would whisper about.

He slapped his belly, which was hairy at the sides and bald in the middle as if his navel was a well in a forest clearing. It wobbled in a troubled manner for a couple of seconds. Viktor stood on his tiptoes, then rocked back on his heels. A ripple ran down his belly from top to bottom, then bounced halfway back again.

Was he putting on weight? Hard to tell. Different mirrors give different verdicts and Viktor looked in so many different mirrors in so many different hotels it was impossible to maintain a very precise idea of his own physical appearance. He consoled himself with the thought that in all probability this was a particularly unflattering mirror and that he was still a bit puffed up after the flight from Belgrade. He sucked his belly in and stood in profile. It could have been worse. Air travel always promoted certain biliousness and it was inflicted on him just as frequently as these blasted mirrors. If he ate a little more healthily and took a little more exercise, it could make a great deal of difference. He toyed with the idea in a half-hearted way as he dressed. All it would take was the odd visit to the swimming pool or an unaccompanied ramble through the streets of whichever town he happened to be in.

It would be simple enough to limit oneself to a single glass of wine – two at most – and opt for the fruit salad instead of the sorbet. He was not a bad-looking man underneath, and his features possessed a certain interest that was preferable to youth or prettiness. Much as he hated to admit it, on the circuit these days appearance seemed to matter more than it did ten or fifteen years ago. The nice-looking speakers increasingly got invitations to events that their mental abilities barely merited.

On the flight from Belgrade he'd noticed as he read the in-flight magazine that something similar seemed to have happened in the world of classical music. Flicking through the pages, he had skim-read the blather about which were the best restaurants in various destinations, confident that he would visit them all eventually, and had briefly been amused by an advertisement of hopeless naivety attempting to lure tourists to a Latvian town significant only for its gas terminal but whose smiling mayor suggested would be worth a visit on account of a local breed of purple pigs, a sports centre, an over-restored castle and a few middling-sized boulders that were supposedly of deep significance.

Then, on the opposite page, he saw a review of a new recording of Schubert's Trout Quintet. He knew nothing much about the genre but recalled that in his student days he had owned a copy of the work which he had played on an old gramophone as he worked through the night on his theses, to mask the sound of people walking past the window of his ground-floor digs and the slurred shouts of fellow students reverberating through the quadrangles as they returned from a long night out.

He could still see the cover of his record – a detail from a nineteenth-century painting of the eponymous fish that he had liked despite its essential incompetence and appalling print quality. In tiny letters beneath the sleeve notes it was revealed that the image came from a painting by a minor Slovene artist and was now part of the collection of the Yugoslav National Gallery. It had amused him, as he sat writing about the politics of Central and Eastern Europe, to think of the tides of history washing back and forth over this Austro-Hungarian trout, the great empire withering and vanishing, the rise of national movements, the wars, revolutions and the formation of new empires like Yugoslavia. It would have amused him even more had he seen his fishy old familiar on the front of this new recording of the Trout Quintet as his airliner flew over Mount Triglav, symbol of an independent Slovenia, while Yugoslavia was now, like Austria-Hungary, less substantial than the shadow the plane cast over the Julian Alps.

Instead, the Trout Quintet was now represented by a photograph of a young pianist of decidedly untrouty appearance. Posing coquettishly next to a piece of repro-Roman statuary and playing with her long scarf as if it had just told her an hilarious anecdote, the young Romanian looked like she modelled for catalogues between movements and probably ate sushi from the lid of her Steinway, which might provide an unconventional link to the trout. Perhaps she was as good as the review said. Perhaps the player who had recorded Viktor's old disc had looked like this, too. But it seemed highly unlikely.

II   BREAKFAST BACON

Viktor never felt truly hungry until he arrived in the breakfast room. There his half-hearted conceptions of fruit salad and Greek yoghurt would be immediately overpowered by the smell of bacon, a drug he had taken up first during his years at Cambridge. Bacon remained one of several Anglophile affectations Viktor retained along with the battered Harris Tweed jacket he used to project an air of the Donnish academician and his habit of pushing his horn-rimmed, half-moon reading spectacles onto his forehead – an apparently casual trait that in fact had been copied from an eminent tutor and practised in front of a more flattering university mirror than the one in his hotel room.

He had even tried to cultivate an appreciation of dry London gin in its pink, sloe and tonicked guises, despite a general aversion to alcohol. He hadn't actually bought one since graduation and despite his best efforts to acclimatise himself to the stuff, never really enjoyed it, but still found himself requesting a gin and tonic when asked at rooftop receptions in Varna, Athens or Dubrovnik.

For all his cerebellum's determined Atlanticism, his liver remained annoyingly in thrall to the vodka of his origins somewhere between the Carpathian and Caucasus mountains. But he avoided vodka at all costs – it inflamed his blood and his passions to such an extent that the merest sniff could see him parting ways with the Enlightenment and descending into the sort of silly irrationality that he loathed. The idea of intentionally blunting one's intellect and capacity for serious thought appalled him almost a much as the suspicion that drinking vodka was a kind of tacit approval of Russia and Russian-ness.

As well as the pleasant memories of Albion provoked by bacon, breakfast brought with it a less enjoyable experience. Pavel Panchev was sitting at one of the better tables, over by the window which framed a handsome view of Tallinn's cold spires. If the mere fact of his presence was not bad enough, directly opposite Panchev was what appeared to be the only free place in the breakfast room neither occupied nor rendered inaccessible by abandoned bread rolls and muesli bowls.

Draaks double-checked the room as he swayed beside the cutlery, bacon in one hand, coffee in the other. There was one other free place after all, in a gloomy corner barely out of blast range of the swing doors to the kitchen – but it was at a table beside a Chinaman. Land of opportunity and an increasingly lucrative lecturing venue it might be, but if Viktor had learned one thing during his years of political proselytizing, it was to be wary of breakfasting with Chinamen. The way they smiled pleasantly and asked pertinent questions over boiled eggs was always highly suspicious, giving the impression that they weren't particularly interested in breakfast at all.

Besides, by now Panchev had seen him... he might even have registered his indecision, which could not be allowed to happen. He must not be allowed to think Draaks was avoiding him. That would be a form of backhanded compliment, confirming that Panchev was some sort of threat and therefore an equal.

Their eyes locked briefly, Draaks doing his best to remain poker-faced as he scrutinised Panchov's remarkably dark eyes and the lick of equally dark hair that flopped to one side of his brow. He would brush it aside every few minutes during his presentations, a habit which Viktor found infuriating, not least because of the unattractiveness of his own russet-coloured topping. Combined with a complexion that managed to be both Mediterranean and pale at the same time, Panchev could have been mistaken for a Central Asian diplomat or perhaps one of the minor, youthful Roman emperors who didn't last long before being intrigued to an early grave by a wily Senator. Viktor had a lot of respect for the Roman Republic and counted a love of Cicero as another of his Cambridge-obtained vices.

In fact Panchev was half-Slovak, half-Hungarian with a Georgian grandmother, allowing him to switch annoyingly between Slavic, Finno-Ugric and Caucasian identities according to the audience he was addressing or the subject under discussion. It won him a lot of invitations – considerably more than he deserved, in Viktor's estimation. His fortunate genetic inheritance, youth, good looks and generally suave manner hid a second-rate mind that valued a quip over an insight. He would have looked perfectly at home next to the pianist on the cover of the Trout Quintet. People would have pointed at them in the street and said what a delightful couple they made.

In Finno-Ugric Tallinn, Panchev would certainly open his remarks with a weak joke about having distant relatives among the audience. This schoolboy obviousness made Viktor smile as he sat down opposite his adversary, removing any suggestion of tension from his demeanour. Even so, it would be fair to say that Viktor Draaks had a distinct aversion to Pavel Panchev.

"Good morning, Paul," Viktor said, Anglicising the name for fun.

Panchev appeared not to mind. "Good morning, professor," he replied. "Please do join me, though I have almost finished."

Viktor decided to let Panchev do the talking if there needed to be any conversation. There was nothing to learn from such an individual.

"I didn't dare to expect you would honour us with your presence here," Panchev said with what may or may not have been a note of sarcasm. "I didn't see you at the welcome reception last night?"

"My flight arrived late," growled Draaks, "Very late. Then there were some important calls I had to make to the 'States." This was a lie. Though the flight had arrived at approaching midnight, Viktor had gone straight to bed after taking a couple of sleeping pills.

Disrupted sleep patterns was just one of the inconveniences heaped upon the worthy heads of real circuit members – admittedly in exchange for conveniences of substantially greater size. Shuttling from one end of the continent to the other, twice a week didn't produce the classical jet lag associated with intercontinental travel but a sort of diluted, domestic version of the same that expressed itself not in a sudden time disjunction but a more insidious, creeping feeling – a sort of personal annoyance with the apparent indecision of clocks. It was as if time was a car with slipping gears and an owner too miserly to take it to the garage.

The symptoms were the same as with most other creeping ailments: irritability, biliousness, night sweats and sudden fatigues. Extended over many years, the cumulative effect had contributed greatly to producing the modern Viktor Draaks. He had held out as long as he could but eventually, as a result of a recommendation by another long-serving member of the circuit, Viktor had taken recourse to pharmaceutical measures to help his ongoing skirmish with Eastern Europe's time zones. He had been reluctant to do so until he noticed how his colleague's presentations gained some definite zest after some well-timed medication. So Viktor had followed suit, doubling up on the monthly prescription from a Czech pharmacist who could be relied upon to provide blue pills that would usher one into the arms of Morpheus and red ones to sharpen the edges of one's intellect in a discreet and reliable manner.

"I was coming directly from the Balkan Security Summit in Belgrade," Viktor continued, seeing an opportunity to put Panchev in his place. "You should have been there, Paul. Some really first-rate, clear-headed thinking, particularly on energy. It was the inaugural event, of course, but I think in future it might develop into something of real regional significance. We gave it a great start. I told the organisers so and they seemed excited by the reaction. In fact keep it between ourselves but they asked me to deliver a keynote next year," Viktor said between forkfuls of bacon.

"I said I would confirm in the next couple of months... if you like I will ask them to send you details of next year's event once the programme has been worked out. Or perhaps you would like me to put your name forward as a participant? They may even want you to sit in on one of the discussion panels if I suggest it – perhaps on an ethnic issue?"

"That's very kind of you, but..."

Viktor waved away Panchev's gratifyingly embarrassed protests with a bread roll.

"It would be no trouble. I must admit there were a few holes in this year's itinerary. You might usefully contribute to filling one of those holes."

"There is really no need, Professor," Panchev said, pushing his lick of black hair back from his brow.

Viktor hoped no hair had dropped onto his bacon.

"In truth Belgrade did ask me along this year but I had to turn it down as I didn't see how I could give keynotes of the required standard both there and here, so close to each other. One cannot be everywhere at once and..." At this point Panchev seemed to sense he was on the verge of implying something unflattering about Viktor doing precisely the same thing and tried to correct himself: "...I mean, not all of us have your powers of endurance." The ingratiating smile. "Perhaps this evening you would be kind enough to give me a précis of the Belgrade discussions? I'm sure they benefited greatly from having someone of your calibre there. Look, here's my room number."

He pulled out a business card far more impressive than the one supplied to Viktor by the Benbo Foundation, whose design appeared not to have been altered for thirty years. Panchev scrawled his room number on the back – Viktor couldn't help noticing it was on a higher floor than his own room – and pushed it across the table to Viktor who placed it in his breast pocket without even looking at it.

"Perhaps when you are free you could call me – I would be delighted to take you out. I'm sure no-one would notice if we slipped away and saw the sights of the city at our own pace for an hour? Now if you'll excuse me I must go and prepare..."

"For what?"

"My panel. I will be moderating the first panel – the three Baltic presidents plus the prime minister? I do need to read today's local newspapers before I take the microphone. It wouldn't do to be unaware of the latest positions of the participants."

Somewhere around the words "presidents" Viktor noticed that continental bacon was never as tasty as Cambridge bacon. It was rubbery, hard to swallow. He had not looked at the conference itinerary in any great detail. After a few years on the circuit one gains a feel for these things, and the only thing that mattered was that he was presenting on the morning of the first day, which meant he was one of the more important speakers.

They always wheeled the Prime Ministers, Presidents and other VIPs on first to say predictable things to keep the dumb oxen of the press happy, but moderating that discussion was the starring role as far as the assembled analysts, academics and experts were concerned. When he had seen Panchev, Viktor had assumed he would be presenting an obscure panel in the afternoon. This news that he was launching the entire event, dictating its tone and timbre was deeply troubling and bordering on the intolerable. It meant that he was following Panchev.

With Viktor still rapt in these revelations, Panchev put his napkin onto his side plate and placed a knife and fork carefully on top of his neatly discarded banana skins and melon rind. "Until this evening, Professor? Let's make sure we are sitting together at dinner..."

"Break a leg," Viktor mumbled.

"...and good luck yourself! Enjoy your time in Riga!" Panchev called over his shoulder as he headed for the lift.

He was following Panchev. Outrageous! It seemed to mark some significant shift in their relationship – indeed in Viktor's relationship with the whole world of geopolitical scholarship. A second-rate mind like Panchev leading a prestigious international conference? It must be an error. A silly error by the organisers who had confused Panchev with someone else. Yet they had made the same mistake in Belgrade... Rather than continue this train of thought, which was making his head swim, Viktor decided to return to his room and prepare for his own panel discussion. It would be infinitely better than Panchev's. It would show him up for the hollow charlatan he was, it would throw into sharp relief his rather obvious interpretation of...

His mind changed gears suddenly. What had he called over his shoulder? "Enjoy Riga?" Viktor looked out of the broad glass windows at the skyline of spires and rooftops. It appeared that Tallinn was Riga after all.

Confusing Berlin and Paris would have been a cause for concern, but mixing up these two Baltic capitals was understandable. They didn't look at all similar, but in geopolitical terms these were lands that didn't really matter, at best narrow buffer zones between the real centres of power. It was a provocative thought with which he was pleased. He could throw it at his audience as his opening gambit – and it would certainly get their attention, then he could cleverly expostulate the reasons why despite "not mattering" they could be made to "matter" in a really very significant way.

He was so pleased he decided to have one more rasher and set off for the steaming hot-trays in pursuit of satisfaction. By the time he had placed more bacon on one plate and more toast on another – there being no room for it on the meat platter – and returned to his table his seat had been usurped by a small, dapper little man dressed in a blue blazer with polished buttons, grey slacks and a white shirt set off by a bright yellow patterned cravat. All he required was a peaked cap with an anchor to look the part of a Greek shipping tycoon about to take the helm of his luxury yacht.

Viktor towered over the nautical midget and harrumphed, standing with a plate in each hand like a statue of Justice weighing up a guilty verdict for bacon sandwiches. The little man looked up at him from his plate of pickled herring and beamed a smile that spread from one rosy cheek to the other. With a papal wave of his fork he gestured beneficently for Viktor to help himself to the seat opposite.

Rather than embark on a lengthy explanation of his prior claim to the table, Viktor decided to let the matter pass and sat down, noticing the unpleasant sensation of the seat pre-warmed by Panchev on his backside as he did so. Before he could even retrace his chain of thought regarding the Baltic lands not mattering much, his uninvited host had commenced what was evidently a well-rehearsed marketing campaign on behalf of the port city of V----.

"Have you tried these?" the tiny tycoon asked, pointing at the marinaded fish with his fork as he continued munching. "Delicious! And produced at a state-of-the-art canning plant in the free-port of V---- owned by a Norwegian company! They chose V---- as a direct result of a successful trade mission to Kristiansand organised by the V---- municipality at the initiative of mayor Anrijs Pletenbergs..."

"Really?" Viktor said to his bacon.

"Have you ever considered locating your business in V----? Whether it's manufacturing or services, V---- has so much to offer and it's a great place to bring up a family."

"I don't have a business and I don't have a family."

"Then you must come as a tourist and discover for yourself," the little man said, refusing to be perturbed. "We have an award-winning beach, a notable castle, a floral clock and several important stones, including the fourth-largest rock in Latvia. Here, have a brochure." From somewhere under the table he produced a glossy publication with an orange cover.

Despite giving it only the briefest of glances as he assembled a new bacon sandwich, Viktor was arrested in mid-creation by the central image. There, surrounded by land- and sea-scapes of what looked like a rather dull provincial town was the dapper little man himself, smiling from the cover in precisely the same way he was now smiling at Viktor.

"But that's you!" Viktor exclaimed without thinking.

"Anrijs Pletenbergs, mayor of V----, extremely delighted to meet you," the little man said, placing his fork down at last and extending his hand across the herring. Viktor took it, again without thinking.

"Do I detect from your accent that you are from Great Britain?" the little man asked excitedly.

Not wanting to give his irritating dining companion any sort of clue as to his actual identity, Viktor nodded. It seemed to delight the little man, his grin becoming even wider.

"Wonderful, wonderful. I love England. I visit regularly to see my tailor. In fact this jacket – no, one should say 'blazer' – is from England. And so are these shoes. Sadly, my trousers are from Moscow. May I ask where in England precisely?"

"Cambridge," Viktor said, making it three in a row for thoughtless responses.

"Ah, Cambridge..." Anrijs Pletenbergs nodded as if dreaming of spires and punting. Then somewhat unexpectedly he asked: "Did PG Wodehouse come from Cambridge?" He looked as if the information was of vital importance and his slight Latvian accent meant he pronounced "Wodehouse" to rhyme with "goat house".

"I don't know," Viktor said. "I'm not really a fan. All I know is that he ended up an American."

"Yes, such a shame," Pletenbergs reflected, as if naturalizing as an American was akin to losing one's leg in a farming accident. Then with the flick of some internal switch, the smile was back. "I am a huge fan of PG Wodehouse. That will be all, Jeeves – ha!"

"If you will excuse me, I must go and prepare, Mr Plat..."

"Pletenbergs. Anrijs Pletenbergs. Mayor of V---- Anrijs Pletenbergs." For a moment there was a hint of anger in his voice, like a child refusing to go to bed.

"Well, as I said, Mr Pletenbergs, I must leave," Viktor said. Something about the little man was intensely annoying and he could not resist trying to put him in is place as he wiped his mouth, placed his napkin on an empty plate and rose from his seat. "You see I will be questioning the three Baltic presidents and your prime minister in half an hour."

"Ha! President Liepiņš! That old hound! I knew him when he was an electrical engineer! He used to come to fix my cranes in V----! If you want a good question for him, ask him how he got licensed to found a bank when all he was qualified for was switching fuses! If he forgets the answer, as he is getting old and forgetful these days, whisper the name Anrijs Pletenbergs in his ear – that'll get a response! As for the prime minister, ask him if he still has the rubber stamp that Anrijs Pletenbergs gave him. He'll know what that means! Prime minister indeed – I can still see him coming out of his little office in the basement of the Transport Ministry with that stamp in his hand. He used to blow on it, as if he was the most important man in the world, then stamp documents to make them legal. Ask him who's got it now!" He dissolved in mirthless laughter.

"Enjoy the conference," Viktor said as he beat a retreat.

"No offence intended, but I am far too busy to sit in a conference hall all day," Pletenbergs called after him. "Breakfast is the best time to catch people, what? But perhaps you could mention V---- and its opportunities in your talk? Nice meeting you!"

III   AN EARLY MISTAKE

Viktor was in better spirits by the time he got back to his room, though he did pause more than once in the carpeted corridors to make sure the pitter-patter of Pletenbergs' feet was not following him. Though the prospect of playing second fiddle to Panchev was intolerable, he would restore the natural order, he mused as he looked out of the window at Riga's now-unmistakable skyline. The only way to respond was for the second fiddle to embarrass the presumptuous lead violin with a display of dazzling virtuosity.

"Ladies and gentlemen, esteemed excellencies, members of the press, I would like to begin with a statement you will find shocking. All I ask is that you hear me out before deporting me!" Here he would pause for laughter. "But sometimes a painful truth can lead us to the most effective course of action. Today I would like to propose to you that this land in which we find ourselves (better to say "land" rather than the name of the country, in case he got it mixed up again), this land and perhaps even this whole region, simply... does... not... matter!"

Here he would pause again for dramatic effect and push his glasses up from his nose to the top of his head to signal the end of the overture and his preparedness to develop the main theme. Already he could tell it would make a provocative paper for the Benbo Foundation, the Washington-based think-tank of which he was professor emeritus.

Harvey Benbo, born Herschel Barenboim, had originally come from the same small Carpathian town as Viktor, made his fortune in the United States as a sausage magnate ("Hot dog, that's a Benbo!") and just before his death in 1978 had used his considerable wealth to create the Benbo Foundation, dedicated to studying and publicising the evils of the Soviet Union. It had survived the alleged collapse of the USSR by applying Benbo's earthy philosophy of "Call it a frank or a Weiner, it's still a goddam sausage" to geopolitics. Thus the fight against the Evil Empire continued, simply redirected against Russia's economic threat instead of the Soviet nuclear threat.

Benbo's foresight gave his eponymous Foundation well-appointed offices near the Lincoln Memorial, a permanent staff of around 40 – half of them globe-trotting academics – and a never-decreasing pool of cash that could be used to attend conferences, publish papers under the Foundation's own banner and generally rally all right-thinking people to the cause of liberty.

Benbo's portrait still hung in every room except the toilets. Unfortunately like many very wealthy men, Benbo had been a recluse and the only existing photograph of him of usable quality was an ill-advised advertising shot from the 1950s which showed him in a straw boater and horn-rimmed glasses, somewhat gingerly holding one of his products in a bun and preparing to take a bite. When the great man had seen the image, he had promptly fired his entire marketing department as well as an unfortunate stenographer who happened to be in the same room.

Over the years, attempts had been made to remove the hot dog from the image to create a more dignified portrait, using first photographic techniques, then airbrushes and latterly computer technology, but the mustard-smothered item caused more trouble than expected. If the sausage was simply removed, it left Benbo's right hand gesticulating in a decidedly obscene manner. If the whole hand and arm was removed from the frame, the angle at which Benbo was leaning forward, and his open mouth made it look as if he was rather the worse for wear.

An expert from a Hollywood computer animation studio had been handed a generous allowance to try the very latest techniques in the 1990s and had managed to close Benbo's mouth, make his hand into a defiant fist and remove the offending meaty treat, but even that had been unsatisfactory – the unmistakable, exaggerated gleam of "I'm about to bite into a Benbo" remained in place behind his thick spectacles, a belated testimony to the skill of the ill-fated advertising executive who had devised the original campaign.

In his warm hotel room Viktor stood so close to the window that the air expelled from his mouth formed a hazy patch on the glass, blotting out a section of the city consisting of blocks of century-old brick warehouses, an Orthodox church with a wooden dome and half of the Soviet skyscraper the locals called 'Stalin's Wedding Cake' as if a Baltic sea mist had suddenly been swallowed by the mouth of the River Daugava. It was a nice image that could perhaps be used as an extended metaphor as his speech progressed, with the indistinct Baltic lands slowly emerging from obscurity into sunlit prominence, their church spires topped with golden cockerels catching the beams of democracy and progress, serving as a beacon and an example to that vast, shadowy land across the border.

By "vast, shadowy land", of course, he meant "Russia" but it never did to simply say "Russia" in the world of geopolitical discussion, in much the same way that serious thespians would never say "Macbeth" in a theatre. Russia must always be alluded to in dramatic, sinister terms. Probably in the press conference after his oration, a journalist would ask him if the "vast, shadowy lands" were Russia, and even then he would reply enigmatically that he would leave interpretation to his listeners. The thought made him chuckle, but the chuckle turned into a hacking cough that sent flecks of spittle onto the hazy patch on the window, reducing the picturesque effect considerably.

His throat was probably still thick from the flight. If he was to give of his best, he would need his usual operatic levels of projection, so decided that one of the Czech pharmacist's red pills was probably in order. He picked up the bottle of tablets from the top of the mini-bar where he had left it, wondering absent-mindedly whether "vast, shadowy lands" or "shadowy, vast lands" would sound better. As he spoke the two alternate phrases out loud, he popped a pill into his mouth. Precisely as he did so, a shaft of sunlight broke through the grey cloud, illuminating the green copper spires of St Jacob's and St Peter's churches, their golden cockerels sparkling briefly. The display made him chuckle, and placed him in such a good mood that he decided a dose of two pills would be permissible to ensure he didn't flag halfway through what was going to be an epic presentation.

After all, Viktor knew that he was in good company in calling upon the services of the Czech pharmacist. He had actually met the tall, elegant, moustachioed man at a Prague conference at which it seemed he knew a large portion of the participants. In a dark blue suit with his grey hair oiled smoothly into place he actually looked like he would make a rather good president of some middle-sized middle-European country himself, and in a civilized conversation during a coffee break had informed Viktor that his clients included a remarkably distinguished selection of the continent's leading minds and decision-takers. Viewed through this prism it had become something of a game among "friends of the Czech" to spot fellow initiates and to guess from the manner of their speeches precisely what sort of pharmaceutical boost they had been given, and knowledge of the names of his fellow subscribers removed any lingering doubts about popping the occasional pep pill.

In his casual manner, the pharmacist revealed that one of the very bulwarks of North Atlanticism had been one of his most enthusiastic customers – indeed, rather too enthusiastic as the pharmacist himself had insisted on reducing the volume of his mood-enhancing shipments for fear that the Lion of the West was either consuming industrial dosages himself or – according to one rumour – passing them on to others in distant lands whose stability could not be relied upon. For the sake of world peace, the pharmacist had dropped his own profit margin and was relieved that his client had eventually complied with his request.

"There are two ways one can deal with the demands made by time and power," said the pharmacist as he bit into a pastry. "The first is to develop the ability to cat-nap. That is what most politicians say they do, but they lie. Hardly anyone can cat-nap effectively. I have a renowned neurological colleague who has researched this. I will be happy to forward you the paper. The more common path is to have help from someone like myself. And why not? If people would just stop to consider for one moment the demands they make of their leaders, they could not fail to see that this is the best solution.

"These people shuttle back and forth in a state of constant sleep deprivation, their every word, action and expression scrutinized in detail, for weeks on end. People think they have power but most live in a state of constant fear – fear they will say or do the wrong thing, fear that they will seem weak or that one of their colleagues or rivals or counterparts will outdo them. The strain is unimaginable. Anything that can reduce this fear and restore confidence must surely be a worthwhile investment in a country's national security.

"In the case of the great man we were just discussing, I'm pleased to say that at the end of his second term of office he wrote me a charming letter explaining that he would no longer need my services, enclosing a gift of fine porcelain, which was a gratifying touch. I was happy to receive it. He went to his country house, slept for a few months and was soon in fine shape. He did some charity work and wrote a book. But now he is starting to get bored and the rumour is that he is planning a comeback in next year's election. As far as my business is concerned, of course, I am delighted, but whether it will be good for world peace is another matter..."

Viktor understood the lesson implicit in the pharmacist's words and had always taken care not to become dependent on the two little bottles of what the pharmacist described as "elevators" and "moderators". In any case, Viktor's was about as far from the addictive personality type as it would be possible to find, and it would sometimes be weeks before he remembered the medication was even packed in his wash bag.

He screwed the cap off a bottle of complimentary water standing on a tray to one side of the small writing desk, feeling the two little red pills colliding briefly on his tongue like billiard balls. Still extremely dry in the throat, he took a deep gulp, letting the cool liquid clean the larynx that would vocalise the best presentation of the season.

In a way it was good that the gauntlet had been thrown down by Panchev, it would give him a chance to show how...

His lungs burned, his stomach heaved, his head spun.

He stood there by the window, staring down at the bottle. It had no label. It was "designer water". He sniffed the bottle. It was not designer water. He picked up the small white card that had been lying on the tray beside the bottle, a whirl of fear forming in his stomach.

"The organisers of the conference and the Riga Distillery Company are pleased to present you with this complimentary bottle of quadruple-distilled vodka which we hope will..."

Without reading on he picked up the pill bottle that he had replaced. He knew it had no label, because it didn't need one. It wasn't full of red pills as it was supposed to be, it was full of the blue ones he'd taken to help him sleep. He hadn't been elevated. He'd been double moderated.

Viktor had read about minds "reeling" but this was the first time his own had performed the trick, spinning in the opposite direction to his stomach. It was not a pleasant sensation, as it was difficult to ascertain how much of the reeling was caused by shock and how much by the effects of the fairly considerable slug he had taken. In a cold frenzy as he imagined the quadruple-distilled Latvian hooch seeping into his bloodstream, he tugged the door of his mini-bar open and reached for a bottle of water. The cap was off and the cold glass neck of the bottle rattled against his teeth as he attempted an immediate dilution of the situation.

It is surprising how frequently we repeat the same elementary mistakes. A man who stubs his toe on a bedpost in the middle of the night on his way to the lavatory will frequently repeat the performance on his way back to bed. A man who has wrenched his back lifting a heavy box will rarely decide to give up and ask for assistance. Rather he will attempt the feat again to prove some unprovable point and will then reflect, as he lies on his back looking up at a light fitting for three weeks, that the only thing he proved was that the box was too heavy for him. It is as if we have some innate Will to Stupidity that sometimes gains control of our motor functions, opens the throttle and points us at the nearest lamppost.

So it was with Viktor Draaks. The second bottle was the same as the first. History had not bothered to repeat itself first as tragedy and then as farce. It had instead eschewed the Marxist approach and gone straight to farce. Or maybe it had shuffled the deck and tragedy still lay ahead.

Viktor started for the bathroom to drink some water from the tap and splash his face with cold water, but first he would try to make himself sick into the toilet. He collapsed to his knees, placed his head above the bowl and moved his hand toward his mouth to tickle his tonsils when a jet of water erupted from the bowl into his face. The surprise sent him sprawling backwards across the bathroom floor into a heated towel rail which, as it no longer had towels on it, was effectively a giant griddle, burning the back of his neck and sending him lurching reflexively forward again. As he gathered his breath on all fours in the middle of the bathroom floor with a cold, wet front of his head and a hot, scorched rear, he had no time to reflect on what earns a hotel a five-star rating as the telephone started ringing in the bedroom.

He crawled out of the bathroom like a giant baby and picked up the receiver noting his shaking hand with alarm.

"Mr Draaks?"

"Grrr, yesh."

"So, Mr Draaks, are you almost ready? So we're hoping to get started in the next couple of minutes and it would be wonderful to have all of today's speakers together for the keynote?" The voice had that whining tone that made everything sound like a question. It registered even more disagreeably than the knowledge that he had just seconds in which to make his presence felt downstairs and that he now had only the most rudimentary grasp of what he would say when he got there. Something about fog and buffers, lands that mattered and didn't matter, shadowy forests extending as far as the imagination could picture.

But he was Viktor Draaks and he had been referred to in print as one of the leading authorities in the field of Eastern European geopolitics. They wanted him in Belgrade and they wanted him here in Tallinn or Riga or Vilnius or whichever one it was. It didn't matter. He got to his feet a little unsteadily, managed to put a rather vague knot in his tie and told himself it would take more than Pavel Panchev, the wrong pills and a few shots of vodka to humiliate Viktor Draaks.

IV A MEMORABLE ADDRESS

The conference hall was of the sort that would have been acceptable a few years ago when the circuit was in its post-Soviet infancy, when it still retained a leftover whiff of samizdat meetings that really pushed events along. But for today's more mature conference market, when palatial hotels and conference centres from the edge of the Sahara to the Arctic Circle – the novelty of their locations now something to be expected – had become mundane, the room was a bit shabby, too small for the number of tables and chairs crammed into it. The air conditioning hummed as if suffering from arrhythmia and had a negligible effect on the atmosphere which was both too warm and too humid.

Viktor made his way towards the stage in a manner he hoped gave no clue as to his fermenting status. Keen to seem ready, he sat in one of the four vacant leather chairs on stage, choosing one of the two in the centre to make sure he was prominent in any photography.

The audience shimmered a little as if a fine mist were filtering into the room, but apart from that, he felt as if he was regaining control of his senses and motor functions, though the air conditioning seemed to be struggling more and more with the amount of body heat being generated by constricting ties around fleshy necks and belts around flabby waists.

The atmosphere was becoming quite oppressive, so Viktor had the excellent idea to loosen his own tie once he held the floor, a nice addition to his spectacle-push routine that would enhance his image as the maverick yet brilliant academic. He tugged the knot he had improvised in his confusion a few minutes earlier to practice, but it must have been some sort of slip knot, as it got tighter. Further attempts to loosen it made it tighter still until he was forced to yank it to one side to try and reduce the constriction of his throat, lending him a less than dandyish aspect.

He saw Panchev enter the room, shaking hands with anyone within reach and smiling that rather too white smile of his. How he could seem so fresh in such a stifling atmosphere was remarkable, almost uncanny. It must be something to do with his mixed blood. He probably had a dash of Bedouin in there somewhere. Gypsy, Eskimo, Pygmy... The drone of the air conditioning got louder still – or was it the muffled sound of voices coming from the translation booth over in the corner? How could they be translating when no-one was speaking? Very curious. But thank god he felt refreshed and sober... apart from the air conditioning which droned on and on...

. . . .

"Excuse me? So, excuse me?" The voice came from far away but was getting closer, slowly closer. It started as the drone of the air conditioning but rapidly transformed itself into the annoying voice he had heard on the telephone in his room. Then a new voice sounded in his other ear.

"Viktor!" Panchev's clear tones awoke him with a start. His rival stared down at him, with a look of concern. Fake concern, Viktor reasoned, before fully realising that he was the object at which Panchev was directing his enigmatic expression while the nameless conference organising minion looked from one to the other of them helplessly.

"Viktor, are you alright? Do you have any medication? Is it your heart?"

Viktor did his bear growl and hauled himself to his feet, pushing Panchev out of the way like a finely cut curtain. Immediately he regretted his action. The room was full of swirling mist. He should have stayed sitting and feigned a heart attack. For an instant he thought of faking a collapse but pride took over and he remembered that there was no situation that Viktor Draaks could not rescue with his erudition and insight.

Panchev's concerned face was replaced by four other faces, wearing expressions that ranged from mild amusement to intense annoyance. The two belonging to the presidents of Lithuania and Estonia were more puzzled than anything else. In contrast, the Latvian president and prime minister seemed less sympathetic, as if they were considering the immediate introduction of legislation to allow the imprisonment without trial of foreign nationals found on a public stage in a state of intoxication.

Even worse, behind the line of leaders was a greater mass of faces, painted with expressions ranging from derision to hilarity.

Viktor would show them. He had already decided to put on a virtuoso performance and that was exactly what he would deliver. Thinking with a rapidity that surprised even himself, he resolved to launch into his provocation without further ado. The disjointed opening might even enhance its dramatic impact. With synapses crackling with electricity he would work this incident into his speech so that finally it would be revealed as a brilliant piece of play-acting. Perhaps something to do with slumbering giants – Russia as a drunken bear waking from its slumbers with a dangerous, confused aggression? It would come to him. The thing to do now was to get started and trust in his marvellous mind. He opened his mouth and spoke to the back of the hall without looking at the audience, just as they had taught him at Cambridge.

"Ladies and gentlemen, her excellency and gentlemen of the press. And members of the press. Let me start by insulting you. This place in which we are standing does not matter! Not one little bit!" As he had rehearsed, he paused, swaying, for dramatic effect and was gratified to hear that a murmur of sorts did indeed rumble from the audience.

"Please let me finish before you insult me. Over the border is a big forest and one day it will... be full of... cockerels in the shadows. Cocks. No. Anyway, there is a big bear and it is probably angry and intoxicated," This provoked more noise from the audience but he continued quickly. "If we wake it up, what will it do? It depends whether we prod it with a stick or a... carrot. Grrrr."

At this point Viktor completely lost his hitherto clear chain of thought because the audience had turned into rabbits. They had not kept their promise to wait until the end of his lecture. They had turned into big, fat rabbits with pink noses and droopy jowls. At Cambridge that would have been regarded as very poor form. An audience of distinguished guests had never metamorphosed into furry ruminants during any of his lectures before. They still wore their pinstriped suits and business skirts and somehow resisted the temptation to gnaw the edges of their collars and ties with their protruding front teeth. He knew they were still people, but somehow there was something completely leporine about the whole lot of them.

Then the fear started to rise up his spine. A creeping coldness that if it ever reached his head would make him horribly aware of what was actually happening. Like a man walking in the dark and hearing footsteps behind him, but refusing to turn around, he wanted to deny the horror by looking straight ahead. He was experiencing something awful, and knew something incomparably more terrible was about to engulf him. He had to get out before the footsteps caught up with him and he felt cold breath on his collar followed by cold steel between his shoulder blades. He had to escape.

He lurched from the podium and headed for the exit as fast as he could, trying to keep his gaze directed at the door rather than the twitching faces of the herbivorous delegates, some of whom were now pointing cameras and gesturing wildly with lettuce leaves. The ranks of chairs on either side of him seemed to close like flood-waters, threatening to engulf him at any moment and pull him back towards the podium. He pressed on, as if wading through the torrent until at last his hand reached the brass handle of the large door to the conference hall.

It was cool to the touch, but Viktor involuntarily noted that considering this was a five-star hotel, it really should have been better polished, particularly for an event attended by three presidents and a prime minister. But the observation made his thought start to drift back towards the current humiliation. It became imperative to open the door and get out, to place some sort of shield between himself and the stifling atmosphere of this room of very important rabbits.

He pulled on the doorknob with all his considerable weight. It creaked a little in its frame but did not open. He pulled again, jerking the handle so hard that it hurt his elbow. Still nothing. Viktor began yanking on the handle like a lunatic in moonbeams, his body squirming and perspiring partly from the unaccustomed exertion and partly from the tide of laughter rising behind his back. He pulled harder and harder, practically suspending his whole body from the dull doorknob. On second thoughts it might be better that it wasn't too polished – it made it easier to grip. But the hinges should have been oiled – how could such an important door be so difficult to open?

Cracks started to appear in the paint around the door frame, such was the energy Viktor was putting into his assault. From the corner of his eye he could see a group of particularly square-headed, short-eared rabbits start to approach him. Their lapel badges made it plain they were bodyguards.

Emitting a sound more like a whimper than his usual bear's growl, Viktor directed all of his remaining energy into one final, strenuous attempt to pull the door towards him. It opened – in the opposite direction, revealing a startled-looking waiter with a tray of half-filled champagne glasses. For perhaps a full second, a heavily-perspiring Viktor Draaks and the young man whose name badge said he was called 'Laimonis' and was happy to help stared at each other as if looking at reflections in a peculiarly gruesome hall of mirrors.

It was many years since Viktor had run – really run as fast as his legs would carry him. But he had not lost the knack and did not look back even with the sound of breaking champagne glasses chasing him out of the hotel lobby.

V   THE CAPITAL OF LATVIA

It is supposed to be impossible to get truly lost in cities that have a large river flowing through them. It is not impossible. The Daugava River divides Riga clearly enough, keeping a broad arm's reach between the old stone spires and new glass towers of the right bank and the creaking wooden houses and quietly crumbling parks of the low-rise left bank. The cruise ships that berth in the shadow of Riga castle rarely make it across to unglamorous Pārdaugava, and if they do it is either to gaze across at the most satisfying view of the Old Town or to indulge in a few minutes of "Ostalgia" at the hulking, curiously childish Soviet memorial in Victory Park, where the Tsar once rendered an unwitting service to his Bolshevik successors by planting a stand of oak trees that came in useful a few decades later for lynching Nazis.

For arrivals from the airport, in contrast, spirits rise as the usual set of car showrooms and supermarkets gives way unexpectedly to the beautiful wooden mansions of Kalnciema street, some restored with their planks stained tar-black to better show the deep golden grain of classical porticoes and carved window surrounds. Here and there amongst the beams and gables the strange symbols of pagan culture are etched and raised like hieroglyphs in a mysterious text that wanders from building to building, disdaining to touch anything made of concrete, steel or glass in case contact with such clean new substances would rob the symbols of their vague meanings accrued over the centuries. Speeding past in their taxis, new arrivals make a mental note to return and explore this part of the city, but invariably forget as soon as the Old Town spirescape rises into view one minute later.

A river such as the Daugava – the sweet-sounding Dvina of the Russians – can act as a sort of mirror, reflecting skylines and road maps, throwing the sense of orientation back on itself and giving a through-the-looking-glass sense of unreality and uncertainty to the uninitiated visitor. Riga is in reality two cities, with only the Daugava working ceaselessly to unite and interweave them in its reflective little wavelets.

Viktor stood in a cobblestoned square with traffic skeeting around trams and trolleybuses in the middle distance, little knots of tourists rotating in front of cameras and lone figures scurrying with clockwork intent in all directions. Viktor stood in the middle feeling robbed of any sense of momentum. By rights he should still be holding forth on stage, approaching his conclusion and the moment when he would return his spectacles to his breast pocket, which usually signalled the start of the applause.

Instead, it would be Panchev taking the plaudits while he stood in the square looking like an inflated version of the statue of the uninteresting knight, Roland, to his left which a group of East Asian tourists were photographing enthusiastically.

The almost total lack of signage and Viktor's already befuddled condition magnified his growing disorientation. There were plenty of traffic signs displaying arrows pointing to the left, right or straight ahead, but for some reason the Latvians chose not to spoil their geometric perfection by appending place names. These signs were strangely philosophical, suggesting that freedom of choice was illusory and that whichever road you chose, the chances are you would end up at precisely the same unnamed destination whether you wanted to or not.

The white arrows on blue backgrounds possessed a certain pleasing purity, as if their designers had taken an artistic stand for the aesthetic over the utilitarian. They were signs to be admired rather than followed. An arrow pointing left, an arrow pointing right and an arrow pointing straight on. Viktor belched and – possessed of a sudden decisiveness that had a definite chemical origin – struck out in the direction of "straight on."

Straight on pointed towards a bar, which was ominous. Viktor hauled his heavy frame towards it, almost slipping on one of the cobblestones worn smooth by centuries of large men seeking liquid refreshment. He stumbled into the road and for a second stood frozen in terror as a sleek Mercedes careened towards him.

In one of the absurdities so typical of moments of mortal danger, he noticed as it bore down on him was that it had smoked glass, which added to its generally sinister appearance. The Mercedes' star was missing from the bonnet and it had a little steel stud located just above the right wheel arch. The flawless bodywork was polished to a liquid sheen. At the moment of his certain demise, Viktor's thought was not of his obituary or the tragic loss his death would be to the political sciences but of how difficult and costly it must be to obtain a missing Mercedes badge for a brand new S-Class.

"You could steal one from another car. Maybe that's what happened to this one. Someone stole it to replace a badge which had been stolen from their own car..."

As he concluded his theory about an eternally-extending chain of Mercedes badge thefts, the shadowy driver of the car hit his brakes, which complied immediately with the order to halt. The rear of the car wiggled as it slumped to a stop like a walrus washed onto a beach by a great wave. Viktor could have reached out and touched the place the missing badge should have been had his muscles not been frozen in place by the expected impact.

For what seemed a very long time, neither car nor Viktor moved. Then the moment passed as if some unseen director had called "cut". Viktor's muscles relaxed slightly. He walked to the other side of the road, noticed that the car had Russian diplomatic registration plates and felt a sudden queasiness in his stomach. Behind the smoked windows there was some sort of movement, as if the occupants were preparing to get out. Fear seized him and he ran off into the tourists thronging Town Hall Square as the car door opened and someone shouted his name. He did not look back and did not stop until he could barely breathe and was beaded with perspiration.

His near-death experience with a Russian car banished any lingering thoughts about sobering up and trying to repair the damage done at the conference. If not exactly glad to be alive, Viktor recognised that it was the only fact of which he could at present be sure. He didn't want to contemplate anything else. He decided to get drunk and start again when he woke up tomorrow.

VI   A TRAIN FROM TORNAKALNS

The first bar was a bore. It was full of laughing tourists served by gaunt Latvians who looked ridiculous in the stripy American uniforms demanded by the franchise which ran the place. A couple of scruffier, swarthier types scowled in the seats nearest to the toilet, murmuring into expensive cellphones in Turkic languages on the lookout for well-scrubbed, fat-walleted Scandinavians who had taken too much advantage of cheap liquor. They looked like mangy Caucasian lions watching over a herd of healthy zebra.

After a tepid beer and vodka chaser, Viktor decamped to a barely-better hotel lobby which said on a board outside it could provide "famous classic cocktails." To his disappointment, the staff appeared never to have heard of Daiquiris or Gibsons, so he contented himself with their own definition of a "classic" in the umbrella-strewn cataclysm of Sex On The Beach, a first for Viktor in every sense.

Subsequent events would suggest the appearance of at least one more bar in the Mesolithic period of his binge, but all he could recall of them afterwards was a vague dispute about a bar bill, the indistinct faces of more swarthy faces peering at him from the shadows, a botched picture of Che Guevara in a Cuban bar and a row of pearly lights extending for a long, long way across a cold and windy bridge.

By the time he reached the final bar, and shed the last remaining ideas of where he was, he had drunk himself partially sober. Trams passed outside every fifteen minutes, their tracks set into cobblestones. This, combined with the bar's position just below street level created a sort of fatalistic shudder as their wheels ground past the window. Each half hour, trains passed on their tracks slightly further away down an embankment – the tram tracks crossed over the railway line on a small bridge just outside the bar – creating an even more sonorous and deep-noted roar. Once an hour or so the passing of the tram and train would occur simultaneously, causing a vibrating roar like thunder echoing in a nearby hell.

The bar gave the impression of being simultaneously filthy and spotlessly clean. It had a damp, musty smell of potatoes that came from a large sack of them kept under the sink in the toilet, as if they were wondering whether to start rotting or wait to be turned into vodka in the small still in the shed on the railway embankment. Yet the floor and counter gleamed as the barmaid pushed a disinfectant-fragranced rag on the end of a stick round the linoleum tiles.

It was still only early evening so the bar was sparsely populated. A very thin man and a very fat woman sat in one corner, studiously avoiding each other's gaze and only occasionally mumbling something to each other, as if they had been sitting there for many years, perhaps since a dim and distant marriage day when she had been thin, he had been strong and their words still came out in unfamiliar order.

Beneath a television screen that silently showed Chuck Norris firing assault rifles in slow motion between advertisements for mobile phone ringtones, a group of three young men, two of them with bruised faces, held a rueful conversation. One was much more intoxicated than the others, and they occasionally pushed him gently back onto his bench when he started to lean forward. Until recently he could have been described as handsome, with high cheekbones and pale blue eyes but already he showed the ravages of long-term drinking which had started to inflate his eyes and make his skin sallow. He sat there, occasionally swearing but mainly just staring through the walls, a self-contained tragedy edging towards an inevitable end. His friends had that air about them that suggested one day they would sober up, raise families and discover another path but he was marked for a confused and wasteful death. The three friends spoke Russian, but the drunk one wore a stained old Latvian football shirt.

No-one turned and stared at Viktor when he walked into the bar. His slurred request for a vodka seemed entirely in keeping with the style of the place, but even while the barmaid was pouring out a generous shot of Moskovskaya, threat presented itself in the form of a square-set man dressed in black fatigues that clashed jarringly with his cropped, reddish hair. He seemed to have been constructed entirely from cubes, from the shape of his head to his breeze-block fists. His head rocked back a little when he noticed Viktor sitting at the bar. He swaggered over and sat on the next stool.

Looking up at a fly circling overhead rather than directly at Viktor, the cuboid man asked in Russian: "Are you a Jew?"

That it was said with an air of vague curiosity made it all the more frightening. Viktor felt the bile of fear perform a rapid circuit of his belly.

Somewhere back in the misty Carpathian past, a Jewish tailor originally from Vilnius with a reputation for extremely comfortable hosiery had made an appearance in Viktor's ancestry. He rarely acknowledged the fact except at conferences in Tel Aviv, where the industrious little cloth-cutter could usefully be employed as proof of Viktor's deep empathy with the Jewish people.

However, given the present circumstances and the look in the black-clad figure's hard eyes in which blood vessels the same colour as his hair looked as if they had been tattooed around the pupils, it seemed that the industrious old Litvak should probably not be called out from the back of his long-liquidated shop.

"I think the Finn who tried to kill me was a Jew," the man mused, still following the progress of the fly, whose awkward, indecisive twisting could have been a dance inspired by Viktor's own thoughts at that moment. "Are you a Jew?" he repeated, turning his square head ninety degrees to look at Viktor finally.

Viktor did speak Russian – or rather he spoke an extremely formal and old-fashioned form of Russian that no-one else spoke, now or probably ever. It allowed him to read Kremlin press releases well enough to scoff at them but not well enough to understand the myriad Russian TV channels he encountered in hotel rooms with their anachronistic offerings of variety spectaculars staged at Moscow theatres, soapy melodramas and low-budget cop shows in which the good guys were helped by faithful police hounds and spat when offered bribes.

It was strange that he was reasonably comfortable with the refined Russian of diplomacy that so intimidated ordinary people but was helpless when faced with a middle-aged man telling jokes dressed as a babushka on TV. He had experienced something similar at Cambridge: the academic English of lectures and debates within the quadrangles of his college seemed so much more reassuring than the impenetrable patois of taxi drivers and shopkeepers. On one occasion he had entered a greengrocer's shop to buy some apples but emerged five minutes later carrying leeks and plums only because the greengrocer turned out to be from East Kilbride, which he later discovered was in Scotland.

Aware of his linguistic limitation, Viktor tried to avoid Russian if at all possible, doing his best to give the impression that this was down to a general disapproval of all things Russian rather than anything else. When cornered at a drinks reception or late-night informal briefing he found that a shrug, a wave of the arm and a quick *kanyeshna* or *davai...** was generally sufficient to give the impression that he was a master of the vernacular. Neither of those would be good replies in the current situation.

At school he had memorised a single Russian poem: Pimen's monologue from "Boris Godunov". Whenever his Russian credentials needed a boost, Viktor would randomly select a line and declaim it in the melodramatic style that Russians adore, all rolling "Rs" and extended vowel sounds. From stage comics to the classics, Dima Bilan to Vladimir Mayakovsky, Russians always listen to a man who is making a point of speaking Russian. And all Russians love Pushkin, most particularly those who never read him.

So far there had been no conversational awkwardness that could not be rescued by Pimen's monologue. To intellectuals it is familiar enough to give a self-satisfied glow of recognition yet obscure enough to win approval for the person quoting it. Whereas to the less well-read it possesses the unmistakeable timbre of Pushkin whilst being indecipherable to just the right degree to seem both profound and applicable to every circumstance.

Quoting Pushkin hardly seemed the most appropriate course of action

---

*Конечно (Russian) – of course; *давай* (Russian) – come on!

with the black-clad, flame-haired thug staring at him. But in his drink-addled and emotionally overwrought state, it was the best he could do.

"The future generations of the Orthodox may know the bygone fortunes of their native land..." he said, his voice cracking into a whimper towards the end.

"Oh, you're Orthodox?" The man said, leaning back. "I thought you looked like a Jew. I have a lot of time for Jews. They could teach us Russians a thing or two. We need to be more like them, except, like you say, Orthodox. They say there are Orthodox Jews, but I don't see how that can be the case."

"I'm not Russian," Viktor said.

"Yes, I can tell by the way you speak. I knew you weren't Russian as soon as I saw you walk past me. Hang on, you're not a Finn, are you?"

Viktor looked puzzled for a moment. The Russian word for "Finn" seemed familiar, but he was having trouble recalling what it meant despite it sounding exactly the same as its English equivalent. Finland cropped up surprisingly rarely in discussions of geopolitics. Not even Finns seemed to talk about it much. The man's face turned slightly red and he clenched his teeth. A vein on the side of his brow began to throb noticeably.

"I said are you a Finn?" he repeated, leaning to within inches of Viktor's beard.

Some deep neural network of self-preservation switched itself on and the Russian word for Finnish - *Finskii*** - flashed before Viktor's eyes. It was absurd. He looked nothing like a Finn. Was that really what he was asking? Maybe it was his size: Finns are all big, aren't they?

"Finland? Finn? No, I'm not from Finland. I'm from... the Carpathians."

The square man raised his square fist and pumped it toward Viktor like a piston. He flinched, instantaneously wondering if he would ever wake up and if so, where. But by the time the fist made contact it had transformed itself into a flat palm and landed not on Viktor's chin but on his broad back in the form of a slap that knocked all the air from his lungs.

"Oh, a Serb!" the man laughed. "Juta, get this brother Slav a drink from me," the man gestured to the woman with the mop. "I have a lot of time for Serbs. They've got guts and they're not afraid to cause trouble. We Russians could learn something from you Serbs. Orthodox, too, now I understand! We could learn something from the Jews as well. Just as long as you're not a Finn!" At the word "Finn" he spat invisibly into the corner of the room.

"Have you ever been to Finland?" he continued.

"Well, I have but..."

"But you left! The best thing you could have done, my Chetnik brother. It's a lousy place. Spend most of the year in snow up to your waist. Can't get a decent drink at a decent price but everyone else seems to be drunk all the

---

*Финский (Russian) – Finnish.

time. Then they lecture you about drinking in the street after you've broken your back for them all day. Helsinki is a hole. I wouldn't go back there. You did the right thing leaving. Riga is much better. Here people have some heart!" The man leaned towards Viktor, hitting himself in the general area of the heart with his fist as he did so.

"Look at this," the man said, hitching up his jumper to show a patch of pock-marked skin below his ribs. That's where the Finn stabbed me."

It looked to Viktor more like an appendectomy scar.

"Why did he stab me?" the man continued, asking himself the question Viktor had already resolved not to ask. "I'll tell you... because he was a filthy Finn! A great big, blond-haired, blue-eyed Finn! No offence, I didn't really think you were one of those miserable fish-eating bastards!"

And he laughed hugely, laying a heavy hand on Viktor's shoulder. "I could show you more. My girl says my body looks like a road map, it has so many scars on it! A badly-folded road map! Folded by a woman, eh Juta?"

Juta smiled a smile that was the opposite of a smile as she piloted the mop for another circuit of the floor.

The thought of Viktor Draaks, scourge of Russia, sitting in a bar full of Russians and drinking a pan-Slavic toast would have been unthinkable a day earlier. But here he was, with a Finn-hating thug, wondering how he had got here and what was going to happen next. Through the alcoholic haze, the dreadful sequence of this morning's debacle replayed itself, prompting him to empty his glass with an unenthusiastic *Na zdorovye*.[*]

"This stuff won't give you a hangover," laughed the Finnophobic security guard, "it won't let you live long enough to get one!" The wreck of a young man in the corner swore loudly *Bla!* to second the motion.

Absurd though he knew it was, Viktor could not prevent himself looking at the door as the clear, strong vodka burned his tongue. He was afraid that Panchev would walk in. It was impossible, of course, but when fear enters one's thoughts, rationality tends to slip out the back door and hide behind the bins. Night is simply an underexposed copy of the day, but that knowledge does not help the man alone in the middle of the forest at sunset to feel less afraid as rural idyll transforms itself into a vast, shadowy maze.

Viktor's heart gave a similar pump of fear as he saw a figure form on the other side of the smoked glass door to the bar and prepare to enter. He choked momentarily at the thought of Panchev's smooth, Saturnine features peering in, fixing him in his tableau of Slavic brotherhood, smiling in a suitably sarcastic manner, then disappearing at speed to inform the rest of the conference about this new, compounded scandal which explained the earlier scandal with the three presidents and one prime minister.

For what better explanation could there be for his performance this

---

[*]*На здоровье!* (Russian) – To your health!

morning than it being some Russian-engineered plot to turn this important regional conference into a laughing stock? It would not be the first time that a supposed critic of Russia had been revealed as one of its agents. In a way, Viktor's long track record of bear-baiting made this interpretation even more credible, for how could he have got away with voicing such criticisms for so long unless it was with the approval of his controllers in Moscow?

It all made sense; the reason he had always limited himself to academic papers instead of writing a book to make his Russia-bashing available to a wider audience; the reason he had never been refused an entry visa to Russia when everyone knew that those on the Kremlin's list of enemies could expect to be subjected to all manner of bureaucratic obstacles and petty inconveniences. Above all it explained why Viktor had become such a constant figure on the convention circuit: because Moscow wanted him there.

In all those strategic discussions, off-the-record briefings, informal consultations and quiet strolls with important men around hotel gardens, he had been there. Moscow's man acted as the most hawkish of hawks, all the time probing, recording and transmitting the thoughts of the real hawks back to his handlers.

And when one stopped to look at what Viktor Draaks had actually contributed over the last 20 years, did it really amount to much more than a crude Russian idea of anti-Russia rhetoric? It was all rather too knee-jerk and predictable – the denunciations, the accusations, the interpretations of hidden significances – was there actually anything original or were they really no more than a rough assemblage of views expressed by other, genuine commentators? Had Viktor ever contributed anything truly unique?

The sham should have been spotted sooner, the delegates would say to each other with shaking heads. They would joke about how as professionals, they could almost admire the way the Russian secret services had created, inserted and used Viktor, allowing him to remain a sleeper for so many years before activating him to such devastating effect. No-one had thought to use the persona of a bumbling alcoholic in geopolitics since the days of Yeltsin. This could even mark the advent of a new threat from the East: the use of what might be termed "absurdist intervention" to undermine the credibility of important Western democratic institutions. NATO was undoubtedly worryingly exposed to this new weapon and should develop strategies to defend against the comedic threat.

And Panchev would get the credit for uncovering the conspiracy. His stock would rise immeasurably. His career would blossom and he would forever be pointed out as the man who exposed that snake in the manger, Viktor Draaks – remember him?

Why had Viktor done it? He didn't seem like a man with unsated appetites, neither sexual nor financial. No doubt a generous pension and pleasant Dacha awaited him somewhere on the banks of the Neva, Volga or Moskva but that was incidental. No, it seemed clear that Viktor's motivation was ideological. He had exhibited the obsession with historical and economic processes that have always been the hallmark of the dyed-in-the-wool Marxist. Probably he shared Vladimir Putin's belief that the collapse of the Soviet Union marked the greatest political catastrophe of the twentieth century. A little research by well-placed contacts would quickly reveal a series of seemingly accidental but undoubtedly significant coincidences between the two men's movements, stretching back years. It was almost certain that Viktor was Vlad's man.

Whether consciously or not, Viktor knew the real answers to those questions. He had never written a book because he viewed the popular approach as unworthy of his academic background. A book would require simplifications and a broadening of appeal to be viable, and the end result would be one of those cliched efforts written by journalists and full of scaremongering and sloppy generalisation.

Subconsciously, he had never written a book because he was afraid lest it suffer in comparison with the hacks' books or, more specifically, with the three books Panchev had already written and which he so shamelessly peddled at every opportunity. So he stayed in the area in which he knew he could outperform the press: dry, factual, meticulously annotated and barely readable academic papers, all of them published by the Benbo Foundation.

He had never had visa problems because, by his reasoning, the Russian authorities knew that to cause such problems would be to acknowledge and even enhance his standing as an important voice. He was convinced that his visa applications always proceeded with suspicious smoothness.

And he had become a constant fixture on the convention circuit for a very simple reason: it was his life. With no family, no sense of permanent attachment to anywhere – certainly not to the grace and favour flat he received from the Benbo Foundation – he was unable to cook, clean, sew or drive a car. Hotels were his home, complimentary meals his sustenance, airport transfers and group tours his means of travel. The convention circuit was not a cycle he slipped into and out of as its amateur participants did. It formed the fabric of his life. And why not? He had no real interests other than geopolitical discussion. He was doing what he enjoyed, he believed he was doing something important and, moreover, it was the one thing he was good at.

Or rather, had been good at. It was hard to imagine a return from this morning's debacle, and that opened up the terrifying prospect of having to do something else with his life.

The door opened, the figure stepped in. It wasn't Panchev. It was a skinny young man with a bandage wrapped around one wrist. He looked around the bar, getting disproving glances from the three friends and even the morose couple in the corner. He walked nervously to the counter, his head twitching slightly. The anti-Finn stared at him, saying nothing, but with a look of utter contempt.

Despite the tension in the room and the patrons' clear dislike of the newcomer, no-one moved toward him. Even the spec-ops torch-headed Slavic hard nut limited his assault to his death's head stare. After a couple of long seconds he rose from his seat at the bar, gave Viktor another meaty slap on the back as he passed and exited through the same door, spitting theatrically into the gutter as he stepped across the threshold.

The newcomer seemed unperturbed, and sat down in the vacant seat next to Viktor, flickering a smile in his direction that looked more like an effort to gauge his disposition than an expression of any genuine happiness. With a delicate, airy flick of his bandaged wrist he gestured toward Juta. She promptly poured him a drink, but this time it was not hard liquor. She yanked a can from the chiller cabinet behind the bar, cracked open the seal and unceremoniously dumped the sweet-smelling red soda into a tall glass, handing it to the young man without once meeting his eyes and promptly returned to her waiting mop as if it was more likely to provide stimulating conversation.

The thin young man's drink smelled of artificial raspberries mixed with syrup and fizzed with chemical fury. It seemed strange that in this hard-drinking establishment Viktor had stumbled upon someone who not only was sober but looked likely to remain that way. Nor did the thin young man look like psychopath – in fact he possessed a rather intelligent, amiable face spoiled only by a slight twitch at the corner of his broad mouth. Almost immediately Viktor's enfeebled mind hit upon what seemed like the most brilliant idea since Democracy: get the little teetotaller to help him home.

"Shcuse me, do you speak Inlish?" Viktor slurred. Shifting on his stool he tried again: "Excuse me, do you speak English?"

The thin man's face seemed to swell and gain colour at hearing the words. "Ja-aa! I mean yes! Are you English? American? What the hell are you doing here?" The word "American" had been spoken with far more excitement than the word "English". "Ja-aa, I lived in the UK two years. It's no good, so I came back. But I plan to go to America soon."

"I live in the United States."

"Really? Where?"

"Washn. Washington."

"Really?"

"Yes, really. The thing is, I did something… foolish… this morning." Memories threatened to flood back in, so Viktor pressed on. "Now I need to go back to my home, to my hotel. Can you tell me how to get there?"

"Sure thing, man," the thin young man said in what was his best shot at an

American accent. Chuck Norris smiled approvingly on the screen above his head as the credits rolled. "But first let me get you a drink…"

"No need, really…"

"Hey, let's just hang out for a minute. You're in my 'hood, Juta!" He made the internationally accepted sign of the refill and Juta obliged with a sigh.

As Viktor reached into his pocket to pull out his wallet, the young man placed his hand on top of Viktor's and forced it firmly back down.

"My father, you know, my 'pop' owns this place. It's a dump, but my friends don't need to pay anything. My name's Kristaps. Call me Kris."

"Viktor," said Viktor. He extended his hand automatically, then realised he was offering it to the thin young man's bandaged hand. Kris waved away his concern.

"Oh, that's nothing, just some medication I have to take. In America you call it drugs, right?"

"Grrr, yes, I suppose so."

"That's funny. So you go to the drug store to buy drugs, yes? And you have a war on drugs? And sex and drugs and rock'n'roll?" Kristaps found the various uses of the world "drug" very amusing.

On the television suspended above them, the news followed on from the exploits of Chuck Norris and his grizzled disciples. Viktor kept one eye on the screen, anxious in case footage appeared showing a leading expert in his field lurching around a stage containing three presidents and one prime minister. He counted off the headlines one by one while Kristaps continued his inane, slightly manic chatter. The lead story was something about buses, trams and queues, the second story depicted an old woman saying something about her cat, the third showed the fireball of a crashed aeroplane in a Russian swamp.

The fourth story did indeed began with a familiar face – thankfully not Viktor's but the small man who had sat opposite him at breakfast that morning. Except, instead of his former annoying ebullience, the man appeared to have met some mishap even greater than Viktor's in the ensuing hours. The broadcast showed him tottering down the steps of some sort of official building on crutches, his entire torso encased in a pastry-coloured surgical corset that gave him the look of a well-baked sausage roll.

The little man spoke into the camera, at first looking as if he would pass out from pain at any second, but then, fielding what must have been a provocative question from the pack of journalists that surrounded him, his expression changed to something approaching anger. He seemed to forget his agonies and even banged his crutches on the ground a couple of times.

Next a row of old women processed towards him like a phalanx of pensionable Praetorians and presented him with lavish bouquets, which restored his good humour and prompted him to hand his crutches to a gaunt man standing behind him who looked like a lawyer, thank the old crones profusely and hop into a waiting Audi that whisked him away.

Viktor leaned towards Kris, flapping a paw up in the direction of the screen. "Whozzat?" he growled.

Kris followed his gaze and started laughing again. "Haha – Pletenbergs! He's the biggest crook in the country! He's always in court but they'll never get him. He's too smart. He's probably paid the judges. They are even bigger crooks!"

At mention of Pletenbergs' name, the dissolute young man in the football shirt shouted something that, luckily, was far too rude to be understood by Viktor, then relaxed back into his semi-comatose state.

"Whassa matter with him?" Viktor asked, indicating Pletenbergs again.

"Nothing. Every time he goes to court he gets ill. It's like a circus. He's the... what do you call the most important one at a circus?"

"Ringmaster."

"No, not ringmaster. Clown. He's the clown. The king clown."

Pletenbergs' smiling face was replaced by a weathergirl whose expression was all strong winds and sleet. Viktor decided it was time to force the pace. "I'm staying at the Grand Hotel Europe. Or Europe Grand Hotel. Some combination of those words. Room 419." Viktor sometimes forgot his hotel but never his room number.

"Those are two different hotels, but they are both veeery niiice! You must be rich."

"I really do need to get back..."

"Sure, my man. I'll see you home. Just as soon as we finish our drinks, yes? It will be best to take the train. The station is just outside, you cruise across the river just one stop and you can see your very nice hotel when you walk out the other end. No problem!"

Downing an unwanted drink seemed a high but unavoidable price to pay, Viktor's numbed brain reasoned. With luck no-one would see him creep back to his room. He would collapse into that comfortable, cool bed, pull the sheets up over his head and pray that when he woke in the morning he would find himself again in a nice bathroom with a toilet that sprayed water and a heated towel rail, a goodie bag from the conference organisers and a busy day's debating ahead of him. If ever originality needed to be avoided, it was now. Though everything felt worryingly real at the moment, he clung to the cliche that it could all be a bad dream.

Summoning the fortitude of his Carpathian forebears, he looked down into the shimmering liquid which glowed inside its thick glass carapace like a dimly-lit bulb. A train and a tram rolled past at intersecting angles outside, making the whole bar vibrate with a low hum. With a flick of his paw, the drink was despatched and he rose to his feet purposefully. The bar stool fell to the floor behind him, though it seemed he had barely touched it as he dismounted. He lurched towards the door and threw it open, noticing with a certain horror that the sky was a deep purple colour. Cold night air did its best to slap him into a more alert state. Kristaps followed, humming 'Hotel California' and doing a little dance as he walked.

Juta trailed behind them both. She emptied her bucket into the drain and went back inside to check up on its partner, the mop.

The path outside had clearly been a cobblestone road at one point, but the construction of the tram bridge over the railway line had truncated it. Old cobblestones sprinkled with sugary dust led down a long slope to a wooden railway station. In the twilight gloom, the white-painted letters of the wooden station nameplate were visible from some distance: "Torņakalns".

The declining road made it easier for Viktor to make progress. Kristaps, or 'Kris' as he insisted on being called, was now walking beside Viktor, occasionally placing an arm around his shoulders or a hand on his back to provide guidance. As they climbed a small set of steps to reach the platform, Viktor noticed a single wooden railway truck on its own, set a few yards off the main line. A large, grey granite stone was placed in front of it with the figure '1941' carved into its front.

"Whassat?" he asked.

"Oh, nothing," Kris said. "They deported people from here. Fifteen thousand in one night."

"To where?" It was a silly question.

"To Disneyland! The one in Siberia. Which is the one in Florida – is that Disneyland or Disneyworld? They sent another four thousand a few years later because they were having so much fun."

Viktor did not reply. He felt a bit more sober but not much. Just four or five people skulked silently under the yellowish lights of the platform. Seventy years earlier there must have been thousands and the terrible noise of lives being warped and disfigured, plans being screwed up and thrown away by the side of the tracks. He badly wanted to be in his hotel room.

"Where can I buy a ticket?" he asked, reaching for his wallet. This time Kristaps' hand was on his forearm before it even reached his pocket.

"No need. The station is closed. You can buy a ticket on the train. But it is only one stop. It takes one minute to cross the river. The inspector probably will not even ask you. If she does you can buy a ticket from her. She will want to go home, too. Here..." Kris handed Viktor a 1 lat coin. "She will give you change. It is cheap to travel from this station."

The thin young man's gift was strangely touching. Viktor was used to receiving gifts from conference organisers grateful for his attendance, souvenirs from tourism departments desperate for journalists to mention their proudly mediocre attractions, books for review and dust-jacket recommendation, sweeteners for donating his valuable time towards the judging of this or that prize. At the very least, lunch from newspapermen making clumsy attempts to cultivate him as a contact. It was a very long time since anyone had handed him something with no expectation of anything in return. A vague memory of a young girl sitting on grass in a Cambridge field raced through his mind faster than a hare, and was gone.

"Thank you. How can I repay you?"

"Buy me a cup of coffee when I am in America. One day soon I will be there and you will be surprised to see me!"

Viktor knew this would never happen. It made accepting the gift easier.

A tram had already crossed the bridge over the railway line, but its clanking was nothing like the bass thunder of the train as it approached with its single bright light nosing through the closing darkness. Only when it stopped at the platform could its full size be appreciated. It was either much taller than the trains he had ridden before or the platform was much lower – or both. Three near-vertical steps led into the passenger compartment. Viktor placed one foot on the first rung and attempted to haul his considerable weight up towards the second rung. It was difficult. Kristaps helped by placing his hands on Viktor's hips and pushing upwards. Reaching the second rung with some effort, Viktor struck out for the third with more confidence. As his leg raised, a tearing sound came from behind him and he felt the cool night air waft gently around his underpants.

Below him, Kristaps laughed. He was still laughing when the train lurched and slowly pulled out of Torņakalns station. There was no-one else in the carriage. Viktor slumped onto the nearest bench, clutching his solitary lat for when the ticket inspector arrived. The cruel laughter had evaporated his feeling of gratitude towards Kristaps. The station lights ambled past, then a line of three beaten-up taxis and one other car waiting on the cobblestones at the station entrance. The car, a sleek black Mercedes, looked somehow familiar, but in a moment it was lost as the train picked up speed, passed a dark landscape of overgrown allotments and ground its way onto a steel bridge across the River Daugava. The lights of the city centre shone brightly. Viktor settled into his seat and waited for the next stop with the hot air from a floor-level heater singeing the exposed hairs on the inside of one trouser leg.

VII   NORTH BY NORTHEAST

The conductor had been decent about getting Viktor off the train. He must have been woken by her approach, the way a rum-soaked sailor would rouse at the approach of some fateful Siren. He still held a sweaty, silver one-lat piece in his hand, as slippery as the writhing fish depicted on its face, and offered it hopefully, his booze-bruised brain not yet registering the dissonance between falling asleep in the dark and waking up in bright morning sunshine.

Her reaction left him in no doubt that one lat wasn't nearly enough, so he reached into his pocket to retrieve his wallet – which was no longer there. In normal circumstances it would have taken him one second to work out what had happened. With his present handicap it took no more than four seconds. Kristaps' carefully placed hands and parting laughter provided an explanation for the missing wallet, but not the steadily growing hole flapping between his legs in the manner of a gasping trout. That would remain a worrying mystery for some time to come.

Trees fell past the train window like dominoes. Viktor heaved a bearish sigh and placed his palms out in a gesture of supplication. He offered no resistance. She looked like a woman who dealt with resistance in a Prussian sort of way, who would without hesitation shoot every tenth fare-dodger *pour encourager les autres.*

One deliberate bat of her magenta eyelids contained all the accusation, condemnation and execution of a drumhead court martial. Viktor merely held his hands up in surrender and shuffled towards the door, a prisoner of war captured no further than the barbed wire.

His discharge from the train at the next stop contained added humiliation when he fell onto what passed for the platform. Used to the low-riding trains of the West, he forgot about the near-vertical ladder of three steps that would have required a belay line to descend safely. His foot felt for air, the backdrop of a wooden hut and pine forest inverted itself and his senses shuddered as he hit the ground. Only the cool breeze wafting through his underpants provided any comfort, and even that had its drawbacks.

A second later he lay sprawled on the mossy embankment looking up at the practical undergarments of old ladies stepping over his prostrate and bruised body who disappeared either into a few waiting old Russian cars with domestic appliances strapped to the roofs or percolated directly into the forest. His guardian angel was among their number, but Fate being in a playful mood, he remained completely unaware of this significant event. Reserve ranks of widows and spinsters pressed their noses to the grimy glass of the train as it pulled away, tut-tutting at another victim of drink as they receded towards a thin, distant cleft in the trees.

The train could still be heard long after it had disappeared from view, as if calling a final warning to Viktor over its shoulder. He stood up, did his best to arrange his trousers in such a way that they did not billow too noticeably in the breeze and walked towards what passed for the station – really no more than a concrete block with the word "Āraiši" picked out in white letters on a large wooden board just as "Torņakalns" had been picked out at the other end of the line, who knew how many hours ago.

He considered his situation. He was lost somewhere in the middle of Latvia at a place he couldn't even pronounce properly, was unable to understand or communicate in the local language, had no identification, disposable income of precisely one lat, a hole in the seat of his trousers and a terrible hangover.

Moreover, he had very recently disgraced himself in front of three presidents and a prime minister, an audience of experts and his main professional rival. His career was more tattered than his trousers and a car of the Russian government appeared to be following him for purposes which remained unclear but were unlikely to be to deliver a season ticket to the Bolshoi.

The situation was less than ideal. However, though he tried hard to apply reason and rationality to all of these existential problems, what was at the forefront of his thoughts was how hungry he was. It was a long time since he had experienced hunger – probably not since Cambridge when three cans of soup had a roughly equivalent value as a second-hand volume of Cato's speeches and therefore could be willingly sacrificed by a scholar hungrier for learning than food.

But on the convention circuit, hunger was kept far over the horizon by an unending round of coffee breaks, lunch breaks, evening dinners, cocktail receptions, buffets and the omnipresent option of free room service. It was no coincidence that virtually all the speakers who talked about the need for lean institutions and vigorous preemptive action were portly at best and in some cases impressively obese. In the street into which he rarely ventured unescorted, Viktor looked and felt fat, but in the company of his fellow geopolitical experts, he was fairly svelte, which only provided one extra reason to stay in their company and benefit from relativism.

He still had his one-lat piece which thankfully had not been accepted by the train Gorgon. It was worth approximately one US dollar. Probably it wouldn't stretch very far, but if he could find a shop, he might be able to get something to eat and drink while he tried to draw up some kind of plan. His initial idea, of walking back through the forest towards Riga along the rust-coloured tracks – though he had no idea how far he had come – would make finding a shop unlikely, so he decided instead to walk along the dusty track from the now deserted stop in the direction the derelict Ladas had gone in hope of finding a village. There he should be able to get something to eat and hopefully find someone to help him. At the very worst he could always retrace his steps to the station and set off down the tracks with provisions or ride the train and do his best to hide from the ticket kommandant.

The other passengers had dispersed into the forest like mist. The sun was shining, birds broadcast their sweet songs and throat-clearing calls in all directions and the smell of the pines' resinous trunks acted like a mild dose smelling salts, putting Viktor's addled thoughts back into order.

The last time he had encountered the same aroma had been at a reception he had attended in Sweden at the invitation of some humanitarian body or other, to discuss human rights in Russia. The Scandinavians had rattled on all day in their earnest fashion about detention without trial, modern-day Gulags and press freedom without ever saying anything very nasty about the Russian government in case it gave offence to its representative, one Deputy Prime Minister Kopeikin, who had been kind enough to attend and seemed more interested in flirting with the prettiest women available than wringing his hands guiltily or becoming indignant at the criticism and haranguing the hosts for their hypocritical hospitality.

In the evening, a select group of speakers including Viktor had been picked up in a Victorian motor launch, ferried across a glass-smooth lake at sunset and disembarked on a small islet where an immaculate silver service spread had been laid out under a canvas canopy. Flaming torches illuminated the reluctantly darkening Swedish night, blond waiters sprang unseen from the shadows when required and hopped back into them at will and the conversation turned gradually away from the facts and figures with which Viktor was comfortable towards more personal and flippant matters. Furrowed brows and nodding heads were replaced with laughter and a shadow play of gesticulation as the Akvavit pushed the conversation along at increasing pace and volume.

Between the main course and the dessert several guests excused themselves at intervals, either to make use of the striped toilet tents which had been thoughtfully erected or to take a constitutional stroll around the tiny island to clear some space in their stomachs. Viktor was among them – mainly to get away from the social chatter he regarded as inane and with which he found it difficult to join in.

Little boats continued to traverse the lake bringing fresh supplies and taking away the silver service staff who were no longer needed. The launches caused bow waves to spread across the surface of the water like evenly spaced harp strings, sometimes creating strange patterns when they crossed each other and reflected the light of the torches, as if the lake itself was a huge linen tablecloth being woven in honour of their banquet. The waves were lapping at Viktor's feet as he walked along a miniature beach of orange sand no more than twenty metres long and two wide. His big feet left deep pawprints which he stopped to examine momentarily. He looked up from them into the face of the Russian Deputy Prime Minister who had approached from the opposite direction.

Viktor averted his gaze but there was no way to avoid the Kremlin crony, who to Viktor's surprise called him by his patronymic, halted in front of him and offered a cigar from a leather case that looked like a clip for an anti-aircraft gun.

"What a wonderful place, eh, Viktor Nikolaievich?" Kopeikin said, facing the lake and lighting his cigar with a blue flame from a Gazprom-branded Dunhill lighter.

"I like Swedes very much. They are an intelligent nation, no doubt about it. But I don't know, Viktor, they lack something as well, don't you think? They are afraid of surprises. They cannot embrace chaos. Their own artists – Bergman, Strindberg, that sort – admit that they have no soul, and they are right."

"I disagree. Chaos is generally the result of neglect or stupidity," Viktor replied.

"Do you think so? I'm not so sure. You see we are standing here on this lake in Sweden and we feel very safe and secure. We know that we can walk around this island, ask for anything we want and it will be given to us. We know that when we are tired of food and drink and good company, we can ask to be taken back to our hotel and the civilised Swedes will do that for us. And tomorrow they will wake us up at precisely the time we asked them to wake us up and again we will know where we are, what we are doing and when we will go to bed in the evening..."

"And your point is?"

"Indulge me, Viktor Nikolaievich. Imagine we are standing on this island still, but now we are in Russia. For as we both know, Russia has many places that can equal or surpass even this delightful scene before us. Just you and I standing here in Russia, talking man to man, discussing life, politics, women... whatever we want. For in spite of some of the things you have written about Russia – and I have read them, Viktor, it is my responsibility to read them – these things, these thoughts, are permitted. Our thoughts and emotions are as free as anyone else's... certainly as free as any Swede's..."

"Talking politics on an island in the middle of a lake is one thing. Criticising the government in a Moscow street is another though, isn't it? We both know what would happen then!"

"No, Viktor, no. This is precisely my point. Standing here on this beautiful Russian island with all of creation spread around us, talking man to man, what will happen? Neither of us know! Anything might happen. We might fight, we might embrace. One of us might throw the other into the lake. We might decide to live here forever. We might decide to meet here on the same night next year or never come here again except to be buried. That is my point – in Russia the possibilities are as boundless as the land itself. It sounds like a poor tourist slogan, but it happens to be true. Not because we have done anything ourselves to make it that way, you understand. Despite what you think and write, no-one controls Russia and no-one ever will. Our greatest rulers were the ones who understood that. Our artists complain of a surfeit of soul, not a lack of soul. But you, Viktor, wish to judge us as if the cosmic laws – if I may use such a word – of this Russian island on which we stand were the same as the petty rules and regulations that govern where on this little Swedish island the latrines can be located."

"It sounds to me as if you have been reading too much Tolstoy, Mr Deputy Prime Minister."

Kopeikin laughed loudly. "One can never read too much Tolstoy, Viktor!" he roared, slapping Viktor on the back with such force that an ember dropped from his cigar into the sand, where it lay smouldering in an unnerving way. Kopeikin kept his hand pressed firmly between Viktor's shoulder blades.

He inclined his intelligent face close to Viktor's, but kept his gaze directed to the little lights that marked the jetty on the other side of the lake. His voice now was barely more than a whisper yet somehow sounded with crystal clarity.

"What I am saying, Viktor Draaks, is that next time you write about the distant shore, perhaps you could imagine yourself standing on it. Columbus thought he had discovered the East Indies and look how wrong he was... and who are we compared to Columbus or Tolstoy?"

He paused and drew on his cigar, then exhaled, sending a rolling blue wraith out over the water. "I know a place near Pskov that is ten times more beautiful than this. One day I will take you there and show you the far shore!" His hand patted Viktor's shoulder twice, like a father promising his son a treat if he behaved himself.

Viktor was at a loss as to how to respond, but he felt that the ensuing silence needed to be broken. Naturally, he reached for Pimen's Monologue.

"Now it is silent and tranquil, few are the faces which memory has preserved," he murmured.

Kopeikin continued with the next line. "...and few are the words which have come down to me. The rest have perished, never to return..."

He smiled. "You see, Viktor, it is not only Tolstoy we read at the ministry." With a chuckle and a wave he walked on as a launch, full of cloudberry cakes, started out from the distant jetty.

Perhaps it wasn't only the smell of the pines that reminded Viktor of his conversation with Kopeikin as he walked along the track in the unknown Latvian forest. The idea of being somewhere beautiful and tranquil that hid an underlying threat was another thing the two places had in common. He had considered that encounter on the Swedish island many times, working out what he should have said and how he should have challenged the Russians' childish belief that they were in some way a special case, as if they had been endowed with twenty percent more destiny and mysticism than other nationalities. One only had to walk through a typical Russian provincial town or look at the wreckage of reinforced concrete and rusting rivets they had left behind them from the Baltic states to Kazakhstan to see the extent of that fallacy.

Every time he replayed the meeting, it became a little more worrying. Had it really been a chance meeting? Highly unlikely. The talk about "anything" being able to happen at any moment and being buried – was that a threat, a way of telling him he was being watched? And the contrasting issues of friendship and enmity, of standing on the other shore – was it perhaps hinting at an overture to "come over" to the Russian side?

Viktor couldn't be sure, but the more he thought about that meeting, the more significant it seemed. It was so typical of the Russians to play those sort of games – how could one ever work out their true intentions? Perhaps their lack of clarity was what they mistook for "cosmic forces". They needed to sort themselves out, not plead "destiny" as the excuse for everything they couldn't be bothered to do by hard work.

But there was still something about Kopeikin he couldn't fathom. It was something to do with that invitation to visit Pskov – what was its significance? His mind started to wander towards another pleasant scene in a Cambridge field thirty years earlier when he had been similarly nonplussed by what seemed a simple conversation... but the sight of a bus stop up ahead brought him back to the present.

He must have covered a couple of kilometres when he reached the bus stop. One lat should be enough to carry him to wherever the terminus was – the minibuses tearing around Riga all had signs saying the price of a ticket was 40 santims, which would leave him 60 santims for food and drink. It might be worth catching the bus, as the sun was getting very warm, which combined with his tweed suit and his infrequent exercise was making for perspirational progress. There was no-one else in sight and the glorified, unmetalled track that served as this main road cut an almost perfectly straight path through the tall pines, restricting his view to a telescoping perspective in two directions. It was quiet, apart from the disinterested commentary of the birds and the sound of a light aeroplane circling at a great distance, perhaps spraying crops.

In the far distance, he noticed a tiny cloud at the limits of his view. It grew steadily, like the first sighting of the Seventh Cavalry in a cowboy film, swelling to become a plume of dust streaking behind a comet-like red car with rattling suspension. Viktor had never hitch-hiked in his life, but as the car came closer he held out his thumb, unable to remember whether it should be pointing upwards like Augustus or downwards like Caligula. He opted for the second option but it made no difference. The rusty old Moskvich didn't exactly speed past, but it moved quickly enough to make it clear the driver hadn't even paused to consider a pickup. Viktor's curse disintegrated into spluttering as the trailing pall of fine dust enveloped him, stinging his eyes and making him bury his head inside the breast of his jacket to try and shield himself from the worst of the sandstorm.

Slowly the dust dissipated, the blue sky and dark green tree tops redefined themselves and Viktor stood again in silence. He was just wondering whether he should start walking when another cloud formed in the opposite direction. Like the first one, it grew, but faster, suggesting this vehicle was really travelling. The accompanying noise was deeper and smoother, consisting mainly of tyre and engine noise, not mechanical parts in perpetual friction.

Viktor stuck his arm out again, this time with thumb pointing up. The gesture seemed to possess magical power as the car immediately started to slow, which caused the trailing dust cloud to catch up and engulf it. The vehicle was now no more than fifty metres away, and almost stationary, but hidden as it was in its billowing cloud it was impossible to see more than a large, vague outline. Viktor took two paces forward, delighted to have saved himself 40 santims, but as he did so, a sudden warm gust of wind ran out of the forest behind him and across the road, whipping the dust backwards again like a stage magician pulling the cloth from a box in which someone lay sawn in half. There crawling towards him was a polished Mercedes car with smoked glass windows, Russian government registration plates, a badge missing from the front and a steel stud above the front wheel arch.

For the second time in as many days, Viktor rediscovered his ability to run, bolting into the treeline with the sound of heavy car doors opening and closing behind him and voices shouting words that were snagged on the branches and stumps of trees so that they reached his ears only as harsh, guttural calls.

It is remarkable how little time and space can separate a benign landscape from a hostile one. The shady floor of the forest with its modest spread of blueberry and wild strawberry plants suddenly became a tangled mass of tripwires and ankle-twisting traps of soft earth, but somehow Viktor kept staggering into the shadows like a brown bear on a hind leg rampage. He did not dare look back but could imagine tall, crop-headed figures weaving in and out of the trees, reaching inside their long leather coats to pull out Makarov pistols. He expected to hear a sharp report at any moment and feel the hot, piercing pain of a bullet between his shoulder blades, but it never came.

When he did finally stop and turn to look back, panting, he was completely alone. If the assassins or kidnappers had followed him, they must have given up the chase long ago because now he was not only alone, he was also completely lost.

If the sense of panic was only marginally reduced, it was surprising how quickly the threat of imminent death diminished its fearful proportions. Though he had stopped running, his exertion still caused the blood to pound in his temples so that it seemed as if now the trees themselves were on the move, hiding behind each other, circling, seething one into the other in a vast swirling folk dance of old oak, birch and pine.

The heavens were collaborating with the forest by drawing a grey veil of cloud across the skies, increasing the sense of directionless uniformity and, completing a conspiracy of disorientation, the birds contributed their unending chatter to fill every second with meaningless songs that echoed and re-echoed in all directions.

The intense but thoughtless fear of death was replaced by what was in some ways a more profound fear – a fear of present reality.

The trees, the smell of damp earth, the slight warmth of sunlight on the skin – all felt dreadfully immediate, too near, as if these things were forcing themselves into Viktor's senses against his will. Thinking, imagining or writing about a place is one thing, but actually being there is another, particularly when you do not want to be there. The circumstances that combine to place you in a specific location at a specific time can seem like vindictiveness on the part of the place itself, as if it has somehow tricked you into putting in an appearance precisely when you were expected.

Viktor wanted to be back in his hotel room, choosing between salted and dry roasted peanuts, or ruminating on the policy implications of this or that draft law in front of someone who respected his opinion. It was a simple life with all the details taken care of by efficient organisers. Out here in the forest, nothing was organised. All was impersonal and indifferent. It did feel as if nature herself had targeted Viktor for a special lesson in how little it cared about him. He could run away from the gunmen – but how could he run away from nature?

Suddenly, away to his left, Viktor spotted movement among the branches. Instinctively he crouched down behind the rotting remains of a giant pine now overgrown with wild raspberry and stringy nettles. His first thought was that the assassins had not given up their pursuit and had used their Spetznaz training to track him through the forest, but he quickly saw that the figure moving towards him was not a tall, pale, special forces assassin in a leather jacket but a short, florid-faced man in a filthy woollen jumper and paint-spattered trousers. On his head was a baseball cap at a skewed angle that would have gone down well at a hiphop gathering had it not featured an incongruous image of a smiling dolphin and sun-soaked letters spelling: "I've been to SEA WORLD!"

His crooked nose, cauliflower ears and puffy eyes spoke of an intimate relationship with cheap vodka, and the smell of his perspiration, which grew stronger as he got nearer, had more than a hint of white spirit about it, as if his whole body was acting as a mobile still. You could pour in purest spring water at one end, and eye-numbing hooch would likely appear at the other a few hours later.

In each hand, the man carried two large plastic buckets that, judging from the designs on them, once contained catering-sized helpings of sunflower oil and butter but which were now completely empty, judging from the way they bumped into each other with a dull drumming rhythm as he walked.

If ever a publication needed an image to depict poverty in Eastern Europe and its associated problem of alcoholism, here it was, Viktor thought. The drunk looked harmless enough, so he rose from behind his fallen tree and addressed him in Russian.

"Hello!"

If the man was startled by Viktor's sudden appearance as Oberon, king of the fairies, he didn't let it break his stride. Maybe long nights in the forest accompanied only by a half-litre of local firewater had inured him to strange sights and apparitions. Whatever the reason, when Viktor repeated his greeting in both Russian and English, the man just shook his head reproachfully and murmured something indistinct but of a negative enough intonation to be understood, like a businessman passing a beggar refusing a request for loose change. Soon he had disappeared into the undergrowth.

It left Viktor alone in the middle of the forest. The first fading of the daylight began. Unseen birds commented in mocking tones upon Viktor's predicament as he resumed his trek through the trees. He was very hungry. The sun was becoming anaemic and the shadows were no longer scared of it.

VIII   THE NON-GUEST HOUSE

He nearly walked straight past the sign, though that was hardly surprising as it was lying flat on its back, in a ditch, behind a hedge. He had walked through the forest for hours, half suspecting that he was describing a large and spiteful circle or that the saplings and seedlings of the forest floor were vindictively rising to premature maturity in front of him as he walked, extending the reach of the forest far in front of him like some sarcastic guard of honour as his leafy Latvian odyssey continued.

Eventually, as the sun brushed its backside along the tops of the trees, he stumbled on a track which became gradually wider and drier before forming a junction with a road of sorts. Like the one earlier, it was formed of pebbles and sand rendered white by layers of dust, flanked by intermittent hedges and broad fields. Release from the clutches of the forest was a relief. When he noticed the sign, it occurred to him that it was the first evidence of civilization he had encountered since the fleeting appearance of the man with the buckets – and whether he even qualified as evidence of civilization was a debatable point.

What had caught Viktor's eye was the flag of the European Union. The usually bland gold stars on their bottomless blue field glowed in the evening sunlight, stimulating a kind of reflex recognition in his retina, so often did the symbol appear on the literature, platforms, banners and menus of the conference circuit. It could be noticed without being recognised, acting as an indicator of a set of familiar faces and satisfied appetites rather than a symbol of pioneering trans-national statehood or diplomatic convenience.

He pushed at the gorse hedge by the side of the road with the sleeve of his tweed jacket. Next to the EU flag, on a wooden board that was starting to swell and crack with exposure to damp and sunlight were the words "Guest House" rendered in English, German and Latvian. Beneath the writing were symbols depicting food and drink, swimming, tennis, skiing, saunas and – most seductive of all – beds. Standing the sign up and almost slipping into the ditch which smelled of stagnant water and algae, he tried to see which direction it was supposed to indicate. Nothing was immediately apparent, until he noticed an arrow and the word "100 m" at the very bottom of the sign, half eaten away by mould and mildew. Sure enough, a little way down the road a freshly surfaced side road led up an attractive avenue of trees that were more formally arranged than the forest which kept its distance at the edge of the fields as if suspicious of this imposed geometry.

He set off up the track, reasoning that it might be possible to get a room without advance payment, use the telephone to call the Benbo Foundation for help and lay low for a few days devising a coherent plan to extricate himself from this ridiculous situation. If it wasn't possible to get a room... he shuddered at the thought.

Walking closer to the little complex of buildings he saw that the symbols on the coyly sited information board had not been misleading. First came two tennis courts with tournament-standard surfaces and high net fences that would not have disgraced any tennis club. Behind them was what looked like a bath-house, in a rustic style but clearly newly built. It sat next to a small pond with a manicured edge. Further away reeds rose their swaying heads from the margins of a larger pond with a jetty on the far side of which was another wooden building that looked like a summer house.

Set on the other side of the complex was a four-bay garage with one of its doors opened to reveal a large, deep blue BMW SUV and beside it a prim little woodshed open on one side to expose thousands of expertly stacked triangular logs. Next to the woodshed were two tall, white flagstaffs with one flying the burgundy and white flag of Latvia, the other the European Union's blue and gold starred ensign again.

At the centre of the complex was a broad, cobblestoned yard with a well that may have been functional or ornamental, as it had yet to acquire any patina of age and beside which was the main building. The ground floor clearly used to be a huge stone barn with massive, purplish rocks set into ancient brickwork and plaster which had recently been professionally rendered. The two upper storeys were of gorgeous dark-stained wood that would have looked impressive on a grand piano, never mind a rustic guest-house. All the windows were double glazed and made to measure from a slightly lighter wood that could have been oak. On top of that was more evidence of no-expense-spared craftsmanship in the soft slope of a vast thatched roof. The golden strands that formed it looked like they must have been finished only moments ago and at the gable ends the sheafs were cut into folkloric criss-crosses.

The sight of this immaculately-appointed location raised Viktor's spirits. He had expected some modest farmhouse with a spare room and the smell of straw, not this lavish and remarkably tasteful facility that could have given some of the locations on the convention circuit a run for their money. He made a mental note to ask for a brochure and mention it to conference organisers as an interesting little place he happened to know that might be good for highly confidential and sensitive discussions of, say, trade tariffs or visa regimes. Then he remembered his most recent experience on the circuit and his spirits ebbed once again as he wondered if he would ever be in a position to recommend anything to a conference organiser. He resolved to concentrate on getting a bed for the night and something to eat.

Somewhere behind the house a dog started barking. As it grew in volume and intensity, Viktor quickened his pace, hoping to reach the brass knocker on the main entrance before the dog could intercept him, but worn out by the day's exertions, he was too slow. Within arm's reach of the door he was transfixed by the appearance of a huge hound, the size of a small pony, which rounded the corner of the building and came to a skidding halt inches away from him with its fleshy jowls dripping long gobbets of drool. It bared its teeth and emitted a long rasping growl like an outboard motor, its yellowish eyes daring him to make the slightest move.

Viktor hoped someone was at home. If not, he might end up standing here all night. He had always found man's best friend to be among his worst enemies – perhaps it was his ursuline appearance – and this great, dribbling beast provided ample evidence why.

Relief came only with the opening of a small window next to the door. A middle-aged blonde woman with her hair cut in a business-like bob peered out, her nominally attractive face screwed up in a vinegary expression of distaste. She screeched something at Viktor, ignoring the hell hound as if it was a figment of his imagination. Viktor did not need to speak Latvian to know that she was expressing something along the lines of "What do you think you're doing?" followed by "Get away from my house!"

Viktor's eyes swivelled in their sockets but he was unwilling to risk a movement of his head. Transfixed by the combined aggression of the slobbering dog and the sour-faced blonde, he was unable to form coherent sentences, instead emitting a series of garbled requests and explanations that were further mixed up when the dog started its ear-splitting barking again at the sound of his voice.

"I saw... (bark bark!) guest house... (bark bark!) room for the night..."

The poison blonde registered that he was speaking English and responded in kind. It seemed to slightly soften her attitude.

"I think there is a mistake. This is not a hotel."

The dog registered that its mistress was displeased with the fearful bear and increased the intensity of its braying, which further flustered Viktor and confused the communications. "Guest house written on sign... (bark bark!) I... (bark bark!) expert covering Eastern Europe... (bark bark!) European Union... (bark bark!) very important... (bark bark!) room."

At the words "European Union" the woman's expression changed abruptly from annoyance to a sort of shock and then something like fear which she attempted to disguise with a smile. At last she addressed the dog in similar terms to those she had originally directed at Viktor and the beast turned and slunk away as if it had just been cheated of a bone, but not before it had given Viktor a lingering look that suggested his moment was yet to come.

By the time Viktor's eyes returned to the door, the woman was standing in its open frame offering her hand.

"Ilze Liepiņš, very nice to meet you. But couldn't you have telephoned in advance?"

"I'm afraid in the circumstances that wasn't possible. This is something of a surprise visit."

"Ah, I see, so that's the way it works, is it? I didn't know that was allowed." She looked slightly offended and eyed him with a degree of suspicion. "Where are your bags?"

Viktor didn't know what she meant, but carried on regardless. "I left them at my hotel in Riga, the Grand Palace Europe…"

"A very nice hotel. My husband takes me there for dinner sometimes." She was impressed, pleased that this bond existed between them.

"My bags will follow. I only arrived from Serbia a day ago."

"You cover Serbia, too?"

"Of course. As I just said, I cover all of Central and Eastern Europe."

"That seems like a lot of responsibility. How many of you are there?"

"Just myself."

"Really? I would have thought there would be more of you. So I suppose we are particularly lucky that you came to visit us here," she said with what may have been sarcasm. "Not that we in Latvia have anything in common with Serbia, do we?"

The question seemed rather odd. "Er, you're both European? Post Communist states with political corruption problems? Though between the two of us I think they have more of an issue with it than you. The Serbian president is little more than a gangster."

"Everything here is in order, as you will see!" the blonde shrieked. She seemed to regain her composure with some effort. "You had better come in. You can stay in the private guest house. My husband has some VERY important visitors arriving this evening. That is why I am surprised you would just arrive like this. It could have caused all sorts of problems. I would have expected the European Union to be better informed. Personally I voted against membership, but never mind," and then she added the phrase used by every fraudster, con artist and hustler from the dawn of time, "We have nothing to hide!"

By now Viktor realised they had been talking at cross purposes, but the promise of a bed for the night was not one he was going to risk by any attempt at clarification. His stomach rumbled to remind him to enquire about food as they walked through an airy hallway, through a huge living room done out in a style best described as modern baronial and out the back of the main building onto a path leading to the smaller villa-like building he had noticed as he walked up the drive.

"Do you have a restaurant?"

"Not exactly a restaurant," the woman said, but added, as if to talk up the property's culinary facilities, "…but we do have excellent catering facilities for banquets, weddings and other special celebrations! You want food?"

"That would be splendid."

"I will make sure you are sent a representative selection."

"Thank you kindly. Oh, I meant to ask – do you accept credit cards? I didn't see anything saying you did when I was looking at the facilities you offer."

"You mean you actually intend to pay?"

The question was odd. "Of course. I'm not carrying much cash but I can get my office to wire funds."

"Our credit card machine is out of order at the moment. But I'm sure we can come to some sort of arrangement," the woman of the house replied.

"One final question. Do you have a telephone?"

"Of course."

"Could I use it? To place an international call?"

"Well, yes, but... can it wait until tomorrow? My husband will be back at any moment. You be staying in here tonight." She pushed open the door of the villa.

"How much will it cost?" Viktor asked. He had been thinking more in the line of a simple single room than an entire luxury villa, despite his familiarity with the latter. Unexpected expense tended to raise eyebrows among Benbo's bean-counters.

The woman eyed him up and down again. "As I said, that can be by... negotiation. I am sure we can agree a very competitive rate. Perhaps tomorrow you can tell us what the usual rate would be – what sort of money you might expect to change hands under the circumstances?"

Viktor had the nasty feeling that this misunderstanding would unravel in a very disagreeable way, but the promise of food and a bed was too valuable to risk.

"I must ask that you do not come outside for any reason at all tonight, or it will cause all sorts of complications. I will need to explain to my husband why you are here. I will have your food sent when it is ready. What's wrong with your trousers?" She pointed at the flap of fabric revealing an unenticing section of Viktor's inside thigh.

"Ah... I caught it on a bramble as I came up the drive."

"What? Where? We trim all the hedges every week! The gardener is meticulous! We have never caused any damage to a guest or their possessions!" She was working herself up into a fit.

"When I say 'drive' I mean just before the drive. It happened on the road."

This pacified her. "There, you see? I told you. We can't be held responsible for what happens in every square inch of Latvia, can we? We just take care of our little corner, and everything here is in order. You'd better give me your trousers. I'll get Magda to sew them up." She gestured abruptly that he should hand over his trousers there and then.

"Magda?" Viktor said, as he sheepishly climbed out of his tweed trousers with the awkwardness of a little boy still struggling with the operation of zips and buttons.

"I suppose you could call her our chambermaid, though she is much more than that. She has a heart of gold. You'd better give me your jacket, too. It looks like it's been dragged through the forest."

"Thank you, you have been very kind," Viktor said, squeezing his legs together and folding his arms across the front of his shirt in a display of embarrassed modesty. He couldn't remember the last time he had been so scantily dressed in front of a woman. "Out of interest, is anyone else staying here, too?"

She eyed him askance. "No," she replied as she opened the door. "The last guests left just this morning. They were a family of Russians and very much enjoyed their stay." The door closed behind her.

Like the rest of the complex, Viktor's villa was expensively but tastefully furnished and would not have been out of place on the circuit as a special residence for one of the senior speakers, a fact he added to his mental note of the complex's suitability. Pleasant though the main room was with its exposed beams and antique furniture, spotless though the kitchen was with its honey-coloured pine table and rustic flagstones, only the bedroom was of immediate interest, the oak bed pulling him in as if he were a worn-out planet being sucked into a flaring sun. His eyes ignored the expert carving on the bedposts and the stags flexing their muscles on the headboard. His whole body collapsed into blissful unconsciousness before even making contact with the grey-brown linen bedcover into which he plunged as into a bottomless pool.

*****

He was woken by a flashing blue light, so slight and soundless it was surprising it had broken his sleep at all. The light played around the walls and ceiling so that for a moment he thought he really was underwater. Next he assumed it was the flashing of LEDs from a bedside clock which had in the past woken him from five-star slumbers in hotel rooms from the Crimea to the Skaggerak. But the only clock in the room was a heavy wooden mantel mechanism that tocked but disdained to tick above the unlit fireplace.

As his senses swam up towards consciousness, he saw the blue light was coming in through the window. He lifted the fine linen curtain to peer outside.

Coming to a halt and shutting off their engines on the other side of the pond was a row of expensive limousines, flanked by tall SUVs all dark and shining in the moonlight as if they were coated in crude oil. But what immediately seized his attention as the last of the blue lights was extinguished was what three of the vehicles had protruding from the bonnet above their right front wheel arches. Each had a small flag of one of the Baltic states – Lithuania, Latvia and Estonia – on little silver flagpoles.

Viktor rubbed his eyes, the way a character in a cartoon might when presented with some unbelievable spectacle. Even as he did it, he was aware of how ridiculous the gesture was – like the drunk who sees a flying elephant, looks at his bottle and throws it over his shoulder – but what else could he do other than hope again that he was dreaming and the scene in front of him was a therapeutic playing-out of the last two days' appalling events.

When he reopened his eyes the cars were still there, and a small army of bodyguards was swarming from the SUVs to the limousines, looking like besuited giants in the moonlight. They seemed relaxed. None of them looked across the pond at the darkened villa, or if they did, none of them noticed the face staring in amazement from the bottom corner of the bedroom window.

Now the three presidents and their aides emerged from the brightly-lit interiors of the cars. The presidents exchanged handshakes in a way that suggested they had been doing so all day, laughed loudly at an unheard joke and began strolling slowly towards the main house, the Latvian president leading the way and explaining something about the complex to his counterparts, probably telling them how much care and expense had gone into the place in a suitably modest manner. At one point he even paused, turned and pointed at the villa, causing Viktor to duck and lie cowering beneath the window, which provided him with an excellent opportunity to wonder what it all meant.

The one consolation Viktor had had during his two-day diversion had been the knowledge that at least he was so hopelessly lost that anyone wanting to confront him about his performance at the conference had no chance of finding him. He had not formed a coherent strategy to explain his behaviour, but a few possibilities were beginning to suggest themselves and he was confident he could come up with something at least half-credible given another day or two.

But there was something terrifying about believing himself to be hopelessly lost when – to the powerful people he had offended – he apparently was not lost at all. The means by which he had arrived at the villa seemed too random and absurd to suggest there was any design behind it but – what if there was? No-one was better placed to control affairs in the Baltic states than the presidents of those countries, and he had no real idea how far their powers extended or worked, except on the international stage, where he routinely referred to them as "minnows".

His speech to the conference launched with a statement that the Baltics "didn't matter" and his unfortunate condition meant he had never had a chance to reach the point at which he reversed the argument and showed that they did, after all. Could the presidents have taken such umbrage at his actions that they had decided to usher him to this spot in the middle of nowhere and do... who knows what?

The more he thought, the more confused he became. What bothered him more than anything else was that he did not have all the necessary facts at his disposal. If there was some sort of conspiracy against him what did it hope to achieve – would he be given a good talking to, told never to darken Baltic shores again or, if the authorities were prepared to go to such extraordinary lengths, might he face a more serious fate? Torture? Imprisonment?

Such things had happened in the past and it was common knowledge that secret prisons existed in the Baltic states for the detention of terror suspects, but surely they could not be used by the Baltics themselves to imprison someone who after all was an American citizen? Then again, if the Americans got something tangible in return – say, the right to site some missiles or a juicy defence contract that would allow them to unload some second-hand fighter planes – then after all Viktor Draaks was only a naturalized citizen from the hazy Carpathians, and what future value would he have after embarrassing three regional allies? Better to cash him in. The theory that he had been a Russian sleeper all along seemed even more credible in the circumstances. The leading expert on the realpolitik of the region did not enjoy the feeling that he might actually be a token of exchange in the very game he had been a commentating upon for all these years.

But it was all too incredible. Could it be engineered that he would walk in a certain direction and find a sign in a ditch? If it really was a charade of breathtaking complexity, it might perhaps explain why the woman in charge of the guest house had been so keen to get him alone in this villa and not let him make a call to Benbo straight away – but why had she spoken her lines in such an odd way? Above all, if they had known where he was all the time, why not simply pick him up in a police van? And if the Baltics were out to teach him a lesson, why were the Russians after him as well?

As if in answer to his question, as he lay hunched on the floor, the blue light returned. Venturing the top half of his head above the window sill again, Viktor saw another car approaching slowly up the long tree-lined driveway he had walked earlier. It was without an escort but just as sleek and sinister as the other vehicles. Like them it displayed an ensign from a silver flagpole sticking up from above the front wheel arch which flapped listlessly in the still night air.

The Baltic presidents noticed the car's approach, too, and waited on the path, with the Latvian president waving cheerily in greeting as it drew closer.

The brightness of the headlights made it difficult to see details until it turned into the parking space which had been reserved for it next to the other limousines. As the headlight beams swung across the pond, briefly illuminating Viktor's startled face, he saw with horror the white, blue, red flag of the Russian Federation. It couldn't be the president – even a secret visit would involve an escort larger than the entire Latvian army – so it must surely be the ambassador. What on earth was he doing here? The sight was enough to stimulate Viktor's professional interest, banishing temporarily his apprehension of a few moments ago as he wondered if he might be on the verge of discovering a geopolitical secret. If it was a big enough revelation it could be his ticket back to the circuit.

However, fear returned anew and even stronger when he saw stepping from the car not the horse-faced Russian ambassador to Latvia but the familiar, jovial features of none other than Deputy Prime Minister Kopeikin.

It was a very long time since Viktor had uttered the oath that escaped his lips at that moment, but like running, it was a skill he appeared not to have forgotten completely.

Kopeikin joined the presidents to launch another round of handshakes before they all walked off towards the main house. For perhaps twenty minutes Viktor lay on the floor in the dark, wondering what to do. Trying to escape was futile – the place was swarming with security personnel and in any case he had no idea where he was or in which direction he should head.

The only thing to do was accept whatever fate had in store with as much dignity as he could muster and enjoy the irony of a chain of events that had seen a man renowned for his stout defence of the Baltics against Russian aggression trapped by an apparent alliance of the Baltics and the Russians.

On a personal level it was terrifying but even as he sat on the bed waiting for the knock on the door he could not suppress a perverse pride that at least his name would go down in the annals of the Benbo Foundation as a martyr to freedom and democracy when the facts eventually emerged, even if it took decades. Perhaps a meeting room of the planned new Benbo Foundation headquarters would be named after him.

And then the knock came, not the rhythmic pounding of the leather-gloved hand that had suddenly destroyed the lives of thousands in the Baltics over the years, but an almost apologetic little tap, which still made him start, followed immediately by the sound of the front door swinging open.

Viktor took a deep breath, stood up as straight as he had for years and walked slowly down the stairs to face his fate, his feet providing a heavy drumbeat accompaniment on the wooden stairs.

To his surprise, fate did not take the form of tall men in long leather coats but trout with potatoes, green beans and a mushroom sauce. It lay on the kitchen table on a white plate, under a stainless steel cover. Next to the plate was a large glass of white wine – his nose said probably Chablis – which, to his surprise, was nicely chilled. As he unfurled a knife and fork from the grey linen napkin in which they were wrapped, he noticed a small, folded piece of paper tucked under the plate. Holding the paper at arm's length – his glasses had been in his jacket's breast pocket – he took a first forkful of juicy fish, nodding approval to himself and began reading.

"We have arranged for you to be thrashed at 1100 tomorrow. Stay in the house until then. Good night." He put the fork down.

So that was it. A barbaric punishment worthy of this barbaric little corner of Europe. Yet it held, surprisingly, less terror than he had expected. The last meal of the condemned man still tasted delicious. He picked the fork up again and let his mind wander as he ate.

In a way he was curious to see exactly what form the thrashing would take. Back in his Cambridge days the dons and even some of his fellow students had so frequently referred to the "thrashings" either handed out or received at the grand old public schools of England that he had almost envied them the experience, as if it were a rite of passage that he had not been asked to undergo in his small Carpathian school run by kindly teachers whose main worry was keeping pace with his developing intelligence.

It had been the same at senior school – provincial professors doing their best to impart real knowledge while staying on the right side of a system that preferred all genuine fact – evolution, economy, even biology – to be tainted to some degree by the pseudo-science of Marxist Leninism. On the whole these timid, worn men and women had done a good job, too – by the time Viktor arrived in Cambridge he had an unquenchable thirst for knowledge that put most of his languid, carefree British contemporaries to shame. They might have more fun on their nights out and trips back home for the holidays, but he always read more, knew more and wrote more. And the more he knew, the more he wanted to know so that it never seemed like a deprivation that he had no money, no real friends and little interest in a social life outside the quadrangles and lecture theatres. As his academic aptitude grew and grew, the outside world shrank and shrivelled until he barely noticed it any more.

His isolation had been accelerated by an incident that still crossed his mind from time to time. A pretty girl called Amelia had approached him in the library one Thursday – he remembered it was a Thursday. He even remembered what he had been reading when it happened – official biographies of Enver Hoxa and Josip Broz Tito issued by their respective Parties. The gaps, contradictions and revisions contained in the accounts of the two great leaders' meetings – particularly as they loathed each other – provided him with a rich seam of material that he had drawn upon first in his thesis and then in his after-dinner speeches ever since.

Amelia had asked if he was Viktor Draaks and, if he was, had he ever been to Budapest? He said that he was and he had. She told him that her parents were originally from the Hungarian capital but had never spoken of the city and now both were dead. She had heard from her course mates that a brilliant scholar from Eastern Europe named Viktor Draaks knew everything about Eastern Europe. She wanted to hear what Budapest was like, any recollections or impressions he might have.

On Saturday they had caught a bus together out of the city to a country pub one of Viktor's more worldly classmates had recommended as suitable for a romantic encounter. He had checked the timetable to be sure of the arrangement and they had been rewarded with a glorious spring day. It was strange walking through the bucolic countryside of Cambridgeshire, crossing little streams on stone bridges, hearing the distant bells of a church with a wedding, all the while talking about the broad sweep of the Danube and gypsies on street corners with accordions and fiddles, but Amelia had listened intently, only rarely interrupting to ask for some fact to be clarified or explained more fully.

After a ploughman's lunch in the pub, which Viktor paid for with the last of his money even though it would mean condensed soup for a week, they sat on the grass in a nearby meadow. His one pint of pale ale had made his conversation more expansive than usual, and he started embellishing his descriptions of domes and avenues, tiled bathhouses and cool beer cellars.

Then something very strange happened. Amelia asked him if he was happy in England.

"Of course. Cambridge is marvellous. If you had told me when I was growing up with sheep and goats that one day I would be attending Cambridge University and sitting here with you, I would not have believed it."

"But do you feel you really belong here?" Amelia asked. "I am a second-generation immigrant, but even I sometimes feel that... well, that England doesn't want me. Don't you feel that you belong over there?"

"I'm not Hungarian."

"I know, but you are from the other side of Europe, the Soviet side. Don't you ever want to return?"

He was about to answer, when the thought struck him. Amelia was attempting to recruit him. He felt cheated and cheapened, but the more he thought about it, the more sense it made. He had never seen her before, he had no way of knowing if her biography was fact or fiction, she had approached him, she had wanted every last detail from him – which was of no value in itself but did showcase his powers of recall – and now she was asking him in effect where his loyalties lay.

The warm beer seemed to curdle in his stomach. He despised his own naivety. Viktor Draaks was known to be a superlative scholar from behind the Iron Curtain. In a way it was remarkable that he hadn't been approached sooner. Maybe he had, but his innocence was such that he might not have noticed. And what other reason could there be for this pretty young girl to ask someone like Viktor Draaks out on a date?

Viktor said it was time they returned to Cambridge, trying to fend off further conversation by answering all questions in the most inane and obvious manner possible. Amelia noticed but said nothing. She simply looked sad and looked at her shoes. By the time they reached the bus stop, conversation had dried up.

They waited and waited, but no bus came. Eventually Viktor realised that when he had checked the times, he must have been looking at the weekday timetable, but he didn't admit his mistake to Amelia. He had no money anyway. There was nothing to do but wait and hope another bus would come. It grew cloudy and cold. Amelia went back to the pub and called for a taxi. It came, and dropped Viktor off at his college. Amelia said she would pay the fare and disappeared in the back of the cab.

He didn't see her again for months, which tended to back up his suspicion about her being a Soviet agent. Then one morning he saw a girl who looked very much like Amelia riding past on a bicycle. It was a sunny day and she was smiling as if her destination held the promise of something enjoyable. For an instant he wanted to call out, but he didn't. If she saw him, she didn't show it. After a few seconds she had disappeared, pedalling in the same direction along the same road in which the taxi had taken her.

The strange thing was that every time he landed in Budapest for a conference, which happened at least twice a year, without fail his first thought would be whether Amelia had visited the city yet and whether she felt his description had been accurate. By the time he got to the customs desk he always caught himself scanning the faces of travellers heading in the opposite direction, just in case Amelia was among them and her expression might reveal something. Then he would decide to drown the memory in a careful study of the conference agenda.

Waiting that night in Latvia for the next day's promised punishment felt a little like waiting for that bus to arrive in the Cambridgeshire village. There was nothing to do but to wait, no alternative action available, so Viktor just sat on the bed with the lights off looking at the insects making ripples on the pond's surface as the orange glow of the bodyguards' cigarettes buzzed around the limousines like fireflies.

But Viktor was not destined to endure a night of simple, stoic contemplation. A bright flame suddenly burst into life by the edge of the pond, billowed a couple of times then died as he squinted through the dark night air to see what had made it. At first he couldn't believe his eyes, but as a long, yellow slit of light played for a few seconds across the pond from a door being opened in the main building, there was no mistaking what he saw: Deputy Prime Minister of the Russian Federation Kopeikin walking slowly around the pond with none other than Pavel Panchev.

He watched in stunned silence as the two men described a full circuit at a leisurely pace, Kopeikin clearly leading the conversation with Panchev listening and occasionally commenting. He wished he could hear what they were saying, but at this distance it was impossible, so his mind had little difficulty serving up an imagined version of what must be passing between them, involving instructions from Moscow, congratulations on Panchev's increasing international profile and what was going to happen to Viktor Draaks.

But at no point did they look at the villa, which seemed odd if they were part of the conspiracy that had put him there. Or was the punishment, as he had supposed, a purely Baltic initiative? And if so, exactly how far did Russia's influence extend? If only there was a way of telling the Benbo Foundation – evidence of Russian meddling on this scale would surely outweigh any embarrassment about his performance at the conference? He could be back on the circuit with a story that would make him top of the bill from Helsinki to Istanbul with the added bonus of turning Pavel Panchev's meteoric rise into a cataclysmic fall. He had to take his "thrashing" tomorrow with gritted teeth, like in pirate films when they gave some sailor a taste of the cat, and look for a chance to escape and tell the world the truth, with the scars to prove it. With such a tale it might even be worth writing a book.

And it was with adventure on the high seas still listing from side to side through his brain that the day finally caught up with Viktor Draaks properly and sent him sinking back into the bottomless bed to fight heroically against all manner of dragons and devils.

IX   A THRASHING

It was a lovely day for a thrashing. A few jolly cumulus clouds wandered lazily across the pale blue sky, looking like piles of fresh cottage cheese. The wind blew with a gentle irregularity that was no stronger than the air escaping Viktor's own nose and mouth as he snored like a bullfrog. Unoffended by his inattention, two ducks had taken up residence in the pond outside the villa and were discussing the day's slim prospects of rain while amphibians practised their diving technique from tiny holes at the water's edge. A pair of pike had taken note of Viktor's continued unconsciousness and after a cursory visit to the surface at daybreak and a brief breakfast decided to emulate him by returning to their reed beds.

Viktor's first thought on waking was that today he would talk about the unrealised strategic potential of gas pipelines in the Baltic states. There were some important possibilities of which policymakers seemed ignorant and which he would be sure to make an impression by explaining. His second thought was that the pillow had been excellent and he would ask for the same type next time he stayed in a hotel of the same chain. His third thought was that his first two thoughts had been based on a false premise and his fourth was that he was lost and about to be whipped like a serf by the presidents of the Baltic states.

Would they wield the whip personally or get one of their goons to do it for them? The former would be more psychologically disturbing, the second more painful. Viktor concluded that it didn't really matter, had a shower, got dressed, went to the kitchen, drank a glass of water and waited.

Contrary to his dreams of gnarled deck-hands dragging him to the poop deck and lashing him to the wheel with hempen ropes, his escort to the flogging ground turned out to be the small blonde woman he had met when he first arrived, whose name he had forgotten and who brought with her his freshly stitched and pressed suit. In a reverse of the previous night's exchange, he climbed into the clothes while they spoke.

She still seemed on edge – probably it was rare for someone to be thrashed, even in Latvia – but after a brief exchange of good mornings and comments on the weather, she asked if he had slept well.

"I slept as well as could be expected in the circumstances," he ironised.

"Our beds are all very comfortable. All our guests say so. I'm sorry if my husband's visitors kept you awake at all but I hope you will understand that it was impossible for you to leave the villa. That's why there are no other guests here at the moment. But we will be welcoming them again next week. Are you ready to go?"

"As ready as I will ever be," Viktor said resignedly as they walked out of the door and along an expertly-laid path made from the circular cross-sections of tree trunks set into sand. After a pause during which he smelled freshly-cut grass and admired the china blue of the sky, he added: "Will it hurt very much?"

"Will what hurt?"

"The thrashing."

"Well, have you ever been thrashed before? It may sting if it is your first time. You will soon get used to it. It becomes quite addictive. When my husband thrashes me, I always tell him not to stop. More, more I shout!"

The casual manner in which she talked about such barbarity was appalling. No wonder Turkey was offended at not being allowed into the European Union when existing member states apparently still looked on flogging as part of everyday domestic life.

He looked around, wondering if this might be his last opportunity to make a break for freedom. All but one of the presidential cars – the Latvian one – and its escorting SUV had departed, so it seemed he would not be punished by a triumvirate of presidents but by the offended host alone. Two burly security guards prowled around the SUV and would be easily able to stop him if he tried running down the driveway. In the other direction the lawn gave way to an abrupt line of forest which looked momentarily more promising until he saw the ugly long lump of the hell hound lounging on the grass in the shade of a tree, its one open eye watching him derisively. It seemed to be daring him to make a break for it.

At a junction in the path, they turned not towards the main building but in the other direction towards the back of the tennis courts.

"Would you like to play tennis first?" the blonde woman asked.

"Would I like to play tennis? No!"

"I'm sure we could find someone to play with you – the gardener, perhaps? I don't think Magda plays. It would be better to play before because you might not have the energy afterward. And we want to make sure you experience everything we have to offer here at the guest house."

This really was the limit. The idea of a jolly little knock-up followed by savage corporal punishment was the sort of thing even English public schools would have regarded as beyond the pale, a sort of cross between Wimbledon and Devil's Island.

By now they had reached the door of the tiny wooden hut next to the smaller pond behind the tennis courts that he had seen on his way into the complex. To Viktor's surprise there were still no burly guards to pin him down or place a leather strop between his teeth.

"You go in and strip off and I will be in after a few minutes," the blonde woman said with a forced smile. "You will be able to recommend this to everyone in the European Union!"

He smelled hot, fiery brimstone as he stepped into the dark interior of the hut. The little room had a wooden bench, a low table in the corner and two more doors, one leading out of the back of the building and another in the direction of a low electrical note and a sudden hiss as if some subterranean geyser was erupting in the next room. As much to escape the heat as anything else he stripped quickly, hanging his clothes on thoughtfuly-provided pegs in this ante-room of hell.

Now wearing just his underpants, he wondered what he was supposed to do next. It felt odd to be standing naked anywhere other than a brightly-lit hotel bathroom. He could feel the hairs on his belly and legs curling slightly as the heat escaping from one of the doors in front of him wrestled with a cool draught from the cracks around the edge of the other door, through which he could just see daylight. He didn't know where to put his hands.

The sense of exposure deepened as the blonde woman came back in. With a laugh she indicated his underpants.

"Hah! Take those off, too. Who ever heard of being thrashed wearing underwear? It would be silly."

"I would rather keep them on if that's all the same," he replied, attempting to assemble a few last shreds of dignity.

"As you wish. But you look ridiculous! Now – in there!" She pointed to the hot door.

He pulled on the warm wooden door handle and stepped through.

The first circle of Hades was always reported as a somewhat mild form of punishment for those unlucky enough to be born in ignorance, and so it proved with Viktor. His personal hell was a very nicely constructed sauna with pine benches that almost glowed with the heat, a pile of fenced-off volcanic rocks in the corner with a tap dripping onto them to boost the humidity and temperature to levels that seemed to boil his blood, and light from six small LED bulbs that phased gradually from blue to purple to red to green and back to blue.

It was silent at first, but after a minute during which he took stock of the situation and pawed ineffectually at his dripping brow, the real torture began when Native American chanting to a triphop backbeat began wafting through the heat box from hidden speakers. He almost wished he had walked straight into the flogging he had originally feared. But that was still to come.

On the verge of passing out as he broiled in this oven, there was as knock at the door. He grabbed a towel which lay folded on the end of one of the benches and wrapped it quickly around his hairy belly, as in stepped not the little blonde woman but a woman at least as large as himself in a blue overall who might charitably have been described as "matronly" and could easily have been a relation of the conductress who had thrown him off the train.

She gestured for him to lie on his belly. He complied. In a movement of speed and dexterity which belied her size, she whipped away the towel around his waist like a conjuror removing a tablecloth without spilling a drop from the wine glasses on the table. The sight of his underpants prompted a sort of Banshee yell, she yanked them down and off his legs in an instant and threw them over her shoulder with a grunt.

In one hand she held half the forest. Long switches of birch, complete with leaves and in some cases catkins formed a fascine in her huge hand which she raised into the air in a Gorgonish manner and brought rasping down in the small of Viktor's back. He whimpered more from the completion of his humiliation than from any actual pain.

The assault was repeated over and again with the whacks getting harder and being interspersed with strange circular motions of the twig bundle so that his manhandler looked more like a cleaner sweeping and beating a rug than a masseuse administering a relaxing spa treatment. Then suddenly she shouted an order with all the sensitivity and politeness of a gulag sentry, gesturing for Viktor to leave the torture chamber at once.

He was so pleased to be offered some respite and the chance to breathe air that did not feel as if it had been spewed out by a volcano that he neglected to wrap himself in his towel, so was taken aback to be greeted on the other side of the door by the small blonde woman, who eyed his glistening, swollen body up and down with a curled lip.

His brawny wrangler pushed past him and out through the back door, letting a brief gust of beautifully cool air into the changing room, but as he gasped it in thirstily, it became clear she had stepped outside to smoke a cigarette. It smelled like a fire in an oil refinery lit using a blowtorch.

"How are you enjoying your thrashing?" the small blonde woman asked. "Is that what you would call it? I don't think there is an exact English word for what happens in our *pirtnīca*."

"You mean the sauna?" Viktor whispered, his voice hoarse from the heat.

"No, no, no, it is not a sauna! It is a *pirts*, a *pirtnīca*. It is completely different and very Latvian," she said, continuing to eye the naked, heavily perspiring and hairy expert in his field up and down. "You look like you needed it!"

"It is... not at all what I was expecting," Viktor puffed, giving thought to the strategic placement of his hands over his nether regions for once rather than the placement of Russian missiles in Kaliningrad.

"But you can feel it making a difference, yes?" the blonde woman continued. "It is extremely good for the blood. It will clean out your organs."

"I don't doubt it," Viktor puffed.

"But as it is your first time, we should not overdo you. I think one more session with Magda will be enough. Did you know that she was Andropov's personal masseuse?"

From a small table in the corner she pulled out a ring binder and flipped through the plastic sheets inside which contained newspaper cuttings in Russian, Latvian and Finnish attesting to the efficacy of Magda's technique. Near the back was a large and lavishly embossed certificate awarded by the Soviet Ministry of Health and on the final page a large photograph of Magda with her chin jutting out almost as far as her ample bosom, upon which was riveted a row of medals.

"Andropov was the one who died unexpectedly, wasn't he?" Viktor said. "I'd heard some theories that he was murdered but never one suggesting massage as the means."

His joke did not cross the cultural divide. "If Andropov had met Magda earlier, perhaps he would still be with us," mused the blonde woman. "Perhaps the Soviet Union would still exist!" she added, seemingly pleased by the originality of her thought.

"I must remember to thank Magda," Viktor wheezed.

"You have your breath again, so in you go!" the blonde chided. "Afterwards it is traditional to run straight out of the door of the pirtnīca and roll in the snow to close the pores of the skin. There is no snow yet, but there is the pool just outside, so when Magda tells you, you must run straight out and jump into the pool. It will feel wonderful and will wake your blood again. After you jump in I will take you back to the villa to rest. It is very important that you lie down after visiting the pirtnīca. Magda!"

Magda re-entered, lacking only a bunch of keys and rubber truncheon to make her appearance complete, and dragged Viktor back into the hothouse where, to make matters even worse, she insisted that he lie on his back so she could sweep her broomstick around parts that were rarely exposed to daylight let alone circulation-enhancing assault.

Viktor found it hard not to think of rumours that had been swirling around the circuit for years about a certain German politician who apparently was prepared to pay a substantial sum of money to be whipped in the dark by Eastern European women. A session with Magda would probably cure him of his secret vice, and if not, he would at least get his money's worth, Viktor mused.

Perhaps there was a semblance of human charity remaining somewhere deep in Magda's formidable breast because just as Viktor again prepared to tunnel towards unconsciousness she prodded him hard in the ribs and barked for him to get out while gesturing for him to go and plunge into the pool. Dizzy from the heat and with perspiration pouring from him in rivulets, he swung his legs off the bench and made a course for the door, picking up speed in the changing room before nearly tearing the door off its hinges and emerging, steaming, into the outside world.

With his head still spinning he looked around for the promised pool. It took a second to see it, and it seemed smaller than he thought. It did not look enticing, with some unhealthy-looking weeds growing from its fringes and water that was translucent at best, but probably in Latvian lore this was good for the skin or some similar folksy nonsense. Pinching his nose and closing his eyes, he launched himself through the air towards the middle of the pool.

It was not the sudden plunge into refreshing depths he had envisaged. Rather it was a slow descent into a nasty, glutinous mass of warm – what? Having failed to submerge further than his chest before his feet hit the bottom he removed his fingers from his nose and breathed in the most obnoxious odour he had ever smelled. He immediately pinched his nose closed again, though by now the revolting reek seemed to have penetrated his every pore and could be experienced orally as well as nasally.

He waved his other arm frantically, succeeding in throwing a fair amount of sewerage into the air to land on his head, and attracting the attention of the Hound of the Baskervilles which bounded joyfully to the edge of the pit and began barking at him in a way that made it clear he would be savaged the moment he tried to exit his disgusting stink-hole. Viktor was caught not between a rock and hard place but between a dog and a soft place.

The commotion summoned the small blonde woman who appeared within a few seconds from the other side of the bath-house. She didn't speak immediately, but brought her hands to her mouth and stood there wide-eyed as the dog continued haranguing Viktor from the sidelines. Then she broke into a shrieking, hysterical laughter that formed a dissonant counterpoint to the barking. All the while Viktor stood helpless, trying to breathe in as little as possible of the noxious vapour that shimmered around him in waves.

"Get me out of here!" he whimpered at last.

"But why did you jump in here?" the blonde woman asked between sobs. "You are supposed to jump into the nice water on the other side!"

"Please!"

The blonde woman scurried back into the bath-house through the back door which had been Viktor's downfall. She returned a moment later with a scowling Magda and some towels which Magda knotted together with the skill of a stevedore and threw towards Viktor so as to avoid having to touch his unclean body directly. At the second attempt he grasped the life-line and the two women – one small, one large – began hauling their large brown catch towards the near shore.

In some ways it was unfortunate that at that very moment the President of Latvia exited the main building and started walking to his limousine accompanied by a bodyguard and the up-and-coming geopolitical commentator and freelance adviser, Pavel Panchev, who had been invited to stay the night in view of his lack of personal transport.

The group walked briskly towards the car before their attention was taken by another small group far away behind the bath-house and the barking of the large dog, which was hidden from their view by the bath-house itself.

"What's happening?" Panchev asked, peering at the curious little scene being enacted.

"That damned dog has jumped into the cess pit again," sighed the President. "Come on, let's get moving before my wife sees us and asks for help. I have to meet the Norwegian ambassador today, and I don't intend to do it covered in paw prints and last month's shit!"

The President quickened his pace, and gave a token wave to his wife who was tugging on the end of the towels like a Volga boatman. She let go of the towel to wave back and blow a kiss in his direction which, while sentimentally touching, had the unfortunate side-effect of dropping Viktor back into the slough of despond. But with Magda acting as sheet anchor on one end of the rope, and with the presidential car disappearing up the driveway, they finally managed to haul Viktor onto dry land where he lay gasping like a large brown trout. With the last of his strength he crawled back through the back door of the bath-house, out of the front door and slithered into the cool water of the plunge pool on the other side, where his collection of accumulated unmentionable filth floated free of his body at last.

X LIFE AT THE SUMMIT

Pavel Panchev was puzzled by the strange scene taking place down by the bath-house, but such was the speed at which the motorcade was instructed to move by the anxious president that by the time he had loosened his seatbelt and turned his neck, they were already far down the tree-lined driveway and the buildings of the Latvian President's pleasant private residence were sinking down into the gently rolling landscape.

The preceding forty-eight hours had given him plenty to think about. While his contact with decision-makers was frequent on the circuit, it tended to be in the sterile confines of conference suites and meeting rooms. The invitation to join the presidents for their informal discussion at the end of the two day conference had been unexpected and had, they told him, been a unanimous decision by themselves after the expert way in which he had conducted their discussion the previous morning, particularly bearing in mind the somewhat awkward manner in which it had commenced with Viktor Draaks lurching around the stage.

Viktor remained in Pavel's thoughts for some reason as he sped down the long drive. Sitting next to him was the Latvian president, who struck him as a pleasant enough man but one who clearly regarded being president as more of an inconvenience complicating his family life than an honour bestowed upon him by the land of his birth. Two years into his four-year term already, by the time they had reached for the brandy after their evening meal he was speculating about walking away from high office in order to spend more time with his wife and dog. His counterparts from Estonia and Lithuania did their best to dissuade him, but their efforts struck Pavel as rather half-hearted. Probably they had heard it all before.

Luckily none of the leaders had known much about the embarrassing inebriate who had launched the morning conference in such an unusual manner. Perhaps it was for the best, Pavel reasoned, and had tactfully decided against identifying his colleague when the dinner-table conversation passed briefly onto previous morning's events. Why Viktor had behaved as he did, Pavel had no idea – perhaps a reaction to medication or food poisoning? Had Viktor eaten mushrooms with his habitual bacon at breakfast that morning? Pavel had been so preoccupied with his preparations for the seminar that it was difficult to remember, but he did have a vague recollection that Viktor had been a little curt in his remarks – perhaps he had already been feeling ill?

As the car bounced along the rough track seeking the main road back to Riga, the escorting SUV up ahead gave an occasional blast from its sirens to frighten away weary country folk who appeared from nowhere by the side of the road carrying large buckets, bags and baskets.

Pavel felt a deepening sense of concern about Viktor, whom he did not know well but did admire. Viktor had been on the circuit so long that he was a sort of permanent fixture, his looming presence lending a sense of security and familiarity to events in locations that were sometimes new and a little intimidating. Viktor must be full of stories about how things had changed over the years and what great figures from the past were like off the record. Pavel wanted to hear those stories and if Viktor was not the easiest person with whom to strike up a friendly conversation, he probably had his reasons. It would have been nice if Viktor could become a mentor of sorts, but as that seemed unlikely to happen, Pavel was content to watch and learn from the older man and hope that increasing familiarity bred friendship rather than contempt.

It was understandable that Viktor might see him as some sort of young pretender, but Pavel wanted to reassure him that he had nothing to fear. He didn't wish to compete and in his moments of honesty with himself – which were becoming more frequent – he wasn't entirely sure whether this was a life he wanted to lead for much longer. Put bluntly, he wasn't sure that he wanted to become Viktor in twenty years' time, which was another reason to study him closely.

Certainly the travel was fun and the endless discussions and intellectual cross-examinations were fine in small doses, but he couldn't escape the growing suspicion that the gap between words and action was much larger than most of the participants ever acknowledged.

And it had to be admitted – though no-one ever did – that most of the people at most of the events had only a slight interest in the items on the agenda. Deputy heads of government departments who were sent in lieu of the boss, academics from second-rate universities looking for something quotable to pad out a thesis, military men who seemed about to pop their buttons from boredom – these accounted for a large proportion of attendees on the circuit. Then there were the journalists sniffing for a provocation or indiscretion who left after the first hour, contrasting with the students who wilted through the course of the day because they didn't realise there was no need to listen to the bitter end.

The genuine experts like Viktor and the real power-brokers – politicians who were still in office (retired ones were generally there for the free food and an ego massage) had their special absurdities too – the unspoken rule that you ask each other pertinent questions even though you have heard each others' presentations a dozen times, the tiresome dance of networking and card exchange, the polite interest in a tedious tour of some miserable castle, and finally the feigned embarrassment and surprise when presented with gaudy gifts from the hosts – before stuffing the lot into your flight bag and moving on to the next conference venue.

In fact it seemed to Pavel that some of the veteran attendees judged the success or failure of a conference largely according to the novelty and expense of the free gifts presented to them. It was remarkable how people who liked to talk at length about the morality of this or that situation and the ethics of this or that course of action could play such extraordinary double games with their own personal ethics. They would recommend austerity from five-star luxury, talk airily about necessary job cuts and epidemics that weren't worth the expense of a vaccine in a manner that condemned thousands of people to unemployment or death as part of a political equation.

Most of these habitues of the circuit were contractually obliged to accept only genuine expenses to avoid accusations of bias or conflict of interest. Usually they would start off on the circuit in a self-righteous frame of mind, insisting on paying their own bar bills and leaving their complimentary bottle of fine wine or olive oil, the local handicrafts and the commemorative album in their rooms at the end of the conference. They would quietly sneer at their colleagues at business class check-in, who seemed so desperate to take shopping and souvenirs back home for the family.

But as they became more familiar with the circuit, they came to view the enticements as less worth worrying about, even as they increased in value. It would be much ruder to spurn a digital audio player loaded with an (easily removable) recording of the conference than to leave a box of chocolates in one's room for the cleaner. A cut crystal decanter engraved with one's own name could never be of use to anyone else and if the provider had already arranged for it to be dispatched to one's home address via special courier, it would cause an awful lot of trouble and offence to get the delivery cancelled.

The craven nature of some of the circuit regulars was staggering. A couple of them could be relied upon to begin the first bar-room conversation of a new conference with the question: "What do you think of the freebie?" They passed it off as a joke but underneath were deadly serious. Answering was dangerous because there was always the chance that attendees of differing importance had been given different presents. A low-caste attendee might have to make do with a commemorative brochure, while an A-list speaker would leave weighed down with enough booty to satisfy a pirate. When one talked to the other, both could end up feeling embarrassed.

He remembered Madrid, where a particularly loathsome delegate from Montenegro had complained that the freebie had consisted of just some olives, cheese and vinegar, which Pavel had thought was actually one of the more enjoyable offerings in that it felt more like a picnic than a bribe.

Looking around the sunlit lobby in which they stood with its Alhambra-like pool of water trickling and deep green broadleaved plants growing from terracotta pots, Pavel replied: "Oh, didn't they leave one of those rare orchids outside your door? I'm not sure how I will get mine home, but I understand they are worth thousands." The next morning, at check-out, the Montenegrin could be seen staggering towards reception with a large yucca plant from the corridor outside his room protruding from his luggage and seemed offended by the hotel manager's request to take it back where it belonged.

On another memorable occasion, the quality of freebie on offer had a sudden and material effect upon the composition of a conference called to discuss the deepening of relations between the countries of the Mediterranean littoral. After a morning session full of forthright views at the venue in Nice, delegates were bussed the short distance to Cannes for lunch in one of the most expensive restaurants in Europe, set back slightly from the famous beach.

As they sat down to lunch in true Gallic style, one of their number spotted an acquaintance walking in a jaunty sort of way along the promenade and called to him. He didn't hear at first, because he had headphones in and was clearly enjoying his rhythmic perambulation along the Riviera. However, when the gentleman, a rather red-faced Dane, was seized from behind by his friend who left the dining table like a greyhound from the traps, he revealed that he was attending another conference taking place in Cannes itself. Furthermore he admitted was just walking off his main course from another fine dining establishment, listening to the latest state-of-the-art personal organiser-cum-camera-cum-musical gizmo provided by the organisers of his conference before rejoining a very select band of colleagues discussing NATO enlargement.

This revelation caused immediate uproar, mainly but not solely because the freebie provided by the Mediterranean littoral conference had been a bottle of lemon liqueur, a packet of biscuits and the biography of a French politician who was the patron of the organising body. The electronic gadget was incomparably more desirable. In addition, the smaller numbers attending the NATO event proved it was a higher-level gathering, so professional egos were bruised, too.

As Pavel watched in amazement, several of his dining colleagues began bad-tempered telephone conversations with press officers and representatives of NATO, demanding to know why they hadn't been informed the Cannes event was taking place. Within minutes, around a dozen delegates had defected to the NATO conference – though not before they had finished their lunch – while others expressed grudging satisfaction that they had won the concession of being sent an electronic item of their own by way of an apology from NATO and an assurance that they had only been omitted from the invitation list as a result of some dreadful mix-up by a junior employee who would now face a stern reprimand. Thus, honour was satisfied and the two conferences continued; one overburdened, the other under-represented.

After being on the circuit only a couple of years, back in his Bratislava flat

Pavel Panchev already had a whole cupboard crammed with complimentary souvenirs he would never need or use. Every time he accepted a jar of truffles, a digital camera, gold cufflinks or a pen spoiled with semi-precious stones he felt a little ashamed, the way he had felt when he was caught as a young boy copying an essay from the boy on the next table. Seizing up his paper and pencil, the teacher had asked: "Don't you have any original thoughts of your own?"

The question had been ringing in Pavel's head ever since and lately he had become surer than ever that the honest answer was: "No."

The Riga conference had provided one freebie in the goody bags handed out to delegates that provided a particularly poignant commentary on the uselessness of life on the circuit. Along with the usual chocolates, vodka, guidebooks and key rings, every bag contained a pair of thick, woollen mittens. Each pair was unique, incorporating the geometric, strangely futuristic designs of Latvian folklore, some in pulses of bright coloured twine, others in the dull tones of roots and last year's leaves.

Pulling his own mittens from the bag which he found in his room after returning from breakfast with Viktor on day one of the conference, Pavel saw that they were of an off-orange colour with large black and white twelve-pointed stars bursting from the palms and backs as if shooting over the top of each other continuously. Pulling them on – a ritual every other delegate must also have performed in their own rooms – Pavel felt the coarse wool tickle the skin on the back of his soft hands, a reminder that the hardest work they ever encountered was playing the tuneless music of a computer keyboard.

An accompanying leaflet explained that the mittens were knitted by hand as part of a project designed to provide an income to elderly women in "isolated rural communities" who were now the only people who knew how to make them the way they had been made for centuries. Seemingly simple, they actually incorporated designs demanding unimaginable complexity of craft, and a canon of folk symbolism that was specific not just to different regions or towns but even to individual farmsteads. Essentially, knitting such mittens required knowledge of a language on the verge of extinction – a way of thinking as much as a way of making.

The thin faces of the old women who did the work looked up from the leaflet, mostly smiling gently, but one or two with enigmatic, blank expressions that would have suited a sphynx or the statues of Easter Island – expressions for which the modern viewer lacks the necessary interpretive power, like slabs of stone bearing unknown hieroglyphs. Each pair of mittens took weeks and sometimes months to create.

Still with the mittens on his hand, Pavel clapped them together, creating a muffled noise like a carpet being beaten that died quickly in the antiseptic hotel room.

It was incomparably more difficult to make these gloves than to write and deliver a lecture about missile sites, bank failures, budget cuts or privatisation plans. Yet here he was sitting in a five star hotel being virtually begged to accept such a majestic work of art for simply running his mouth for a few minutes, creating nothing more substantial than an echo from the back of the lecture hall. However one looked at it, the system of value and exchange was absurdly inverted. Carefully he took the mittens off and laid them down on the bed, feeling almost embarrassed to have put them on. The stars continued fizzing from deep within their orange galaxy as they lay on top of the blank white sheets.

His session with the presidents and the prime minister, which had met with universal approval from those present, was clearly the high point of his career, yet it felt like a disappointment. He had been suave, perceptive, struck just the right balance between affability and rigour and everyone was able to end the discussion feeling they had acquitted themselves well despite undergoing a proper, penetrating inquisition.

All of that came from practice and a gradual process of acclimatisation during his time on the circuit, yet throughout the whole session, while his mouth said the right things and his body struck the right poses, the one thing that kept repeating in his head was: "None of them could knit a mitten. No-one in this room could knit a mitten. But we all have them."

In a way he even admired Viktor's curious curtain-raiser – at least his inner conflicts had been clearly visible on the surface, not buried deep within him like Pavel's. Perhaps that was what he had to look forward to – being regarded as a great mind until one day the demons broke free, after which you could be regarded as no mind at all.

To be described as influential did not necessarily mean that one had genuine influence. To present a critique of a problem, no matter how penetrating, was not the same as suggesting a practical solution, and Panchev sensed the time was approaching to leap the ideological wall and become a political player rather than just one of the small army of commentators, analysts and experts who trained their sights on the politicians but never possessed the power or inclination to pull the trigger.

That's why it had been doubly fascinating to see the Baltic presidents in action up close, particularly when Kopeikin had arrived for a visit that Pavel was told was to remain strictly unofficial and off the record.

Though interesting, the evening at the grand house in the country had not exactly been full of high diplomacy.

The Latvian President had tried to act the affable host but as an unpretentious and somewhat ineffectual individual – he was elected by parliament chiefly because he seemed the candidate least likely to meddle in affairs of state – he clearly would have preferred a quiet night in with his wife, a pretty but somewhat shrill woman more than twenty years his junior.

The Lithuanian President was a droll bon viveur with hooded eyelids who seemed less interested in discussing anything remotely resembling business than reminiscing about which were the best restaurants and even the best individual courses he had tasted in an official capacity. His description of lunchtime risotto at the Villa d'Este on Lake Como brought actual tears to his eyes, understandable perhaps for someone whose most typical indigenous national cuisine was a large ball of dough called a Zeppelin. However, his constant references to unforgettable and extraordinary cuisine of the globe rather put the trout and potatoes served up by the first lady into perspective and her discomfort grew noticeably as the evening got later. Pavel put the Lithuanian President down as a definite future fixture on the convention circuit.

In contrast the Estonian President was something of an intellectual and an ascetic. A well-known sportsman keen on cross-country skiing and mountain biking, he politely refused the dessert of profiteroles as he was competing in a road race the next day – a further slight to the hostess' efforts – and repeatedly tried to turn the conversation away from light-hearted banter onto electricity grid connections, joint defence procurement and the relative merits of different nuclear power station designs. His lack of success in this direction made him rather taciturn towards the end of the meeting and he was first to leave, somewhat archly mentioning the poor condition of the local roads as a factor contributing to his early departure.

The Estonian President's nose also seemed to have put out of joint by the presence of Kopeikin at the dinner table. Partly this was frustration at his inability to understand Russian when the others used it to explain a joke or abstract concept – having been born to emigre parents in Norway, he had not lived in the Baltic states during the years of Soviet occupation – but mainly it was fear that Kopeikin's presence would be leaked to the nationalist Estonian press who would start to ask all sorts of awkward questions about why he was having secret meetings with senior members of the Russian government. The true reason why he was there: "Because he invited himself and the Latvians didn't feel they could refuse" simply would not do, so he would have to make something up about taking a tough line with money laundering or cross-border smuggling.

But at least Pavel had been provided with an excellent chance to get to know Kopeikin as they strolled around the pond together. To his surprise, Kopeikin seemed to know him already, using his patronymic and indicating that he had read a few of his papers. He then delivered an enigmatic monologue about "standing on the distant shore," though the far side of the pond was barely a stone's throw away. He had even invited Panchev to his dacha near Pskov, which he assured him was in an even more beautiful setting than the Latvian President's, even if it was not on such a grand scale.

"Still, that is because – though it may surprise you – the Kremlin keeps a closer watch on its money than Brussels!" Kopeikin laughed as he lit a cigar with his Gazprom-branded Dunhill lighter.

"What do you mean?" Panchev asked.

"Come, come, surely you know?" Kopeikin said, waving at the whole complex with his cigar. "No? Then it will be my pleasure to explain – and though I must insist that the source of these words is, of course, confidential, I will not have the slightest objection to you mentioning these facts in print or in public... if you happen to find them of interest."

He inhaled in a dreamy manner, puffed out a blue cloud with a satisfied shake of the head and placed his arm around Panchev's shoulder as they continued their circuit around the pond. It seemed a strange gesture but Pavel had met enough Russians to know that their concept of personal space tended to change dramatically according to their mood.

"This delightful place in which we find ourselves is not all that it seems. You see, it only looks like the private residence of the Latvian President. In fact it is a sort of bed and breakfast establishment..."

"You mean it isn't where he actually lives?"

"Oh, it's where he lives alright, and where he has lived in the four years since he built it with no expense spared. But if you, as I have, had read the relevant tax and land registry documents – all available in the public domain quite freely, no espionage required – you would see that technically speaking it is, well, a motel. This whole complex is listed as a guest house, not a private residence. So in a sense Mr President is a temporary lodger in his own home."

"Is that important?"

"Only if you regard the embezzlement of large amounts of European Union taxpayers' money as important. Do you?"

"I do."

"Then let me elucidate." Kopeikin drew again on his cigar, clearly relishing the process of imparting knowledge to an eager student and the chance to show off his English-language vocabulary by using the word "elucidate".

"When Mr President was still just a lowly bank chairman, he decided it would be a good idea to open a luxury guest house. It would stimulate the local economy, give employment to builders, attract tourists to a neglected part of the country and so on. So he wrote all of that down and applied for co-financing from Brussels, which they were happy to agree with, particularly as the person responsible for approving the project at the Latvian end happened to be a member of his own family. So Mr President spent a little bit of his own money and something equivalent to one million dollars of EU money to construct this delightful ensemble. Incidentally I must say I cannot fault his taste."

Kopeikin was now in full flow. "But as you may have noticed during our brief stay today, there aren't an awful lot of other guests. In fact there have never been any guests and there never will be – apart from Mr President himself and his family. You will not find this 'guest house' listed in any tourist directories or advertised in any brochures. It does not have a website. If you call into the helpful tourist information office in the very charming little town of Cesis twenty kilometres from here, they will not be able to book you a room or even tell you how to get here. Why, there is not even a sign at the end of the driveway to capture passing trade which I admit is an extremely remote possibility. There was a sign for a few hours after it 'opened', purely to conform with the requirements for co-financing, you understand. I'm sure vandals or a lightning strike took care of it fairly quickly."

"He stole the money?"

"Only in a moral sense, not a legal one. He hasn't broken any rules per se. But he was a little careless or lazy, whichever you prefer. This is not a rare occurrence, there are dozens of similar 'guest houses' across the Baltic states. But it does mean he could face an embarrassing question or two if he is ever quizzed about the use of EU funds. Really he should have sold the complex to himself for a good price, in which case he could have changed its registered use to residential. Or simply sold it to someone else at market value. With the EU footing the bill for most of the construction costs he would have made a handsome profit. I might even have bought it myself seeing as we, Russians, can now apply for a residence permit if we buy expensive real estate here!"

Kopeikin roared with laughter and flicked his half-smoked cigar into the pond. It arced through the air like a tracer round.

"Or perhaps I should just rent that villa for a few weeks," Kopeikin said, indicating the handsome building they had passed on the other side of the pond. "I wonder how much Mr President charges? Theoretically, at least. Come, we had better rejoin the others. We wouldn't want them to think we are conspirators. For all I know, Mr President may have installed secret microphones in the water lilies. You would be surprised the lengths certain parties go to. By the way, how well do you know Viktor Draaks?"

Panchev answered with the truth, edited slightly for Russian consumption – that he did not know him well but that he admired his intellect and found his arguments provocative and stimulating even if he did not always agree with them.

"Do you have any idea what Viktor is working on at the moment?" Kopeikin asked, fishing for information.

"No, I do not and to be perfectly frank, Mr Deputy Prime Minister, even if I did, I am not sure it would be entirely ethical of me to tell you."

"Very correct!" Kopeikin laughed. "I understand your reticence absolutely. But between you and me I am a little concerned for Viktor's welfare. You may find it hard to believe, but despite the scurrilous lies he writes about Russia's intentions and ambitions, I too quite like him. And if nothing else he serves a useful purpose in giving us a steady stream of unsubstantiated claims and silly rumours which we are happy to deny and clarify. If Viktor did not exist, it would be necessary for Russia to invent him. It would be a shame if he just... disappeared, as seems to have happened. For a start, I might get the blame, and that would not do at all. I don't know why he behaved as he did yesterday morning, but I would like to clear the matter up one way or another. I noticed you took the opportunity to keep silent about Viktor over dinner."

"As did you. If he has disappeared as you say, I'm sure he has a reason," Panchev said, trying to convince himself as much as Kopeikin. "Viktor is not a man who does things on a whim. Who knows – maybe everything that happened yesterday was part of some larger plan? He is an intelligent man. He may yet have the last laugh."

"Perhaps you are right," Kopeikin conceded, though he now sounded like the doubtful one. "In any case if you do happen to see Viktor, please tell him that I would be grateful if he would call me as soon as possible, and assure him of my good intentions. Perhaps you could give him my card – and here is one for yourself as well. I hope we will be seeing more of each other in the future. The way you handled the presidents was very impressive. You reminded me a little of my uncle Ilya, God rest his soul. He was a wonderful teacher of five-year-olds."

XI   A HERO OF OUR TIME

Kopeikin was as slippery an operator as Pavel had ever met and the conversation had only strengthened Panchev's concern about Viktor's welfare and whereabouts. He had a couple of days before the next conference in Tallinn and resolved to try to find his colleague as soon as he returned to his hotel, but first there was another engagement to take care of. He was to take part in a question and answer session at the Latvian Association, a quasi-governmental body charged with promoting and developing the country's overseas image, though from Pavel's experience its main activity seemed to be sending out a monthly newsletter in which it wrote primarily about its strategy of buying thirty second advertisement slots on cable TV channels that nobody watched.

Its second most important duty was to tell Latvians about any famous, semi-famous or potentially famous people who had expressed any sort of passing interest in the country and then try to claim credit for planting the seeds of that mention in their minds. In short, it was desperate to justify its existence and, more importantly, its budget. Pavel Panchev barely fell into the "potentially famous" category but, aware of the opportunity to raise his profile by a few more microns, he had perhaps rashly agreed to take part in a question and answer session on the subject of Baltic and Latvian identity.

The president was giving an introductory speech at the event, which he candidly told Pavel would last "two minutes… at most" as they sped through the gorgeously unspoiled, untrammelled countryside.

"Just tell 'em what they want to hear," the president advised. "You have heard of Latvia, you understand its suffering and it has a great future. Oh, and something about being at a strategic location between east an west always goes down well, even if everyone from Arensburg to Almaty says the same thing. Whatever you do, don't get into the ethnic question!" he advised, his faraway look of pain suggesting that either he had made that mistake himself too many times in the past or that he was a martyr to haemorrhoids despite his limousine's soft suspension.

After driving in confusing circles around and through Riga, the limousine came to a sudden halt beside a large brick building next to a pleasant park which turned out to be the University of Latvia. They were ushered through the high hallway into an even higher auditorium where an audience of several hundred eager young faces turned as one to see them enter and a tall, lean man in late middle age with white hair and a beard trimmed in intellectual style stepped forward to shake their hands.

After shaking the president's hand he did the same to Panchev, his soft and slender fingers revealing a life spent pushing paper and stroking his beard.

"Oskars Riekstiņš," he said with an ingratiating smile in a strong Australian accent. "I will be chairing today's discussion."

"Pleased to meet you," Panchev started to say, but before he had even finished the sentence, Oskars Riekstiņš talked over the top of him.

"I was the first Latvian ambassador to Australia after we regained independence," he confided as if this was significant information. "I grew up in Australia and was actually a well-known television presenter with Channel 8. Have you ever watched Australian television?"

"No."

"Channel 8 was the second-most-popular channel back in those days. Of course, it's different now... Anyway, we had better get on. The president will speak for around fifteen minutes, then the roundtable will begin. There is no actual table, but you get my meaning." This, apparently, was a joke.

"Roundtable? I was told I would just be taking part in a question and answer session."

"Yes, I will open it out to the hall once the roundtable is complete. Perhaps if you could take your seat, we will begin."

Pavel climbed onto the platform where four high-backed chairs had been arranged in an arc. Each had a small side table next to it with a microphone and glass of water on top. Two men were already occupying the outermost seats and were glancing at each other in a way that suggested long-standing antipathy. Both nodded and smiled at Panchev and Riekstiņš as they took up their places in the central seats beneath the venerable vaulted roof of the Univeristy of Latvia's main lecture hall.

A lectern was placed to one side, at which the tall figure of the President stood and began his introductory speech. He said what a pleasure it was to be invited to open the debate and that he was sure they would all learn something new from these respected thinkers. Then he mentioned something about youth being the future of the country, stepped away from the lectern to polite applause and walked out of the auditorium escorted by his bodyguard. Panchev had timed the whole thing, which took precisely 1 minute and 27 seconds.

Riekstiņš didn't seem at all distressed by the brevity of the President's address, immediately sitting forward in his seat and beginning to introduce the participants. He spoke clearly, without pausing for thought, and had a curious habit of staring intently into the middle distance as if reading his lines from an invisible autocue. This was clearly causing some discomfort to a group of students in the fourth row back who thought he was speaking directly to them for an unknown reason.

"To my left is the well-known economist and journalist Juris Laptevs..."

"Yuri Laptev," an emaciated-looking, balding man in a cable-knit sweater sighed. He could have been any age from 25 to 55. "Please have the decency to use my real name, not the ridiculous construction forced on me by Latvia's language Gestapo."

Pavel sensed the next hour could be a trying one.

The unflappable Riekstiņš continued, "...and next to me here is Mr Pavel Panchev, who I'm told is one of the most in-demand speakers on Central and Eastern Europe at the moment, though, of course, we consider ourselves here to be in Northern Europe these days. He has kindly agreed to share his international perspective after taking part in the Riga conference over the last few days." Pavel nodded to the audience politely, noting in particular the presence of some rather attractive female students in the front row who looked up at him coquettishly. Maybe the hour wouldn't be so bad after all.

"Over there to my right – in more than one sense – is Ivars Dzintars, who made headlines last year when he said on television that condemned pork past its use-by date should be sold to Russians. Mr Dzintars is the chairman of FLACID..."

"Flay-kid!" interjected Dzintars.

"...the Free Latvian Association of Chicago, Indiana and Detroit which promotes Latvia and the Latvian language in a large part of the United States. At this point I should probably declare an interest. During my time as a television presenter on Australia's popular Channel 8 I did attend one of FLACID's summer camps in my role as co-director of the Australian Baltic Brotherhood Association, ABBA, and great fun it was too. Mr Dzintars is also the owner of one of the largest pig farms in the Baltic states and is a major donor to the nationalist 'Latvian Sacrifice' political party. So to get the ball rolling, let me start with a question. When the rest of the world hears the word 'Latvia' what do they think? Yuri, perhaps I could come to you first?"

"His name is Juris!" interrupted Dzintars. "We're in goddam Latvia and there is only one state language – Latvian. So if he insists on staying in our country as our unwanted guest, he had better get used to being Juris. If he wants to be Yuri, I will be happy to drive him to the border right now!" Dzintars had looked like such an anonymous sort of man when Panchev had first seen him that he was startled to find himself sitting next to this raging lunatic whose face was turning more crimson by the second. It had started the colour of an under-ripe raspberry and was steadily moving towards wild strawberry.

Riekstiņš sat nodding absent-mindedly with his gaze still fixed at an indeterminate location in the middle of the hall, just like a cutaway shot during an interview. As if receiving some unheard cue, he went live again with: "A fair point, Ivars, but seeing as this debate is taking place in English, which also is not the state language, I suppose we can extend Mr Laptev the small courtesy of dropping the 'esses' from his name."

Dzintars scowled and turned the colour of a red apple. His outburst did provoke a reaction from Laptev, who spoke with the quiet, bored-sounding and condescending tone that is so often the hallmark of the Russian intellectual. Rocking his chair back onto its rear legs he waved one arm dismissively as he spoke as if conducting an unseen orchestra.

"Here we see a typical piece of nonsense from the neo-fascist right. I would rather not dirty myself by entering into this conversattion which we have heard a thousand times, but would simply remind Mr Dzintars that unlike him, I was actually born in Latvia and have lived here all my life. But as a non-citizen I am part of a minority that is oppressed for no reason other than an accident of birth. It is hard to believe that a country that is a member of the European Union and regards itself as civilised could be allowed to carry out such racist policies without international condemnation, which is why Russia has a legitimate right to point out the inequalities and deprivation that continue to exist."

Pavel remembered the President's advice not to get involved in the ethnic question, while the two antagonists continued baiting each other, arguments flying from side to side like a game of ideological tennis.

"Then if you're so proud of coming from Latvia, why don't you naturalize?" Dzintars asked. "It should be no trouble for a smart guy like you who I'm told speaks Latvian fairly well. The tests are so easy one of my pigs could pass!"

"Why should I be made to sit through a series of tests that require me to give a crypto-fascist account of history in order to obtain a passport for the country in which I was born? And if I might throw the question back on you, why haven't you – whom I am also told speaks fairly good Latvian – taken a Latvian passport? Until you do so, you have no moral right to criticise me."

"I am an American citizen, but my blood is pure Latvian, unlike yours. As soon as dual citizenship is allowed…"

"Given this country's history I rather doubt there is any such thing as 'pure Latvian' blood. All this reveals is your pseudo-scientific belief in bloodlines that serious scientists recognised were false from the moment the Third Reich fell. But your answer tells me all I need to know. Being Latvian is just a hobby to you," Laptev said with a wave of his bony wrist.

This was too much, for Dzintars who leaped up, scarlet, and made for the startled Laptev, who in turn lost his balance and tumbled backwards on his chair. Oskars Riekstiņš didn't move but asked the middle distance if Ivars would please sit down. Fearing Dzintars might actually physically assault the surprised intellectual, Panchev stood up and grabbed Dzintars by the shoulder to restrain him. Dzintars turned instantly, a look of pure hate in his bloodshot eyes.

"I might have known it. You Slavs always stick together!" Then he spat, clearly intending to hit Panchev in the face with his spittle but owing to his comparatively small stature managed only to cover Panchev's tie in a gobbet of purest Latvian-American phlegm.

Our actions in moments of crisis are not always explicable, no matter how often we examine them subsequently. In later days Pavel sometimes thought his next act was prompted by the fact that the tie had been a gift from a lovely Croatian girl of whom he had particularly fond memories, at others he wondered if he had been affronted at being assumed to be a Slav when he was at least half Finno-Ugric. But probably he simply decided that Ivars Dzintars was an annoying little shit who deserved to be punched – which is precisely what he did.

The entire auditorium gasped as he connected with Dzintars' left cheek. The annoying nationalist went sprawling backwards, ending up on top of the terrified Laptev. Pavel's first reaction was surprise that he still had the right cross he had used as a junior boxer, the second thought was fear that he had just done something very wrong, but the third was a certain masculine pride that swelled when the pretty girls in the front row started clapping and giggling. The clapping was taken up by the second row, then the third and fourth. Within seconds, the whole auditorium was applauding him, drowning out Riekstiņš' attempts to smooth the way towards a commercial break and Dzintars' Anglo-Saxon expletives as he struggled to extricate himself from the Russian intellectual's woolly jumper. Pavel pushed back the lock of black hair back which had fallen rakishly over his brow as he delivered the punch and walked out of the auditorium to a chorus of cheers and whistles.

He hadn't noticed reporters or television cameras at the event – probably because most Latvian journalists dress and look like students – but back at the hotel an hour later it was clear that his right cross had already gained a certain fame. His phone was ringing every few minutes with questions from newspapers which he did his best to answer with apology and explanation. Turning on the television lunchtime news he saw slow-motion replays of the incident, an interview with an incandescent Dzintars – complete with a swollen eye that would be black before morning – who said he would be contacting the US embassy for legal advice, another interview with Oskars Riekstiņš who looked delighted to be on camera and took the opportunity to mention the valuable work the Latvian Association did, and interviews with members of the audience who had witnessed the extraordinary spectacle – which Pavel was pleased to see included the pretty girls from the front row.

For the second time in as many days, a leading expert in his field had experienced an unfortunate set of circumstances on stage that had brought a premature end to his discussion. As far as Pavel Panchev was concerned, it increased one hundred-fold his doubts about his continued involvement in the circuit. It also reminded him to find out what had happened to Viktor Draaks and he put a call in to reception asking to be connected to Viktor's room.

"Mr Draaks has not been in his room for two days, Sir," the receptionist said. "He was supposed to check out today but has left some personal items in his room. Are you a friend of Mr Draaks?"

He thought about his answer: "Yes, I am."

"Then would it be possible for you to collect his things, please? We are fully booked for the next few days and his items have been placed in our left luggage room. I will tell the concierge to give the items to you."

"Very well," Pavel agreed. As he rose to go downstairs, the telephone rang again. He prepared to repeat another apologetic explanation for his actions.

"May I congratulate you? If it was in my power, I would award you the Pushkin Medal. Or possibly the world middleweight boxing title! Someone should have done what you did a long time ago. Russia thanks you." It was the familiar, jovial voice of Deputy Prime Minister Kopeikin.

"I didn't do it for Russia. I lost my temper. It was a mistake. Was there a reason for your call?"

"Indeed there was, thank you for reminding me. I have some interesting information regarding our mutual friend Viktor Draaks. It seems he caught a train in the early hours of yesterday morning."

"A train? To where? I just spoke with reception here. He has not been to his room and left his bags behind."

"Yes, I already knew that, thanks to a certain contact at the hotel. His destination was apparently the small forest stop that just happens to be the closest one to the presidential guest house we visited last night. Intriguing, don't you think, particularly given the very confidential nature of my visit?"

"Intriguing is the word."

"I will be returning to Latvia in a few days' time. I and the Russian government would be extremely grateful if you would postpone your other plans and stay on at the hotel at our expense until I arrive. You will, of course, be paid for your time at whatever rate you deem appropriate. Is that possible?"

"Yes, it is possible. I'll stay put."

"Thank you. Would you like to move to a better room? The suites on the top floor are wonderful for entertaining..."

"No, this one is fine."

"I'm sorry I have to ask this, but it must be done. Did you tell Viktor my meeting with the presidents would be taking place? I'm asking as one gentleman to another."

"No, I did not. I didn't even know about it myself until you arrived."

"I didn't think so. Well, see you in a few days." The line went dead.

Kopeikin's offer of generous paid leave had not taken much thought to accept. Some time for reflection on the future would be very welcome, and

Pavel could for once pass time doing things he wanted to do, seeing the sights he wanted to see and perhaps learning something about the country in which he found himself rather than simply arriving, lecturing and leaving.

He pulled out a scrap of paper from his pocket with a telephone number written in a girlish hand. They had been very cute in the front row, after all, and there is no better way to discover a city than with a local guide.

XII   AN INSPECTOR DEPARTS

"I hope this won't be in your report. After all, you must admit it was your own fault that you jumped in the wrong pool. Have another tea. I make it myself from linden flowers. It will clean your blood."

Viktor grunted his assent while pondering how clean one's blood could actually become and ate another oatmeal biscuit, which he was assured was also homemade and very popular with the elusive other guests. Despite a series of hot showers and a long lie down, most of which was spent in the foetal position, he could still detect the faint smell of unpleasantness in his nostrils and while pleased not to have been flogged, he nevertheless remained puzzled as to the exact status of both himself and the guestless guest house. But as the small blonde woman continued with her criticism in the middle of her huge fitted kitchen, the mystery slowly started to resolve itself.

"You won't mention it, will you? It would be an embarrassment to my husband. You wouldn't want to be responsible for – what do they call it – a diplomatic happening, would you?"

"A diplomatic incident."

"Exactly. And think of poor Magda. She has her professional reputation to consider."

Viktor doubted Magda's reputation was in serious jeopardy unless the threat came from the fact that she hadn't finished him off. "Well, I suppose I could omit it... from my report I mean..."

"Thank you, Mr... I'm sorry, I don't believe I have asked your name. I don't suppose that's a secret, too."

"Delors," Viktor replied, saying the first European Union-type name that occurred to him. "Viktor Delors."

"Well, Mr Delors, I'm afraid your bags still haven't arrived. Do you think there may have been a problem?"

"If I could perhaps make a telephone call, I could check..."

"And there is also the matter of payment that you mentioned. As you have kindly agreed not to mention the incident this morning, perhaps I could waive payment as a gesture of goodwill? I mean, would that be allowed under EU rules? It wouldn't be seen as a bribe, I hope?"

"No, that is quite alright. Happens all the time."

"Does it?"

"Perhaps if I could make that call now?"

She led him into a study that would not have looked out of place on the top floor of a Manhattan skyscraper and indicated a telephone lying on top of the desk.

"I will be in the kitchen," she said. "Perhaps when you have finished we can discuss what you would like to do next. We could take you to see the ski slope. Of course, there is no snow at this time of year and the hill is small, but you can see the lift that we have installed and that our guests so love to use. As we said in our application for funding, we understand how important it is to have something worth visiting the whole year round. Which we are. And everyone in Latvia loves skiing, even though we have no mountains. Are you sure you don't want to play tennis? The courts are well maintained. That's why so many sportsmen like to stay with us," she added rather too hastily.

"Quite sure, thank you. I saw the courts on my way in. Very nice."

He waited until long after she had left the room, looking around at the well-stocked mahogany bookshelves, the plump leather club chairs, a drinks cabinet in a wooden globe and some old Latvian landscapes on the walls. They contained a series of bucolic Romantic images: ferrymen at work on rivers, fishermen mending their nets on the Courland coastline, a castle above lofty cliffs. In some ways it was a world that had disappeared forever: the towering cliffs long submerged thanks to Soviet hydro-electric projects that left just a few of the castle's stones protruding from the water. But the ramshackle farmhouses and the log barns with storks resident in cylindrical nests on top were identical to those he had seen from the windows of the train, and along the coast fishermen still smoked their catches in wooden huts that smelled of drying fish flesh and smouldering birchwood, the aroma unchanged for centuries.

As Viktor sat in the revolving chair and reached for the telephone, he noticed a family portrait beside it on the heavy oak desk. It showed two young girls, a teenage boy going through the surly stage, the small blonde woman and the President of Latvia. The President had his arm around the small blonde woman and was looking at the little girls with doting eyes. On the floor in front of them lay the ugly hound that had trapped Viktor in his personal swamp earlier that day. Just the sight of it was enough to make him feel uneasy. Even reduced in size in two dimensions it seemed to be looking for an excuse to savage him.

It was almost disappointing to see his grand conspiracy collapse into ridiculous coincidence and misunderstanding. The persecution theory had at least provided a form of certainty, a malignant rationality to the sequence of events in which he was trapped. But now, sitting in the President's study with his wife in the kitchen apparently under some sort of delusion that he was a hotel inspector... everything was messy again. Where did Panchev and Kopeikin fit in? What did Benbo know? Where would he be in a day's or a week's time? There was no itinerary to which he could refer.

Still mulling the possibilities, Viktor dialled the directory enquiries number the First Lady of Latvia had given him and an English-speaking operator patched him through to the Grand Hotel Europe. It took a few seconds, during which time the earpiece clicked a couple of times and the sound became slightly more resonant, presumably as she made the connection.

"This is Viktor Draaks, room 419. I have been unavoidably detained due to circumstances well beyond my control. I wondered if my room was still free and if my bags were safe?"

"Mr Draaks, thank you for calling. I'm afraid your room has been taken as the booking was for only two nights, but you have nothing to worry about. The conference organisers have taken care of all expenses and your friend Mr Panchev is looking after your bags."

"My friend Mr Panchev?"

"Yes, Sir, just a few moments ago, in fact. Some messages were also left for you. Will you be able to collect them?"

"No, you'd better read them out."

"A Mr Jameson from the Benbo Foundation in Washington DC called to enquire about your whereabouts. He asked that you contact him as soon as possible."

"Did he leave a number?"

"No, Sir, he said you would be sure to have his number. I took the message myself. He said an exceptionally large bar bill appeared to have been charged to the Benbo Foundation's credit card in Riga. He sounded extremely annoyed, Sir."

"You said there was another message?"

"Yes, Sir. The second message was also asking that you make contact at your earliest convenience. It was from a Mr Kopeikin of the Russian government. Will there be anything else, Sir?"

"No. Thank you."

"Thank you for staying at the Grand Hotel Europe, Mr Draaks. We look forward to welcoming you again soon." The line went dead.

Viktor was more confused than ever. So Kopeikin really WAS looking for him – in which case why hadn't he made contact last night? Or didn't he know he had been just a few yards away? And why had Panchev taken possession of his bags? Had he done so on behalf of Kopeikin? If only the idiot Jameson had thought to leave his number, Viktor would at least have been able to contact Benbo, though his vague recollection of an argument over a bar bill would hardly do to explain what might be a huge hit on Benbo's plastic if Viktor had fallen victim to one of Riga's notorious scams. That alone would be enough to make Jameson in the accounts department annoyed, but it did nothing to confirm whether he had heard about the incident with the three presidents and the prime minister.

Viktor placed his hands on his temples and tried to concentrate. What was the number of the Benbo Foundation? He had called it often enough and the first few digits appeared momentarily in his mind before being chased away by the confusing need to place international and regional dialling codes in front of the numerals. He decided to call the operator again and see if she could get hold of the Benbo Foundation's number from some international directory, but as he reached for the receiver, the door of the study burst open and the First Lady of Latvia came flying into the room wearing the same scowl she had worn at their first meeting on the porch.

"So!" she shouted, "your name is not Delors at all, is it Mr Draaks?"

Viktor was shocked. "You were listening in!" he blustered. "Of all the nerve! You should be ashamed!"

"Me? You're the one who should be ashamed! Do you have any idea how much trouble you will be in when I tell my husband about this? I took you in under false pretences, thinking you were from the European Union and sent to inspect us because of these stupid regulations about hotels and guest houses. I treated you well, I fed you..." a look of horror passed over her face, "my God, I even saw you naked! You exposed yourself to me, you sex criminal! I don't know where you are from but we have ways of dealing with people like you here in Latvia! Who are you, Viktor Draaks and why are you here?"

"Yes, madam, my name is Viktor Draaks. But I am an inspector from the European Union. Do you think we use our real names? We are not amateurs, madam, and when we have reason to believe that an inspection is required it is sometimes necessary to use covert means and to arrive unannounced under an assumed name! As you heard me talking, you will have heard that indeed I have been staying at the Grand Hotel Europe, that my bags are there and also that I am a personal friend of Mr Panchev and Mr Kopeikin, who were your dinner guests here last night! Hardly the actions of some vagrant seeking a bed for the night and a mediocre braised trout, I think you will agree?"

Viktor wasn't sure where this magnificent series of lies was coming from, but he was happy to let them continue. The put-down of the trout in particular had struck home judging by the First Lady's expression.

"What better way to test the facilities available than to arrive with nothing at all and see to what lengths the staff will go to provide service to the random traveller? I must tell you, madam, that some of the things I have seen here have raised serious concerns that I feel compelled to include in my report. The suspicious lack of guests for one, which surely is linked to the fact that the main signpost to this place is located in a ditch. The presence of unrestrained and dangerous dogs for another. You have also kindly provided me with proof that the owners of the property routinely listen in on the telephone calls of their guests. And last but not least, a lack of suitable signage that in my case almost led to a fatal drowning incident! I will also need to research whether the therapist Magda has obtained any EU-standard certification as a healthcare professional, without which her Soviet qualifications are about as useful as the Order of Lenin!" He thumped the top of the desk with the palm of his hand for effect.

His performance had temporarily thwarted her attack, but it wouldn't take long for the effect of his indignant bluff to wear off. It was certainly time to bid adieu to the blonde woman, her revolting dog and Magda, her evil henchwoman. Thrusting his head back imperiously, Viktor rose from the chair as if it were his own and walked towards the front door where he turned and delivered one final fusillade of falsehood.

"I bid you a very good day, Mrs Liepiņš." He surprised himself by remembering the name she had only mentioned once. "You will be hearing in an official capacity from my department in the very near future! I am sure it is a matter you will wish to discuss with your husband... at length! Of course, in keeping with the European Union's commitment to transparency, the report will be placed in the public domain and I am sure will be of great interest to people here in Latvia."

As the door closed behind him, the little blonde woman looked as if she was actually starting to cry. Before she could say anything though, Viktor was striding majestically away down the tree-lined avenue. Only when he was safely out of view of the main building did he begin running back into the forest which for a few minutes at least seemed like a welcome refuge rather than a frightening maze.

XIII DEEP IN THE WOODS

Soon Viktor was lost again, his confused mind willfully misleading him. His uncertainty about the recent chain of events, Panchev and Kopeikin's motivations, his own current reputation and questionable future all found expression in a convoluted path through the forest until with evening falling he could have done twenty kilometres in a straight line or two in a circle. Just as it seemed that he might spend the rest of his life locked in this never-ending timbered prison, he was relieved to see a door. The surprising thing was that it was not attached to any house but appeared to be just a rough wooden door standing alone in a clearing, like an abandoned work by some minor Magritte copyist.

Viktor approached uncertainly, as if he was hallucinating a rather too obvious metaphor. Close to, he could see that in fact the doorway did lead if not into the bowels of the earth then at least into its gorge. It was the door to a small room not much larger than a bear pit. Coughing loudly in case someone was in residence, Viktor pushed the door open and inched inside, his eyes slowly adjusting to the gloom.

As accommodation went, it formed a stark contrast with the luxuries of the villa he had stayed in the previous night. In essence it was a hole in the ground – or rather a hole dug sideways into a mound – with rough birch planks forming almost the entire inner structure – floor, walls and a sort of bunk bed arrangement that wasn't free-standing but formed by simply linking the four stout pine beams that prevented the whole structure collapsing. There was no window, just the door which would have required even a small man to stoop as he entered and forced Viktor to bend nearly double. The only other ventilation came from a flue in the roof which was linked by a length of steel tubing to a rusty iron stove. It still had a small dome-like cap visible among the heather growing over the top of the mound in which the whole thing was located – the only evidence available to the casual passer-by that this formation represented anything other than another sandy hillock in the middle of nowhere.

Someone had been here recently. Lying on the lower level of the bare bunk bed was a single pink flower, looking like something between a carnation and a rose. It was still fresh, but there was nothing else to suggest another human being had seen the inside of this little cave for years – other than the fact that it was spotlessly clean with none of the dirt, dust and mould that must maintain an unending offensive to take possession of the bunker.

For that is what it was – the sort of structure that an officer might possess while his men outside squatted in their trenches. With the light fading fast Viktor was resigned to spending the night here. He would at least be out of the wind and the rain which looked like it might come from angry looking clouds that were beginning to clamber one on top of another and form a dark grey sheet above the tree tops. He thought he could hear distant thunder, but it might just as easily have been the sound of a tree falling somewhere in the forest or a logging truck passing on some distant track, such was the muddled nature of sound bouncing around.

He regretted his lack of matches, thinking that the bunker could be almost cosy with a fire burning in the stove, but a closer examination of the rusty flue made him think lighting a fire would be more likely to kill him from carbon monoxide poisoning or smoke inhalation than hypothermia. He might be found years from now interred in this spacious coffin complete with floral tribute. Leave it a few centuries, and future generations would no doubt assume him to be some late twentieth century chieftain interred in ritual fashion.

He lay on the lower bunk, placing the flower gently on the top bunk first, wondering who had placed it there and why, trying to stop his thoughts becoming too macabre. It grew colder and darker. He counted himself lucky to have a jacket of quality old English tweed which kept him warmer than something more modern and fashionable. He tucked his socks into his trousers, finding a piece of dusty hessian sacking underneath the bunk as he stooped down to do so. It could almost have been a feather duvet for the feeling of unexpected delight it gave him. Its only drawback was its modest size. He tried to decide whether it would be most effective covering the third of his body from the feet to the knees, the third from the knees to the stomach or the third from the stomach to the neck. Every time he woke in the night – which was many times – he tried a different position but still came to no definite conclusion.

He swung his feet up onto the bunk and lay down, pulling the sack over his midriff. The wood felt cold on the back of his head at first, but quickly warmed, so that whenever he changed position he felt its chill anew and wriggled back to his original spot. Surprisingly, he could actually feel the grain of the wood through the reddish hair on the back of his neck and chuckled to himself that this was not something he had ever been offered on any hotel's pillow menu.

"I will be sure to recommend wooden pillows," he said out loud. His voice had no reverberation in this enclosed hole and sounded thin and uncanny.

"My name is Viktor Draaks and I am here to tell you that this place in which we find ourselves doesn't matter!" he tried with more volume. "Or maybe it does. Who can tell? It's dry and it's free, so I suppose that's worth something after all..." He started to fall asleep.

At some time in the early hours he thought he heard a bell tolling, which gave an uncanny immediacy to the feeling of being prematurely buried, but after a few moments he realised it was heavy raindrops falling on the little dome sticking through the turf above his head and sending their resonant impact down the rusty flue like a Victorian speaking tube connecting a ship's captain to the engine room. The sound of the rain was soothing and it sent him back to sleep.

Later he woke to a dull rhythmic pounding which seemed to be coming from outside. It was on the edge of perception, but such was its remorseless timbre that it was impossible to ignore. At first he thought some heavy-footed animal such as a deer or moose might be stamping the ground above his head, but it seemed too regular a beat for that.

His second theory involved an imagined car somewhere in the nearby forest with teenagers drinking, smoking and screwing in the back seat with the doors open and the stereo blasting out lumpen europop. It seemed plausible for a while, but if it was indeed music, it was the longest single track he had ever heard, its thump-thump-thump extending for hours. He put his fingers in his ears to regain silence in an attempt to gauge how loud the sound actually was but, to his surprise, the steady bass drumbeat got louder, not quieter. He had been listening to his own heartbeat.

There was something appalling about the sound, as if one was not supposed to eavesdrop on the workings of one's own heart. Not only did it provide a rather obvious reminder of the fragile nature of mortality, it also reminded him that Viktor Draaks was, in the final analysis, not a great intellect with freedom to roam the world of knowledge as it pleased, but a cold lump of muscle and gristle emitting nothing but a repetitious thump-thump-thump. The wonderful mind able to leap from thesis to antithesis to analysis and forward again to synthesis and conclusion was entirely reliant on this prosaic little organ maintaining its most predictable and unimaginative task. He pulled the hessian sack up from his knees to his chest and shifted his body as the pressure of the board on his hips became uncomfortable.

Had anyone been there in the middle of the forest to witness Viktor waking, they could not fail to agree that the growl he emitted was entirely appropriate. It was worthy of marking the end of a hibernation lasting months, not the few fitful, shivering hours he had managed under a sack wishing the door would close more than three quarters of the way, leaving him an unsettling chink of forest to watch in his wakeful moments.

True to his academic roots, his first lucid thought on waking was that he should have read more Thoreau. He had read plenty of Thoreau's political stuff, along with Paine and Jefferson and anyone else who might be called upon to lend posthumous support to the work of the Benbo Foundation, but had only ever skimmed his natural histories. At the time he had thought them pointless and repetitive but now, with mysterious birds transmitting their coded messages above him, the trees whispering their own arcane commentary and everything else in nature there for the reading to those who knew how to decipher it, Viktor wished he had at least picked up from the sage of Walden a few practical tips on how to find something to eat and which direction was most likely to lead to what passed for civilization in this part of the world.

The amount of sensory stimulation provided by the forest at night had been remarkable. It was the certain knowledge that a lot was going on out there that bred terror in Viktor's breast more than any particular incident or sense of immediate danger. For after all, he had survived his night in the bunker. But a rustling in the undergrowth a hundred metres away which may have been caused by wind, bird or beast was a source of unfailing apprehension, let alone the unseen flitting of winged things overhead – bat, moth and owl.

When three glow worms had lit their thoraxes in the thin slit of forest visible through the door, Viktor had experienced genuine terror. In the double gloom it had been impossible to judge how far away the three glowing forms were. At first it seemed they were a sign of some distant habitation but then when they started gently vibrating and flickering off and on they became will o' the wisps, then more malevolent swamp wights advancing slowly to drag him down to some abysmal region. Only when he stood up to face his fate, abandoning the slight warmth his body had impregnated into the wood, did he realise that in fact he was being confronted by three small insects on a little hillock just outside the door who seemed indifferent to his presence and showed no sign of malicious intent. Yet even when he realised what they were, the very fact that he knew nothing about glow worms, or insects in general, or forests, or being outside at night, or sleeping in anything other than a bed with a very precise choice of pillow firmness made them only marginally less terrifying.

But now with the first tentative rays of morning light turning the forest outside a warm pink, the fear of the immediate subsided and a different, creeping fear began to rise: a fear of the future.

Viktor lowered his legs from the boards, feeling stiffness in his whole body as if he had himself turned into one of the planks, and ran his hands quickly across his face and head. As he did so, the door swung open, causing him to rise as a reflex and bang his head hard on the upper bunk which in turn made him sit back down, slightly dazed.

She carried a besom broom and old as she was, this inevitably lent her the air of being a witch. But whereas Viktor was startled by the sudden appearance of the old woman, she acted as if she had expected to find him there and began sweeping the floor. He hopped out of the way of the roaming broom, edging perplexedly towards the door while the woman muttered some strange little spell to herself, pulled a rag from the pocket of her grimy coat and gave the decrepit stove a polish. Only when she got to the bed on which Viktor had been lying did she put the brush aside and speak to him in indecipherable Latvian, rather angrily asking him a question and peering at him suspiciously with green eyes that still sparkled despite her advanced years.

Then she noticed the single flower he had placed on the upper bunk, which seemed to satisfy her. She returned it to its rightful place on the lower bunk, shooing him out of the way, gave the bunker one last inspection that necessitated the removal of a freshly-spun cobweb from one corner, and left with as little ceremony as she had appeared. At the door she paused and looked around at Viktor expectantly. He understood he was supposed to follow. His diary being fairly open, that is what he did, his big body trailing along behind her shrunken frame like a cruise ship towed by a tug.

She moved faster than he would have thought possible. Or perhaps he simply moved more slowly than usual, the blood in his arteries feeling as if it contained ice crystals. The pink light of sunrise was fading, to be replaced by the pure white of morning proper which warmed him like a fire moving from tinder to kindling. The sun's warmth made the trunks of the birch trees glow like fluorescent tubes and warmed the pines to a texture of orange peel. He had never breathed such clean air in his life and it seemed hard to believe that this place of such beauty and tranquility could only a few hours ago have expressed such menace.

XIV   GRETEL'S COTTAGE

The woman's home looked like the cottage in the story of Hansel and Gretel. Or rather, it looked as that cottage would had it been built by Hans Andersen at the peak of his popularity and then left to quietly collapse ever since. The workmanship of carpenters and turners whose skills were now lost forever was still there, but eaten away by time, rot, the teeth of squirrels, the mandibles of insects and the corrosive juices secreted by generations of worms, slugs and snails.

"There is a wind that will undo knots," the old woman said as she hung her washing outside in the yard, one end of the line tied to one of the upright posts holding up the small wooden-shingled roof above a well with a bucket rocking indecisively over the void on a length of chain. "There is another one that will do them up again. Sometimes both will blow and you will notice your clothes on the line in a different order!"

Such wisdom was lost on Viktor, who watched her long, bony hands work quickly clamping the clothes in place with simple pegs made of split birch twigs. He could smell the woodsmoke rising slowly from the chimney of the little cottage. It mingled with the fresh morning air to produce an intoxicating combination, somehow clean and dirty at the same time - a bit like gin and tonic.

The old woman's speech sounded like the chattering of some dusty old forest partridge. Like birdsong, it possessed a definite but elusive rhythm and - unless he was mistaken - her words even rhymed with greater frequency than could be accounted for by chance, as if her instructions were interspersed with aphorisms and maxims to demonstrate or reinforce her statement.

Between simple instructions to pick this up or look at that, which required no language skills to understand, she twittered away in little stanzas that sounded like they might develop into poems but always stopped short just when Viktor thought he might be able to anticipate the next sound. It was as if Schopenhauer's aphorisms were being rendered as nursery rhymes, a combination certain to produce an interesting younger generation.

In this curious way, the old woman reminded him of his Cambridge tutors. They would certainly be baffled by the purpose and operation of a clothes peg, but they too used to spend more time quoting Xenophon or Tacitus than they would expressing their own thoughts, as if thinking for oneself was merely a kind of vanity. Whatever you wanted to say, it was certain that some genius of antiquity had had already expressed the same thought in a far more elegant manner a thousand years earlier.

"Originality is a very over-rated thing," his old Polish tutor had told Viktor during an assessment of his essay on political structures in the Polish-

Lithuanian Commonwealth. "Socrates said as much," he added, handing back the paper marked with the best grade in the class. At the time Viktor had thought the old Pole was saying his work was original, but thinking about the words again, it seemed clear he had meant precisely the opposite. Far from being retrospectively offended, Viktor smiled as a burst of birdsong brought him back from the past's honeyed spires and into his present smoke-stained home.

It was still early morning and the air was suffused with moisture from the dew outside. Inside however, the fire burning in the brick oven behind a small open iron door dried the atmosphere so completely he could almost feel his own flesh slowly curing like a prize ham. He held his hands towards the fire, a gesture which immediately prompted the old woman to recite one of her little rhymes.

From one of two iron hot plates set into the top of the stove the old woman conjured a pot of coffee and poured its thick, black contents into two tiny cups resting on top of saucers of different sizes and colours. Each cup had a fuzzy image of flowers. One of them had a chipped rim – the one she pushed across a pine table the colour of honey towards Viktor, waving her other arm to make him sit opposite her in a pine chair with a cane back.

It was the best coffee he had ever tasted. The old woman must have pre-loaded the cups with honey because the liquid was sweet in a soft, warming way very different from the effect produced by sugar. Mixed with the small amount of strong coffee it formed a glutinous tar-like mixture that slid down the throat with luxuriant slowness and melted into Viktor's intestines like rain soaking into dry sand. He closed his eyes to savour the moment. When he opened them again, the old woman was holding a piece of burnt wood under his nose.

Reaching for the little charred log, he discovered that it wasn't wood after all but a chunk of hard, black bread. Like the coffee, like the room, like the old woman herself, the bread smelled of black smoke. The universe inhabited by this old woman was a universe of black smoke. Omniscient, inevitable, overpowering, the greater part of humanity's existence in this Baltic edge of the world had been flavoured by this acrid accompaniment, from birth in a "black" bath-house, through countless fires in home and forest for work or comfort, through the smokehouses that would seduce meat, fish and cheese with their inescapable aroma to ensure existence through the cold winter months when the smell of black smoke called the frostbitten traveller back from despair or death. And when death eventually came, filling the noses of the dying with the same tarry fragrance from tallow candles, what more appropriate way to dispose of the blackened, exhausted old body than by sending it up into the sky in a final billow of rolling black smoke.

Viktor had seen black bread at many a breakfast buffet, but had never taken any. Just as the old woman's coffee tasted nothing like hotel coffee, so this bread tasted nothing like hotel bread. It tasted – satisfying. He didn't go into a rapture over it, nor did he spit it out. He appreciated its filling effect. It proved efficient at soaking up his saliva as he thought of hot, sizzling bacon. And with that pleasant thought he drifted to sleep, his big, bearish body slumping forward in his chair with the hot coffee and heavy bread combining to warm the inside of his belly, while his forehead was drawn as if by magnets down onto the smooth, beeswax-smelling table top. His last sensation was of the heat of the coffee pot radiating onto his right cheek as if half his head was in sunlight and the other in shadow.

He slept for a long time.

When he awoke, he was lying in another room on an uncomfortable bed, one of those folding Belarusian contraptions that were supposed to save space in tiny Soviet apartment blocks and which it takes a conjuror's hand to fold and unfold. A deep crease runs where the backrest meets the seat, creating an uncomfortable ditch in the middle of the mattress when folded down as a bed in which unwary arms and legs are all too easily trapped. A pale pink sheet was below him and a very old but very warm woollen blanket on top of him. He was wearing only underpants, shirt and socks. How he had got there was a mystery. It was impossible to believe the tiny old woman had carried him, so she must have used one of her spells to spirit him across the room.

His tweed jacket and trousers hung on the back of the door on a hanger and looked as though they had been brushed clean. The old woman was nowhere to be seen as he hauled himself out of his Belarusian trench and sat up to look at his surroundings.

Rag rugs were carefully aligned with the bed and the few other pieces of furniture in the room. They looked as old as his blanket and made by the same hand. A pleasant, slightly resinous smell tickled his nostril hairs coming from the unvarnished pine floorboards which were worn more noticeably in places where feet had dawdled over the decades, in the same way the forest outside had deer tracks traced through its heart. The walls too were of wood, made of hewn logs placed lengthwise and on which hung faded black and white photographs of families whose unsmiling faces betrayed their primitive wariness of the camera. In the centre of the gallery a young, thinly-moustachioed man in an uncomfortable uniform did his best to look martial but his soft, watery eyes spoke of a soul that could never kill without doing itself a mortal injury in the process.

Apart from a transistor radio with Russian cities' names printed on the dial which looked like it was made in the 1970s, the room could easily belong to an ethnographic museum. On a cane-backed chair in another corner of the room lay a pair of knitting needles with what looked like a half-finished orange and black mitten impaled on them. Perhaps she had been knitting while he slept?

A billow of air made the linen curtains yawn as it tumbled into the room, bringing with it the moist, cool air that confirmed it was morning. Possibly it was the same morning on which he had come to the cottage and eaten black bread with coffee, but Viktor felt so refreshed – practically reborn – that he suspected he had slept the previous day through and this was a new dawn.

Viktor coughed theatrically, but there was no response. It was remarkable that the old woman had left him, a complete stranger, alone in her house. It was an act of either rare compassion or of someone suffering from a mental condition, likely dementia. The latter explanation was more likely, perhaps because it was the explanation which Viktor could more easily understand.

He settled back into bed to ponder Lenin's question of What Is To Be Done? but as he did so, the old woman suddenly appeared, as if summoned by his thoughts like some character in a fairy-tale. He heard her feet and the wooden beat of her walking stick on the boards on the porch, and a second later the door opened and she was moving towards him.

She had a scarf tied around her head and rubber galoshes on her feet. She smiled proudly and in each hand held a large wicker basket. As she drew next to him he peered into the baskets at what at first he took to be marzipan fondants or the crescent-shaped pastries called "pīrāgi" which were served at every Latvian coffee break. A strange odour of slightly musty apricots wafted from the baskets which discounted both of those theories and with the old woman now standing directly over him wearing a beatific smile he realised that the strange little morsels were in fact mushrooms.

He had no time to absorb this information. The old crone's expression suddenly changed from simple joy to one that would have resulted from standing on a stinging nettle in bare feet. With surprising speed she placed both baskets on the floor, seized her walking stick from its resting place hanging on her forearm and with a swishing arc whacked it into the bed not an inch from Viktor's startled body. The force sent thousands of dust motes spinning into the air like asteroids escaping the gravitational pull of a massive planet. It was not the kind of wake-up call to which Viktor was accustomed and from the look in the old woman's eyes, there was unlikely to be a 10-minute snooze option.

The brandishing of the old woman's magic wand certainly did the trick. Remembering the train conductress, the First Lady and Magda, Viktor wondered if there was something about Latvian womanhood that demanded obedience.

Ten minutes after the stick smote the bed, Viktor was to be found back out in the forest with the dew returning to the clouds via a thin white mist rising from the damp earth carpeted with moss, decaying leaves and the wiry tangle of blueberry plants. The bright morning sun scattered splashes of white light onto tree stumps and trunks, while tiny birds hopped and jumped through the canopy above.

The last time Viktor had been out in the forest he had been cold, alone and afraid, an overgrown babe in an overgrown wood. He retained his wariness of the unfamiliar environment, not least because he wasn't entirely sure what he was supposed to be doing. He was equipped with one of the now empty wicker baskets (the original contents of which were soaking in a large earthenware crock of cold spring water back in the cottage) and a knife with a blade so worn by repeated grinding and washing that it was no more than a thin triangle of steel with a razor's edge.

The old woman issued orders at length in her twittering language as if he understood every word. Clearly he was supposed to be gathering mushrooms, but her battle plan meant nothing to him, despite the fact that he nodded along politely. After walking some distance into the forest he had yet to spot a single boletus.

Over the years he had eaten considerable quantities of portobellos, morels, truffles (white and black), button champignons and sundry other varieties of funghi in the hors d'oeuvres, soups, salads and sauces supplied on the circuit's dinners but had always assumed that however florid the descriptions afforded to them – particularly in Italy – they must be produced by some regulated industrial process. That someone had been walking through a beech or oak forest and rooting in the undergrowth a few hours before delegates sat down to their high-class degustations had never occurred to him.

He studied the old woman closely, mirroring her actions as accurately as his clumsy limbs and poor sense of coordination would allow as they stalked through the forest. She stood some ten metres to the east of him. He was proud of having deduced the direction from the fact that the morning sun had been rising up the tree trunks behind her, creating an ethereal glow around her thin body as if a Renaissance painter had just received a fresh delivery of vermillion and was keen to splash it all over his canvas of some beatified old mother superior.

She moved forwards and occasionally backwards in her typical manner, like a small bird looking for worms, rarely taking a pace to either side. Her gaze was not quite blank but not quite present either, as if she were peering into a clear pond at fish circling its depths. She placed her feet carefully but with no softening of her step among the tangled undergrowth and spongy moss with the handle of her wicker basket slung over her bony, bare forearm and a knife in her hand that looked disturbingly like a German military dagger from the Second World War.

Every few seconds the old woman stooped, brushed the earth with one hand then stood up again, usually bearing some sort of fungus which was shaken, scrutinized and placed into her basket. As well as the now-familiar chanterelles her wickerwork treasury quickly filled with purple mushrooms of a colour so deep they seemed to have been dyed, slightly slimy brown forms that looked none too appetising but elicited a squeak of delight from her every time she saw a fresh group of them and smaller numbers of other varieties, some almost black, others a creamy off-white.

Viktor mirrored her movements but where she found something behind every tree stump he saw nothing and the harder he tried to focus, the less he saw. Her basket was already a quarter full by the time he had spotted his first chanterelle, which to his surprise gave him a brief thrill of recognition. Peeking out from a pad of damp moss and cranberry plants was a flash of that unmistakeable chanterelle gold. Carefully he peeled back the moss with his meaty fingers, revealing that what he had seen was just a tiny part of a larger fruit body that seemed well worth the effort of picking it up.

He placed thumb and forefinger around the head of the mushroom and pulled gently. The chanterelle immediately disintegrated into damp, useless pieces. Growling to himself he walked on, noticing too late that with his very first step his foot descended to crush an even more promising specimen.

The old woman must have seen him as she let out the giggle of a four-year-old child but then, perhaps noticing the flush that coursed through Viktor's cheeks which turned his beard redder than usual, she signalled with a fluid movement of her hand that he should slow down and cut the stalks of the mushrooms at the base rather than attempt to pull them up like carrots.

The leading expert in his field took a deep breath and rejoined the hunt. After another ten fruitless minutes or maybe longer – time seemed to have stayed behind in the ticking mantel clock – he finally saw his quarry, and it had been worth the wait.

Approaching silently as if scared that it would run away, Viktor stalked a large, pale brown specimen similar to one he had seen the old woman placing into her basket with reverence. Its cap was a perfect hemisphere the colour of well-tanned leather, its underside and stalk like ice cream. It looked appetising even as it stood. Fried in bacon it might make a delicate treat – a thought that had the juices swirling around the inside of Viktor's mouth.

Looming downwind from his target he breathed softly, tracing the firm stem down through the bed of mouldy leaves from which it rose and well into the earth below. Holding his breath he reached for his knife and with a single sideways flash of the blade despatched his unwitting victim before it knew what had happened. A most humane kill.

Rising to his feet again he held it aloft for inspection. The sun gratifyingly shone a spotlight onto his find which now looked even finer than it had in the shade of the forest floor, its firm body and spreading dome the very embodiment of a handsome mushroom.

The old woman noticed Viktor bathed in a shaft of sunlight like an Arthurian knight brandishing the results of his arduous quest through magical realms. Squinting, she seemed impressed and shuffled over to him. Even in all her years of mushroom gathering she could rarely have come across such an obvious Adonis among funghi. In a sudden moment of inspiration, Viktor realised it would make an excellent strategic gift – in the same way that conference goody bags did – and held it out to her gallantly.

To his annoyance instead of clapping her hands or curtseying, the old woman snatched it from his grasp in an ill-mannered fashion and proceeded to mutilate it. First she sliced it in half through its crown, exposing the pure white flesh inside. As he prepared to voice his protest, the magnificent mushroom turned first a lurid off-yellow and then the sort of dark blue-green that results from mixing all the paints in a set of watercolours together at once. Next the old woman chopped a stumpy section from the stem and very quickly dabbed it onto her tongue, which caused her to pull the sort of face Viktor generally reserved for badly corked Burgundy.

Finally, the wizened old vandal sliced an identical piece from the stem and held it towards Viktor, signalling that he should stick his tongue out. Meekly he did so and she dabbed it onto his tongue just as she had her own. At first he felt nothing but the disappearance of his sizzling bacon fantasy and resolved to voice his disapproval, only to discover that his tongue was now as numb it had been as the last time he had visited his dentist for root canal work.

Luckily the sensation didn't last more than a few seconds. Unluckily it was replaced by a far more unpleasant sensation, a taste of stale urine with the intensity of chilli pepper. He spat repeatedly into the undergrowth but it made no difference as the taste intensified to eye-watering strength and seeped into his whole body from his mouth. He felt as if he had just had his head flushed down the bowl of a public convenience shortly after large-scale redundancies in the municipal cleaning department. Even the smell of his unintentional plunge pool two days before had been preferable.

Worse even than the taste though was the feeling of humiliation, not so much for misidentifying a poisonous mushroom but because it as a clear case of him lacking knowledge. As someone who had always defined himself and was defined by others as "a clever man", a demonstrable lack of knowledge was the worst deficiency of all, even in an area as far removed from his area of expertise as picking mushrooms. It is the curse of clever men that they must always think themselves clever – and particularly cleverer than other people. That is why academics so often fail to heed the well-informed instructions of people they feel are their intellectual inferiors and are at their happiest left to theorise about the true motives behind a pipeline project, a cabinet reshuffle or an invasion while someone else cooks their meals and washes the dishes.

It is also why the cleverest journalists tend to ask the most convoluted and least interesting questions: they are more concerned to maintain their aura of being well-informed themselves than to communicate the essential information to the wretched masses.

The last time Viktor had felt such intense humiliation – apart from the recent incidents involving the presidents and the bath of sewerage – had been during his first term at Cambridge. He had delivered a dissertation in confident fashion on the political philosophy of Montesquieu. He was regarded as a rising academic star, and an intriguing figure at a time when few students from Eastern Europe attended the college. An elderly emigre Polish professor who had escaped to England before the war had taken him under his wing and it was to his class that Viktor was discoursing in a manner already notable for its authority and confidence.

At the end of Viktor's speech he had expected positive commentary, some cross-examination that he could deal with robustly and perhaps even applause. Yet looking at the rows of other young faces, all he could read was a mixture of bemusement and amusement. There was a dreadful, puzzled silence, broken eventually by the elderly Pole clearing his throat.

"Very nicely delivered, Mr Draaks. I should however point out that when you referred throughout your monologue to Montaigne, you did in fact mean to say Montesquieu..."

But that was not the worst of it. His next comment was what made Viktor shudder even now: "It may be some consolation that this is a not uncommon mistake by students encountering the great thinkers for the first time."

His cheeks, eyes and brain all burned at the same time in an inferno of humiliation. Part of him wanted to run from the class, return to the Carpathians and never show his face in Cambridge again. Instead he sat quietly down and swore to become a better academic than the old Pole, who died the next year.

Absurd though the comparison seemed, Viktor felt something similar now confronted by his malignant mushroom. But perhaps in the intervening decades, or even the last few days, he had changed somehow because instead of sitting quietly down he hurled first his basket at the nearest birch tree and then his knife down to the ground where, to his surprise, it struck a rotten tree stump point first and stuck upright, wobbling from side to side in a way that amounted to sarcasm from an inanimate object.

The old woman reacted with the same *sang froid* as his old Polish professor. He had turned to a new page in the study book and proceeded with the seminar, and now she bent over and picked up a chanterelle from the patch of earth within Viktor's shadow. Next she walked to the basket he had thrown, placed it right side up on a patch of moss and put the chanterelle inside. Then, without a word or a glance she walked back to exactly where she had broken off her own search and resumed filling her basket, slipping into her ineffable rhythm and moving slowly away from where he stood.

Just before she disappeared from view he wrenched the knife from the tree stump in another minor Arthurian gesture, picked up his basket and followed, parallel with her again, wondering to himself how many times he would have to practice to manage a repeat of his knife-throwing trick and whether apparent expertise really could sometimes be no more than bluff or luck.

Somewhere far away in the forest a cuckoo took his cue and started an unwelcome commentary on the whole incident.

By the time they returned to the cottage the sun was directly overhead and Viktor was ready to eat anything except mushrooms. Inevitably, mushrooms featured prominently on the menu. While the old woman replaced her original haul of soaking mushrooms with the new arrivals, Viktor was allowed to take charge of a sack of potatoes and told to practice his knifework in a more menial fashion. His first efforts made it difficult to tell the potatoes from the peelings, but he improved steadily and after a few minutes was turning out passable pieces of tuberous sculpture at a rate that even won a nod of approval from the old woman – which again reminded him of the old Polish political professor.

Both the washing of the mushrooms and the peeling of the potatoes were accompanied by more of the old woman's folk poetry, but rather than being annoyed by her twittering voice, Viktor was starting to find the predictable rhythms welcome. It seemed odd to spend so much time in someone else's company without words of some sort passing between them – even mutually unintelligible ones – and in his life on the circuit, the sound of conversation was a constant accompaniment.

So sometimes in the gaps between the recitation of her little spells, he began to contribute to the conversation too, asking "When do you think the average defence spending of the Baltic states will exceed 2 percent of GDP per annum?"

She replied with a tra-la-la about the dangers of picking mushrooms on a full moon or somesuch, which he took to be a reasonable enough response.

"But if that's the case, then perhaps a co-ordinated legislative approach is required. But should that be achieved at domestic level or through NATO do you think?" he countered.

And so conversation returned to the house. Even without understanding, it was enjoyable and served a purpose of sorts. The old woman seemed happy enough with her side of it and Viktor was pleased with his, allowing him to think aloud about treaties, pipelines, power grids and borders.

In many ways the old woman's nonsense responses were more conducive to creative thinking than the ones he would hear at late night off-the-record briefings in hotel rooftop bars. As a man who "knew" things, he wasn't particularly interested in other people's views of what he knew already. Etiquette, or at least the fact that the person proffering an opinion was one of the conference sponsors, demanded that he nod and respond with "an interesting point" or even a "*kanyeshna*", but he never really listened to what they were saying, just as a teacher isn't really interested in what his pupils answer other than to confirm that they have understood what he wants them to understand.

With the potatoes consigned to a boiling fate in a large iron bowl on top of the brick kitchen range, Viktor was sent to await the arrival of the gala dinner in the other room which served as lounge, dining room and his bedroom. With not even the ticking of the clock to pass the time – the one on the heavy wooden sideboard was now frozen at sixteen minutes to eight – he took the opportunity to re-examine the family photographs in their frames, none of them larger than a postcard.

Dating a photograph from fashions, haircuts and film stock is a fairly straightforward process in the West, where all these things change on a decade-by-decade cycle. But the Soviet Union's mania for standardization, its roughcut modes of production and its tendency to produce goods that were fit for purpose but no more, and then continue making them until they were no longer fit for purpose – including black and white film stock – makes it difficult to date images the same way. Photographs of young couples smiling on swings in the 1920s could have been taken in the 1980s. The group of moustachioed hunters in trapping gear showing off the body of a huge wild boar could have been even older, or the boar's rich dark meat could still be swinging in the sausages hanging from racks in the kitchen.

Only the degree to which the images had faded gave any clue as to their age, and in the pale, greyish Baltic light even that process took longer than it would at lower latitudes. Certain faces seemed to age from one frame to the next, but with strong family resemblances running through the portraits of people standing on top of hay ricks or looking uncomfortable in their best clothes, it was easy to confuse grandfather with grandson or assume both were the same person.

Several photographs featured the same watery-eyed, thinly moustachioed young man, suggesting he was a brother, a lover or husband of the old lady. There didn't seem to be any of him as an older man, unless the gruff, gaunt man with a much thicker moustache and deeply lined face walking through deep snow with a scowl was him, in which case the years had performed a cruel transformation on the sallow youth. There were two photographs of what might have been the old woman as a young woman in which she looked shy but strong and happy, but there were no photographs of her with children.

Viktor's gaze moved along the wall from picture to picture, all of them safe in their secrets, their stories and the circumstances that had caused them to be taken. A fat man in a dressing gown stood on a beach smiling with a briefcase in his hand. Three middle-aged women in aprons linked arms and looked defiantly at a photographer who must have been a man they didn't like.

A neat set of farm buildings was photographed from a distant rise. Cows stood in one field and strange, giant shapes in another. Viktor peered closer and realised they were formed by hay piled on top of A-shaped ricks that leaned against each other to dry out the grass in strange Baltic pyramids. As he scrutinised the tiny details, one of the outbuildings caught his attention and he realised it was the cottage in which he was standing. In the image it was one of several minor buildings, dwarfed by a long farmhouse, vast barns, a cattle shed and what might have been a dairy. But now it stood completely alone. Everything else was gone, and the forest had closed in on the fields, eaten up the hay ricks and grazing cows and now had just one small cottage left to devour.

The last photograph in the row contained an even greater shock. The young man with the thin moustache was back, this time in uniform once again. He looked even less confident and confrontational than in the other pictures, almost apologetic, in fact – which made the presence of the SS thunderflash on the collar of his rough tunic all the more surprising.

Before Viktor had time to look more or formulate a theory to explain it all, the old woman came into the room carrying two steaming bowls which she placed on the table. She motioned with her head for Viktor to come and sit. One bowl was piled high with a mountain of potatoes smothered in a thick white sauce with pieces of mushroom glowing out of it like fragments of heated amber. The other bowl contained fewer potatoes and much less of the mushroom sauce. The smell of the food was better than Viktor had expected, and he decided to act the gentleman by taking two wooden chairs from the corner of the room and putting them at the table, even offering to seat the old woman at the smaller portion of food the way waiters had done for him on countless occasions. The old woman sat down and Viktor took his place opposite her, picked up his knife and fork and prepared to commence hostilities with the potatoes as the steam from the sauce condensed on his beard.

"Bon appetit!" he said jovially, to which the old woman replied with a rap on his knuckles from her fork that made him flinch. She wagged her finger in his face and smiled a knowing smile which was accompanied by "*Labu apetīti*" as she switched the plates around.

Now she had the mountain of potatoes and Viktor was left looking down at his reduced portion like the smallest of the Three Bears wondering who had eaten all his porridge. The amount of mushroom on his plate seemed to correspond with what he had actually collected that morning, but still it seemed unfair that a little old lady should get such a huge helping and a large, middle aged man such a modest one. Even so, he ate the lot and thought the meal delicious. So did she.

In the evening the old woman put him to work again. First he was required to help her make bread, a function he had never before performed and which he was amazed to discover was both difficult and labour-intensive.

At one point, after kneading rubbery dough for what seemed like the full duration of a five-year plan, he began musing on how he would have to revise his evaluation of inflation indicators in light of this revelation. How many people still made bread by hand this way? Even commercial bakeries must have a lot of dead time in their schedules as they waited for bread to rise. How could this be made more efficient? He had underestimated the importance of yeast as a resource. Who actually made yeast? Where did it come from? A strange thing, dead and dry, summoned to life by a splash of water then killed off again in the heat of the oven. Poor old yeast. Viktor sympathized with it.

As soon as the bread was baking in the brick oven, Viktor was set to work again by the old woman, who seemed to be following a schedule of of domestic chores she had memorised and streamlined years ago so that not a moment of the day was left unaccounted for. Her economic efficiency might make some fascinating graphs for one of Viktor's economic analyst colleagues at Benbo, Viktor pondered as he raked hay and leaves amid lengthening shadows on the square patch of grass behind the cottage. His instructress had demonstrated the correct technique after his initial efforts had had a plough-like effect as he dragged the old iron rake head over the ground. Reciting another educational rhyme that matched the rhythm of her movements the old woman showed how the correct technique was more like sweeping than ploughing, dry grass and sun-blanched grass leaping in front of her strokes as she advanced over the miniature meadow.

Zeme raud uz arāja,
Vecainē gulēdama;
Arājs raud uz Dieviņa,
Nava laba kumeliņa.[*]

---

[*] Lying fallow, earth is crying
For a ploughman;
Ploughman's crying to the God,
Being without mighty steed. (Latvian folksong)

After handing the rake back to Viktor, she scuttled inside while he continued the task, discovering that if he worked too slowly his movements became much more awkward than if he emulated the old woman's tempo. He started muttering under his breath a rough approximation of what he'd heard her say:

Zimy zimy lala lala
Tiddle tiddle doodle-dah
And the diddle diddle fiddle
Hic hac hoc and there you are!

He was breathing heavily, but enjoying the sensation with his muscles warm, and his torso turning from side to side as he inched forward to intersect with the cool shadows of the treeline edging across the tiny field towards the cottage. The ubiquitous smells of pine resin and woodsmoke, the incongruity of his situation – all combined into one emotion which he expressed by laughing. Leading academic Viktor Draaks, raking hay on a small Latvian farmstead for bed and board. He laughed again, thinking what Jameson and the rest of the staff of the Benbo Foundation would think if they could see him now. And then he checked that thought and found that in fact he did not want them to see him like this – not because he was embarrassed, ashamed or amused by the picturesque scene, but because they would never understand that he was laughing for another reason entirely. He was laughing because it felt good. The absurdity was not that geopolitical expert Viktor Draaks was raking hay on a Latvian farmstead. The absurdity was that humorless fools like Jameson, drier even than the grass he shook from the rake head, should find it amusing.

He was still leaning on the rake, looking at the birch smoke rise from the chimney of the cottage when he heard the vehicle. His first thought was of the Russian Mercedes but this engine note was very different with a rougher edge, and altogether less refined than that long, sleek piece of German engineering.

He resumed his raking, thinking the noise came from a passing forester's truck or a tractor on its way to pull a stump from the swamp. He had already learned that such things could be heard at great distances as a result of the acoustic pinball the forest enjoyed playing. Trees could act as sounding boards, tuning forks or deflectors according to the atmosphere and its mood. Noise travelled not in nice neat waves but in temperamental bursts and eddies, skimming quickly along the surfaces of lakes and streams, picking up a farm dog's bark from a stony yard, whipping it across fields and through the trees to deposit it miles away in a clearing where it would cause a fresh uproar among the cowering creatures.

As Viktor pulled another rakeful of crackling grass across the ground the engine noise got louder, like an approaching storm until it felt like whatever it was propelling might bulldoze its way straight through the little cottage, splintering it into matchsticks. It stopped with a squeal of brakes just before the anticipated demolition, then a car door was slammed – again, sounding tinny compared to the bassy 'thunk' of the Russian Mercedes.

Responding to the cue, another noise could now be heard coming from inside the cottage itself. It was a frantic scratching, as if a bird had flown down the chimney and become trapped inside. It sounded wrong. Placing his rake safely against the woodshed the way the old woman had shown him, Viktor went inside, a look of concern on his face.

His expression was justified, for what he found when he opened the door of the little cottage was – for reasons he did not understand – the most disturbing sight he had ever witnessed.

Over in the furthest, darkest corner of the room was the old woman, looking even smaller and more shrunken than usual. Her face was turned away from his, towards the wall. She pressed herself into the very corner, as if the meeting point of the walls would part like curtains and allow her to hide behind them. Her forehead touched the smoke-stained old timber. Above it, almost on a level with the ceiling was a small wooden cross that he had never before noticed.

Clasped in her hands, pressed against her apron was the framed photograph of the moustachioed young man who had never come home from the war. She moaned a pitiful monotone, her voice now completely bereft of its customary rhythm and rhyme.

Viktor could never explain why this little tableau of distress seemed so terrible, but it perhaps had something to do with the injustice of seeing indignity visited upon the elderly. Illogical it may be but fate is not expected to take much interest in the elderly. Death has already pronounced sentence and will be round to execute it shortly, so it is assumed the elderly will be given the courtesies of the condemned. But if Fate rushes into the celestial courtroom brandishing fresh charges and demanding fresh punishments in addition to the ultimate sentence already pronounced, it seems to be acting in poor taste, perversely calling for the proceedings to be recommenced.

If Viktor could not understand why the scene made such a lasting impression, he did immediately understand something else: his own recent humiliations in front of the presidents and the prime minister had been nothing compared to this solitary, unheard humiliation that must surely have happened many times. There was something ritualistic about the old woman's actions, suggesting the sound of the engine was the direct cause of seizing the photograph, going to the corner beneath the wooden cross and beginning the wordless intonation of anguish.

Before he could go to the old woman to offer some sort of comfort – though how to do so he had no idea – the front door opened.

XV THE PATRIOT

There in the doorway stood a wholly unremarkable man. Given the old woman's frantic reaction to his approach, Viktor had expected something far more sinister, a golem of some kind perhaps. Instead there was a brown-haired man of average build, average height and middle age. Even his dress was nondescript: a navy blue polo shirt and windcheater with beige chinos and brown deck shoes. He looked as if he had just stepped out of the pages of a mail-order clothing catalogue for middle-income everymen. Just one thing drew the attention: a fresh black eye.

Yet the sight of this unexceptional individual only heightened the old woman's distress. She began clawing at the wall as if interred, her voice more strangulated by the minute.

Viktor knew something had to be done. His stomach surged with unfamiliar emotions. He took a great lurching bear step forward, placing his not insubstantial frame between the Old Woman and the Ordinary Man.

The figure in the doorway stepped back, clearly disconcerted to see Viktor emerging from the shadows to bar his way. A pause followed which both men spent eyeing each other up and down, gauging their respective levels of threat, then the ordinary-looking man spoke in a rather bland voice notable for just one thing. He spoke in American-accented English.

"Who the hell are you?"

Startled to hear his adopted tongue, Viktor did not instantly respond. Taking his muteness for incomprehension, the man switched to Latvian, though from his stammering delivery, the language evidently was not his mother tongue.

"*Kas tu esi*, er I mean *kas jūs esi... esat?*"

He may have been speaking Latvian, but the sounds coming from his mouth were nothing like the old woman's semi-musical chirruping. The words might derive from the Baltic shore, but the accent remained very definitely on the other side of the Atlantic.

Viktor was on the point of responding, but the ordinary-looking American man beat him to it again. He took two steps forward and jabbed his finger towards Viktor.

"Jesus Christ, you do speak Latvian, don't you? Don't tell me you're another goddam thieving Russian!" A look of contempt transformed his neutral face into a mask of intense hatred which seemed to swell red all the way down his neck to his neat little collar.

"You gavaritye the Russkie, da? Da?"

It seemed he might leap forward at any moment like an attack dog, which is probably what prompted the leading academic to break his unintended silence.

"Actually I do speak English. Viktor Draaks, pleased to meet you."

The ordinary-looking man could not have been more surprised if Viktor had introduced himself as James Hoffa lately of Chicago and would he happen to know the score of last night's Cubs game? But the ordinary-looking man's reaction was as nothing compared to Viktor's after the next words spoken.

"Viktor Draaks? Really? But... I KNOW YOU!"

Viktor felt as if he had swallowed a heavy weight. It could mean just one thing – his fears of infamy had been confirmed. If this random American had heard of his disastrous encounters with the presidents and the prime minister, his name must already have become a laughing stock not only within the circuit but in the press and online. He could imagine his drunken speech being posted and shared across cyberspace, turning his life's work into something for bored office workers to while away a few moments.

On top of that, it meant Benbo would be fully cognisant of the manner in which its leading academic had been performing his duties. Jameson would have little doubt about the origin of the enormous bar bill.

As if to confirm his thought, the American added: "BENBO!"

The sound of the sausage tycoon's name being shouted out in a small wooden cottage in the middle of Latvia was the silliest thing Viktor had ever heard.

"You're Viktor Draaks from the Benbo Foundation? I mean, what the hell are you doing here? I'm sorry... my name's Ivars Dzintars. Say, maybe YOU'VE heard of ME?"

Ivars Dzintars' face looked so happy and expectant it was almost a shame to disappoint him. The memory of his hateful expression a few moments earlier quickly removed any feelings of regret.

"No, I'm afraid I haven't heard of you..."

"Oh," he looked a little disappointed. "I just thought maybe you had. You know, through FLACID." He pronounced it 'flay-kid'.

"We're huge fans of the Foundation," he continued before Viktor could ask what "Flay-kid" meant. "Benbo was a great man. We need more like him today. We've gone soft. I still refuse to buy any other brand of frank, provided Benbo is available. But they don't seem to be as easy to find as they used to be – has the distributor changed?"

"I have no idea," Viktor answered with complete honesty.

"Hey, we can talk about that later. What I wanted to say was anyone who's with Benbo is okay with me, Mr Draaks!"

"Call me Viktor, please."

"Okay then, Viktor!" Dzintars stepped forward, took Viktor's paw between his two soft hands and pumped enthusiastically, looking into his eyes with an almost awed expression. "You really call those thieving Russians sons of guns out, that's what I like about what you write. All their conspiracies, all their envy, you're not afraid to tell the world! The only way I disagree with you is when it comes to military options. I say strike first. We all know that's what it's gonna come to in the end, so why not do it now, while we have the upper hand? Give those Russians and inch and they will take more than a mile, right? Look at Abrene! Pytalovo my ass! It's in the goddam Constitution, it's Latvian land! Latvia should take it back! Their military is a shambles, a few hundred Georgians in pick-up trucks nearly beat them!"

Ivars Dzintars started to rave. This mild-mannered man needed only the slightest of excuses to embark on a long monologue centred on the Evil Empire, how the Cold War had never ended and the Kremlin was hatching all manner of evil plots to steal unspecified treasures, ideas, and above all "freedoms" from an equally ill-defined entity called the West. Only a new suspicion halted his slew of recycled soundbites and conspiracy theories.

"Say, what are you doing here anyway?"

Perhaps it was the fact that he was thinking in English again that switched Viktor's brain on. Whatever the reason, he surprised himself with the speed of his response.

"Research."

"RE-search? But what kind of research can you do HERE?"

"Research into people living on the fringes of the European Union. Existing on the poverty line in the post-Soviet space." It didn't sound quite convincing enough, so he decided to invoke the help of St Benbo. "The Benbo Foundation is very keen to see the view from the borderlands, getting boots on the ground in the places where the politicians in Washington and Brussels would never dare to go."

"Really? Well, hats off to good old Benbo! I always knew Benbo was different from those other academics in their irony towers," he Malapropped. "Anyhow, you're wasting your time with this old witch. She's not living in poverty. Well, she is, but she doesn't have to. I've offered to buy this hole from her a hundred times, and for more money than she would get anywhere else!"

His voice and temper were on the rise again. "And the joke is it's not even hers to sell! This is my family's farm! When they had to run for their lives in 1940 from those Red rapists, she was just one of the farm hands left behind. Some gratitude she showed, treating the place as her own all the way through the Soviet occupation, playing footsie with Ivan all the time, I'll bet. The Russians turned it into a collective farm which ruined it, then I came to claim my rightful inheritance after Latvia won its independence back and this goddam witch refuses to leave! If she was a Russian, I'd have brought my M-16 with me and problem solved. She's lucky she's a Latvian, but she's the worst sort, a Russified Latvian!"

To Viktor's amazement, at this point Dzintars actually spat on the floor of what he claimed was his ancestral home. It had never occurred to Viktor to speak Russian to the old woman and she had never spoken it to him. But now was not the time to wonder – he had to get back to Riga somehow, and however unstable Ivars Dzintars seemed, he was his best hope.

"Are you driving to Riga?"

"Sure, do you need a lift?" Dzintars looked delighted.

"It would be appreciated. I think I have learned all I can here. Perhaps if you would go outside, I could talk to her – about selling, I mean. I could suggest that she consider it."

"Nice idea, Viktor, but there's nothing to consider! Just tell her I have a big fat bundle of cash, more money than she has ever seen before." To prove the point he pulled a wad of notes from inside his windcheater and waved it in the air, flicking his thumb through the ends of the notes so that they buzzed like a honey bee.

"She doesn't have to live in this stinking dump any more. With my money she can move into a nice warm flat in town, go to the *kafejnīca* for her *solyanka* every day and count herself lucky that she's living under NATO protection and that I'm a generous guy who doesn't hold a grudge!"

Viktor nodded. His dislike of Dzintars was becoming stronger by the minute, but he had to keep him onside if he was to make it back to Riga and attempt to piece his life back together.

After a final flourish of the cash, Dzintars left, but not before he had spouted another garbled mixture of Latvian and English at the little woman in the corner, who had fallen silent and watched Dzintars and Viktor with frightened eyes as they conversed in their unknown language.

With the lunatic out of the room, Viktor moved slowly towards the old woman. She flinched, but he placed his hand on her thin, bony arm and led her gently to sit opposite him at the table where they had eaten potatoes with mushroom sauce for lunch. He had no intention of getting mixed up with Dzintars' land grab no matter how justified his claim might be. But he did want a chance to say goodbye to his old woman as it seemed unlikely they would ever meet again.

For a moment he considered addressing her in Russian, but the faded black and white photograph which she still cradled told him not to. They sat looking mutely at each other, the bird-like woman and the bear-like man, the bonds between them destined to remain forever unspoken. Viktor had the uncanny feeling that they were not alone, that many unseen figures stood around the table with them and looked down from the walls. Viktor took the hand of the woman who had possibly saved his life, and pressed it between his hands, feeling the sharp bones beneath the thin skin. He inclined his head as if about to speak, but no words would come. He went to look for Ivars Dzintars outside.

The distance from the cottage to Riga turned out to be around 90 kilometres according to the tachometer in Dzintars' preposterously oversized SUV. The clock said the trip took just over an hour, yet it seemed one of the longest journeys Viktor had ever endured as he was regaled with the average-looking American's incoherent chatter and further evidence of his heady mental mixture of sociopathy, psychopathy and xenophobia.

After lying that he had pressed the benefits of selling up to the old woman, Viktor was treated to a precis of what passed for Dzintars' philosophy – really no more than recycled soundbites about bombing various other nations and religions "back to the stone age" and invitations to the rest of the planet's population to kiss his ass – all underpinned by a never-questioned assumption that the United States of America was effectively heaven on earth and that citizens of all other nations yearned to either become American citizens themselves or to destroy America – by becoming American citizens. He was solidly against either option, seeing no contradiction in closing the borders of a nation established as a state open to all.

Anyone giving less than wholehearted support to Ivars Dzintars' entire canon of political theorising was encouraged to "get out of Dodge" in tandem with a fresh bout of ass kissing.

A yellow-painted church slid by next to an oddly-shaped lake with little wooden huts like large dog kennels on an island in the middle. A minute later a stone windmill waved goodbye from a small hill to the right and a sign confirmed the scene of their departure from Āraiši, which Viktor recalled seeing written once before, though in the gathering gloom only an old school building with a pillared portico provided evidence of human habitation.

"Crazy place this," Dzintars said in a rare detour from insanity. "Those huts on the lake are a reconstruction of an old settlement they dug up, an artificial island with a village on top. No-one's sure who lived in these parts before the Crusaders showed up. Other parts of Latvia had the Livs and the Letts, but round here was some outfit called the Wends and no-one knows who the hell they were, where they came from or where they went."

"A sort of lost tribe..." Viktor thought out loud.

"They weren't Jews!" Dzintars exploded. Just as Viktor assumed he was about to launch into an anti-Semitic tirade, a look of deep confusion crossed his swollen face, deflating it momentarily. "I mean, I support the state of Israel," Dzintars mumbled, "they're better than all those ragheads. But they're all mixed up in the New World Order, too, so that's bad. They want to take over America. But I guess they do more for America than the Latinos. Though technically they are both members of the white race, aren't they? Or are they?"

To Viktor's horror, this was asked as a genuine question, as if Dzintars' overstretched brain needed some guidance as it wrestled with the paradox of disliking Jews on racial grounds and supporting the Jewish state of Israel. Viktor stared fixedly out of the window as the SUV turned onto a main road with a derelict cafe at the junction, its walls and floor ripped back to bare boards so that it looked like a larger version of the little huts on the island. The silence seemed to last a very long time. He didn't want to look at Dzintars in case he was still looking at him expectantly for an answer.

Dzintars suddenly reached forward, flicked open the truck's glovebox and – with his eyes ignoring the road ahead as they veered toward the trees – pulled out a handgun which he brandished in front of Viktor's wide-eyed face, just as he had done with the cash in front of the old woman. The vehicle swerved back onto the road from the grassy verge.

With courage that actually surprised himself, Viktor decided at that moment that if he was going to be forced to answer Dzintars preposterous question, he would tell the madman straight out that there was no such thing as "the white race" and that he himself had a Jewish ancestor of which he was proud. If it meant being shot, then so be it, but Viktor Draaks was not going to feign that sort of ridiculous stupidity just to save his own skin. Better to have a bullet in the brain than to dishonour that same organ by giving credence to Dzintars' obnoxious idiocy. He was about to say all that, but Dzintars opened his mouth first.

"Glock 21," he barked, as if reading directly from the pages of *Guns 'n' Ammo*. "I'd have preferred something with Made in America stamped on the barrel, but if the US Marine Corps trusts it, it's good enough for me and a hundred times better than the crappy Russian Makarovs that are all you can buy here. I wouldn't dirty my hand with one of those. The little Glocks like the 19 are fun but any self-respecting American has gotta have something with a .45 calibre! Standard magazine carries 13 shells – a dirty dozen for the bad guys and one left over for yourself to avoid capture! Only trouble here is getting hold of high-grade ammo. I tried mail-ordering some, but it caused a bit of trouble with the Latvian postal service. They act like the Commies are still in charge! For Chrissakes, what the hell business is it of theirs what I send through the post? Here, have a try!"

Dzintars spun the pistol round expertly so that the butt was facing Viktor and the barrel was aimed directly at the logo on his preppy polo shirt. At that moment the car hit a huge pothole. Viktor flinched. But Fate inexplicably passed up the chance to rid the world of Ivars Dzintars for good, saving him for the future.

For the first time since arriving in Latvia, Viktor felt that he had actually been lucky. While his current situation was bad, it would have been immeasurably worse having to explain how he happened to be the sole passenger in an SUV with an illegal firearm driven by a dead American known for his rabidly anti-Russian views. His reputation as an elite Kremlin agent would surely be sealed.

Never having held a firearm in his life, Viktor did his best to study it in a manner approximating the way Chuck Norris had eyed up a sidearm from the wall of the Tornakalns bar. It didn't impress Dzintars, who seized it from him as they careened over another pothole, shouting: "I said have a TRY, not have a look!"

He pushed the electric window control in the truck's central console with the muzzle of the gun. Simultaneously, all the car's windows retracted, taking cover in the doors and admitting a huge roar of air into the cabin as the vehicle piled on towards a dusty sunset. Ivars Dzintars stuck his arm out of the window and began firing booming shots into the forest at random, the large recoil taking his hand up above the roofline with each report.

"Sweet, ain't she?" Dzintars laughed as the windows closed and he threw the Glock, smelling strongly of cordite, back into the glovebox.

"Very impressive," Viktor replied timidly.

More surprising than the contrast between his generally unprepossessing manner and underlying aggression was the discovery that Ivars Dzintars didn't even think of himself as an American first and foremost. He called himself a "Latvian" or occasionally a "Latvian American" but never an "American Latvian". He was Latvian and he was proud of it, as he reminded his relatives every summer when he came over to visit for a month.

Viktor let Dzintars carry on talking, relieved that he was no longer firing bullets and too tired to challenge his paranoia. Dzintars himself took this to be tacit approval from a leading strategist of the Benbo Foundation. He appeared to be seeking encouragement for a contribution of his own to the Foundation, clearly coveting the fame that would accrue to him among the rabid nationalist online community as a result of being published by Benbo.

Viktor humored his ambition while being careful not to make any promises. Whenever the conversation became awkward, he feigned an interest in the ramshackle farmhouses and collapsing brick buildings that moved past the smoked glass windows, giving way as they neared Riga to dormitory settlements of newer houses competing for space on small plots of land, Soviet era apartment blocks screened from the road by rows of thin birches and finally the distribution warehouses, car dealerships and cheaper suburbs, all the while trying to form a realistic plan of action.

All he could think of was to return to his hotel, recruit the receptionist's help by saying he had been the victim of a robbery – which was true in a way – and use the hotel's telephone to contact the Benbo Foundation, explaining that the bar bill was caused by fraud and that a pickpocket had lifted his wallet. As for the drunken incident with the three presidents and one prime minister – if they knew about it – he might try telling the truth. But as he attempted to frame appropriate phrases, it sounded just too silly. He decided instead to claim an allergic reaction to something he had eaten at breakfast – perhaps a bad Baltic herring?

If he could make his tale stick, calling upon his exemplary record to that point and his standing within the Foundation and the circuit, they might be willing to pay for a room, wire him some money and book him a flight back to Washington. But speed was of the essence – sooner or later they would find out the whole story and by the time they did, he needed to have a strategic response ready. But just a day or two would be enough for him to think his way out of it.

By the time they approached Riga proper, Dzintars cut short a soliloquy on the subject of Russian colonisation by stealth using higher birth rates, in order to ask Viktor where exactly he wanted to be dropped.

"The Europe Grand Hotel, please."

"Nice. They sure take care of you at the Benbo Foundation. So how much would they pay for one of your papers?"

"I really couldn't say. Probably not as much as you might imagine."

"...but enough to keep the wolf from the door, eh?" Dzintars laughed knowingly, as they sped down the broad boulevards, traffic lights easing the passage of the big lump of Detroit metal as if even they wanted to spend as little time as possible in Dzintars' presence.

Few cities in the world have been kinder to architects than Riga. There it often seems that their plans have all been executed without alteration or dilution. The Jugendstil boulevards still retain a feeling that they have only just been sketched with a set square and had Art Deco fancies doodled on top in a daydream between pencil sharpenings. If the decoration fails to quite satisfy, there is no need to reach for an eraser to rub them out and start again, because there is always the equally voluminous building next door to work on, its five or six regular storeys waiting to be filled in like the blank staves of a musical score.

In this way, what started as a filigree flower at one end of the street can undergo numerous changes as one walks along the boulevard with the trams and trolleybuses rattling past, the flower metamorphosing first into watchful birds, then sphynx-like creatures, contorted faces or spiralling ribbons, reaching a near-perfection as an abstract form around a window or a piece of plaster geometry that looks both organic and mechanical. But then the long-extended row of buildings is suddenly truncated by an arhytmic car lot or tin-shelled shack and the street's train of thought is lost, the way an old man with white hair and thick glasses far down below stops at the doors of an intruding supermarket, having forgotten what it was he wanted to buy.

The Old Town's mediaeval street plan is as opportunistic as the merchants that competed in its haphazard creation. The lines of the original city walls survive only in the minds of the historically inclined, while the name of

Smilšu iela – Sand street – gives the only clue that a tributary of the Daugava once flowed where the boutiques and international offices now stand, doing their best not to look bored.

The architecture extends not just up, but in broad expanses of cobblestones that try to nudge their way through history by working themselves free from the sand in which they are set with the help of winter's ice which cracks and squeezes them loose. Then in summer the men with rubber mallets, pieces of string and long wooden boards return to set them straight, but not always in the same order. Over a few centuries some of the cobblestones have managed to work their way from one side of Dome square to the other, executing a long-term plan to reach the edge of the Daugava, teeter for a decade or two and finally dive to the bottom of the river.

The wooden houses of Āgenskalns and Torņakalns show that the Latvian artisans commissioned to construct them could match the efforts of their esteemed German peers on the other side of the river, using seasoned timbers and symbols from their songs and folk tales to balance the latest brick-built aesthetic philosophies brought on the train from Berlin and Konigsberg.

Then there are the dozens of forgotten masterworks, the brick buildings created by master layers able to turn their dull rectangles of crushed rock into smooth curves, sharp corners and endlessly aligned walls in the Spīķeri warehouses that cluster around the Central Market, through the tenements of the Maskatchka district and the old workshops and factories of Pārdaugava. The fact that these buildings, a hundred years old, still stand straight and strong when newer concrete blocks are crumbling all around their feet or even when they have been compromised by the imposition of a ramshackle roof bears lasting testimony to the craft and pride of their creators.

Sprinkled across Riga so that even the most humdrum districts might have a building of which to be proud are the brick-built "Red Schools" which manage to be folkloric, ecclesiastical and progressively practical all at once. But the brick style finds its apogee in the extravagant Baltic Gothic of the national art academy in whose spires, towers and curtain walls the Venice of the Doges, Egypt of the Pharaohs, Dresden of the Burghers and London of the Victorians dance and collide in an apparently effortless mosaic of red and black brick.

Even the Soviet-era appointees of later years enjoyed a freedom in this Westernmost province that they rarely experienced in Russia proper. Their huge apartment blocks at Imanta and Ķengarags which still house a large part of the population stand in counterpoised groups, performing a slowing dance around each other long after the music has ceased playing, stepping carefully over the communal gardens and playgrounds as they crumble quietly to grey dust and are abandoned for newer, less nimble blocks built to almost-modern, almost-European standards.

Yes, architects are a select breed in Latvia and are still granted a special status given to a handful of professions – or rather vocations. Being an architect, a choirmaster, a brewer, a farmer, a dancer or a poet wins a special respect, perhaps because these are the few professions in which it is impossible to rely on luck and bluff. It also explains why politicians and businessmen are viewed with such disdain.

"Here we are, home sweet home!" Dzintars said as they turned into the parking lot of a hotel that looked completely unfamiliar.

Viktor hoped that when they walked to the front of the building he would experience a sudden rush of recognition, but they rounded the corner and walked through a terrace where residents were leisurely sipping drinks in the moonlight reflected with benevolence from the upper windows of an apartment block with the numerals "1904" sewn in plaster on its apex. The building's art deco facade confirmed just one thing – this was not his hotel.

The words of the Torņakalns pickpocket returned to him – there was the Grand Palace Europa and the Europa Grand Palace. Whichever one this was, it was the wrong one. Should he ask to be taken to the other one? Or should he try playing the distressed but potentially wealthy client here? It did look rather nicer than the one the conference organisers had opted for. But there was also the matter of his bags which, while they contained nothing of value, did provide a necessary link to discovering Panchev's game.

Before he could make a decision, a voice rang out across the tops of the orange-foaming beers and wine glasses glowing the same deep blood-red of the Latvian flag hanging limply from the building opposite.

"Oi-oi! Over 'ere, Eye-vars!"

With a shudder, Viktor was transported instantly back to Cambridge and run-ins with taxi drivers and barmen. Gesturing to the two of them from the middle of the terrace was a bullet-headed figure in a white linen shirt, shorts and sandals with a pair of sunglasses wrapped around his shining pate like a band for non-existent hair. A glass filled with ice and lemon, a packet of cigarettes, a showy mobile phone and a Zippo lighter with a Union Flag were on the table in front of him.

"Hey, Jonny!" laughed Dzintars, leading Viktor over to the table from which the man had shouted. "John Smith, let me introduce you to my good friend here, Viktor Draaks. Viktor is one of the most important voices on the region. He writes for the Benbo Foundation!"

"The fackin' who?"

"Typical. I forgot you have the brain of a rabbit and the morals to match, Jonny. Viktor, don't trust a word this man tells you. But he's okay really, even if he is a Limey. At least he's not a Russian!"

This last sentence was said just that little bit too loud and, as he had intended, attracted a few disapproving glances from neighbouring tables.

The Englishman brushed aside Dzintars' critical portrait and subsequent showboating, standing and extending his hand. He had the too-sincere smile and firm grip of a seasoned negotiator. Viktor had seen the same almost irresistible affability dozens of times from members of the diplomatic corps. It was always the friendly ones who gave the impression of performing their duties as a slightly tiresome hobby who turned out to be the most devious and dedicated. The ones who were grave and businesslike were usually either shamming or attempting to cover up their lack of seniority.

"Pleased to meet you, Vic. My name's John Smith. Before you say anything, yes, really. Will you gents join me for a cheeky one?"

Dzintars said he had to get home and warned Viktor again in a half-joking way and a nodding finger not to fall in with John Smith too closely, which felt like Caligula advising about someone else having an unpredictable streak. "Here's my card. If you need any help, gimme a call. I'll send my article in a few days, okay? Next week at the latest. If Benbo could get it published by the Fourth of July, it would make FLACID's year! I'm so proud to be associated with Benbo and I'm looking forward to setting the world straight about Russian crimes in Latvia. It's a tale that needs to be told!"

Viktor didn't remember commissioning anything from the unquiet American, but Dzintars clearly thought he was about to embark on a dazzling new career as a geopolitical analyst rather than his current employment as – Viktor looked down at the business card – an adviser to the pig farming industry. He was already gone, waving gleefully from the wheel of his compensatory SUV as he rolled off into the night.

"S'funny Vic, the Letts dwink 'orrible gin and tonic by the gallon in great big cans and bottles, but this is the only place in town you can get a proper one," mused John Smith as he examined his glass. "They call it a 'long drink' which I s'pose tells you something or other. No joke, I once asked for a gin and tonic in a bar here and the bloke behind the counter asked me what went in it! Fackin' 'ell what a cantry, eh?"

"You're English?" Viktor said for want of anything better to say.

"Not only am I English, but as far as Latvia is concerned, I AM fackin' English."

Viktor felt he must have misheard. Or perhaps it was something to do with this impenetrable accent of the shopkeepers and taxi drivers of Cambridge and London who spoke such a different form of the language than the Dons, the tutors and the students from whom Viktor had picked up his own understanding and accent. It was a different English to the internationalised version with which he was surrounded on the circuit, too. But before he could reason or explain further, the man carrried on, speaking quickly and loudly with a smile that sent his eyes recessing into his domed skull and jerky movements of his thick, bulldog neck.

"Yes, I'm English. My name's John Smith and I've heard all the jokes already so don't bother. My parents didn't have much imagination and even less of a sense of fackin' 'umour. I'm a payroll accountant, at least I was in the UK. Can't do that here because no-one understands payroll and in any case everyone gets paid in brown fackin' envelopes. So now, if anyone asks, I am a fackin' business consultant. Most of the time all they want is to have someone foreign hanging around the building for a few days telling them they're all doing a great job but not to use so many fackin' paper clips. They're happy and I'm happy, 'cos it's money for old rope. Fackin' 'ell, what a place!"

Clearly this was his catchphrase.

"But I do voiceovers, too, see? If they want an English voice to say "Top quality" or "We're crayzeeee!", they give me a call. I sometimes do American and Irish, too, but my accent's not much good. Most of 'em don't fackin' notice, mind. Fackin' 'ell, what a place!"

"You know when I come here fifteen fackin' years ago the price of this drink could've bought you any bird in this bar. Yeah, even that fackin' stunner over there by the fackin' bay tree. Why'd they put all these stupid fackin' trees out here anyway? It's too fackin' cold for 'em in winter and they all fackin' die, then they have to buy a fresh lot next year. Just 'cos you can sit outside for thirty fackin' days a year, they think this is the Costa fackin' Brava. Fackin' 'ell, what a place!"

"Why you hanging around with that crazy fackin' Yank? Did he tell you how he got that black eye? Some fackin' Hungarian prof clocked him in front of four 'undred fackin' students. Straight up! Ivars is alright, but more than once I've thought about doing the same thing. Violence solves nothing, that's right innit? But I'd buy that fackin' Honved a drink, I tell you! Anway what's your game, Viktor, how do you earn a shekel?"

"At the moment you might say I'm between jobs, taking something of a forced sabbatical."

John Smith straightened in his chair and stared at Viktor.

"Say that again!" he demanded.

"What?"

"Say it again. About taking a sabbatiwhatchamacallit!"

"I am presently of neutral employment status."

"Again."

"My current professional position remains a matter of some conjecture. I'm sorry but I'm not sure I understand precisely what is happening."

"Yes!" John Smith said, as if his football team had just scored a goal. "What's your name again?"

"Viktor, Viktor Draaks. Actually I was at Cambridge and…"

"Viktor's a bit old fashioned and I don't know what the fack Drax is all about but never mind. Listen, Viktor, you could be a big help to me. Could you do me a favour? It won't take more than an hour and there's some quick cash in it, though I don't suppose you need that if you're staying here..."

"Well, actually a bit of cash would be useful... what would I need to do?"

"Thing is, I've agreed to do a little bit of voiceover work for a mate, but I can't do it. I've, er, I've got a consultancy job to do instead, for good money. But tell you what, with that nice English voice of yours, how about you pop along and do it for me. I'll make it worth your while."

"Well, actually I was wondering..."

"Smashin'! Good lad, Viktor, I knew I could rely on you. Tell you what, here's the address." John Smith ripped the top off his cigarette packet, flattened it on the table in front of him and began scrawling on it with a stub of pencil he produced from his pocket. "I'll point you in the right direction, you can't go wrong, it's ten minutes by Shanks's Pony. Tell them John Smith sent you and you are going to do the English part. They'll take good fackin' care of you, trust me, they'll probably fackin' feed you up and all. When you've finished, come back here and I'll give you fifty of the folding. You done any speaking before?"

"Yes, I've spoken in public many times. Mainly about Russia and..."

"Perfect, most of 'em are fackin' Russians anyway, so you should get on like a house on fire. Say what you like about the Russkies, they know how to have a good time, eh?" He flicked a cigarette out of the decapitated pack straight into his mouth and lit it in a single movement with the lighter, which Viktor could now see had what looked like the crest of an Oxford college and the motto "Ubique Quo Fas et Gloria Ducunt" on the reverse of the side with the Union Jack.

"Were you at Oxbridge, too?" Viktor asked, unable to hide the incredulity in his voice.

"Eh? I've been to Uxbridge. What about it?"

"No, Oxford, Cambridge. Ubique Quo Fas et Gloria Ducunt," Viktor said, indicating the lighter.

John Smith giggled uncontrollably. "Oh, Ubique! No mate, that's my old mob – the Royal Engineers. I never made it to Oxford, but they have their handy little school of Military Engineering not far away in Bicester which taught me a thing or two, mainly how to fackin' blow things up. Happy days! Anyway V, we'd better get a wiggle on, can't stop here gassing all fackin' night!"

Viktor smiled uncertainly. Whatever fool's errand John Smith was sending him on, it couldn't be worse than another night in the forest or on a park bench, and in his present circumstances 50 lats was a small fortune that might be his passport out of this insane little statelet – though more would be better.

"Make it 100 lats and you've got a deal," he said with uncharacteristic boldness.

"Bloody 'ell, Vic, we only met five minutes ago and you're already trying to give me a fackin' shakedown. But alright, a hundred it is. You're a proper card, Vic..."

While he spoke John Smith had already put his possessions back in his pocket, finished his drink, beckoned Viktor to do likewise and pointed over his shoulder along one of the looming boulevards of Riga's central district.

"That's where you're headed. If you get to a house with a lion on top of it, you've gone too far. See you here later, Vic! If I'm not around, ask Andris behind the bar to give me a tinkle. Break a leg! Everywhere Where Right And Glory Lead, eh?"

"I beg your pardon?"

"Ubique Quo Fas et Gloria Ducunt. You want to ask for your money back from Oxbridge, Vic! See ya!"

With nothing but a scrawled address and the promise of Russians in his future, Right and Glory seemed like remote possibilities.

John Smith was at least right about the ease with which Viktor found the address and the fact that the people he was to meet were mainly Russians, with a Ukrainian and a Belarusian thrown in. However, the excitable Englishman had been a bit less candid about the nature of the voiceover work.

After climbing five flights of stairs covered in the remains of old, cracked tiles that might once have been elegant, his clothes absorbing the smell of damp plaster and dust, Viktor found himself pushing open a wooden door that seemed to correspond with what was written on his cigarette packet instructions. The door opened to reveal a warehouse. A wan light filtered in through some of the large, dirty windows closest to him, but the windows towards the other end of the vast room had been covered with sheets of assorted colours and patterns, causing them to glow in a confusion of dim light. Placed between the parallel rows of windows was what at first looked like a brightly lit altar. Upon it some form of ritual human sacrifice appeared to be taking place.

XVI A STIFF UPPER LIP

A draught caused by his opening of the door rushed past Viktor and slammed the door shut behind him. The noise caused the priest and the victim of the sacrifice to turn and look at him, both of them uttering something in Russian that required little translation.

The man started turning circles of the small stage upon which he stood, waving his arms and complaining in a voice that echoed back and forth around the warehouse while he lit a cigarette. The woman reached into a handbag placed just off the stage and started disinterestedly making a phone call. Both of them were completely naked and the man sported an impressive if rapidly diminishing erection.

Viktor remained frozen. From somewhere in the shadows, another wiry, balding man dressed in a metallic purple shirt and black leather trousers appeared and demanded to know who Viktor was and what he was doing here, again in Russian. With some effort, the leading academic in his field whispered "John Smith sent me!" and held the top of the cigarette packet out. The man seized it imperiously, scrutinized its scruffy hieroglyphs and broke into a broad and genuine smile.

"Ah, our gentleman has arrived! Such a shame John couldn't make it but he speaks highly of you. He says you are an experienced performer." The man spoke the flawless, fluid English of the educated Russian with the merest hint of an accent.

"I am... well... I mean not like that!" Viktor spluttered, gesturing at the two naked figures who were now smoking cigarettes and chatting. Every few seconds between puffs, the woman gave a rapid tug on the man's member in an effort to maintain his status.

"Tatiana!" the purple-shirted man screeched. A young redhead – fully clothed – appeared beside him. "Take our new star..."

"Viktor."

"Take Viktor to make-up please. He is perhaps a little... fuller in the figure than I would have preferred but that's no matter. Viktor, do you know where the rain in Spain falls."

"Mainly on the plain?" Viktor snorted.

"Excellent, perfect. Viktor, by Jove you've got it – the part, that is. But we must do something about the name. Think about it while Tatiana takes care of you." With that he clapped his hands and reassumed control of the porn shoot, summoning a tiny band from the shadows that consisted of a stooping sound recordist with spots, a stern-looking female assistant with a clipboard who could easily have been another relative of the train ticket inspector and Magda, and finally a large, swarthy man in a blue T-shirt with a tool belt who evidently was responsible for props and set construction – and in this case his efforts had created an interesting zero-budget rendering of an Edwardian drawing room.

The expressive man in the purple shirt was called Vladimir – not Vlad, but Vladimir with the stress very correctly on the second syllable. He explained Viktor's duties, while Tatiana stripped him to his underwear then helped pour him into a butler's full fig, complete with starched collar and studded shirt front, tails and, most ridiculous of all, a monocle.

"You are Javes the Butler – the vowel has been altered for copyright reasons – the essential English gentleman's gentleman. Your role is to interrupt the proceedings at regular intervals with tea, cucumber sandwiches and amusing messages from Aunt Agnese," Vladimir elucidated.

Still unable to take in what was happening to him, Viktor simply protested that a butler would never have worn a monocle.

"A valid observation," Vladimir agreed, flicking through an old copy of 'Cahiers du Cinema' as Tatiana dabbed powder onto Viktor's cheeks with a brush that felt like a small rodent running over his face, "however, the executive producer of the film insists that a monocle must feature in the *mise en scene*, and what the executive producer wants, he gets. If even Tarkovsky and Welles were unable to secure final cut for their pictures, I can hardly complain about this."

He spoke with a good deal of irony, one thin eyebrow slightly raised and was clearly relishing the chance to display his English-language skills.

"Have you ever considered how difficult it would be to retain a monocle while engaged in the carnal act and approaching a spectacular climax, Viktor?"

Viktor admitted he had not with a shake of the head that earned him a poke in the eye from Tatiana's brush.

"The only other option would be to give the monocle to our leading lady, which would I suppose lend the piece certain Dietrich-like Weimar decadence, but again, it would play havoc with the money shot. Who knows what might happen? The poor girl could be blinded. Therefore the only remaining option is for you to don the monocle, my dear Viktor, for monocle we must have."

Vladimir said he was happy to let Viktor improvise his lines provided they reflected "the spirit of the roaring twenties" in his supporting role as Javes the butler. As a result they consisted almost entirely of: "Dinner is served", "You rang, Milord?" and "A telegram from Aunt Agnese, Sir," all delivered in his constricting black dinner suit, bow tie and preposterous monocle which gave Viktor the look of a minor Turkish bey.

The maestro Vladimir was unsure whether Viktor would be better playing his interruption of the orgy as an unflappable and discreet gentleman's gentleman or as a representative from below stairs outraged by the acts of depravity he encountered while clearing away the tea set but restrained from objecting by his inferior social position.

Vladimir commented drolly that the second scenario was more interesting in terms of class struggle and bourgeois decadence so would have been of more interest to Eisenstein, who, he informed Viktor, incidentally had been born in Riga. But sadly, as a full Eisensteinean treatment would require a bigger budget, generous shooting schedule and cast of thousands, he resolved to make Viktor perform his entrances twice, the first time maintaining the proverbial stiff upper lip as bodies writhed and groaned all around him and the second time encouraging a hammy performance full of raised eyebrows, puffed cheeks, rolling eyes and "Good griefs!"

Viktor found the first set of takes fairly easy – he simply pretended none of this was really happening – and while his secondary attempts at melodrama were reminiscent of the worst over-acting of the silent era, Vladimir and the crew thought them hilarious. Even the stern Belarusian woman with the clipboard broke into a smile, while the hulking set builder stood with his hands on his hips and a look of comedic rapture on his squashed face.

"Viktor, you are a star!" Vladimir called from behind the camera. "Have you ever considered taking your pants off?"

"No."

"Quite right, too. It would ruin your mystique. Now once more, this time with the tea tray a little higher and when you pour the tea, let it overflow the cup as if your thoughts are elsewhere! Oh, the symbolism, the symbolism!"

Being to all intents and purposes asexual, Viktor was the perfect type to work on a porn set. He shared the total disinterest of Tatiana the make-up girl, all of his co-stars and even Vladimir himself, which made working in porn so much easier. The last thing required on a porn set is an enthusiast. Viktor lacked the familiarity that the others had developed creating and watching hour upon hour of digital penetration, but was surprised how quickly the most outrageously explicit acts seemed to lose their power to shock. Only the set-builder, who seemed to be called Baba, professed any degree of arousal with occasional stiff-armed gestures and lewd comments, but even these seemed more like attempts to pass the time than genuine expression of any carnal appetite.

It was a cold, draughty warehouse of commercial depravity. The pale light of the veiled windows faded paler still until Vladimir suddenly exclaimed "That's a wrap" in his best Hollywood accent. The actors immediately pulled on their clothes and collected brown envelopes containing their fees from Vladimir's assistant, Alexandra who was a former performer herself and therefore the perfect on-set disciplinarian. The girl's envelope was thin, but the man's was even thinner. Viktor thought ruefully of the "performance fees" he was accustomed to receiving from the organisers of conferences, which usually took the form of generous tax-deductible donations to the Benbo Foundation, a part of which eventually trickled back into his personal account by mysterious means from offshore holding companies. Alexandra, Tatiana the makeup girl, the nameless slack-backed sound boy and Baba had already disappeared, as if Vladimir's cry of "That's a wrap" had sent them instantaneously back to fairy land.

Soon only Vladimir and Viktor remained.

"Thank you, Viktor," said Vladimir. "Between you and me, you gave a much better performance than Mr Smith could ever have given. He is perhaps too English to play an Englishman, or at least to play an Englishman the way we Russians like to have our Englishmen, which is the old-fashioned *gentylmen*. You, on the other hand, are far too English to really be English. Where are you from?"

"Originally from the Carpathians, but I went to Cambridge."

"Fascinating. Now you'd better put that costume back on the hanger or Tatiana will murder me tomorrow. And here is your fee." He pulled the slimmest envelope yet from his pocket. Inside were two 10-lat notes and one 5-lat note.

"John Smith said I would get 100 lats," he stammered.

"Did he really? Well, that is his business. I agreed to pay him twenty-five lats. As you were such a pleasure to work with – and never tell anyone I am doing this – I will make it up to thirty." He pulled another five-lat note from the pocket of his leather trousers. Viktor took it.

"I would not place too much trust in Mr Smith if I were you, Viktor," said Vladimir. "He is a harmless enough character for the most part, but not someone I would leave alone with my sister or my dog, to use a Russian proverb. He is a man with loyalty only to himself who has a price rather than principles."

"He told me to meet him at a cafe tonight..."

"It is very late, and Mr Smith is notoriously poor at keeping appointments. I should be astonished if he attended your little rendezvous. But worry not, I will remind him of his obligations next time I speak to him."

Viktor sighed a deep bear sigh. "Do you know anywhere I can stay for twenty... or for ten lats?" he asked.

"Viktor! A man of your breeding and intelligence with no roof over his head?" Vladimir paused in thought for a moment as if weighing up a course of action.

"Very well. You can stay here, in the studio. For one night. My personal flat is upstairs, but I will be busy editing today's masterpiece for most of the night and I do not wish to be disturbed. In return you will act as nightwatchman. You can come up for breakfast. Are we agreed?"

"Agreed."

"Very well. Good night, Viktor, and thank you for your performance today. It was full of naive charm."

Vladimir walked into the shadows, deepening them by turning off the remaining light bulbs as he went. There was the sound of his Cuban heels ascending a wooden staircase followed by the sound of a door closing too hard thanks to the draughts that continued to chase each other through the empty and silent space in which Viktor found himself. By the last of the daylight he pulled off his dinner suit, and the rest of his clownish costume and lay down on the couch which had played an even more important supporting role than himself over the last couple of hours. Unsurprisingly its springs were flaccid and it gave off the unsavoury odour of a thousand naked bodies mingled with cleaning products and cheap perfume. He looked around at the Edwardian drawing room painted on cardboard all around him. As he fell asleep, his eyes rested on the painted clock on top of the painted mantelpiece above the painted fire. It reminded him of the clock in the old woman's cottage. Both had hands that never moved.

He fell asleep almost immediately and dreamed of John Smith being buggered in a Cambridge park by Baba the props man, while Vladimir filmed the leaves falling from the trees and called for one more take.

He was woken, what seemed like seconds later, by a shaft of sunlight that had somehow negotiated the dirt on the outside of the window panes and the rags on the inside to point a teasing finger in his face. In contrast to most of his recent awakenings, he immediately knew exactly where he was and the circumstances by which he had come to be there. For several minutes he stared up at the iron beams supporting the ceiling, still looking secure a century after some Baltic German master builder had hammered the glowing steel rivets into place, causing a few orange sparks to fall approximately where he now lay.

The ray of sunlight picked out the dust and fibres circulating in the air like a miniature solar system. It was perfectly quiet and must still have been very early because the rolling background noise of the city, made up of trams, traffic and footsteps was absent. Riga sounded as if it had wandered off somewhere else in the night, and Viktor could almost believe that outside the warehouse, the damp leaves and creaking pines of the last two days had swirled into place outside the building and reassembled to monitor his continuing progress through their land. Perhaps they wanted to ask him if he still thought the place didn't matter.

His hypnogogic thoughts were interrupted by the creak of a wooden door and Vladimir's voice calling down from above: "Javes, if you would like a cup of coffee and a shower, come up now." After a pause and with a barely suppressed giggle he added: "Pip pip, Javes!"

The apartment upstairs was like a negative of the studio downstairs. Where that was black, this was white. Where that was dusty, this was clinically clean and where that had an atmosphere of age, this seemed pristinely modern, with the very same small Baltic German bricks painted a glossy white, vast bookshelves crammed with art and photography volumes on the lower shelves and photographic paraphernalia of all eras on the upper shelves, and the sort of straight-edged geometric furniture that can only belong to someone with no children.

It was open plan, a spacious living area with white and beige sofas grouped around a huge television screen connected to various boxes of electronics and computers, the purposes of which Viktor could only guess at. A smaller television, presumably for domestic use, loitered apologetically in another corner.

On a ceramic hob in the kitchen area, an espresso kettle burbled pleasantly, and it was from here that Vladimir approached carrying a small cup with a constructivist design that looked like it had been rescued from some junk shop by the keen eye of a collector.

"Did you sleep well, Viktor?" he asked. He was dressed in identical fashion to the day before, save for the fact that his shiny purple shirt had been replaced by a shiny blue silk shirt.

"I think so," Viktor replied. "It seemed I woke as soon as I fell asleep."

"Ah, our Baltic nights," Vladimir rhapsodised with his customary irony. "They may not be as long as St Petersburg's white nights, but they can still scramble one's sleep patterns. It is small consolation that we also have the endless nights of winter when we can never seem to wake up completely. But that only starts to affect one after a year or two, I am told. How long have you been here?"

"Three... four days. I think. I'm not sure. It's all been rather confusing. It's a long story, but if you have a moment..."

"Later, Viktor, later. I must ask you to drink your coffee quickly. There is some bread and fruit on the table if you are hungry. The bathroom is through that door if you would like to clean yourself up. You may use the red towel which I have placed there for you. But you must be quick. I have an important business meeting this morning and I know you will understand if I ask for your discretion. Perhaps you could go and find John Smith and collect your hard-earned money? Then feel free to come back here later and tell me your story. It is always good to talk to an intelligent fellow, as Dostoyevsky observed more than once."

"I will, and..." Viktor paused as his brain wrestled with an unfamiliar concept. "...I would like to thank you for..."

Vladimir shooed him away. "Quickly, Viktor, quickly. Time will be happy to keep his appointments when we are all dead."

After days of dirt, the shower was unimaginably luxurious, and as the water cascaded down his back, Viktor wondered whether the pristine white cubicle would be graded as a four- or five-star facility on the circuit. He stayed in the stream a long time – so long in fact that the supply of hot water suddenly ceased and he was shaken to life by a jet of cold water that sent him hurdling out of the cubicle towards the folded red towel Vladimir had left on a small table by the sink. In a hotel, leaving a towel thusly would signal his willingness to use it again and therefore underwrite the continued existence of life on planet earth, whereas dropping it on the floor would be a way of communicating his desire to have the towels replaced without the inconvenience of speaking to the chambermaid.

The towel was a little rough and would not have won even a four-star rating, but as he looked at himself in the mirror it seemed his paunch had shrunk noticeably and his skin had taken on a bit more colour than usual. When he slapped his belly, the shockwave still rippled through him but didn't bounce back again from his extremities the way it had in the hotel bathroom a few days previously.

In fact he looked healthy, by his standards, and the realisation made him smile – which unfortunately caused him to notice the yellowish tinge his teeth had acquired from neglect, honey and strong coffee – which prompted thoughts of breakfast. Making good with a tube of toothpaste and a length of toilet paper, he did his best to polish his molars to a more respectable hue while wondering if there was any bacon in Vladimir's sculptural refrigerator.

He felt, if not a new man, then a more coherent middle-aged man. He decided to take Vladimir's advice and return to the cafe where he had spoken with John Smith. Another one hundred lats to add to the thirty in his pocket would give him a respectable amount of cash to live on for a few days. A bar chart of average monthly incomes in Eastern Europe projected itself inside his head, giving him the firm conviction that 130 lats was nearly half the average monthly wage in Latgale, the poorest Eastern part of Latvia – the bit that borders the "shadowy and vast" land to the east. The Benbo Foundation could cable him some funds or book a plane ticket for him – provided he could negotiate his way around Jameson with a plausible explanation for the bar bill and, if necessary, the episode with the three presidents and one prime minister.

However it happened, the priority now was to get out of Latvia at the earliest opportunity. Back in the offices of the Benbo Foundation he would find it much easier to use his respected position to justify his behaviour, disappearance and subsequent reappearance. The story he had devised for the benefit of Ivars Dzintars about grass-roots research to see the lives of ordinary people might even be worth elaboration and embellishment.

Nevertheless there remained the possibility that by now the Benbo

Foundation had been fully informed of his disgrace – it would take only a call from Panchev to do so, and it was Panchev's exact role that the whole game hinged on. If his young rival wanted to usurp Viktor's position at Benbo, it would be child's play. He also had Viktor's bags, though for what reason was a mystery, as was the purpose of his taking a nocturnal ramble with Kopeikin at the meeting of the presidents.

The thought was terrifying. Panchev might have ended Viktor's career already. He could imagine his desk cleared at the Benbo Foundation, the books removed from the shelves, the complimentary photographs of him at conferences with the great, the good and the not-so-good removed from the walls like a soldier having his stripes ripped off and being drummed out of the army. Then in would walk Panchev, a sardonic smirk on his handsome face, sitting down in Viktor's chair, putting his feet on the desk and flicking through his diary to see where he must fly to next week.

Panchev had become a figure not of hatred, as he had been when they sat down to breakfast together – how many days ago? – but a Janus-like figure offering hope on one face and ruin on the other. It all depended which way he turned, and it convinced Viktor he could only contact Benbo when he was sure he had a convincing story to account for everything.

Several explanations were already circulating in his mind to complement the grass-roots research gambit: allergic reactions, sudden blows to the head, poisoning by Russian agents... which was uncomfortably close to reality if the Russian-plated Mercedes car really was continuing its sinister pursuit.

In a strange way, it would be good if the Russians were trying to get him. If he could get some sort of evidence that the FSB was taking an active interest, not only would it offer an explanation for the last days' chaos, it could even enhance his reputation on the circuit. Panchev had never been followed by a black Russian government car, after all. It was the sort of thrilling tale that made a speaker all the more bookable... provided he was still around to tell it and not having his fate debated by everyone else on the circuit.

But getting such evidence would be dangerous and involve having to make contact with the drivers of the car to obtain information about their mission. He would need an accomplice to help ensure his safety, for simply climbing into the back of the car would result in a one-way trip to a shallow grave or, more likely a lingering disappearance in some latter-day gulag.

No matter how friendly he might seem, as a Russian, Vladimir was out of the question. John Smith was clearly untrustworthy, and asking Panchev for help would be unthinkable until he knew what he was up to.

If anyone would be willing to expose a tale of Russian deviousness, it would be Ivars Dzintars, though teaming up with such a clearly unbalanced individual would carry risks of its own, not the least of which would be that the gung-ho American would be unable to restrain his confused patriotism and start shooting at the slightest provocation.

These ruminations had already taken some time while he dressed, and Viktor decided to continue them on his way back to find John Smith. He still had the Englishman's scrawled directions on the cigarette packet in his pocket, so he only needed to follow them in reverse to find his way back to the hotel, where the barman would be able to locate the slippery Englishman.

Viktor stomped back into the kitchen to bid farewell to Vladimir, and reconnoitre the prospect of bacon. The Russian looked up sharply from a sofa in the main living area of the apartment as he opened the door and clicked off the large television screen with the remote control – but not before Viktor had caught a glimpse on screen of what looked like an earthquake in a sausage factory and his own face reacting as any self-respecting English butler must react – by not reacting.

Only then did he see Vladimir was no longer alone. Opposite him sat a small man dressed in a dapper combination of royal blue blazer and trousers rendered in a tartan that must have been favoured by a colour-blind clan. Upon Viktor's entrance, the little man momentarily flinched but instantly corrected his expression to a pleasant smile.

"And who is this, Vladimir?" the man asked in Russian between clenched teeth.

"Viktor, I thought you had gone!" Vladimir castigated in English. Then he, too, regained his composure. "This is Viktor, our English star," he continued in Russian.

The dapper little man himself switched to English at this point. "Very pleased to meet you, Viktor," he said with a slight Latvian accent. "Have we met before? Your face seems familiar."

"I don't think so," Viktor lied. Perhaps it was due to the fact that he had bacon on his mind that he instantly recognised this as the man who had extolled the virtues of the town of V---- over breakfast immediately after Pavel Panchev had left the table.

"I am a regular visitor to your country, which I find fascinating. Do you know Jermyn Street? It's where my tailor resides. He made these trousers, as a matter of fact. Do you approve?"

"Absolutely."

"Tell me have you ever worked as a butler? You seem very convincing in the role. I must admit I have always dreamed of having my own gentleman's gentleman, but I don't suppose they exist any more."

"Sadly, I am a mere amateur," Viktor said, responding to the man's clear Anglophilia. Then, deploying his inside knowledge of his Wodehouse obsession he added the word "Sir", which made the dapper little man smile more broadly than ever.

"Such manners!" the little man said. "Wherever do you learn such manners? We Latvians are such peasants – not that there is anything wrong in being a peasant. We are honest and hardworking but, how is it you say – there is no substitute for breeding. Like an Ascot racehorse!"

"Indeed," Viktor said, then added another "Sir" to see if it would have the same effect. It did. In light of the man's flattery he became expansive, while Vladimir looked on in his customary ironical manner. "I had the good fortune to attend Cambridge, which I suppose must be where I learned the rules of social etiquette. Before then, well, I must admit I did not know a knife from a fork!"

"Ah, Cambridge," the dapper man said, pronouncing the first syllable to rhyme with "ham". "I wanted to send my son, Aivars, but he insisted on Harvard or Yale. The Ivy League, of course, is the best education that money can buy but it doesn't have the history. Are you sure we have not met before?"

"Quite, sir."

"Viktor, didn't you say you had an urgent appointment with Mr Smith?" Vladimir asked with an archly raised eyebrow.

It took Viktor a moment to take the hint. "Yes, you are right. It was very good to meet you, Mr..." He just stopped himself adding "again".

"It was charming to meet you, too," the man said, ignoring the invitation to give his name. "Now Vladimir and I have business to discuss. About dull matters such as pipelines and ports and such like."

He turned towards Vladimir, whose eyes were telling Viktor to leave immediately. "You would not believe how awkward it can be dealing with Russian gas companies. They try to tie one in knots, Vladimir, do they not?"

Vladimir nodded in a way that spoke of his complete bafflement at the subject.

By now Viktor was almost out of the door, but mention of Russian gas companies stopped him abruptly. The dapper little man's next words made him turn back around.

"Yes, Vladimir, can you believe they are trying to convince me that selling gas on to Belarus would be impossible. It would be a marginal profit anyway, and the logistical task would be vast, but after all I am a businessman and a profit is a profit!"

"Goodbye, Viktor!" said Vladimir.

"It's not marginal at all!" Viktor growled.

"What?" the dapper man said, his smile disappeared.

"How can it possibly be a marginal profit?" Viktor roared. "Since the Belarusian tariff was raised to 400 dollars per 1,000 cubic metres by the Kremlin, they have been paying punitive rates. Latvia is importing from Russia at something more like 350 dollars, giving you a far from marginal profit!"

Vladimir rose to his feet, but the dapper little man waved him down.

"And so what? How do you think this gas reaches Belarus? Float a barge down the Daugava? Do you have any idea how many tankers I would need to operate, and the costs of keeping them on the road, plus the money I would need to pay to ensure they didn't meet any delays at the border?"

"Yes, I know," said Viktor. "You would not need to operate tankers. You can patch up the Potemkin pipeline fairly easily and send it through there."

"A fine idea were it not for the fact Potemkin flows east to west!"

"Yes, but it doesn't have to. It can be reverse flowed quite simply, the same way the Czechs and Slovaks did in 2009. If it was a more modern pipeline, it would be more difficult. The fact that it is a simple old Soviet line is good news. Making it reverse flow capable would cost less than a quarter of the profit you could expect if you delivered just 1 billion cubic metres over three years. At a rough estimate the owner of Potemkin would stand to make..."

"A lot of money!" said the dapper little man, standing, his eyes shining. "You seem very well informed, where did you learn all of this, Mr...?"

It was Viktor's turn to remain silent – not from any strategy, but because he had suddenly realised that he might have just ruined his chance of escape once again. He had spoken as a reflex action and from intellecctual pride – no-one knew more about the 'Pipeline Politics of Eastern Europe' than Viktor Draaks because he had delivered a lecture with precisely that title dozens of times over the years – but only now did he consider that it might have been smarter for him to remain a homeless man who occasionally gave cameos in porn films.

"Cambridge," he whispered.

"Of course, Cambridge!" said the dapper little man, his smile once again on full show. "Viktor, come and sit down," he said, "You are a man of many talents, I see. Anrijs Pletenbergs always enjoys talking to an intelligent man. Are you sure we have never met before, your face does seem familiar? Vladimir, make us a cup of tea – with milk."

XVII THE STAGS

Following the call from Kopeikin, Pavel had been looking forward to a few relaxing evenings out with no need to develop contacts, no need to say intelligent things about strategic possibilities he barely cared about and above all no need to play the childish games of intellectual one-upmanship that passed for conversation on the convention circuit.

His three young fans from the front row of the pugilistic discussion had been charming, intelligent and even more beautiful than he had remembered, and as final-year students of politics and international relations had been able to fill out his sketchy knowledge of the Latvian political landscape, which became more disjointed and absurd the more they revealed.

According to them, the de facto ruler of the country was not the president or prime minster, let alone the Latvian people themselves, but the mayor of a provincial town named Pletenbergs who happened to be the country's richest man, had a political party called ZZZ in his pocket as surely as the silk squares peeking from the breast of his blazer, and was always the party's candidate for Prime Minister while having no intention of taking up the post as to do so would distract him from his business interests. The girls despaired of anything ever changing.

In the words of Baiba, the redhead in whom Pavel was becoming increasingly interested: "Pletenbergs is a thief but a clever thief. It is as if someone points a gun at you and asks for your wallet. They take all the money out and put in in their pocket, but before they leave, they give you back ten lats. So now, instead of feeling angry that someone has stolen one hundred from you, you feel grateful that he has given you ten. That is how Pletenbergs and the other oligarchs behave. They steal from us and we Latvians thank them for it."

As well as Latvian political education, Baiba and friends worked just as hard to tackle Pavel's complete ignorance of where in Riga the best bars and clubs were to be found. They inducted him into the hazy bohemianism of the Teātris Bar, where his leading man looks and fine speaking voice made him fit in nicely with actors and dramatists. Then on they went through the ironic chic of Brasla Bar with its Soviet furniture and DJs mixing tunes from old Russian TV shows and – his favourite – a series of restaurants and pubs at the back of the huge Zeppelin hangars that housed the Central Market. There he found a Georgian restaurant where the spices of fresh *adzika* and *kharcho* soup reminded him of his grandmother's cooking and gave him an excuse to reminisce about his childhood with Baiba over a glass of Mukuzani wine.

The only annoyance during his few days of freedom had been the frequency with which he had been recognised in the street. Several people, mainly but not exclusively speaking Russian had approached him in the street, asked if he was the man who had hit Dzintars and, regardless of whether he confirmed or denied the fact, insisted on shaking his hand. One teenage boy had even asked him for his autograph, and on several occasions Pavel had suspected that the tourists lounging in the same bars as himself with their cameras at the ready might have been press photographers following him around to try and make something of his micro-celebrity.

He was half tempted to think they might be there on behalf of his new friend Kopeikin, but was sure that if the FSB was on his tail it would be sufficiently professional that he would never notice. Nevertheless he made sure his behaviour with the girls and their friends from bar to bar was always perfectly correct, and he kept a close eye on how much alcohol he consumed.

He quickly developed a particularly close rapport with Baiba, who unusually for Latvia, was a redhead with green eyes, fetching freckles and a slight overbite, a feature he always found irresistible. She was extremely intelligent and Pavel found the degree to which she planned out her days and even her future terrifyingly comprehensive. She had received provisional acceptance to study in the US, had already spent a year in Sweden, used her holidays to attend summer schools in the UK and Germany and spent three nights a week doing voluntary work with charities. It threw the dubious benefits of sitting in a conference hall discussing things that probably would never happen into sharper relief than ever.

At the weekend, when Baiba allowed herself a day without study or good deeds, they went fishing. Pavel had never fished in his life, but it turned out that Baiba was a recent convert to the cause, having been initiated into angling by the gilded youth of the Brasla Bar. In a curious twist on the fashion for trendy retro-authenticity it transpired that, lacking the swollen waves required for surfing or the steepling mountains required for snowboarding, young Latvians had adopted fishing as the pastime that would best show off the fine gradations of style necessary to impress each other.

Latvia's generous supply of lakes, rivers and coastline was the destination every weekend for hundreds of trendy types in reconditioned Moskvitches and the boxy Ladas known locally as Zhigulis. Instead of surf boards or festival tents, the old Soviet cars were crammed with fishing gear – preferably old tackle inherited from a relative or picked up in a junk shop. The modern rods, nylon keep-nets and electronic scales of latter-day anglers were frowned upon in favour of wickerwork baskets, cork handles and hand-tied flies.

An hour out of Riga driving in a pea-green Zhigulis loaned by one of Baiba's friends for the occasion they turned off the main road and onto a chalky track that wound laconically through some of the tallest pines Pavel had ever seen. Occasionally stacks of tree trunks would appear at the side of the road, waiting for a truck to whisk them away to a furniture factory, but apart from that there was little sign of habitation. Then, after turning onto an even smaller track that looked as if something pulled by a horse had been the last traffic, they crested a small hillock and a landscape of small but breathtaking beauty slid into place before them, like scenery pushed into place in a child's paper theatre.

Baiba parked the car on a small sandbank next to a derelict water mill. A square hole in the side wall of the building showed where a large water wheel must once have been fixed to catch the water falling a good three metres from the overflow of a large mill pond lying on the other side of the sandy track they had come down. Now just some rubble and a few rotten beams remained of the wheel mechanism, delaying but failing to stop the constant flow of the water tumbling down on them from above, where a small, unstable-looking stone bridge carried the track over the tiny torrent.

Climbing out of the car the two of them stood at the very tip of the crescent-shaped millpond, listening to the sound of the water sliding over a concrete lip, down under the bridge and onto the debris of the water wheel.

In front of them the water was glassy, except where it rumpled like a sheet near the overflow point. It was difficult to categorize – larger than a pond but smaller than a lake, extending a few hundred metres before curving gently to the right and becoming swamp land. The left bank was all meadow in urgent need of cutting, choked with wild orchids and waist-high grasses, while the right bank remained under the jurisdiction of the forest except where at intervals, yellowed stumps of wood showed where beavers had been busy, sending white birches crashing into the water at odd angles with half their trunks still on land and the uppermost branches lingering on and below the surface of the water.

Reeds grew around most of the edge of the water and became much thicker in places, extending almost into the middle of the lake. Emerging from the depths from each side, subsequent stands of reeds created a curtaining effect, making it seem like this was not a single body of water but a series of smaller ponds screened from each other and linked by narrow channels that glittered as the sun increased its strength to warm the water.

Baiba opened the trunk of the car and they began unloading fishing gear. "This one was my uncle's," Baiba said, piecing together a cork-covered handle and sections of a green wooden rod, the muscles in her thin arms flexing as she forced the pieces into place, holding the assembled rod proudly above her head like a laughing Artemis.

She leaned her rod against the side of the car and handed another bundle of pieces in a canvas bag to Pavel.

"This one is yours – my grandfather's. The lucky one."

"This is my first time, so I will need all the luck I can get," Pavel replied, holding up the different pieces and assembling the rod, glancing occasionally at Baiba's for reference. "I really will be hopeless at this," he underlined.

"I hope not," Baiba replied, pointing at a frying pan left in the trunk of the car. "We will be eating what we catch, so you had better perform or we will starve to death."

With Pavel now equipped and shaking his head ruefully, Baiba led the way through the tall meadow grass along the left bank of the pond. Pavel followed in the narrow furrow she created with wild flowers of pale blue, pink and white leaning out of her way to left and right like the wake of a ship. The meadow had looked a solid mass of vegetation from the car, but once inside it, inhaling the dryness of the grass and delicate fragrace of the flowers, Pavel could see dozens of other tracks crisscrossing their own path.

"It looks as if someone has beaten us to the fish," he said, pointing at the nearest line of trampled grass.

"Rubbish!" Baiba replied. "No-one else knows about this place but me. Those were made by deer. That big one was probably an elk."

At last they came to a spot Baiba deemed suitable. With a little skip she jumped straight into the reeds but instead of the expected splash of water, she stayed upright, standing on a little spur of earth sticking into the lake that was completely invisible from the bank, making it appear almost as if she was walking on water. She gestured to Pavel to follow.

"You need to jump the first bit," she instructed. "A big jump or you will get wet."

They both laughed as Pavel hesitated before his jump into the unknown, then with a helping "One, two, THREE!" from Baiba he took his leap of faith. The surprise of landing on ground that was spongy but definitely not liquid almost made him fall over and sent a lock of dark hair falling over one eye, but with a stumble he stood up, pushed his hair back and struck the pose of an Olympic long jump champion having just broken a world record.

"My hero!" Baiba giggled. "Come on, let's catch fish!"

That proved easier said than done as before victims could be sought Baiba had to instruct Pavel in the full ritual of setting the rods, casting and drawing the flies in a manner that produced a passable enough simulation of a tasty insect wandering across the surface of the water that would not cause suspicion in the porter-black depths below.

With the clouds dispersing overhead and warmth slowly seeping into the day as the wind whispered among the birches opposite, it was an idyllic scene, but his eyes spent more time locked on Baiba than the landscape. She, in contrast, was staring into the water and at the banks so intently that the muscle in her cheek flicked and her green eyes darted from one patch of reeds to another – with her red hair and sharp little movements of her head she looked like a squirrel, Pavel thought, and smiled to himself just as his fly dipped momentarily and he felt an immediate and strong pull on the line.

"Something's happening!" he said, his voice trembling slightly to his surprise, causing Baiba to immediately put her own rod down and skip over, placing her arms around his waist and her hands on top of his.

Given the amount of shaking and fooling that followed it was a minor miracle that the fish was ever landed, but it was, and soon Baiba was clapping ecstatically as a large brown trout wiggled between the golden reeds and green grass at their feet, wearing an expression of immense irritation.

"I told you it was lucky, I told you it was lucky!" she squealed. She pulled off her sandal and was about to deal the fish a fatal blow with her heel when Pavel intervened.

"What are you doing?"

"I'm going to stun it. It's more human and it tastes better if you kill it quick."

"Humane," Pavel corrected, though looking at the fish's definite pout, he wasn't sure if Baiba had been more accurate after all. "Why not put it back?"

"Who would have thought my great hero would be squeamish about killing a fish?" Baiba said. "Well, you caught it so it is your choice. But I meant what I said about eating what we catch. If you don't catch another one, you will be eating just potatoes."

Pavel considered for a moment, realising that in fact he was squeamish about killing this puffed-up and helpless brown trout that had been going about its business without causing any problems to anyone when it had been yanked from its pool. Somehow, even if it was as delicious as Baiba believed, he knew it would taste wrong.

"Let's put it back," he decided. "As it is my first fish it gains an extra life. The next one will not be so lucky."

"Ha – you sound like a Roman Emperor. I'm not sure my grandfather would approve, but if you want to send this ugly little man back home, here you are." Baiba picked up the gasping trout in one hand and thrust it into Pavel's face.

"It is your lucky day, my friend," Pavel addressed the fish as he clasped it in both hands, feeling its body twist. It did not look particularly grateful for its last-minute reprieve.

"I hereby grant you an imperial pardon and decree that you return to where you belong," he announced before adding with extra gravitas: "...but I urge you to remember this brief exile in another element and learn from the experience. Stay away from hooks but remember that they are around and don't forget your fishy friends who fall victim to them. Now go!"

Going down on one knee, he leaned forward and pushed the trout through a small gap in the reeds. After a second in which it could not quite believe its luck, the fish flexed powerfully and dived deep into the black water.

"A nice speech," commented Baiba, wagging her finger. "You can make the same speech into the empty frying pan later. That is the world's luckiest fish. I am going to catch one of its brothers."

They resumed their positions and after a brief hiatus in which they listened to the buzzing of dragonflies that flashed across their field of vision. From somewhere out of sight around the bend of the creek came the sound of water being disturbed, perhaps from ducks landing or a beaver thrashing the surface with its tail.

Baiba was true to her word. She let out a delighted scream as the whole top half of the rod dipped towards a clump of reeds between herself and where Pavel stood. It was his turn to put his rod down and help her, but as he got within a couple of paces she waved him away with one hand even though it looked as if the cork handle might leap out of her grasp at any moment.

"This one will not get away!" she yelped, her whole body tensing as she wrestled with her invisible foe.

The ensuing struggle between human and fish was of such epic proportions it made Pavel's own struggle seem like a bar brawl compared to Ragnarok. After nearly half an hour of strain and counter strain, victory finally went to the flame-haired biped as a monstrous green and silver Kraken emerged from the depths thrashing its tail furiously. For some reason the pike fixed Pavel with a defiant eye, as if news of his pacifist tendencies was already widespread among pond life.

The mighty fish thrashed repeatedly as Baiba lowered it onto the grass. She pulled off her sandal and with a war cry of which any Banshee would have been proud rapped it on the head. This only enraged it further and its clamp-like mouth seized her shoe and began tearing it to pieces in a green frenzy of grass and flashing scales, despite the hook still protruding from its lower lip.

Pavel pulled off the handle of his rod and brought it smashing down between the pike's skull and backbone. The first blow halved its thrashing, the second saw it cease completely. They all looked glad it was over, pike included, whose mouth now wore the suggestion of a smile.

"It's a good job I put mine back," Pavel said. "That thing is easily big enough for two."

And so it proved. With a rug spread out on the sandbank next to the old mill, chunks of their former adversary bubbled contentedly in a fish stew while the blue flame of the gas stove roared its approval. Baiba deemed the expedition a definite success and was glad that her grandfather's rod had been honored by notching up another victim after all, even if it was at the opposite end to usual. She and Pavel clinked glasses of sweet, black *kvass*, its bottle chilled in the pond while the stew was prepared. Into the pot went onions, tomatoes, water scooped from where it overflowed and tumbled down to the mill wreckage and handfulls of chicory, watercress, clover flowers and the spinach-like wild cabbage leaves she called *skabenes* which magically thickened the whole thing up.

It tasted ten times better than anything Pavel had ever eaten on the lecture circuit, the exact opposite of those formal dinners with rarefied ingredients served on bone china and eaten with silver. Here they had a few chipped plates, an assortment of mismatched cutlery and a loaf of heavy black bread, but it was redolent of life and spontaneity.

"It's delicious," he told her. "I should do this more often."

"Not bad, but too many bones. Your trout would have been tastier," she replied.

After they had finished, they stowed the kitchen and dining room in the back of the old Russian jalopy before setting out on the return to Riga. Before reaching the main road Baiba took what evidently was a wrong turn, as the track narrowed and the forest became thicker and darker on both sides. It was impossible to turn around as the trees were barely missing the wing mirrors, forcing them to continue over a small rise until a clearing appeared with a tumbledown wooden cottage in the middle like something from a fairy tale.

In front of it, an old woman was taking in her washing from a long line. Baiba waved to her as they turned the car around on a freshly-raked patch of grass but she didn't seem to notice and within a few seconds they were heading back the way they had come. They reached Riga before nightfall and made love for the first time in Pavel's hotel room.

In the evening they went out for cocktails. Pavel was full of that dreamy, replete feeling of surprise that comes with the start of a new emotional and physical connection, mixed with the germ of fear that comes from not knowing if or how it will develop.

Sitting outside at the Labais Krasts beer terrace next to Riga castle, where big paper lampshades swung in the wind under a canopy above their heads, he said how he admired her work ethic and voiced his growing doubts about the course of his own life and its relevance to the real world, but Baiba didn't immediately understand.

"But you are... international," she said, as if it meant something specific.

"If you mean I travel a lot, yes, I do. But most airports, most hotels and most conference centres look the same. Even the food is standardised, in a way. In Italy you will get the food of the best Italian restaurants, in France the food of the best French restaurants. It's all very nice, but really it's all the same. The views from the window change, but if you are always on the wrong side of the window, does it really make any difference?"

Not wanting to sound negative towards the end of such a wonderful day, he changed the subject. "What will you do in Latvia when you come back after your studies?"

"Come back? Don't be silly, I won't come back – except to visit my family. You don't understand Latvians at all. We all love the country, but none of us actually want to live in it."

"And the Russians?"

"They don't love the country but they do want to live in it. Crazy, no?"

Down on the Daugava embankment, some students lit Chinese lanterns and stood clapping as the orange orbs rose slowly into the sky, for a moment threatening to set fire to the presidential flag on top of the castle's round western tower, but then they caught an updraught from the old castle walls that took them arcing over the river towards the huge curved facade of a Swedish bank headquarters where their reflections were multiplied a dozen times in the mirrored windows as they sailed by. One lantern went much higher than the other, which started wandering off to the right toward Ķīpsala island with its expensive renovated wooden villas and squalid un-renovated villas. There was a sudden cloudburst, but the lamps seemed unaffected, as if they had already said their farewells and were racing ahead of the rain in divergent directions.

The rain, which drummed on the plastic canopy above them, brought a group of nine new arrivals to the terrace which had a few trendy young patrons as well as a table of Swedish tourists from the cruise ship docked just a few hundred metres away on the far side of the Vanšu bridge. There was also a businessman whose post-work pint had multiplied into a slightly depressing bender and two athletic-looking men in shorts who were showing each other pictures of their children.

The nine newcomers wore identical printed T-shirts declaring that they were members of "Stevos Rega Stag Do" and had clearly spent most of the day in bars. They were loud, vulgar and proud to be English according to the football songs which they occasionally burst into like sufferers of a collective form of Tourette's Syndrome. They occupied a couple of large tables next to the low and ancient stone wall which ran along the castle side of the terrace, shouted for "lager" and began baiting the girl who brought the beers on a tray.

The atmosphere became immediately tense. As the stag party continued its baboon rituals the Swedes rose and left, placing their money under an ashtray. One of the stags, whose T-shirt identified him as "Hammo" promptly stole the money before the waitress could retrieve it, causing much hilarity among his comrades. The owner of the bar whispered something to another barmaid who slipped out of the side entrance, but not before another stag named "Dazzler" had pulled one of the ancient stones from the wall and thrown it onto the road below, narrowly missing her.

"Shall we go back to the hotel?" Pavel asked Baiba.

She sighed and nodded. They stood up, Pavel put his money on the bar out of reach of the feral pack and placed his arm around Baiba as they walked out of the entrance opposite the well respected English gentlemen. He ignored the vulgar comments being shouted in their direction, but at that point a tenth member of the party appeared, to raucous cheers from his fellow Morlocks, walking directly towards Pavel and Baiba. He was still buttoning up his flies after urinating on the red-brick Anglican Church which stood in semi-shadow next to the bar. Built on soil specially imported from England by patriotic Victorian merchants, he had thus unwittingly been pissing on his homeland.

Then, as the he drew level with Baiba, the urinator reversed his unbuttoning process, pulled out a singularly unimpressive member and waved it left and right rapidly in one hand, as if fencing with a chipolata sausage.

The laughter behind Pavel went supersonic, then for the briefest of seconds everything seemed silent and still. Pavel saw the first of the Chinese lanterns still flying high and heading towards the airport, while the other began a slow descent in the direction of the Gulf of Riga. It probably wouldn't make it to the sea and would land in an overgrown field near the small town of Bolderāja. Perhaps it would set fire to something.

Back on terra firma he saw the gurning face of a person labelled "Woody" in front of him. It wasn't the the piggy eyes, lardy skin, blotchy tattoo, spittle-flecked lips or even the shrivelled little prick that Pavel took exception to. It was the total lack of empathy for another human being, the inability to consider anything but its own gratification as if actions never had consequences. "Woody" represented an even more debased version of the Ivars Dzintars type, lacking even an ideology to justify his actions.

So Pavel Panchev uncorked another right cross that poleaxed Woody even more comprehensively than it had Ivars. Within a second, Woody lay face up on one of the tables with his pathetic little penis still hanging out of his trousers like a strangled slug, an expression of bewilderment arranged on his flabby features.

The stags were onto Pavel in seconds. Punches and kicks rained down on him but perhaps because they were too drunk to be accurate or there were so many of them that they got in each others' way, none of them seemed to hurt very much. He got in a few of his own, but as Baiba ran behind the bar with the staff, Pavel went down to the floor. There was no fear, but at that point he decided once and for all that he was wasting his time on the circuit.

Two police wagons screeched to a halt next to the church and a squad dressed in riot gear leaped out. It was all over surprisingly quickly with the members of "Stevos Rega Stag Do" screaming incoherently about their rights and the British ambassador. It would be another busy night for the duty officer at the British embassy.

Apart from a few cuts and bruises, Pavel was fine. He accepted the barman's offer of a drink on the house, and both the barman and Baiba seemed to satisfy the few questions asked by the senior police officer including one about whether this really was the same man who had felled Dzintars earlier in the week. Pavel feared confirmation might count against him but on the contrary, it made the policeman laugh – perhaps because as the fabric name badge on his uniform showed, he had a Russian surname. When the last of the stags had been loaded up, he saluted and left. The last they saw of the sons of Albion, they were peering with frightened eyes from the rear windows of the riot van looking less like a marauding army than sheep on their way to slaughter.

XVIII   THE HELPFUL MR SMITH

The terrace of the Grand Hotel Europe showcased a wholly different clientele despite being less than a minute's walk from the scene of Pavel's priapic punch-up. Here the beautiful and not-so-beautiful people with serious money mingled with a second stratum of society – those with no real money of their own but routine access to generous business expense accounts which evaporated in a heady haze of good champagne, Cuban cigars and "Pacific Rim Fusion" food which had replaced the traditional caviar as the badge of intercontinental sophistication.

A few old-fashioned Russian and Ukrainian swindlers still ordered a pot or two of Iranian beluga that had been sold on several times to enable it to be placed in faux-imperial packaging, and they still washed it down with the best vodka money could buy, but such actions no longer impressed and today's cosmopolitan jet-set considered them vulgar.

The cuisine of steaming South-East Asia is especially inappropriate on frigid Baltic shores with the vibrant reds and milky greens of Thailand, Burma and Korea appearing to be satirical when contrasted with the grey peas, brown grains and plain dairy products that form a large part of the indigenous diet. The clearest contrast of all came with the seafood. Indonesian crabs and Malaysian deep sea snappers had novelties of form, colour and preparation unheard of in the sturdy and handsome local herring, sprats and mackerel whether smoked or marinated.

Magnificent though it is, the definitive Baltic dish of marinated herring with boiled potatoes, dill, raw sliced onions and a pile of cottage cheese is a virtual definition of the unexotic: lacking colour, novelty and rarity. It can be prepared equally well by anyone, is impossible to mess up badly enough to make it inedible and is cheap.

It is not on the menu at the Grand Hotel Europe or Europe Grand Hotel, but it is in all places worth eating in Latvia.

The surge of adrenalin Pavel had experienced during his latest altercation meant that he didn't want to go straight to bed – not even with Baiba. It would have been all too easy to get her back to his room after what had just happened. Instead he kissed her deeply as they parted at the street corner, rather relieved when she had said that it wasn't necessary for him to escort her home.

The rain shower had passed and the humidity returned, so the broad terrace outside the hotel was already busy. A table of three gorgeous gold-diggers in their late twenties stared at him hungrily and seemed on the verge of inviting him to join them when he noticed a free space at a table with just one man sitting alone. Despite his shaven head he looked like an affable character, so Pavel asked if the chair was free.

"'Elp yerself, always glad to see a new face!" the man said. "Fancy a fag?"

For a moment Pavel thought he might be heading towards yet another confrontation and his whole body tensed, but seeing the offered packet of cigarettes his shoulders relaxed. He took a cigarette despite having given up six months earlier, feeling that he had earned one. The man flicked open a Zippo lighter with a Union Flag emblazoned on one side and lit the cigarette.

"John Smith," the smiling Englishman said. They shook hands as the first sweet smoke stroked the back of Pavel's tongue. He put his lighter down on the table and Pavel saw a coat of arms featuring a crown and Latin script on the other side.

"Pavel Panchev. You're English?"

"As tea with the Queen, old boy," he said with a reasonably convincing mock aristocratic accent.

"I just encountered a few of your countrymen," Pavel said. "They didn't do much for your international reputation, I'm afraid."

"Stag, was it?"

"Something like that."

"Fackin' 'ell. Sorry 'bout that. Mind you the Latvians are half to blame. They moan until the fackin' cows come 'ome about stag parties, then open up a load of strip bars selling cheap booze. What a fackin' country! As you can see we're not all fackin' nutters. Maybe I could buy you a drink by way of evening up the score?"

"That's very kind. I'll have whatever you're having."

"Gin and tonic?"

"Perfect."

With an ease that suggested he was a terrace habitue, John Smith caught the waiter's eye, indicated two more of the same and carried on the conversation.

"So what's your line of work, Pavel?" The use of his first name was significant, Pavel noted. It showed that John Smith was listening rather carefully to what he said despite his air of being a simple Cockney character.

"That's a good question. You could say I'm between jobs at the moment."

"Fack me! You're the second bloke this week who's said that to me. Either I'm the only one around here with a fackin' job or I've got a mug no-one trusts!" John Smith laughed as the drinks arrived, placed on circular paper mats with the ice tinkling invitingly. "Chin chin!"

They raised glasses and John Smith continued as two curls of grey-blue smoke rose from Pavel's nostrils with delicious bitterness.

"What was his name? Fackin' Vincent or summat. No, Viktor, Viktor Drax. Funny character he was, but an educated man like yourself, and…"

"Viktor Draaks? You were talking to Viktor Draaks? When?"

"A few days ago. You know him?"

"Yes, I know him. Do you know where he is now?"

Pavel could see the curtains start to be drawn across John Smith's small, pale blue eyes, even as he maintained his good-natured exterior. He was no comic character, he was a player, though what the game was remained to be seen. Pavel eased off and tried not seem too eager to get the information he wanted so badly, commenting that the gin and tonic was a good one.

"Why are you so keen to see this Viktor character?" John Smith asked. The accent was the same, but there was something different in the way he spoke.

"Oh, he and I did some work together. To tell you the truth he owes me some money," Pavel lied.

"That's funny, because I owe him some money," John Smith said. "He was supposed to come back here to collect it but he never showed up. So I don't think I can help you. It's a small world, eh?"

"How could you owe him money?"

"I put a bit of work his way. I was doing him a favour, he looked a bit down on his luck."

"What sort of work?"

"That's between me and him. I'd love to tell you but you know, client confidentiality and all that."

"Of course."

"How much money does he owe you?"

"I'd love to tell you. Client confidentiality and all that." Pavel smiled sourly at John Smith and felt the ice cubes rattle against his teeth as he finished his drink. "Thanks for the drink. It was... like a little piece of England here in Latvia." He stood up.

"Don't be like that, Pavel! Let's have another. We can work something out. Is it a lot of money he owes you? I mean maybe we can help each other settle our debts?" John Smith repeated his cocktail semaphore and the waiter responded with message understood.

"Well... perhaps..." Pavel sat down, trying to do his best to look like someone who was going to walk away at any moment.

"So say I did point you in the right direction, it would be worth you paying a small finder's fee?"

"Perhaps."

"Perhaps never solved anything, Pavel, me old chum. Twenty percent of whatever he owes."

At that point the negotiations were interrupted by the arrival of the three lithe ladies who had noticed Pavel's arrival. John Smith looked immensely pleased by their presence and started pulling empty chairs from other tables, though they studiously ignored him.

"Good evening, gentlemen," the spokesperson for the Blondes' Union said with a strong Russian accent that only increased John Smith's interest, judging from the puppyish look in his watery eyes. "I am sorry to interrupt your drink, but my friends and I wanted to say that what you did to that… that idiot was the best thing we have ever seen. Can we have a photo with you, please?"

Pavel groaned inwardly but assented, much to the delight of the three women. They immediately snapped into formation, one on each side puckering up next to his cheeks, and the blonde-in chief placing her arms around his neck and turning her head to look back at the camera which to his disappointment had been thrust into John Smith's hands.

"Say 'Seeeeex'," he leered as a bright flash immortalised the moment.

"What the fack was all that about? What a fackin' country!" the Englishman commented as the blondes sashayed into the night with little waves and giggles, his former character restored in all its fackin' glory.

"It's ridiculous really. I got involved in a little disagreement with someone at the University. It was just a heat of the moment thing…"

"Fack me, you're the fackin' Magyar!" John Smith shouted, loud enough to make at least half the people on the terrace turn to look. "You're the one that clocked my mate Ivars. That puts a different spin on things."

Pavel cursed the timing of his fan club's arrival. He had crossed Viktor's trail, but it seemed he was not going to be able to follow it any further. At least he knew Viktor had still been in Riga recently. Perhaps Kopeikin's network of informers could turn something more precise up? But then John Smith surprised him.

"Seeing as you're the one that gave Ivars one in the kisser, let's say ten per cent. Deal?"

"I'll tell you tomorrow," Pavel said. "I'll need to talk to someone first." This seemed to please John Smith a great deal and he smiled knowingly. They clinked glasses.

Back in his room, Pavel asked for an outside line and pulled Kopeikin's extravagantly embossed business card from his pocket. Despite the late hour he was put through immediately and told the Russian – who seemed to be in the middle of a family meal judging by the sound of rattling dishes and children's shouts in the background – a rough outline of his encounter with John Smith and the sighting-at-one-remove of Viktor.

"A fascinating coincidence," Kopeikin said, "if that is what it was. I will see what I can find out about this helpful Mr Smith, he sounds worthy of investigation. By the way, did you know you have become something of a celebrity here in Russia? At least three people have sent me internet links to your little display of the noble art of boxing and even Zhirinovsky admitted he couldn't have done any better."

"High praise indeed."

"You should not underestimate the effects of popularity, Pavel. In my experience it comes in two sorts: temporary and permanent. If you are lucky, it is temporary, but if you were born under a bad star – which is to say a lucky one – you will be permanently popular and never know peace again. Try not to do anything too praiseworthy for a little while."

"I'll do my best."

"I'm just finalising my travel plans now. I should be there in two days. With luck we will find Viktor Draaks alive and well and put him back on the lecture circuit where he can't do any harm. Incidentally would you like to come back to Russia with me?"

"What?"

"Don't be silly, Pavel, no-one crosses over any more, it simply isn't necessary. We're all friends. I thought you might like a holiday and I did promise to show you my dacha. Built with my own money, I might add. You would have to endure being hero-worshipped by my sons, but I'm sure I can keep everyone else at bay."

"I'll think about it."

"Good. Was there anything else? I am about to be attacked by these three little terrors." Kopeikin made the sound of a bear away from the receiver and Pavel heard young boys' voices screaming in mock terror.

"There was one thing. Does that offer of a room upgrade still stand?"

"Of course. Consider it done. The red-headed girl? She looks a delightful creature, very Latvian. Be careful you don't get stuck in the Baltic, Pavel, or I may never leave you alone. Be seeing you!"

The line went dead halfway through the Deputy Prime Minister telling his boy to stop giving food to the dog.

Pavel sat on the bed and wondered if it was too late to call Baiba. A warm body and arms around his neck would be wonderful, but he decided that his relationship with Baiba – if it even merited that description in the few days they had known each other – should be one of those things to be decided when Viktor had been found.

Kopeikin had been right that Viktor needed to be put back on the circuit – either because as Kopeikin thought it was where he could do the least damage or because it was actually where he belonged. After all, what else could Viktor do? At least recent events had convinced Pavel once and for all that he did not want to end up with the same comfortable, respectful and utterly repetitive life.

A change would have to be made but only when Viktor had been slotted back into the only place that would fit him. Then perhaps Pavel would be able to see what new space had opened up as a result, like one of those puzzles made up of squares in a frame that slide against each other and only form a coherent picture after an awful lot of fiddling around.

The telephone rang, startling him. He half expected to hear Kopeikin's family dinner continuing or perhaps an avaricious John Smith trying to rattle a quick decision out of him. Or perhaps it would be Baiba, yearning for arms around her neck, too. Instead he heard an unexpected voice.

"Is that Pavel Panchev? This is Viktor Draaks speaking. Pavel, I need your help."

XIX AN EXPERT AGAIN

Viktor Draaks was an expert once again. The more he explained to Pletenbergs, convincing him that vast profits could be generated in relatively short order by investing merely large sums of money, the happier the little man became, extending his smile's reach east to west while his head nodded north to south.

Yet even as Viktor explained away, sitting in Vladimir's comfortable studio, the more he doubted the wisdom of revealing his full story to this devious little schemer.

He admitted to his academic background – not only did Pletenbergs swoon at every mention of Merrie Olde England, but it was necessary to prove that he really knew what he was talking about – and he mentioned his work with foreign foundations and think-tanks while carefully avoiding naming them in case Pletenbergs took it upon himself to start calling them up.

Finally Pletenbergs seemed satisfied, settling back in his sofa and playing with his silk tie in a manner that was supposed to look absent-minded but gave the impression of cold calculation.

"This is all wonderful, Viktor. You have given me, Anrijs Pletenbergs, advice that would have cost me thousands from a consultant, even if they had known the subject as well as you – which I seriously doubt. I can always find work and rewards for men with special skills who are ready to support me and help me do the best for my town and my country. But, and please forgive the blunt manner in which I ask this, but as anyone who knows Anrijs Pletenbergs knows, bluntness is one of my qualities. I simply must ask," at this point he dropped his tie and stared Viktor square in the eyes, "what are you doing pulling faces in a... film of this nature?"

Viktor was used to fielding questions at the end of his geopolitical discourses and usually did so in a breezy manner that reinforced the idea he was a total master of his subject. Perhaps that is what helped him answer. It was almost as if someone else, some more worldly, confident and less timid Viktor was giving the answer to Pletenbergs.

"A fair question, Mr Pletenbergs, and one that I hope you will forgive me for answering with another question: what are you doing watching me pulling faces, as you put it, in a film of a decidedly fruity nature?"

For perhaps four seconds it was as if all of the air had been sucked out of the room. Vladimir spluttered into his tea slightly, then a single eyebrow rose in ironic appreciation of the moment and expectation of Pletenbergs' reply.

The dapper little man chuckled to himself quietly and resumed playing with the end of his tie. "That too is a fair question, Viktor. We all have our little secrets, don't we? There's nothing wrong with that – who gets hurt after all? Let's move away from such trifles. Anrijs Pletenbergs always keeps the bigger picture in mind. Viktor, I could use a man like you: educated, experienced, not afraid to say what he thinks and with an international outlook. How about you come back to V---- with me and help me make it an even better city?"

Viktor was about to interrupt, but Pletenbergs waved him away.

"I know what you are going to say – that you have other things to do. You cannot commit your future to me. I understand. But come with me, see what you think for a month, or just for a week. I guarantee you will fall in love with V----, you'll see what I am trying to do there. After that, if you want to leave, I will be happy to let you go and see you off. But I know you will want to stay! I know you are for Anrijs Pletenbergs, not against him! What do you say?"

Having bluffed his way into such a position and with no prospect of a regular roof over his head or food on his plate, Viktor knew he had little choice but to accept, all the while doing his best to look as if his decision was no easy matter.

"Good man, Viktor," said Pletenbergs, pumping his hand with manic intensity. "Now, let me ask you something..."

Over the next few days, Pletenbergs was to repeat those same words many times.

After saying goodbye to Vladimir, who invited Viktor with a light sprinkling of sarcasm to drop in next time he was in town, Viktor and his new patron – now resplendent in herringbone overcoat and matching deerstalker – emerged onto the windy street where Pletenbergs' chauffeur-driven Audi was waiting, its twin exhausts grumbling impatiently.

The car's lustrous black shine reminded Viktor again of the Russian Mercedes that was pursuing him. They drove past and in parallel with any number of cars that could have been his Russian hunters as they exited Riga, but a quick glance at the bonnet showed that all of their badges were in place. Even so, the sense of being pursued and disoriented put him back on his guard so that now he released only very general information about himself while continuing to enhance his credentials as an expert, guiding Pletenbergs through the various gas and oil pipeline networks of the region, their geopolitical significance, their untapped potential and their over- or undervalued status.

By the time they were an hour out of Riga, Viktor had outlined a scheme that seemed to meet the little man's approval. As they waited at the latest in a series of temporary traffic lights erected for invisible roadworks on the main Riga to V---- road, Viktor ran out of things to say, something that had never happened to him before in all his years on the circuit. In a conference you knew you had to speak for ten, twenty or thirty minutes – there was never the question of speaking for as long as it took to say everything there was to be said.

Pletenbergs listened carefully throughout, occasionally asking a pertinent question but for the most part simply smiling, nodding and playing sinisterly with his thick, smooth silk tie. With Viktor a spent force, Anrijs Pletenbergs, who clearly viewed any silence as a potential advertising opportunity, took over, turning the second hour of the journey to V---- into another sales pitch. It was like listening to a ham actor read a bad play based on the case notes of a delusional paranoiac.

According to Pletenbergs, the world was divided into two camps: loyal supporters and scheming opponents. For everyone had strong opinions about Pletenbergs, chief among them being Pletenbergs himself who liked to talk about himself in the third person, as if dictating his biography on a minute by minute basis.

By default, most of the world fell into the "scheming opponents" faction, but only because they had never met with and been charmed by his impish grin, tailored jackets and impeccable manners. Those that had had the pleasure of a personal audience almost inevitably transferred themselves to the "loyal supporters" fold immediately afterward.

Those who obstinately refused to become more amenable were part of a powerful cabal out to undermine and impoverish him. They would stop at nothing in their attempts to destroy a man of the people, seize his and his town's gas transit wealth and ruin the work he had accomplished in 20 years as mayor of V----.

Corruption, bribery, tax evasion, money laundering, fraud... the charges Pletenbergs was contesting in court sounded off-putting, he freely admitted. But they were supposed to – his foreign enemies had made sure of that.

"But Anrijs Pletenbergs has never been convicted of a crime in any court of law anywhere in the world! Mr Gates, Mr Buffet and Mr Branson may be powerful men, aided by the little helpers they have bought here in Latvia, but they cannot dig up so much as a parking ticket against Pletenbergs!" he explained.

Viktor wondered what the chances were of being killed jumping from a car moving at 80 kilometres an hour. Just about too high to be worth the gamble, but the more of Pletenbergs' bizarre delusions he heard, the more tempting a sudden appointment with asphalt became.

"No, dear gentlemen in your expensive apartments in New York, London and Monte Carlo, you cannot buy all of our precious Latvian assets and honest Latvian workers with your dirty gold! They underestimate the good-hearted people of V---- and the man who has the honour to be their mayor, Anrijs Pletenbergs!"

Right on cue they rolled through the security gates and up the gravel drive to the place Pletenbergs called home. Viktor had never been so pleased to see such an ugly house.

It was an extraordinary construction. Viktor's first impression was that this was the old woman's cottage built by the Disney corporation as a resort hotel of breath-taking gaudiness. It took the form of the largest log cabin he had ever seen, its size so out of whack with one's usual idea of a log cabin that Viktor wondered if he had wandered into the Brobdingnagian kingdom. With the Lilliputian Pletenbergs standing proudly on the vast porch between two turned wooden posts made from huge single tree trunks and opening his arms in a gesture of welcome, the effect of scale gone haywire was emphasised all the more.

Carved, lace-like wooden cornices wound around windows whose open shutters had flowers painted on them. Real flowers poked their blooms down from hanging baskets and up from deep wooden troughs placed at regular intervals along the porch, while flat lawns cut in the English style extended in all directions as far as the high adobe wall which encircled the entire compound and against which the dark brown shadows of Doberman hounds raced back and forth.

"This way, please," said Pletenbergs. "Welcome to my humble home. We will find you a place of your own soon enough, but for now I hope you won't object to being my guest?" The question was asked in such a way that it did not require a response and in any case, what alternative could Viktor have provided for himself other than to outrun the Dobermans, vault the wall and set up home in the nearest pile of leaves?

The interior decor made some effort to match the Sylvanian stylings of the exterior, but the presence of numerous large television screens, leather suites decorated with abominable patterns and hundreds of gilt-framed photographs – most of them featuring a smiling Pletenbergs and various VIPs – rather undermined the attempt at rustic charm. Viktor could identify just a few – Russian businessmen, some retired western politicians, surprised-looking pop stars and actors plus assorted members of clergy, all of them being treated to the full glare of the Pletenbergs grin. But most of the photographs showed the great man in the company of mere mortals – pensioners gazing adoringly at their benefactor, young sportsmen trying to play the game to win a sponsorship deal, members of various societies watching Pletenbergs snip a ribbon with scissors and, above all, lots and lots of images of wary schoolchildren presenting him with extravagant bunches of flowers.

There was just one painting – a flattering portrait above the marble fireplace that attempted to do for Pletenbergs what David did for Bonaparte but merely succeeded in making him look like he couldn't decide which of his many toilets was closest to his study and whether he would make it there in time.

"Very nice," Viktor said.

"Do you like it? My one piece of vanity, I admit. Now, my assistant will show you to your room. Katy – her name is Katrīna, but I prefer the English Katy, such a sweet name – Katy!"

Within seconds, a smartly-dressed woman with severely-tied hair and a leather-bound notebook in her hand had appeared by their side. She nodded to Viktor in a businesslike manner.

"Katy, would you be so kind as to show Mr... Viktor to his room? He will be staying with us until further notice. And to make him feel at home we will speak only the Queen's English in his presence. Look through our list of properties to see if we have somewhere suitable for him to live for the next month or two. Where would you prefer, Viktor, near the sea or in the forest? It will need to be somewhere quiet, so you can work undisturbed."

"Sea?" Viktor replied. The thought of waking up in a forest again appalled him almost as much as the phrase "the next month or two."

"Very well, somewhere near the sea. Strolls on the sand are so productive. I have made some of my most important deals with the waves lapping at my feet, did you know that, Viktor? And I think we will soon be making some more, what?"

The final "what" was utterly preposterous, but Viktor deployed his newly-acquired skill of keeping his mouth shut, nodded and followed Katy up a curving wooden staircase that looked like a slave galley standing on end, to a small, sparsely furnished guest room. From the window the lawns looked even more expansive than they had from the porch. The Dobermans, tired from their earlier exertions, lay lazily in the shadow of the high wall, drooling. Somewhere near the sea would be preferable to this superior sort of prison camp. But for now at least there was a bed.

The next morning when Viktor came downstairs, Anrijs Pletenbergs was already breakfasting on ham and eggs and motioned to Viktor to join him. He was dressed in an extraordinary orange and green tracksuit with a purple pig embroidered on its breast and back. This was the symbol of the town of V----, based on a rare local breed that reputedly played a vital role in producing the best sausages in Latvia.

"I thought you deserved a lie in after your exertions yesterday," beamed the little man. "And I intend to get my money's worth from you," he added with a wag of the finger that was only half-playful. "Would you like some of this?" he asked, pointing down at his bacon with a triangle of toast.

For some strange reason Viktor decided for the first time in years that he did not want bacon for breakfast. He shook his head. "Just coffee and bread. Marmalade if you have some."

Pletenbergs was delighted. "Marmalade, of course! What else would an English gentleman want for breakfast? Katy! Bring the marmalade to Viktor, my dear."

Ever-reliable, Katy appeared instantly form the kitchen carrying a tray with a rack of toast, a pat of butter and a jar of marmalade.

"Katy, what would I do without you? Now, what do we have on today's agenda?"

Katy informed him in flawless English that though today was a Sunday he had a busy itinerary commencing with firing the starting pistol of the V---- half marathon, presenting medals to the winners at the end and then forming part of a judging panel for a talent show for under 16s to be staged at the Pletenbergs Olympic Sports Hall and Conference Centre. He would present the winner's cheque, in all probability to a 15-year-old blonde singer he had watched performing several times already.

Between these two main duties was a brief visit to a retirement home to remind the pensioners that it was he who cared for their interests ahead of the next elections, and throughout the day he would field business calls and media interviews on subjects as varied as whether he hoped to be officially nominated for the post of prime minister at the next election and whether Latvia's slightly-salted gherkins tasted as good as they used to or whether the sale of a major gherkin bottler to a Dutch conglomerate had spoiled the flavour.

"What do I think about the gherkins?" Pletenbergs asked Katy, while Viktor reflected that the coffee wasn't as good as the old woman's in the forest.

"Usually we would say that the taste had definitely degenerated since the company was sold overseas. But bearing in mind that the same company is considering opening a bottling plant here in V----, perhaps we might say the taste had changed slightly but not necessarily for the worse. All new things take time to be accepted."

"Excellent! A busy day is not a wasted day. Someone said that, I forget whom," Pletenbergs said, standing up and performing a star jump. "And you, Viktor, can start typing up a report for me. Just say everything you told me in the car!" He jogged out of the room and through the front door into his waiting car.

Back in his room, Viktor did as he was asked, ordering his thoughts first on reams of paper supplied by Katy and then, after lunch was brought up to him after what seemed like minutes, he started typing them up on a laptop which was brought in for the purpose.

"Is there any chance of an internet connection?" he asked Katy as she flicked the on switch.

She looked at him almost with pity before replying: "I'm sorry, Viktor. We have a problem with internet access at the moment. I will let you know when it is fixed. Do you need anything else?"

"I suppose a telephone call is out of the question?"

"Yes. It is. The telephone line and internet access are suffering the same problem."

"Somehow I thought they might..." Viktor muttered under his breath.

Katy seemed about to say something but instead pursed her lips for an instant, looked at Viktor intently for a couple of seconds, then turned and left, saying "Dinner will be at seven."

All afternoon he restated the clear case for reverse flow capability through the Potemkin pipeline along with estimated costs, timescales and revenues at which he diligently worked in the absence of any other distractions. Every time he paused for thought and looked across the elegant lawn towards the perimeter wall, the sleek shadow of one of the dogs moving in front of it prompted him to return to his task.

In fact it proved to be a useful exercise disregarding the uses to which Pletenbergs would put his plan, as it allowed him to reappraise and improve his own somewhat dated lecture on the Pipeline Politics of Eastern Europe.

In the evening Pletenbergs returned and they talked once again as they turned laps of the great log construction. Now returned to his blazer and flannels, the dapper little man stooped every few metres to smell the flowers that seemed to be in permanent bloom. When they returned to the outsized porch, Pletenbergs congratulated Viktor on his progress and urged him to redouble his efforts "for the good of yourself, V---- and Anrijs Pletenbergs." The wall looked higher than it had the day before.

The Potemkin pipeline project was quickly turning into a practical proposition. The facts and figures Viktor had produced during the day were sucked up greedily by Pletenbergs who took a strange, almost sensual pleasure in each numeral.

A similar pattern continued at breakfast the next day, with Pletenbergs complimenting Viktor on his progress and urging him to even greater exertions, except this time Pletenbergs seemed slightly nervous, playing with his bacon and eggs distractedly.

"Are you quite alright, Mr Pletenbergs?" asked Viktor. "You seem somewhat out of sorts."

"Out of sorts. A very nice phrase, Viktor. Thank you for asking but don't worry yourself on my account. I always get a little tense before a day in court. It's the pressure, you see. It's like an actor about to give a great performance. Nerves are necessary, only in my case I will be battling not just the lines of the play but this disgusting attack by my enemies. They are powerful men who can bring a lot of pressure to bear, believe me. But Anrijs Pletenbergs is up to the task. I will go on to the end, whatever the cost, just as your great Winston Churchill said!"

He puffed up considerably during his little speech, as if in imitation of Churchill himself and proceeded to unburden himself to Viktor, all the while maintaining the persona of the indefatigable fighter for justice, putting the greater good before his own welfare.

"It would be easy for a lesser man to give in – but not Anrijs Pletenbergs!" was a phrase that recurred several times with characteristic immodesty.

At first, he had been upset by the court cases brought against him by embittered business partners, most of them foreign corporations who had piled into V---- smelling quick profits, he told Viktor.

The legal proceedings clearly struck Anrijs as a form of ingratitude, causing him genuine sleepless nights which sapped him of his usual energy and caused him to be unwell, as his personal physician at V---- general hospital had regularly to inform the judge. The stress and worry tended to manifest themselves in spasms of the lower back which caused lengthy delays in the hearings of his many complex and interlinked fraud cases. When some particularly vindictive judge – probably in the pay of his enemies – insisted upon his appearance despite medical advice, Pletenbergs would make his way to the courtroom in an ambulance requisitioned from V---- general hospital with his torso supported by the remarkable surgical corset Viktor had seen on television during his watershed evening in the Torņakalns bar.

In excruciating agony he would haul himself forwards on crutches, uttering sighs of pain, as he reached his correct position in the courtroom whereupon he would unbuckle himself with the help of his lawyer, smooth out his blazer, straighten his tie and sit down. At the end of the session he had no option but to repeat the entire performance in reverse, a very conspicuous victim of a cruel legal system.

Outside, on the steps to the courthouse, he would pause to regain his breath and receive bunches of flowers from the small army of old women who regarded him as the sort of man they would like to have as a nephew.

Finally, before disappearing back into the patiently waiting ambulance, he would spare a few minutes for the press, or more specifically for his favourite newspaper, *Reality*. With the rest of the media clearly controlled by the shadowy forces arraigned against him, he had bought *Reality* some years earlier to make sure the truth of the plots against him was recorded. He was proud that the paper's journalists were more intelligent and balanced than their counterparts on the Riga titles and he regarded the editor as a personal friend, which, Viktor deduced, was probably why he had got the job.

To Anrijs' surprise, as the hearings stretched from days to months to years, never really changing or advancing, he started to realise they were working to his advantage. They no longer held fear of the unknown and once he had established that his lawyers were easily a match for whatever prosecutors could not be persuaded to step aside, he felt confident turning any line of questioning into further evidence of the conspiracy against him. If he did not exactly look forward to his days in court, and if he still got nervous before another session, he at least felt that they were not a waste of time. The longer they dragged on, the more confident he became that the very notion of a final verdict was receding at a pace roughly equivalent to the speed of the legal proceedings themselves. He no longer had to win the case, he just had to endlessly perpetuate it.

"Forgive me, Viktor, for pouring my heart out to you, but I know I can I trust you," Anrijs said at the end of his exposition before adding: "I hope that one day soon, you will feel able to confide in me in the same way. Are you sure you want only bread and coffee? This bacon is really excellent – it comes from our famous purple pigs. In fact I can claim some share of the credit for rescuing the breed from extinction, did you know that? Which reminds me – I have one or two other small projects I would like you to take a look at – nothing as important as Potemkin of course, but I would think of it as a personal favour if you could spare a few minutes. I don't want that great mind of yours to go stale."

XX   THE THIRD LARGEST ROCK

The "small projects" turned out to be a curious mixture of measures designed to improve V----'s attractiveness to foreign visitors, in most cases amounting to little more than checking or improving the English language versions of brochures describing V----'s main tourist attractions. These included two farms breeding the "famous purple pigs" of which he had never heard until reading his in-flight magazine en route to Latvia, the site of a middling Russian imperial palace which had been completely razed to the ground three hundred years previously and spa treatment centres which for some reason were always rendered as 'SPA' treatment centres, in capitals.

Querying the information and images on the leaflets, which seemed to rely upon the same bland blond family smiling at each location, Viktor learned from Katy that his ignorance of famous purple pigs was clearly an aberration – after all, a purple pig walking trail had for some years been established through the streets of V---- at Pletenbergs' own suggestion.

It extended over four kilometres and featured more than a dozen purple pigs of various sizes, interpreted by local and international sculptors. The largest of these pigs was some five metres tall and resplendent in a fibreglass straw boater and monocle for enigmatic reasons. It was where any tourists who happened to be marooned in V---- would inevitably pose for that once-in-a-lifetime photo and was apparently a particular favourite with the Japanese.

"So you see, Viktor, you have no excuse not to have heard about the purple pigs," Katy said, with what Viktor was starting to suspect may have been a hint of sarcasm – a quality he had always had trouble identifying.

Even so Viktor was able to suggest some revolutionary enhancements to the Purple Pig experience, the most important of which was the establishment of a small souvenir charcuterie booth at the trail's start/finish point to remedy the unfortunate fact that the world famous Purple Pig ham, bacon and sausages were not actually available anywhere other than the two remote farms on which the renowned porkers lived their legendary lives.

On the case of the Tsarina's palace, Viktor's work was more straightforward. He suggested that the three pages of information about the acetate storage facility which now covered three quarters of the site could usefully be dispensed with and that perhaps an information board with any available engravings, drawings or actual facts about the disappeared palace – such as the dates and manner of its construction and demolition – might at least prevent confused tourists wandering around an industrial estate seeking a stately home that did not in fact exist.

This was viewed as an extremely radical suggestion by the local tourist information authorities who treated it with initial suspicion, but once the owner of the acetate storage facility – one Anrijs Pletenbergs – had signalled he thought the plan to be "capital", it was executed within 24 hours and the *Reality* news daily even ran a front page story about the opening of the new information board by Mayor Pletenbergs. The little man came in waving a copy happily that evening.

But the strangest of Viktor's adventures chez Pletenbergs centred on a fairly large chunk of granite in the middle of a field just outside V----.

It started with a passing comment by Viktor who was in, by his standards, a combative mood. The stability of the last few days, plus the knowledge that what he was producing was actually quite a fresh idea, had restored some of his confidence. He was also increasingly aware of how important his work was to Pletenbergs and that it was a commodity that should be traded for an expensive price – his freedom.

As ever, Pletenbergs was at breakfast before Viktor, perusing some papers as he munched energetically. He waved Viktor into place opposite him without taking his eyes from the pile of papers, and asked absent-mindedly through a forkful of albumen what he thought of the pleasant town of V----.

Viktor replied with a degree of irony that from the limited opportunity he had had so far to survey the town – which amounted to no more than a few chimneys and half-roofs over the perimeter wall – it did indeed seem pleasant, even if it lacked what might be called natural wonders.

Anrijs Pletenbergs stopped chewing his scrambled eggs as Viktor settled to his new passion, black bread dripping with honey.

"But we have the fourth largest rock in Latvia!" protested Anrijs.

"I beg your pardon?"

"The fourth largest rock in Latvia! It's right here in V----!"

"The FOURTH largest? With the best will in the world if it's not in the top three, it's not going to win any medals," Viktor chuckled, pleased with his little jest.

Pletenbergs didn't see the joke. On the contrary, he turned pensive, as if someone had told him his shares had just tanked or one of his ships had sunk with forged insurance paperwork. He chewed scrambled egg erratically, his masticating rhythm all to pot. Viktor feared an eruption.

"You are right! Why has no-one told me about this before? Who cares about the fourth-largest rock? It needs to be in the top three to be of interest to tourists, of course it does! Viktor, take care of it, will you? I have to travel, I won't be back for a day or two. I will be taking your wonderful work with me" – he tapped the pile of papers with his fork – "and I hope to bring exciting news back!"

All he left behind was a crumpled napkin, a half-eaten plate of eggs and a faint smell of his nameless cologne.

That is how Viktor was given the job of "taking care" of the fourth largest rock in Latvia.

As soon as breakfast was over, the omnipresent Katy knocked at his door and told him he was leaving.

"You mean...?"

"The rock," Katy said. "Mr Pletenbergs told me to take you to it. And before you ask, yes, I came into your room when you were in the bathroom, took a copy of your work and printed it out – most of it, anyway – for Mr Pletenbergs. I am sorry to have stooped to such subterfuge. I will wait for you downstairs."

Within half an hour, Viktor was at the very rock. It was good to get out of the compound, but for a supposed tourist attraction, the location was not the most picturesque, reinforcing his original point about V---- being under-supplied in the National Geographic department.

The town of V---- itself was a greyish smudge on the horizon and while the location of the rock was not within sight of the sea, the huge sky to the west had all the marks of the maritime mood. Far away on the horizon a grey gauze of rain fell on fishermen returning to port while in other places patches of virgin blue squeezed past boiling clouds to keep hope of a bright day alive but constantly thwarted.

The air carried the tang of salt, but it was whipped across his nose at such speed by a gusting wind that it tickled his nostril hair. In his English days, Viktor would have described the conditions as "bracing" but for now they were simply a welcome change from the stuffiness of Pletenbergs' compound in which even the air itself acted as if it had been waved in by the security guard at the gate in strictly controlled amounts so as not to offer a threat to the master's offbeat idea of domestic bliss.

Facing Viktor and Katy in the middle of a field of coarse marram grass with a half-sandy, half-muddy track leading to it from one direction only was the fourth largest rock in Latvia. It was not difficult to believe it was the fourth largest rock in Latvia, even for someone who had never previously considered the country's geological gems. It was indeed a large rock, looking uncannily like a baked potato the size of a small family car. It would not rate as a noteworthy rock in Spain or Italy but perhaps in Luxembourg or San Marino it might have merited a mention as the site of some ancient duel or lovers' tryst.

"This is the rock," Katy said.

"Really?" Viktor said as he circled the unfamous lump. "I had guessed as much." Immediately he felt that his sarcasm had been a little unfair, but when he looked at Katy to offer an apology, he saw that she was attempting to stifle a smile. That in turn made him smile, and they laughed together.

"I'm sorry," Katy began. "It was a silly thing to say."

"Yes," agreed Viktor, "but what else was there to say, really? And I can't fault your accuracy. This is indeed The Rock." They both laughed again, as Viktor continued to circle the rock, looking as if he expected to find instructions pinned on one of its faces.

"Katy, what am I supposed to do? I'm perfectly willing to believe that this is the fourth largest rock in Latvia, but what exactly does that have to do with me?"

"From your conversation with Mr Pletenbergs this morning, I understood he wanted it to be promoted?"

"The rock?"

"Yes. It is officially a tourist attraction, but no-one comes to see it. You've been very good at promoting some of the other hidden attractions of V----, so Mr Pletenbergs thought you might..."

"Might what?"

"I don't know. Have an idea?"

"It was just a joke. To be brutally honest, it's not much to look at, is it?"

"No."

"If it had a hole in it or looked like a human head, or any body part for that matter..." they both laughed again, "then it would at least have some novelty value, some story we could tell."

Katy looked hopeful. "Oh, lots of stones in Latvia have stories. Usually about how Peter the Great or Gustavus Adolphus - or both - buried silver teaspoons under them after having a picnic. Or stories about them as sites of pagan sacrifice. There is even a special word for them - *lielakmeņi*."

"What does it mean?"

"Literally, it means big stones. It loses something in the translation, trust me."

Viktor raised his eyebrows. "Does this rock have any stories like that attached to it?"

"No."

"So not only is it the fourth largest rock, and a rock of singularly unassuming appearance, it is also devoid of cultural, historical and folkloric significance."

"It seems so. But - pardon me, but I know how Mr Pletenbergs' mind works - I think it was not the rock's qualities that were affecting Mr Pletenbergs this morning so much as the fact that it is - as you pointed out - not in the top three."

"Not on the podium at the rock Olympics?"

"You could put it like that. When I said the rock needed to be promoted, I meant it not just in a marketing sense..."

"But, Katy, this is insane." She gave him the tiniest nod of the head and roll of the eyes, then, thinking better of it, straightened her jacket and resumed a more formal tone.

"You are a clever man, Viktor. You will think of something."

"I could be Albert Einstein's older and wiser brother but I would not be able to make rocks grow larger overnight! If I could I would probably be trading diamonds in Antwerp. Logically, the only alternative would be for one of the top three rocks to disappear or shrink!"

"Aha!" Katy said, her informal, friendly manner restored.

"Aha what? Do you think I can put a rock in my pocket that by definition is even bigger than this great big ugly lump? No offence intended, rock." He extended his arm and patted the fourth largest rock in Latvia. Katy watched expectantly.

"I can't believe I'm saying this, but never mind. Katy, will you help me place this rock, as it were, on a pedestal? Will you help me find this fine hunk of igneous matter its rightful place in the world?"

"Of course, Viktor!"

"Then, Katy, I will need every scrap of information you can glean about the THIRD largest rock in Latvia. Dimensions, rock type, age, estimated mass, any other geological information, associated myths and legends, appearances in history or art, information about its site, ease of access, favourite colour, shoe size, allergies *et cetera, ad infinitum, ad nauseum*. I want to know everything about the rotten third largest rock in Latvia in order to find the chink, so to speak, in its armour. Then our friend here will ascend to glory!"

"Yes, Viktor! I will get straight on it. Let's rock!"

It was a very weak joke, one that Viktor would have harrumphed at a few days ago. But now he just groaned, and Katy did likewise, both of them recognising that it meant they were now joint collaborators rather than Pletenbergs' right arm and Pletenbergs' prisoner respectively.

By the time Viktor sat down alone at the dinner table that evening, Katy had assembled the requested dossier on the third largest rock, but she waited until Viktor's meal was on the table before placing it carefully next to him. As she walked out of the room, Viktor called after her.

"Don't go. Why don't you come and eat with me? It is no fun eating alone."

"Mr Pletenbergs insists that the dining room is only for his use and yours."

"Well, Mr Pletenbergs isn't here, so I suppose that gives me – or you, perhaps – the right to select whichever dinner guests I wish. So please join me. It would be my honour."

Katy looked from side to side as if Pletenbergs might walk in at any moment. Catching herself in the act she threw back her head, shook it from side to side a few times and stared at Viktor again, her formality gone.

"Viktor, you're right. I will be delighted to join you for dinner."

As they ate, Katy summarised the contents of the dossier, occasionally breaking off to reaffirm the absurdity of their task, but the necessity of carrying it out to the best of their abilities. It turned out that the third largest rock was located on a beach in the Gulf of Riga and formed part of what was known in an attached and eccentrically-translated tourism brochure as the "Vidzeme rocky sea coast". It was partially submerged, with the Baltic Sea's small tidal range slowly undercutting it so that it looked a bit like an eggcup thrown by a novice potter.

The stone had served for centuries as a marker for fishermen working the coastal waters and the local youths reputedly viewed an ascent of its slippery sides as a minor rite of passage, but on the whole it was not a renowned rock. Despite its inclusion in the brochure it could barely be classed as a tourist attraction as thanks to the gently-shelving coastline it was too far out to sea to be easily visited. Nevertheless, the brochure did its best to talk it up as both an "ancient standing stone" (which seemed guaranteed to deliver druidic disappointment) and an "anomal rocky outcrop."

This last phrase was seized upon by Viktor, and not only for its grammatical clumsiness.

"But what is it, a stone or an outcrop?"

"I don't understand," Katy responded.

"If it is a single stone – standing or otherwise – then it deserves its top three status. But if it is an outcrop, why, then it is not even a rock at all. It would be part of the underlying bedrock. That I think would disqualify it from third place in the geological equivalent of a dope test..."

"I will call the Latvian geological survey at once, Viktor!"

While Viktor commenced demolition of a fruit salad with a satisfied air, Katy made her call from Pletenbergs' office. When she returned a few minutes later, her smile confirmed Viktor's theory before she even spoke a word.

"They said they will need to check to be one hundred per cent sure but they were pretty certain that that rock is no rock at all. You were right – it is an upcrop! I told them about Mr Pletenbergs' interest in the matter. They promised to confirm its status in a few weeks when it will be re-classified."

Viktor laughed. "An outcrop." The telephone rang. "That's probably the fourth largest rock ringing to thank us."

In a way it was – after taking the call, Katy confirmed it had been Pletenbergs from location unknown. She passed on Pletenbergs' effusive congratulations but looked distracted. Viktor asked what the trouble was.

"He was really calling to make sure that his guest was being taken care of – and wasn't causing me any problems by trying to leave."

"Were you supposed to tell me that?" Viktor asked.

"No. But I can see how he is taking advantage of you. I don't like it. Forgive me for saying so but you are so naive – you don't realise that Anrijs Pletenbergs is a dangerous man. Perhaps you should be thinking of leaving –

are you? If I was in your place... I don't want you to be hurt."

"Then why do you work for him? Why don't you leave?"

"And go where? Latvia is very small. It is a very difficult place to hide, particularly from a man with as many connections as Anrijs Pletenbergs. I have my plans, but now is not the time to discuss them."

An awkward silence followed with Katy staring down at the table. Viktor tried chewing his fruit salad, but the noise of juice oozing around his jaws seemed ridiculous. Eventually it was Katy who spoke again.

"Mr Pletenbergs said something else, too. Something... what was the word you used earlier? Insane?"

"What did he say?"

"He said that if the fourth largest rock can become the third largest rock so quickly, then probably it could also become the second largest rock."

To her surprise, Viktor burst out laughing. "Yes, insane was the word! I half expected as much. Well, you know what we must do tomorrow. Time to research the second largest rock in Latvia. This fruit salad really is marvellous. What are these berries?"

"Cranberries."

"Really? But they are enormous. I'm not sure I've ever had real cranberries before," Viktor laughed. Whether his levity was caused by the taste of proper cranberries, the absurdity of his rock-related tasks or perhaps even the novelty of being alone at dinner with an attractive companion, he wasn't sure. But he did know that he felt less scared and more confident than he should have, given all the facts at his disposal.

XXI   THE SECOND LARGEST ROCK

The second largest rock in Latvia proved to be a tougher one to crack in every respect than the third. Nearly twice the size of their own, adopted V---- rock, it had the added complications of being unequivocally a single lump of red-grey granite deposited as the glaciers retreated. Furthermore, it was thought to be a pagan cult site of some importance owing to a deep cleft in the centre which gave it the appearance of – according to your religion – a sacred heart, or a pair of fertility-enhancing breasts. The regular appearance of candles and small bunches of wild flowers around its base suggested that it was still venerated to some degree by latter-day pagans.

More positively, the bactrian stone was located deep in the forests of Latgale, on the opposite side of the country from V----. It seemed that its location was known only to the candle carriers plus a few archaeologists, anthropologists and folklorists. Despite the prestige of being Latvia's silver medal rock, it did not feature in any of the promotional materials Katy was able to produce by lunchtime the next day.

Viktor studied the photographs and the accumulated data regarding its tonnage, girth and composition carefully. He ruminated upon a Caesar salad, looked at the photographs again, wiped his lips with a napkin and said in a rather casual way: "Eureka, Katy, Eureka."

"What did you say, Viktor? More Caesar?"

"No, I have it!"

"But you've nearly finished."

"Not the salad – damn the salad – though compliments to the chef, it was very tasty. I have the answer to our second stone conundrum. How difficult would it be to gain access to a fairly large quantity of dry ice?"

"It could be done. I'm sure the acetate factory or one of the V---- port facilities must use it."

"Excellent. And we'll need some heavy duty tarpaulin, or better yet large sheets of heavy duty rubber."

"Again, not a problem."

"Then let me explain my plan. It will sound a little extreme, but I think it might not be as bad as it seems. Probably fulfills some ancient prophecy or some such thing…"

As it turned out, it took nearly a week for news of the stone's fate to reach the Latgale press. A passing pagan showed up only to discover that the stone had split in two. The central fissure had extended to the very base, "rending it in twain" as the bearded pagan described it with a medieval linguistic flourish in Latgalian dialect. Probably it had been struck by lightning during a recent electrical storm, an ominous omen of division for modern Latvia. An alternative theory by a local geologist posited that rainwater had somehow gathered in the central fissure, froze, expanded and split the rock as a result, which was mechanically possible but puzzling, as it had not dropped below freezing in Latgale for several months. A climatologist rode to the rescue with an explanation of the ability of heavily-forested areas to generate their own microclimates, often considerably at variance with the prevailing weather conditions.

Long before that news was printed, Viktor and Katy had inevitably been charged with a final piece of geological assassination by Pletenbergs, who was getting more erratic by the minute. He seemed to be on an unusual schedule, coming and going for a few hours before disappearing for a day or more. When he was present he spent less time with Viktor than previously, and when he did so, it was generally to expound one of his crackpot conspiracy theories about secret plans to flood Latvia with African immigrants or that American burger chains were rendering Latvian men infertile by means of hormones injected into the pigs that made up their products.

Neither theory was shaken by Viktor's attempts at reason, pointing out that most Africans probably had never heard of Latvia, let alone craved residence and that "hamburgers" were actually made from beef, not pork. Now, when they walked around the grounds of his residence he occasionally plucked up a flower, examined it and let it drop a few paces further on.

Following the same path with Katy some hours later, she told Viktor the court cases were not going well, a fact which was borne out by the sudden re-appearance of Anrijs' body corset in the hallway along with other accessories including a neck brace, crutches and a fake colostomy bag that his lawyer had persuaded him could be pressed into service in an emergency to bring proceedings to a halt.

"He is worried, I have never seen him like this before," Katy whispered as they walked along the perimeter wall like prisoners of war planning a tunnel. "A court in the US has traced some of his offshore assets and ordered a freeze on them. It's not major in itself, but he is worried more important assets will soon be treated the same way. It is fuelling his fantasy about rich Americans trying to bring him down."

"This idea of disposing of the biggest rock is very ill-advised," Viktor said as they passed a clump of begonias. "I've read your dossier – we couldn't possibly get rid of anything so well known. It's on a banknote, for God's sake!"

"Not only that. The Daina Stone is classed as a cultural monument of the first rank. It is part of our history. I may be Anrijs Pletenbergs' personal assistant, but I am also a proud Latvian. It's like asking me to burn down Riga castle or demolish the Freedom Monument!"

"Well, if he ever becomes Prime Minister – which I understand is a possibility - that might be worth considering," Viktor replied. "But regarding this stone – what can we do? I went along with the first two because it seemed a fairly harmless exercise, something of an intellectual challenge to relieve the boredom of these endless Potemkin revisions he keeps asking me for. And I enjoy working with you."

Katy didn't seem to have heard the last phrase. "We need to play for time," she said. "Let's tell him we will take care of it, but that it will take a while. That we have a plan, but it is very complex and we need to wait for the right moment. He trusts you. You've never let him down, and until you do he assumes you are with him one hundred percent."

"What about you? Have you ever let him down?"

"Not in any way that he has ever been aware of. But I'm starting to think the time might be approaching when I will have to. If you will help me?" She turned to face him, looking up into his eyes with a disarmingly open stare.

"Of course... I mean..."

"We can't talk now, Viktor. He's coming." Indeed he was, his little legs scurrying across the lawn towards them with his old beaming grin restored.

"My friends! No not just friends – my two pillars, Katy and Viktor! May Anrijs Pletenbergs join you? Ah the begonias are wonderful this year – such scent! Intoxicating!" If he had been depressed earlier he now seemed to have swung into full-strength mania.

"You look well," Viktor said.

"I do, I do!" the smiling tycoon replied, slapping the thigh of his immaculately pressed trousers for good measure. If he had picked up a fishing rod and gone to sit on a toadstool, he could not have looked more like a jolly little gnome.

"A good day in court?" Katy asked, fully her efficient self once again.

"Yes, partly that," Pletenbergs said. "I'm more confident that the foreign dogs – excuse me, Viktor – will not get their hands on Anrijs Pletenbergs' hard-won funds. They won't stop me continuing to build V---- into the envy of other nations and exposing their hypocrisy and lies! The new judge seems a lot more reasonable than the last one and it was partly thanks to you, Katy, that we were able to find the disgraceful information to get that idiot thrown off my case." He placed his arm around Katy. Viktor didn't like the gesture and Katy seemed ill at ease, too, her body going stiff.

"Yes, Viktor was just saying how nice the begonias are, too," she said to break an awkward silence. It served its purpose and Pletenbergs turned his attention toward Viktor.

"My second pillar, my rock, Viktor!" he said, taking his other arm and placing it on Viktor's back – right where someone would stab you, Viktor thought.

"You are the other reason I am in this merry mood. I presented your Potemkin proposals today to some extremely important people and I am delighted to say they were impressed. Very impressed. We are going to the next stage!" he said, without elaborating on what that stage might be.

"Tonight, we celebrate!" Pletenbergs announced, hanging between the two of them like a superannuated puppet. "My twin pillars of support, Viktor and Katy. Anrijs Pletenbergs is a lucky man indeed to have two such friends!"

Katy looked at Viktor across the top of Pletenbergs' thinning crown and nodded once.

XXII SEA SALT

At seven o'clock that evening, Viktor came downstairs to find Pletenbergs and Katy dressed for dinner and waiting for him. Pletenbergs wore a navy blazer and grey flannels as if he had just stepped away from Cowes regatta, while Katy looked delicious in a geometric black dress and white shawl, her eyes even more attractive than usual thanks to some subtle mascara and her dark hair freed of its restricting band.

Viktor had been provided with a white shirt, a purple tie bearing the V---- crest and a surprisingly well-fitting navy blue suit for the occasion.

"You look a new man, Viktor!" Pletenbergs said. "I must admit it was not run up by my London tailor, but here in V---- the tailoring options are limited, especially for a man of your size. But I think Katy estimated well, you look very presentable indeed! I will need to be careful or people will think I am your assistant!" he laughed, unaware of the veiled insult his words carried. "By the way, have you ever been to Jermyn Street?"

"I am sure I have walked along it. Just behind Piccadilly, isn't it?"

"Exactly. That's where I get all my clothes run up. My tailor always says 'Rich men flock to Saville Row, but gentlemen prefer Jermyn Street'. I think that's very good."

"Very good."

Pletenbergs took up a position at Viktor's side and attempted to place his short arm around Viktor's shoulder, exposing a crisp white cuff fastened with a golden link. The disparity between Viktor's bearish frame and his own diminutive stature made the gesture awkward, so he changed his mind and gave Viktor what was evidently intended as a hearty slap on the back instead. It reminded Viktor of similarly significant slaps he'd already received from the thug in the Torņakalns bar, from John Smith, from Deputy Prime Minister Kopeikin and even of the attentions of the monstrous Magda. That in turn reminded Viktor of his currently penniless status (save for the money he had received from Vladimir in return for his thespian exertions), a matter he resolved to raise with Pletenbergs at the next available opportunity, which might then enable him to slip away from V----.

"Viktor, you have been helping me for a week now, and I want you to know that your work is appreciated," Pletenbergs said. "Anrijs Pletenbergs does not forget those who help him – nor those who hinder him! I know we are still strangers to each other in many ways, but I know that as an English gentleman you feel the same way I do – that trust is the most important quality a man can give or receive. You have trusted me by coming here to V---- and I have trusted that you know what you are talking about. My trust was well placed. The reaction to your Potemkin proposals has been very positive and I hope to move soon to implement them. For reasons that I'm sure you understand must remain confidential, I have kept your name – which incidentally I still do not know – out of discussions, but I want you to know that doesn't mean I regard you as an anonymous figure. Anrijs Pletenbergs is proud to know you and hopes the feeling is mutual. Which is why tonight we celebrate in style at my restaurant, "Sea Salt" where we may even encounter some surprises!"

And so it proved. The three of them were driven twenty minutes to a pleasant art nouveau restaurant with its own section of beach for a sunset seafood meal that would certainly have merited a five star rating on the circuit. Viktor and Anrijs had pride of place. The only other diners were members of Pletenbergs' staff: Katy and his chauffeur on an adjoining table, then the gardener, a security man, and a few other factoti Viktor had not seen before, all of whom smiled and nodded without saying a word and kept their own conversations to a whisper on the other tables. Evidently Pletenbergs had booked the whole place for his private use as no-one came in and no-one left without his say-so.

Even one of the Dobermans was in attendance. It passed up the offered crab, lobster and langoustine from the a la carte menu, instead ordering something cooked blood rare from the grill menu to slobber over while chained to the front door.

By the time dessert arrived and the kitchen staff had been dismissed, Pletenbergs had become more effusively friendly than ever. Unfortunately, the concerted effort to be especially pleasant and informal only succeeded in making him seem even more scheming and insincere than usual, even to someone with Viktor's narrow – but quickly broadening – sense of emotional intelligence.

"It's clear that we work well together. I think – I hope – that by now you realise that Anrijs Pletenbergs is a man of honour and that he will take care of you just as you take care of him. Now you find yourself in a position many people would envy. You have great influence – admittedly anonymously, though I get the impression you are not unhappy with that. You have no need to worry about providing yourself with a roof, food or even clothes. Incidentally, I want to say again Katy has done a remarkably good job with that suit, you cut quite an impressive figure."

Anrijs removed his wire-rimmed glasses and started playing with them on the white tablecloth while he spoke.

"But you are not a man who has sprung from nowhere, Viktor, even if your arrival was in the most unexpected of circumstances. With that in mind, I think the time has come for us to deepen the bond that ties us."

The conversation was not heading in a positive direction. Since the third glass of Rioja, Viktor had entertained tentative hopes that he was about to be freed from his gilded cage. Talk of "deepening the bond" was worrying.

"If our relationship is to blossom, I do need to know more about you," Anrijs continued. "Not much, you understand, but enough so that I can be sure there are no unpleasant surprises that could be turned to their advantage by my powerful enemies. And to prove to you that Anrijs Pletenbergs is sincere and will guard this information in strictest confidence, I am going to make my own gesture of trust."

He leaned over to Katy, who was as ever just out of sight but just within earshot. He whispered a few words, she nodded and almost silently she swept the other diners out of the room until Viktor and Anrijs Pletenbergs were completely alone, apart from the hound at the door.

The princeling settled back in his seat, as if about to embark on a fresh chapter, all the time rotating his spectacles through the fingers of both hands.

"Dear Viktor, you have probably been wondering about the circumstances under which we met. It really was most extraordinary, was it not? I will come to your role later, but here is my own side." He was choosing his words carefully, speaking more slowly than usual.

"You once asked what I was doing at the house of a man engaged in the production of... erotic entertainment. The fact is, Viktor, that Vladimir is an old friend of mine. He is an honest man and a true professional. He has even produced some of my campaign films over the years, which everyone agreed played an important role in my success at the polls. Much better production values than my rivals – but that is neither here nor there, as the English say. Vladimir is also an artist and like most artists he needs funds to pursue his dreams. I provide those funds. But I never provide hand-outs or charity, Viktor. I prefer to make investments, mutually beneficial investments."

He cleared his throat and stared at the basket of bread rolls on the table between them, his spectacles slithering between his fingers all the time.

"I suggested to Vladimir that he should produce some high-quality erotic entertainment to help fund his artistic projects. He resisted at first, but the commercial scope of Latvian cinema is so tiny that I was able to persuade him that by entering the erotica market he might develop a sideline that would prove lucrative enough to subsidise his more... philosophical works."

Pletenbergs put his glasses down and began buttering a bread roll, a gesture that for some reason struck Viktor as mildly obscene.

"I provide financing for Vladimir's commercial film making efforts – via companies I control – in order to help him produce work of the highest quality. And I am happy to say that my commercial instincts proved as accurate as ever. The returns of 'Russian Sluts in Riga' Volumes one to four have been sufficient to put Vladimir's film about Old Believers in Latgale into pre-production, and his brand new series of erotic features inspired by works of English literature – in which you had a role – should allow him to start shooting next spring. As well as Wodehouse he will be producing hardcore entertainments based on Graham Greene, Sir Arthur Conan Doyle and Charles Dickens, then next year we will be adapting some of the great works of Russian literature: Gogol, Chekhov, Pushkin. The possibilities are enormous."

"I have never told anyone else about this, Viktor, and it will never be made known to anyone other than yourself," Pletenbergs concluded, popping a fully-buttered roll into his mouth and chewing in a self-satisfied manner.

It seemed clear to Viktor that this was at best a half truth and that somewhere in his huge log cabin, Pletenbergs probably had an impressive cache of "erotic entertainment" salted away for his private pleasure.

"So now it is my turn to ask you – how did you come to be starring in 'Up My Ass Please, Javes' and where did you acquire your knowledge of gas pipelines?" Pletenbergs asked.

A week earlier, Viktor might have had trouble dealing with such a question. But in the intervening period he had been placed in such extraordinary situations that he was starting to develop a sort of cunning that was proving much more useful than mere intelligence. The Rioja probably helped, too.

Whatever the reason, he realised that he needed to do what Pletenbergs himself had done – swallow as much of the truth as was necessary but with a few of the more awkward corners smoothed down for ease of passage, particularly as he was certain that if the Potemkin pipeline was involved, the unnamed parties for which Pletenbergs was seeking reassurance must necessarily be Russians with close links to the Kremlin.

Finding insincerity an attractive strategy for perhaps the first time in his life, Viktor began his own edited biography, leaning heavily on Pletenbergs' obvious Anglophile streak.

"Mister Pletenbergs – may I call you Henry?"

The dapper little man nodded his assent, delighted to be addressed in the English style.

"I have indeed come to respect you during out brief acquaintance, and I wish to thank you for the sincere trust you have just shown me here, at this table, tonight." Again Pletenbergs nodded in a manner that would have befitted Her Majesty. To his surprise, Viktor realised that lying through his teeth was actually rather enjoyable.

"My name is Victor King and I am a leading academic, dividing my time between Princeton and the Berger Institute, a think-tank promoting international trade ties in Eastern Europe. When we met at Vladimir's flat you asked if we had met before. In fact you were right. We did meet, albeit briefly, at breakfast on the first day of the Riga conference when you told me about the opportunities available in your lovely town of V----."

Anrijs laughed. "I knew it! Ah, this explains why you know so much about gas pipelines! Carry on, carry on, Viktor!"

And so Viktor continued spinning his rudimentary but curiously believable web. King's College Cambridge had been his alma mater and the derivation of the Berger Institute's name was a mere mouthful away from the sausage-inspired Benbo Foundation. He sketched in real enough details of life on a fictional circuit that ran parallel to the one of his experience, dropped a few of the better known names in his contacts book and talked up the tremendous influence exerted by the Berger Institute and other similar bodies such as the Tybone Trust and Benbo Foundation.

Pletenbergs took it all in with his customary grin, and Viktor moved on to the circumstances by which he came to land his supporting role in the erotic entertainment. He conjured up an inspired tale of being drugged in a Riga bar and having his wallet and passport stolen – a notorious entrapment scam well known both inside and outside the country – being shamefully turned away from the British embassy because the ambassador was on holiday and finally accepting help offered by a compatriot with the name Tom Jones.

Pletenbergs waved away further explanation. "Details, Viktor, details which do not concern me. You have told me the important facts which answer my original questions and for that you have my thanks. But I am intrigued by this Berger Institute you work with and the others you mentioned. Are they really so influential?"

"Certainly! For example, the Benbo Foundation advises the British Foreign Office and the US State Department. I myself regularly give comment as one of the most respected academics in my field to the Washington Post, Financial Times, El Pais..." It suddenly occurred to him how close he had come to saying he actually worked for Benbo, not Berger and how he was now releasing information that could easily be double-checked.

There was a long pause during which Pletenbergs was deep in thought. To Viktor's relief, he did not seem to have noticed his slip, but what he said next made him think that perhaps it would have been better if he had and the whole game could be over and done with.

"One of the most respected in your field, Viktor? One of? Is that really good enough? I have had a wonderful thought – YOU have given me a wonderful idea, Viktor! How would you like to head the Pletenbergs Foundation, dedicated to the promotion of business and democracy plus of course the exposure of the dirty conspiracies of Mister Buffet, Mister Gates, Mister Trump, Mister Branson and the rest of them? With a generous budget, all the staff and support you could wish for, a purpose-built headquarters here in V---- and best of all, the chance to help Anrijs Pletenbergs change the world!"

For an instant Viktor assumed Pletenbergs was joking but the light of megalomaniacal insanity burned bright in his eyes as he stared across the table with a crumb in the corner of his mouth. It was the same insanely misplaced inspiration he had seen burning in the eyes of Ivars Dzintars and it was not something that could ever be persuaded to change by reason. And Viktor realised, as a psychological aside, that despite his smiles, his air of good humour and his propensity for laughing at the most trifling things, Anrijs Pletenbergs was constitutionally incapable of ever making a genuine joke.

"You would have complete freedom, naturally," Pletenbergs enthused. "I would only need to give final approval like I do with *Reality* and they have never, ever complained about dropping inappropriate stories. That's how high their standards are. Imagine it, Viktor, a chance to influence the tides of history and commerce, enhancing your own reputation while simultaneously performing the valuable mission of telling the truth about Anrijs Pletenbergs to the whole world!"

Pletenbergs wore a rapt expression. Viktor could not break the spell by telling him that he was clearly deluded and asking why anyone outside V---- would have the slightest interest in his tinpot fiefdom and crackpot conspiracy theories.

So Viktor did what he was becoming quite good at: he lied to save his own skin.

"Henry, I really don't know what to say..."

"Say yes!"

"It is indeed a tremendously generous idea... an inspirational thought..."

"Say yes!"

"It is very tempting... but I have commitments to the Institute, to my students. I can't just walk away from them and..."

"Details, details, details! Men like us should never bother with details – that is for the smaller men to deal with. All of that can be taken care of. Say yes, Viktor!" And again, quieter but with more menace, "Say yes."

"Well... I suppose... how can I refuse?"

"Capital!" he said, preposterously, then called out towards the door, "Katy, bring champagne, the second best bottle on the wine list! We must toast the foundation of the... what should we call it, Viktor? The Anrijs Pletenbergs Foundation? That sounds odd. Shall we call it the Henry Pletenberg Institute?"

"Perhaps simply the Pletenberg Institute?"

"Your first executive decision, Viktor, I approve! That's why I keep you around – you are a clever man who has the best interests of Anrijs Pletenbergs at heart!"

And so it was agreed that the already crowded world of geopolitical pseudo-analysis would get a little more crowded with the formation of the Pletenberg Institute, to be headed by the renowned non-existent academic

Viktor King, based in the unknown Latvian gas transit town of V----.

Anrijs instructed that a special founding conference should be organised by Viktor within two months to bring a galaxy of influential politicians, businessmen and thinkers together for what would inevitably be referred to as "Davos on the Baltic" by lazy journalists. More immediately, a high-profile launch event would need to be staged within days at V----'s own small but ripe-for-expansion Pletenbergs Olympic Sports Hall and Conference Centre to introduce the Institute, make it known that men of genius inhabited V---- and allow Pletenbergs himself to speak to the international media.

While Pletenbergs continued expounding on the future importance of the PI, Viktor's mind raced as bubbles leaped from the champagne glass onto his nose hair. He had no doubt that Katy would be told to check up on his fictitious biography. If he was lucky she would discover nothing at all, which might cause her to keep on trying for a few days until she stumbled upon Viktor Draaks and the Benbo Foundation. If he was unlucky, she would discover the truth straight away, along with the unfortunate episode with the three Baltic presidents and one prime minister.

Pletenbergs' dreams of power and influence via his newly-minted Institute would be revealed to be absurd fantasy and Viktor could only shudder at the thought of how such an egomaniac would react when confronted with his own vanity and idiocy, particularly given his current mood swings. No-one was aware of Viktor's presence chez Pletenbergs and consequently no-one would notice his sudden disappearance.

Meanwhile, another delicate subject had to be broached.

"Henry, about the rock..."

"Which rock?"

"The largest rock in Latvia..."

"Oh, that rock."

"Yes, that rock. Are you sure you want it – taken care of?"

"What do you mean? You've done the other ones. Viktor, you're not going to let me down, are you? At this moment of all moments? You're not going to let Anrijs Pletenbergs down?" Viktor's fear had been realised. Pletenbergs' mood had switched. Emotion was swelling within him. The crazy look in his eye made it difficult to judge whether he was about to burst into tears or attack Viktor with the butter knife.

"No, I will not let you down. It's just that this rock is rather higher-profile than the others – in every respect." The joke did not register. "It will take a little longer to sort out. I'm just saying it will take some time. I have some ideas already and I'm sure I can..."

"Time? Time?" Pletenbergs burst out laughing, but it was a laugh mixed with equal parts joy and fear. "Time is not a problem, Viktor, I don't expect everything done immediately! Anrijs Pletenbergs is not an unreasonable man.

he knows that when one of his friends promises to do something, it will be done, he does not worry about small details like time! Take as much time as you like! As long as it is done by the time the Pletenbergs Institute is launched, it matters not at all!"

That meant he had a matter of days, but as Viktor had come to realise, buying time, like lying in the cause of self-preservation, was a skill that should not be undervalued. Pletenbergs' interminable court cases provided ample evidence of that.

Suddenly Pletenbergs' mood changed again. He leaned right across the table and spoke in a whisper.

"That rock will go. V---- was fourth, then third, now it's second. It must be first. We will be first. It is inevitable. Potemkin will flow backwards. Anrijs Pletenbergs will be first. All those who stand in his way will be destroyed like those rocks. Now do you understand why it is so important?"

Viktor nodded slowly, now more convinced than ever Anrijs Pletenbergs was the maddest mayor in Eastern Europe, which – as an experienced traveller in a region where golden statues of Bruce Lee had been erected and illegally parked cars had been crushed under the wheels of municipal heads driving armoured personnel carriers – was quite a distinction.

Anrijs had one more surprise for Viktor that evening. Switching immediately back into affable host mode, he shouted for the waiter to bring in more champagne. Katy and the head of security – who, it turned out, was called Jānis – were invited to the table and politely acquiesced while Anrijs began another little speech in the manner he generally reserved for the opening of a new children's playground or the inauguration of a much-demanded bus route to one of V----'s less pleasant suburbs.

"Viktor, do you like it here? Be honest."

"Why, yes, from the little I have seen, V---- looks a very nice place." In fact, on his brief trip to the former fourth largest rock, Viktor had reached the opposite conclusion but he knew nothing would be more certain to provoke Pletenbergs' rage than criticism of his rotten little pocket borough.

For all that he abused and defrauded the place to grow his personal fortune, Pletenbergs did seem to harbour genuine affection for his home town and believed himself to be the only thing maintaining its prosperity in the face of the global conspiracy sworn to destroying him. And if Anrijs Pletenbergs was destroyed, V---- would surely slide beneath the waves of the Baltic like an extravagant sand castle built too close to the water's edge.

"Yes, of course, you like V----, that goes without saying. But I mean right here, the Sea Salt restaurant."

"Ah. Yes, the food was excellent."

"And the location?"

"I didn't see too much as we arrived because it was dark, but if it's on the coast it must be very good."

"I hoped you would think so. Do you remember that I recently asked if you would prefer to live by the sea or in the forest? I find that people generally prefer one or the other. I'm like you, I prefer the sea. Though the forest has a lot to recommend it as well..."

"Very true," Viktor replied, wishing Pletenbergs would get to the point. The champagne and the stress of avoiding saying the wrong thing was making him feel very tired.

"As a reward for your efforts on behalf of Anrijs Pletenbergs," the dapper little man began, like a monarch bestowing favours, "I have arranged for you to move to a very pleasant apartment upstairs, here at Sea Salt. You will have Jānis and his team on hand to protect you," Janis smiled briefly, "and Katy will supervise your day-to-day diary and take care of your domestic needs. How does that strike you?"

"It sounds... very agreeable. Thank you." He was still thinking about from whom he was being protected.

"I thought you might appreciate a degree of independence. The intellectual mind needs space and sunlight in which to thrive. You will be very busy organising the launch of the Pletenbergs Institute, so I would not expect you to leave the immediate vicinity, but the beach is close at hand, and a table in the restaurant will be reserved for you every night. It might prove stimulating, no?"

"Very much so."

"Then it is settled. I will be away again for a few days – more pointless court appearances inflicted on me by international speculators. But it will give me heart to know that while I am fighting to protect Latvia against them, you, Viktor, will be preparing my counter strike! And in one week's time, we launch!"

Over by the door, the Doberman looked like it was still hungry.

XXIII A PLAN

That night the sea air and the lingering effects of champagne did their best to give Viktor a good night's sleep in his pleasant new room above the Sea Salt Restaurant, but it was still a restless few hours as he tried to devise a way out of his Latvian labyrinth. Ironically, it was not his formidable conscious intelligence that eventually suggested a path, but his subconscious mind.

All the experiences he had endured in the days since his first arrival in this peculiar little country mixed and melded over and into each other like the sticky, yeasty dough he had kneaded with the old woman in her fairytale cottage. Dreams of endless forest, ranks of staring creatures in ties and tight collars, birch twigs flailing through the air, birds reciting miniature poems, missing pictures on wooden walls, mushrooms growing from the bottom of vodka glasses and huge black dogs pacing endlessly back and forth all passed through his imagination like a fever until he awoke to the tranquil sound of the Baltic Sea stroking handfuls of sand along the shoreline below his window.

The endless rhythm was reassuring so that despite his fitful night Viktor Draaks awoke in good spirits, relaxed and ready with a fully-formed plan that was – on one level – as insane as anything Anrijs Pletenbergs could dream up but which he knew gave him his only chance of extricating himself from the situation. Equally surprising was the fact that he didn't particularly care what happened afterwards. Getting away from Pletenbergs was all that really mattered and the attractions of the circuit had waned despite the ease of life on that international merry-go-round. If he ended up back on the ride, then well and good. If not, well, there was no reason Viktor Draaks couldn't do something else with his life.

There was a knock at the door and Katy's voice asked, "Viktor, are you decent? Breakfast's ready."

"I am decidedly decent," Viktor bellowed in a great bear growl. "Though probably not for much longer!" he chuckled to himself.

"I brought your things," Katy said as she pushed the door open, his "things" consisting of his now extremely battered tweed suit on a wooden hanger and his freshly-polished brogues, "though why you insist on having this old tweed suit is a mystery to me. Did you know it is extremely unflattering? It makes you look fat when in fact you are not fat at all. You are... solid, not fat. You are a striking-looking man, so why pretend you are some boring, bloated old professor."

"Bless you for saying so, Katy, though were I less of a gentleman than Anrijs seems to think I am, I might remind you that you also looked rather different – in an entirely preferable way – last night. Did you not know that having your hair tied back in that noose-like contraption is extremely unflattering?"

Katy smiled. "The sea air seems to agree with you."

"Oh, yes, it's 'capital'," Viktor said, rifling through the pockets of his jacket and trousers. They both laughed. He pulled out a small collection of business cards, scraps of paper and a torn cigarette packet, fanning them out in front of Katy's bemused eyes like a Mississippi card sharp showing his dexterity with a marked if slightly soiled deck.

"Very impressive," Katy said. "Naturally I've already seen them – not that I learned much as a result."

"These, my dear Katy, are our tickets out of this madhouse!" Viktor laughed and, without really thinking about it, kissed her on the cheek. "Did you say breakfast was ready? For the chef's sake I hope he has some bacon!" By the time he had finished his sentence, he was already halfway down the stairs, leaving a surprised Katy to follow him with the feeling of his bristly beard still tingling her cheek.

Indeed there was bacon – a good omen – and between mouthfuls, each one of which he savoured with expressive relish and lavish praise of the purple pigs of V----, Viktor outlined his plan. To Katy's disappointment the scheme seemed to involve nothing more than doing exactly what Pletenbergs had asked him to do. He would organise a press conference-cum-seminar to mark the launch of the Pletenbergs Institute, which he informed her would hereinafter be referred to as PI, pronounced "pie" and which would have a stylized logo based on the Greek symbol for the most elusive number in mathematics.

Katy was to organise the design work and the production of suitable literature introducing the work of PI, the text of which would be given to her in coming days by Viktor himself. He would need to make some telephone calls to ensure some big names from his contacts book were on the list and the venue would need to be booked. Katy assured him that getting use of the Pletenbergs Olympic Sports Hall and Conference Center was unlikely to prove an obstacle even if it meant the postponement at short notice of the V---- Annual Cat and Dog Gymkhana.

It was a plan that seemed to resolve nothing at all. Katy humanely waited until he had digested his beloved bacon before voicing her concern.

"If you think launching his Institute will satisfy Anrijs, you are not as smart as I thought you were, Viktor. Would you prefer it if I called you Viktor King or your real name, Viktor Draaks?" she asked.

His eyebrows jumped above the rim of the coffee cup from which he was drinking, but more in amusement than surprise.

"How long have you known?"

"A few days. But only after Anrijs asked me to find out everything did I discover... well, everything – your name, the Benbo Foundation, the day you arrived from Belgrade and which hotel you stayed at, your reputation as an expert, your unfortunate appearance at the conference last week..."

Surprisingly, mention of the great humiliation no longer stirred feelings of shame and embarrassment in Viktor's chest. He chuckled again. "Well, it seems you know everything about me. Have you told Anrijs?"

"Of course not. I have told him that Viktor King appears to be real, but that it is taking me some time to get the full facts. I was hoping you might give me one of those "tickets out of here" you mentioned upstairs. From the moment I saw you I knew you were the only person who might be clever enough to out-manoeuvre Anrijs. That's why I have done my best to protect you by telling Anrijs as little as possible – and why I have been editing your work on Potemkin without your knowledge, changing a few facts and figures, removing other information that might have made you disposable. If Anrijs – and more importantly the people he is negotiating with – ever have all the facts together in one place at one time, they will no longer need Viktor Draaks. Even so, I thought you might have something left in reserve, but from here it looks as if you are just trying to buy time."

"So if I was to leave, you would want to come with me?" Viktor asked.

"No, Viktor. I like you, but I can't leave. Anrijs' time has come. As you have noticed, he is becoming more paranoid every day. But that isn't what makes me hate him. It is not even the way he bends the law and buys people off. What I hate is that he has become too stupid to see that his businesses would make much more money and do a lot more good if they were run properly, legally. The gas transit, shipping, construction, the acetate factory... everything!

"Believe it or not, he was not always like he is now. He used to be a genuinely good businessman. He was always playing games with the law, but he saw opportunities that others didn't and he took them without hesitation when other people did hesitate. He deserved his success and his wealth. But when others started to do the same sorts of things to him that he had done in the past, something changed.

"The court cases became a kind of obsession. Because he became so used to denying his guilt, he started to think he had never done anything wrong, that he was in some way infallible. He felt victimised and became more and more defensive. This phantom conspiracy was born. None of the people he fears have even heard of him. Now he clings to his businesses in such stupid, crooked little ways. But, worst of all, he no longer cares about the people of V----. He thinks he does, and he believes they love him, but the truth is different."

Katy continued her history of the rise and fall of Anrijs Pletenbergs. First she made it clear that Pletenbergs never resorted to violence. True, once or twice businessmen linked to him had been shot dead while they pruned their roses or sipped a glass of wine on the terrace while birds hopped gaily across the lawn, but whoever had carried out these efficient "hits" had not been acting on Pletenbergs' behalf, even when he stood to be the clear beneficiary of an untimely demise.

On the contrary – Pletenbergs felt threatened and uncertain in the presence of violence. His grip on power relied ironically on rule of law, and on the days when a former associate was found oozing blood into the begonias, Pletenbergs stayed in his room, fretting endlessly and calling the security company he owned to make sure they had all the most modern personal protection equipment. They in turn came to recognise their boss' concerns and would have a car stationed outside the gates of his home sometimes before news of the hit had even made it to the local police station.

For the truth was that Pletenbergs had no need of violence or threats of violence. In his fiefdom of family-friendly V----, everything was made easy. Healthcare, education, policing, recreation – all were provided to high standards using gas transit money with the tacit understanding that in return the townsfolk remained loyal to their mayor and didn't concern themselves overmuch with where the rest of the gas transit money ended up. And for the most part they did and they didn't, respectively.

Anyone who persisted in being less cooperative did not find themselves threatened with broken bones or arson attacks. Instead, they started to find things a bit less straightforward than previously. Waits for a hospital appointment got a little longer. Their children started to be awarded worse grades at their well-equipped schools. Planning officers arrived to query small additions made to houses or ask why a woodshed had been built without the relevant permit. Paperwork mounted and appointments to clear up the paperwork always seemed to occur at awkward hours. Almost as if they too were experiencing hitherto unimagined inconveniences, neighbours became less friendly and less helpful.

In the end, people generally relented and remembered how it was Pletenbergs who had created such a pleasant initial atmosphere. Persistent rebels moved to Riga where they could experience similar levels of incompetence and indifference but without the suspicion that they were being given special treatment.

Thus neither fear nor threat were Pletenbergs' means of accruing power. He held onto and increased his influence rather via the selective application of awkwardness, bureaucracy and frustration. People could quickly become heroes or martyrs standing up to intimidation and violence, but no-one ever felt heroic wasting hours in a council waiting room only to be told they had filled in a form incorrectly.

"His whole empire has become dysfunctional and inefficient, but it doesn't need to be," Katy said. "It's not too late. It could easily be cleaned up, turned around and made into something that makes four times as much money without paying a single bribe, without making the people of V---- feel like miserable serfs in their own town and without any more of these ridiculous court cases."

"I have the feeling you know someone who could do that cleaning up job," Viktor said.

"I do. Which is why I was hoping you might come up with something more imaginative to end all of this than one of those conferences you must have been to a thousand times. Did any of them ever change anything at all?"

Viktor thought for a few seconds, treating the question seriously. "Probably not. Not until the last one, anyway. That changed quite a lot, for me at least. At risk of sounding like our absent mutual friend, you should trust me more, Katy. I admit that I am not exactly a man of the world, but did you really think I would be so naive as to fill my Potemkin brief with all the requisite data? All of the important sections were doctored – I just hope that in your subsequent editing you haven't inadvertently provided the correct details!"

Katy's eyes widened, though it was difficult to tell if it was from admiration or horror.

"Between you and I, the more I have thought about Potemkin, the less likely I believe it is that reverse flow will ever work. Even if it does, the costs are likely to make it economic suicide."

"Then why did you suggest it in the first place?" Katy asked.

"It was pure intellectual hubris. I didn't like the fact that someone else was telling me about pipelines – me, the author of 'Pipeline Politics of Eastern Europe'. So like a spoiled child I blurted out a theory about Potemkin – which is theoretically possible but practically preposterous. I always included a section about Potemkin in my lecture. Only during the last few days when I have thought about it properly have I seen how silly the whole thing would be and how silly my lecture was *in toto*." He paused to laugh at himself for a moment.

"When I said I would get us out of here, I meant it, as both Viktor King and Viktor Draaks. If you will trust me and help me, you will get your chance to take over Anrijs' empire. What you do after that is your business. Will we trust and help each other?"

It was Katy's turn to think.

"Don't forget," Viktor chided, "we have already taken the fourth-largest rock in Latvia and made it the second-largest. How many people could have done that?"

Katy let out a long sigh and looked him square in the eye, the start of a smile playing on the ends of her lips.

"Very well, Viktor, I trust you. Speaking of the rock – what are we going to do about it?"

"I think I know someone who will have an idea. He is what you might call a possible friend of a possible friend. I will need to make some calls. Over the last week my opinions have changed so often that I no longer have any real idea of people's motivations, their ambitions or their honesty. So I am going to rely on gut instinct. Perhaps, like Anrijs, I have judged people to be enemies simply because it made me feel important. The people I am talking about have never actually done anything to harm me but I have taken their attempts at friendship to be dark stratagems. When you spend all day speculating on a country's secret plans and spheres of influence, perhaps it is not surprising that these things seep into and infect your private thoughts. So I have decided to purge my system of this poison. I'm going to ask for help and see if it comes. If it doesn't, at least I will have a real reason to take against these people. Now, would you show me where the telephone is, please?"

XXIV A NEW DAWN IN V----

In the town of V----, even the sun was on Anrijs Pletenbergs' payroll. The day of the launch of the Pletenbergs Institute dawned as the most beautiful of the year with sea and sky daring each other to ever deeper shades of blue punctuated by impressionistic flecks of white cloud and spume. A dry wind blew gently from the land, skipped down the beach and leaped into the waves to cool off as a small squad of rotund, retired gentlemen moved in the opposite direction with towels wrapped around their necks. Having taken their early morning constitutionals they set off in pursuit of ham and egg breakfasts and strong, black coffee with a little brandy to aid the digestion.

The day's first brides and grooms posed for photographs on little footbridges above the brook that wandered through V---- municipal park, laughing off their grandmothers' warnings about rainy days making for happy marriages – a decidedly Baltic world view.

Ice cream sellers down by the neat little promenade, with its panoramic view of the slag heaps and silos on the other side of the port, felt even luckier and called their suppliers on the telephone as they opened their kiosks and erected their umbrellas, anticipating having to call for reinforcements by lunchtime. Over in the hardware stores that fringed one side of the market square, shopkeepers moved their selections of umbrellas and tarpaulins to their storerooms and brought out watering cans and garden furniture instead.

In front of them the market transformed itself like the pages of a child's colouring book. The bare wooden benches rapidly filled with scrubbed-clean fruit and vegetables that still clung to their dirt. Flowers of all colours became more brilliant still in the brightening sunlight which made jars of home-grown honey glow like amber lamps, a display rivalled by long tables laid with smoked and fresh fish, eels and lamprey. Small mackerel lay in rows like the scales of some far larger fish. Living carp pondered their fate in large plastic barrels while silver and brown trout rested in peace on the fishmongers' slabs, inviting passers-by to consider the merits of butter lemon, salt and a hot skillet.

Further still along the promenade, the gates of the Livonian Order castle swung open on their massive hinges as they had done for 800 years, delighted that they had not been assaulted for hundreds of years except by busloads of tourists, a few of whom were already squinting into the sunlight through their viewfinders and wondering why their cameras took such poor pictures as their flashes popped impotently.

Out on the farms that ringed the town itself, purple pigs smiled into the sky and rolled in the mud which was already becoming luxuriantly warm, feeling it dry in patches, crack and fall from their bristly backs.

Further away still, at the end of a mud path whose fringes had been freshly strimmed a day earlier by the V---- municipal works department, the second-largest rock in Latvia sat contentedly, happily casting a dark shadow to its west and ever so slowly moving it as the minutes ticked by.

If the rock lay on the outer fringe of V----, its beating heart was elsewhere, at the Pletenbergs Olympic Sports Hall and Conference Centre, with Viktor Draaks at the very nub, the still point from which everything else radiated.

In the kitchens the students of the V---- School of Catering and Hotel Management lined up and launched their canapes and pastries into ovens. In the main hall healthy young men in white shirts and black trousers placed seats in neat rows for the expected guests. Others with complexions as pale as wraiths huddled in the corner around tables with pieces of audio-visual equipment sprouting wires in all directions. At the front of the hall a huge video screen flickered into life and switched from one aspect ratio to another, occasionally pausing to display the words "Test" and the V---- coat of arms which shone benevolently through the whole hall like a second sun.

Viktor was on the stage, rifling through notes and dressed once again in the suit Katy had chosen for him. His beard and hair were trimmed and he looked as if he had lost more weight than seemed possible during a little more than a week since his arrival in Latvia.

Surprisingly he felt little nervousness, in the same way a soldier on a mission fraught with danger and death feels far less anxiety than one on a routine, repetitive patrol. He would do what he had planned to do and after that, let the consequences be as they may.

The smell from the kitchens distracted him from his notes for a moment – the purple pigs of V---- really did make excellent bacon – and looking up he saw Katy walking towards him with a bacon roll on a plate in one hand and a cup of steaming coffee in the other. She sat down next to him, placing the plate and cup next to his notes.

"How did you know I wanted one of these?" he asked.

"You know I am paid to keep an eye on you. It is my job to know these things." She smiled. "Are you ready?"

"I think so, Katy, I think so. Thank you for helping me, and for trusting me."

"As you said, Viktor, at some point you do have to place your trust in someone else's hands – even without knowing everything."

"I was quoting Anrijs, as I recall."

"I know, but I won't hold it against you. Anyway, this is just as likely as anything else to achieve what we want. Quicker, too. Speaking of our little emperor, he says he will come in on your cue. He loves the idea that he makes a grand entrance rather than sitting here from the beginning trying to look modest. The photographers will like it, too. And I think he is going to say something about Potemkin. He wouldn't tell me what, but he sounded very pleased with himself. I think he might go public with the plan."

"Excellent." Viktor took an enormous bite of his bacon roll, closing his eyes to indulge the moment. "You know, when all of this is yours," he said with a sweep of his arm, "the first thing you should do is shake up the V---- meat packing plant. There must be an export market for this bacon, it is quite delicious. It knocks old Benbo's sausages into a cocked hat."

"Thanks for the advice. I'll put your testimonial on the packet."

Viktor laughed his great bear laugh, almost choking on his bacon roll. Katy patted him on the back.

"Viktor, are you still eating that same bacon roll?" said a different but familiar voice. Standing at the side of the stage was Pavel Panchev with a very pretty redhead. "Sorry to sneak up on you, but I had to come in the back way to avoid the photographers. This is Baiba."

In a gesture that showed the depths of his feeling, Viktor put his bacon sandwich aside and rose to shake Pavel's hand warmly between both paws, before giving Baiba a slightly more restrained shake of the hand.

"Delighted to meet you, Baiba. Pavel, thank you so much for coming. And thank you both for your help. It seems we have both had eventful weeks in Latvia. Somehow it feels like much longer – in a good way."

"I know what you mean," Pavel replied. "I'm pleased to see you looking so well. Being on the run suits you!"

Viktor remembered Katy standing beside him. "I'm so sorry, how rude of me. Pavel, Baiba, this is Katy. Without her, I don't know what I would have done."

Pavel bowed and smiled, his black forelock falling down across his brow to make him look even more handsome.

"A pleasure to meet you, Katy. Any friend of Viktor's is a friend of mine."

Katy laughed. "That's funny – just a few days ago Viktor was saying what a terrible person you were."

"He was right, Pavel is terrible," Baiba interjected. "What time do we start?"

The hall was quickly filling up. Bold female photographers from *Reality* and the rest of the Latvian press were already crouching and firing their flashes up at Pavel as he spoke to Viktor and Katy. The presence of this new-forged celebrity to give the keynote had guaranteed a large press turnout from Latvia, Estonia and Russia. Anrijs, too, had been delighted when he was told such a well-known speaker would launch proceedings.

"We start as soon as the hall is full," Viktor said. "Any minute now."

"Good luck," Katy said, and pecked him on the cheek, which made him smile while he finished his bacon roll and coffee.

****

When the crowd had settled down and the cameramen had signalled that their cameras were rolling, the launch of the Pletenbergs Institute (PI) commenced.

Viktor rose to his feet, and walked to the speaking position feeling the first twinges of nerves as a bright spotlight poured its beam over him. His mind replayed the events of a little over a week earlier when he had woken up on stage, spoken nonsense and the audience had turned into rabbits in front of his eyes. A bead of sweat formed on his brow. He growled, clenched and unclenched his fists and took a deep breath before speaking into the microphone.

"Your excellencies, ministers, lords, ladies and gentlemen," he began in his best Cambridge voice. There were no lords, but all the other ranks were in evidence and it seemed proper to turn on the pomp.

"Today is an historic day not only for V---- or even for Latvia, but potentially for the whole world. I am not exaggerating when I say that, for I have spent more than twenty years on the international political circuit meeting leaders from all nations, of various political persuasions and I can truly say with hand on heart that in all that time I have never met a man quite like Anrijs Pletenbergs."

Applause erupted, causing joy to the great man himself who was having the last of his make-up applied in an adjoining room.

"I have met wise men far cleverer than myself," Viktor continued. "I have met charismatic men and men with that curious ability to do the right thing at the right time when all the evidence says otherwise – which we call 'luck' but which is really a talent just like any other – and I have met great humanitarians who have done things for their fellow beings that make the rest of us wonder why we have done so little. Some of you here today might place Anrijs Pletenbergs in any one of those categories," – he glanced down at the front row of Pletenbergs' political cronies and the old women carrying extravagant blooms to give to their hero – "but I would not. I believe Anrijs Pletenbergs belongs in a category all of his own. I am delighted to be able to introduce a good friend of mine to tell you more. Please welcome the renowned international expert, Mr Pavel Panchev!"

The applause that greeted Pavel was even louder than the first burst in honour of Pletenbergs as the crowd showed its appreciation of Pavel Panchev, loved by Russians and intellectuals for punching a boorish extremist, loved by women for being handsome and masculine, and loved by Latvians for single-handedly subduing a rampaging party of British sex criminals, which is how the press had reported the incident with the stag party.

In his dressing room, Anrijs Pletenbergs' toes curled with pleasure and anticipation at the wild applause. He looked at himself in the mirror as the make-up artist dabbed some dark powder onto his crown to disguise his slight balding patch. He bared his pearl-white teeth and screwed his eyes up to examine the lines in his face. "Do you think I need a facelift?" he asked the cosmetician.

"No! You have the skin of a twenty year old!" she lied. Anrijs didn't look entirely convinced. He had seen pictures of Pavel Panchev, too. Viktor had told him it would take around twenty minutes to dispense with the introductory speeches and work the audience to a suitable pitch of enthusiasm, at which point the V---- town bugler would strike up a fanfare and Anrijs would enter the arena on a wave of adulation.

He looked at the make-up girl, a young blonde, in the mirror. "Have you ever wanted to be in films?" he asked.

Back on the stage, the applause, cheers and even a few girlish screams finally abated.

"Hello everyone, I am truly delighted to be here with you today," said Pavel. "As you may know, I have had a fairly eventful week here in Latvia..." More applause and laughter. "...and I have come to realise that this is a complex, fascinating country with complex, fascinating people. Many of us in other countries talk in sweeping generalisations about Latvia and its neighbours. We have only a vague idea of where it is, we know next to nothing of its history and its language baffles us because it doesn't sound like anything we have ever heard before. But that ignorance is our fault, not yours. Sadly, it is something that will not go away very quickly, and with your help I hope we can slowly educate ourselves."

Pavel shifted his position at the dais and changed his tone with the ease of a natural orator. "However, the fault does not always lie with us, ignorant foreigners," he continued. "Sometimes Latvia does things that fuel the stereotype of an Eastern European country with corrupt politicians, crooked businessmen and people whose fame and fortune are based on the flimsiest pretexts, who are tolerated not in spite of their ignorant opinions, shameless crimes and contempt for the law but precisely because of those qualities."

A certain unease could be detected in the audience at this point, but Pletenbergs' supporters felt sure he was working towards a damning indictment of Bill Gates, Warren Buffet, Richard Branson, international finance and the various conspiracies of Jews, Freemasons, Catholics, Chinese, Germans, Anglo-Saxons, financiers, corporations and schoolteachers, among the many groups to which Pletenbergs would allude in his weekly *Reality* interview.

"Of that class of person," Panchev continued, brushing his forelock away with one hand, "there is no more prominent, ridiculous and shameful example than the man we are all here to discuss today, Anrijs Pletenbergs!"

The mention of the name even now brought forth a round of applause from Pletenbergs' more dimwitted supporters, and the MPs, government officials and ambassadors sitting at the front who assumed there was a problem with the simultaneous translation in their headphones or simply weren't paying enough attention to care what was being said. In contrast, the majority of journalists and photographers, possessing that strange news sense that told them something worth writing about was about to happen, all leaned forward with a rustle of fresh pages being turned to in notebooks.

Pavel decided clarity was required. "This Pletenbergs should not be thought of as a favourite son of Latvia!" he said. "He is not a great businessman, a philanthropist or a patriot. He is not someone children should listen to for advice and only the foolish and the misguided would ever look to him as an example."

The flashes strobed at high speed, while television reporters signalled to their cameramen to pay attention and keep rolling.

"So what sort of man is Anrijs Pletenbergs?" Pavel asked as the tension in the hall grew by the second. "Well, in my opinion and the opinion of my colleague Mr Draaks, Anrijs Pletenbergs is really no more than a huckster, a con artist, a snake oil salesman. A crooked little pickpocket with spiteful views of everyone but himself who stole from his own family – that's you, people of V---- and Latvia – and who now demands your thanks for doing so. Some people call him an oligarch, but that flatters him – I'd prefer to call him a 'microgarch'. But don't take my word for any of this. Here's a short film that will say more than I ever could."

The lights went out before anyone could move and the giant screen sprang into life with a full-face portrait of Anrijs Pletenbergs, his smile literally beaming out across the auditorium. What followed was a very professional documentary film in four parts. The first showed how V---- was run as one huge racket, with shots of documents that proved the point and more information supplied by Katy which revealed the location and size of Pletenbergs' undeclared offshore assets which could be found everywhere from the Bahamas to Cyprus, Liechtenstein and Jersey.

Next came an analysis by Baiba and her fellow political science students of how the ZZZ party only initiated and backed legislation that benefited Pletenbergs both directly and indirectly, raising serious conflict of interest questions. This was book-ended by vox pops from mainly young people in V---- revealing their frustration at having to pay obeisance to a man most people seemed to dislike in private even if they supported him in public.

Section three was fronted by Viktor, who outlined the Potemkin pipeline plan showing how, if it went ahead, Pletenbergs would be stealing hundreds of millions of dollars every year from state coffers and compromising the country's energy independence.

By this point the hall was in uproar, but just when it seemed as if some of the angrier elements in the crowd might storm the stage, the fourth and final section began which rooted them to the spot.

It was a brief history of Anrijs Pletenbergs' involvement in the adult entertainment industry – complete with unreleased rushes showing a clearly approving Anrijs' presence on the edges of the set while a succession of blonde actresses earned their pay the hard way. Brief excerpts of some of the more ingenious scenes left little to the imagination despite the judicious application of pixelation, and lest anyone should be in any doubt as to the exact nature of Pletenbergs' involvement, there was even a schoolboyish sketch in his own hand which expressed precisely the effect he was after during the shooting of 'The Elementary Entry of Sherlock Holmes'.

At Viktor's insistence, one of the sequences included his own appearance in 'Up My Ass Please, Javes'. The sight of his perspiring face in full butler rig reacting with a nicely-timed "Well, really!" and withdrawing stage left prompted a gasp from the crowd and an outburst of laughter from Katy.

The film finished with the return of Pletenbergs' perpetually smiling face which faded away to be followed by brief credits revealing the director to be none other than Vladimir, who displayed all the creativity, imagination and wit in his documentary that he had never been able to express while churning out Pletenbergs' peculiar porno.

As the lights came up at the end of the film, Viktor returned to the speaking position beaming with pride. The hall was completely silent as the majority of the audience sat wide-eyed and slack jawed. He leaned toward the microphone and said: "Here he is, the man responsible for all of this, Anrijs Pletenbergs!"

The V---- town bugler struck up a flowery fanfare to welcome Anrijs Pletenbergs, saviour of Latvia. The spotlight picked him out at the back of the hall and he stepped forward in a brand new chalkstripe suit, his head cocked modestly to show the side he had decided in the dressing room had fewer lines around the eyes.

It took him perhaps ten seconds to realise that something was not quite right. He received the expected gratifying barrage of flash photography, but couldn't understand why his offered token handshakes were not being taken up with more enthusiasm by his adoring public. Sooner than he thought, he was preparing to receive the bouquets he had ordered the previous day which it was agreed would be handed to him by his ever-reliable blue-rinsed Myrmidons. The moment he finally understood something was very, very wrong was when one of these devoted flower ladies stepped forward and instead of the usual coquettish curtsey and brief words of gratitude, she flung the flowers into his face and began informing him that he was a "depraved viper and a menace to all decent folk".

Looking down on the bald patch exposed mercilessly by the spotlight,

Viktor almost felt sorry for the dapper little man. Just over a week earlier he had been the one desperate to leave the scene of his own very public humiliation, but whereas he had been trapped by the intransigence of a door that opened the wrong way, Anrijs Pletenbergs was caught in a trap of his own making. All his former allies from the churches and other broadcasters of conventional wholesomeness were transformed into indignant enemies desperate to distance themselves from the pocket-sized pervert.

Those who had always disapproved of him now had more ammunition than they could ever need to justify their opposition. Politically, financially and municipally, Anrijs Pletenbergs was finished.

Even the sun expressed its disapproval in the sky above V---- by moving behind a cloud, which in turn caused the purple pigs to grunt in annoyance and seek the warmth of their sty.

Viktor, Pavel, Baiba and Katy made for the rear entrance pursued by the press who were peppering them with questions. Katy handed out multilingual press releases in response, complete with a link to a website where Vladimir's film could be watched by millions and turned into news stories by hardpressed editors looking for a bit of amusing colour from the Baltic states. For the one thing the locals had never quite realised was that the words Estonia, Latvia and Lithuania were intrinsically funny in an English language that had degenerated to the point where "Ruritania" was too difficult to spell.

As they stepped through the fire door, Katy hung back.

"Come on," Viktor chided. "I think we'd better leave Anrijs to do the rest of the explaining."

"I'm not going anywhere – someone will need to clear up this mess you have created." Her smile was only half happy.

Viktor found himself feeling the way he had when he had said goodnight to Amelia all those years ago in Cambridge. He decided not to let the same thing happen again.

"I'll be back – soon. I'll help you clear it up. I don't think I will be going back to Benbo. V---- is as good a place as any. Might that room at Sea Salt still be available?"

"Don't take too long or I might rent it out to Pavel," Katy said. Pavel gave a gentlemanly smile, pleased to have made an impression, which prompted Baiba to dig him in the ribs with her elbow. "And anyway, I know you will really be coming back for the bacon," Katy told Viktor.

XXV TWO BIRDS WITH ONE STONE

For thousands of years, strange things had happened at the Daina Stone. Given the place's reputation as a site of sorcery and sacrifice it was entirely appropriate that as the witching hour drew to a close, a shadowy figure detached itself from the surrounding gloom and inched up the small hill towards the large, solitary standing stone. Bats circled high in the cold air as dawn prepared to take a new day's first breaths. The path to the Daina Stone, worn by thousands of feet, bare and shod, over the centuries shone as a pale streak as the moon dashed from one cloud to another. Far away in the dark mist of forest that blurred the horizon a feral dog howled a lament. The only other sound came from a low buzzing of invisible insects' wings and the rare passage of a car along a road that skirted the bottom of the small valley formed by the Daina Hill and its six little companion hills, like dark blue bruises on the body of the landscape.

The figure, which was made to look unnaturally broad and squat by the large pack on its back, reached the top of the hill at last and placed one hand on the mystic stone, steadying itself or perhaps communing with it across the ages. The hooded head nodded sagely as if receiving its answer and exhaled deeply, either from the import of what it had decided or from the exertion of its travails up the hill. The nocturnal communicant placed a hand on its breast, first on one side, then the other, from whence it pulled out a small, brilliantly white oblong box.

It paused to glimpse furtively from side to side one more time, and suddenly a bright flame burst into life at the base of the Daina Stone. Illuminated at last, the figure uttered five words: "Fack me, what a country!" and lit its cigarette. Then, cursing himself, John Smith remembered the first thing he had been taught during basic training at Aldershot and cupped the cigarette in his hand so that its glowing tip was no longer visible to enemy snipers.

There was a brief rustle somewhere in the ferns that ringed the crown of the hill at a respectful distance as a bird or badger pushed its way through the undergrowth. John Smith froze for a moment, strained his ears and carried on puffing.

With the cigarette done he set to work at last, placing the large backpack on the ground ten paces from the Daina Stone and removed its contents carefully, placing a series of small plastic canisters, angled metal strips, curled wires, rolls of coloured tape and orange clips in a careful sequence on the ground. He picked up the backpack, strode heavily down the hill and pulled a larger black plastic box from the bottom of the bag, laying both on the ground hidden behind a hemlock that could be clearly seen from the top of the hill. Then it was another breathless hike up the hill, as he told himself he should cut down on his smoking. He lit another cigarette to ponder this before the final task began.

Working in the fast, efficient, mindless manner that comes from repeated drilling, John Smith started placing the charges around the base of the Daina Stone, arranging the canisters, wires and strips in a pleasingly symmetrical spider's web pattern. He seemed happy in his work, not at all concerned that he was about to assassinate a rock of immense cultural significance and rob Latvia of one side of its 20 lat banknote. He even started whistling a martial air through his teeth before the memory of a red-faced sergeant major caused him to seal his lips as he taped the last of the charges to the age-worn rock.

A few times cars passed on the road below, their exhausts wheezing and axles creaking as they rattled between the dairy farms that studded the Zemgale landscape, second-hand German motors and agricultural pick-up trucks in the main. Another car came along the road too, emitting less noise and with a deeper engine note, but John Smith paid it no attention as his hands finished placing clips and tape with practised ease.

The explosives were placed not to destroy the rock in its entirety – that would have required serious ordnance – but to blow a section out of the base that would cause the great boulder to fall and, with a bit of luck, roll down the hill. Quite why his new paymasters wanted this to happen was a mystery, but at the price they were offering he was quite prepared to leave it an open question.

He suspected that this was simply an initial test to check that his sapping skills were still intact and that the real work lay ahead, which may have accounted for the irresistible feeling that he was being watched. He was extremely wary of getting into bed with the Russians, but what could he do? As a freelance he had to pay the bills somehow and this certainly beat voiceovers for nightclubs. Provided they weren't asking him to do anything directly against Queen and Country, or blow up anything that lived and breathed, what was the problem?

He could always tell London about it and play the double game. They'd be grateful and it would work in his favour. After all, they'd turned him loose and made him go freelance precisely because nothing ever happened in Latvia that they were interested in. Now here he was not only with some evidence of Russian activity but right in the middle of it, and all without any help from the stuck-up ponces on the bank of the Thames who had been so dismissive of his earlier efforts.

Meanwhile he would be making more money than any of them, all of which could be easily salted away thanks to several Latvian banks' well-practised expertise in keeping money from the east sloshing around this corner of the European Union. What a fackin' country.

With his task nearly complete he reached for another cigarette, but again the shrill voice of the sergeant major silently upbraided him for his stupidity. There was no danger of setting anything off – these were plastics after all – but something like the collective memory of the Royal Engineers intervened to make him push the filter tip back down into its box.

He walked back down towards the blasting box, letting a spool of electrical wire roll out behind him with a low hiss. Halfway down the hill a voice called out of the darkness: "Take one more step and I'll blow your head off, you Russian bastard!"

John Smith froze. His smile fell silently to the ground.

A small bush stood up near the blasting box, one branch extended menacingly in his direction. It signalled for him to drop to his knees. He did so, placing his hands on the back of his head. The tree walked over to him, keeping what looked like a bird's nest trained on him all the time. With a swift movement, it jerked the hood off the Englishman's head, revealing his bald pate and blue eyes.

"John? What the f...?"

"Ivars? What the f...?"

Both men spoke at once. Simultaneously a rapid "pfft pfft" sounded from the heather as if a bird had taken wing and was flying towards them at high speed. John Smith reached for the side of his neck, his eyes rolled into the top of his head as if in search of his brain and he slumped forwards onto the grass.

Ivars Dzintars sensed a sharp pain in his left upper arm. He looked down at it and saw a dart sticking out of his camouflaged fatigues. His first thought was that it seemed unfair that he had gone to the trouble of wearing a combat vest and had spent hours on assembling his extravagant foliage in a manner he had seen demonstrated on a TV show about US Marine snipers only for someone to shoot him in his unprotected arm. Then, with his eyes already growing heavy he tried to do what Chuck Norris would do – pull the dart out – but he was instinctively unwilling to let go of the gun in his other hand.

Unable to resolve this impossible quandary, he directed the last of his strength to his trigger finger. He wheeled around crazily a couple of times, firing off random shots, the big .45 bullets sounding like cannon fire in the darkness and sending birds and rodents scattering in all directions. Sinking to his knees, Ivars Dzintars' senses closed in around him. He felt scared. All he could see now was the huge Daina Stone looming over him at the top of the hill. It seemed to be laughing at him. He raised his pistol one last time and managed to get two shots off at the mocking rock which raised orange sparks as the bullets sheered off into the darkness. Then Ivars Dzintars toppled forward just as John Smith had, with the laughter of the Daina Stone still ringing in his ears.

It was silent for a long time. The night predators, the foxes and martens, stoats and wildcats watching from the shadows took a while to be convinced the two men had finished their strange ritual, though it was perhaps no stranger than others that had been played out here over the centuries.

Then creatures began to stir again, aware that their hunting job needed to be completed in good time so that they could slink back to their holes before daybreak. Two tall figures rose from the ferns and walked over to the two prostrate bodies. They shook their heads ruefully, then set about completing their night's work in silence.

****

The hunters had been prompted to set out even earlier than usual by reports of an unusually large wild boar in the area which a pair of Russian game tourists had blabbed about in the local bar the previous day. They had seen it rooting around the base of the Daina Stone, they said, but it had scented them and disappeared like a thoroughbred before they had even unslung their rifles, let alone got off a shot. For they were true hunters and cultured men, they insisted. Having read their Turgenev they would consider it bad form to take an "ignoble" shot at such a handsome beast.

The locals had taken good note of the strangers' words and while Russians weren't always the most welcome guests in this part of Latvia, they recognised brother hunters when they saw them. If men who said they had shot from Siberia to the Serengeti had been impressed by the enormous boar, it must be a prize indeed. The powerful, expensive rifles they carried in aluminium flight boxes with incredible sights corroborated their story and had the local hunters examining them half in admiration, half in envy.

Figuring that local knowledge and numbers would easily compensate for their lack of such equipment, they fed their dogs early, gave their trusty guns a final lucky wipe with oilcloths and told their wives they would be back in time for breakfast.

But the king of boars, if he had ever existed, was safe that day. When they arrived at their Daina Stone rendezvous, they were greeted by evidence of a rather different type of porcine behaviour from the one they had been expecting. There, propped up against the sacred stone itself were two figures, snoring away with evidence of their night's revel all around them in empty beer bottles strewn across the grass.

One of the two – the bald one – wore a white T-shirt bearing the foreign words "Stevos Rega Stag Do". The hunters had heard of stag parties and the disgusting things they got up to when they came to Latvia. The other individual was dressed in full combat fatigues – at least from the waist up. Only a pair of underpants kept the cold at bay between his webbing waist belt and jungle boots. As farming men of traditional values who invariably voted ZZZ at election time, the hunters grew more disapproving by the minute. One of them called the police, while the others calmed down one of their number who was rather too theatrically declaring himself in favour of shooting the degenerates on the spot.

But that wasn't the worst of it. Around the other side of the stone, the hunters with their keen sense of smell noticed that someone appeared to have urinated on the Daina stone, an act of barbarism only rivalled by the evidence of freshly-exposed pits in the ancient stone's surface that looked very much like someone had been taking pot-shots at the holy site. Sure enough a quick search of the brush revealed a ludicrously outsized .45 calibre Glock 21 automatic pistol with a half-spent magazine. Not a weapon any hunter would ever use.

By now the two revellers were regaining consciousness. A ring of angry, offended and armed farmers was not the best sight for bleary eyes. Ivars Dzintars' attempts at explanation in his broken and accented Latvian were incomprehensible to the sons of the soil, merely confirming that these were foreigners who held the fatherland in contempt. John Smith said nothing but "What a fackin' country" over and over again. The two were even more pleased than the hunters to see a police car bouncing towards them along the road below and climbed into the back without offering the slightest resistance.

XXVI THE LEAVING OF LATVIA

Kopeikin's car was parked a block away in the special VIP parking area next to the fruit and vegetable market arranged for important attendees at the launch of the Pletenbergs Institute. His familiar long, black Mercedes with its gold-fringed Russian standard blended in nicely with the other ambassadors' cars. As Viktor, Pavel and Baiba approached, the rear window slid down and a smiling Kopeikin beckoned them inside. They joined him on the back seat, Baiba sitting on Pavel's knee, and he pulled out a demi of champagne from the chilled central compartment, popped the cork expertly and filled four vodka glasses with the sparkling liquid.

"Apologies for the glasses," he said. "Standard government issue, I'm afraid. If I may propose a toast? To a job well done."

They clinked glasses, making sure to maintain eye contact as they did so in the Russian fashion.

"I understand everything went smoothly," Kopeikin said rather than asked.

"That rather depends upon your perspective," Viktor said. "I don't suppose Anrijs Pletenbergs will ever be able to show his face again without being laughed at, so that must count as some sort of result."

"A refill?" Kopeikin asked as the car began to move. "I must say, Viktor, in Vladimir you appear to have uncovered a new genius of Russian film. It would not surprise me in the least if his documentary won a prize at the Moscow film festival this year."

"And what about the other side of the bargain?" Viktor asked. "The stone?"

"All taken care of," Kopeikin said. "Our friends Mr Smith and Mr Dzintars will also have trouble showing their faces again after they are released in a few weeks. The behaviour of the British stags has been in the news ever since Pavel's intervention last week, but their actions at the holy Daina Stone are a new low. But it's funny that the Latvians seem far more worried about the fact that someone urinated there than anything else – even Dzintars shooting it! I would have thought the idea of a great Latvian patriot shooting at a national monument would have been the headline, but not everything is predictable."

"Shots were fired?" Panchev said. "You said no-one would be hurt."

"And indeed they were not, apart from some sore heads. Dzintars' enthusiasm for firing at the least provocation was a surprising but happy coincidence. I suppose the rumour he heard of an imminent Russian plot to blow up the Daina Stone had made his trigger finger rather itchy and I imagine he was understandably anxious to regain his reputation as a great patriot after being knocked down by Pavel. The men who carried out the operation said they had never seen the like. They thought it was his lack of military experience. He had no respect for his weapon. He could easily have killed someone, most probably himself."

"What about Smith?" Panchev asked.

"You were right about him, he really is a most interesting character. He hadn't previously come to our attention, but once we had the name and description it wasn't difficult to find out more. It seems our Mr Smith was a former Royal Engineer who drifted to Riga chasing the long legs of Latvian ladies – excuse me for being vulgar, my dear – then made a peripatetic life for himself by performing extremely low-grade espionage simply because London could not afford to have its own station in Riga. He was paid so badly he had to supplement it with various other odd jobs. So he was really a sort of freelance spy, which is why he was so pleased to be contacted by us. Of course he could never be of the slightest use to us, but he saw that we could be of use to him, and the financial side of things clearly attracted him. I feel almost sorry for London these days, it used to be so much more fun when we were evenly matched... but no matter."

"The important thing is that we all ended happily ever after, is it not? Viktor, you have revealed a huge plot involving Russian gas pipelines as a result of your incredible research methods which I am sure will dazzle the convention circuit for the forseeable future. Pavel has had the misfortune to become extremely popular across a large swathe of Eastern Europe and I would venture to say is now extremely electable. Plus of course he has had the good fortune to meet this charming lady who graces us with her presence."

He inclined his head in gallant fashion to Baiba who returned the gesture with a degree of sarcasm.

"In addition, Latvia and V---- have been purged of Anrijs Pletenbergs and our frustrated artist Vladimir has had his career launched. Two extremely objectionable individuals have been taught a lesson that while unpleasant in the short term will probably save them from making much more serious mistakes in the future. Not bad work from the sinister Russian bear – and his friends – I think. More champagne is definitely required."

"But I don't understand what you get from all of this," Viktor said. "When I saw you and Pavel strolling around the pond together and when your men were after me, it wasn't difficult to realise you were trying to influence events, but what you have done doesn't seem to have benefited you or Russia at all."

"I'm sorry to disappoint you, Viktor," Kopeikin said, placing his hand around Viktor's shoulder the way he had at the Swedish lake months earlier. "I have certainly benefited. As a humble deputy prime minister I need successes to get noticed and the last week has been a very definite success, for me personally. As for Russia, well, she has benefited even more – or rather she will from this moment on. For one thing, Viktor Draaks, the implacable critic of the motherland has, I hope, seen that we are not all bent on causing chaos for no reason." Viktor nodded cautiously.

"More importantly, we have cleared Pletenbergs out of the way. Your report was far too good, Viktor, despite those errors you placed in it – yes, we noticed those. Potemkin does have reverse flow potential, but not yet. We will have to wait a long time before that is put into action and when it does happen it will not be with someone like Pletenbergs. He would have made too much money – too much of OUR money that is. And, believe it or not, we do not enjoy dealing with such men. They are unpredictable and as we have just seen, prone to sudden changes of fortune. Much better to talk state-to-state. We have our standards too, you know! Please, have another glass."

"But I think our best result is yet to come. Pavel here has a sickeningly bright future ahead of him – and I don't mean delivering lectures. Whether he acknowledges it in public or not, I hope he will always have fond memories of a helpful Russian deputy prime minister when he is something far more senior, so will perhaps not be afraid to cooperate in future. Who knows, Viktor, perhaps one day there will be another pipeline that you can get angry about and that you will hear about from both sides? Then we will all be happy!" Kopeikin dissolved into laughter as he poured more tiny glasses of champagne.

"Now, you will do me the honour of visiting me in Pskov? My family would be deeply offended if you refused. Unless of course you feel it is more urgent to get to the Tallinn conference? I'm sure they are discussing something terribly important such as what sort of light bulbs will save the world."

"Tallinn doesn't matter," Viktor said. "It will still be there next year."

****

Kopeikin's car sped on along the Vidzeme highway with the distance to Pskov – signposted in Latvian as 'Pleskava' – counting down the kilometres steadily with the road surface gradually worsening the further they got from Riga.

Baiba had been dropped off in Riga after extracting a promise from Kopeikin to return Pavel to her within a week.

"A wonderful young woman," Kopeikin said to Pavel as his car pulled away from the run-down Imanta block in which she lived. "With that red hair, clearly she has some Russian blood. She will make an excellent first lady, I think."

The three men continued talking about nothing in particular. Kopeikin had a diplomat's talent for alighting on a subject, talking around it without ever reaching a conclusion and moving seamlessly on to something else.

ishing, the intervals between roof replacements, likely developments in aerospace technology, how finely coffee should be ground – all these were covered and to Viktor's amazement he found himself joining in with the conversation. He knew nothing about any of the subjects, and a week ago would have had to sit sullen and mute until the conversation returned to Russian expansionism, energy security or the toxic mix of state and monopolistic businesses. For perhaps the first time in his life he was chatting aimlessly.

As he looked out of the window, through his own reflection which flickered on the inside of the car's darkened glass when the sun caught it at just the right angle, he had a suddenly uncanny feeling. Something to do with the topography, the way the forest approached and then receded from the road like a verdant tide was very familiar. And then, up on top of a small hill to the left was a stone windmill, its bare wooden sails motionless so that it looked like a figure trying to catch his attention. It was the same windmill he had passed travelling the other way with Ivars Dzintars.

"Turn left here!" he said, trying to re-trace the route in reverse.

Kopeikin signalled his assent to the driver and only then asked what the matter was.

"There's someone I'd like to call on if that's okay," Viktor said. "It will only take a moment."

Kopeikin shrugged, but Pavel studied Viktor, as if this was not the Viktor Draaks with which he was familiar from the circuit.

Viktor guided the car back past the sign saying "Āraiši", past the old school building where the road became deeply pitted, and the windmill hid again behind a hill, down to the lake with its tiny wooden huts on an artificial island and the massive foundations of a Livonian Order castle, up past the yellow-painted church with its russet roof and up and over the brow of a hill where the gravel road turned to a barely perceptible track and finally down, down into thick forest until finally there it was – the little fairytale cottage looking just as it had when he left.

Wordlessly he climbed out of the car, wishing he had brought some token of gratitude – flowers, a cake, anything. Kopeikin and Panchev waited inside, while he went to the front door and knocked. There was no answer. He tried again, but still there was no response. He peered in through the window. Everything seemed to be in order. On top of the table was half a loaf of black bread, a bowl of butter and a jar of honey. The pictures were in place on the walls and even the old woman's knitting needles still lay on the chair, skewering an almost complete mitten. His timing had been unlucky. The old woman was out in the forest somewhere.

With a feeling of disappointment he climbed back into the car and they began reversing back the way they had come, so narrow was the last section of track leading to the house. Suddenly the rear parking sensors beeped and the driver stood on the brakes, causing Kopeikin to curse creatively in Russian. Standing behind the car was the drunk with the big plastic buckets Viktor had seen during his forest odyssey. With barely a look at the car he carried on walking, heading back into the trees.

Viktor leaped from the car, followed by a curious Panchev and Kopeikin. "Wait!" Viktor shouted. The man seemed to take no notice, so Kopeikin echoed the cry first in Russian, which also garnered no response, then in Latvian: "*Gaidiet!*" The man turned his bleary eyes onto the three besuited men in the sleek black limousine as if it was a common enough sight in this part of the forest.

"Your buckets," Viktor said. "How much for your buckets?"

Kopeikin provided a translation, but the man did not seem to understand. Viktor walked over to him and tried to take an empty bucket from his hand, but the man guarded it jealously. Kopeikin came up behind Viktor and pulled a roll of banknotes from his pocket held together with a clip bearing the twin-headed imperial Russian eagle. He pulled off four twenty-lat notes bearing the image of the Daina Stone and waved them in the old man's face. At the sight of the money the man thought to himself for a moment, as if wondering whether four empty plastic buckets were actually worth much more than 80 lats. Kopeikin sighed and added another note, which was enough to seal the deal. He put his buckets on the ground and walked back the way he had come. In twenty seconds he was made completely invisible by the dense forest.

"Congratulations," Kopeikin said. "You are now the owner of the most expensive buckets in the world. Quite how I am going to record this on my expense sheet I do not know. Shall we resume our journey?"

"Not quite yet," Viktor said. "Friends, we are going to get some fresh air and be productive at the same time. It will make a nice change from stuffy conference halls, I think. Here's a bucket for each. Kopeikin, get the driver to join in too, he deserves to stretch his legs. Now form a line a few metres apart from each other. Good. Now, do what I do. Happy hunting!"

And so four smartly-dressed men, all leading experts in their fields, began stalking the Latvian forests for mushrooms. Rain showers the previous evening had brought the funghi out in large numbers and at certain parts of the forest the musty smell was overpowering, telling Viktor that treasure was there to be plundered even before his eyes caught sight of the golden chanterelles and brown baravikas. Panchev turned out to be a natural, attracting mushrooms almost as effectively as he attracted women, while Kopeikin complained in a joking sort of way that his family had spent four generations trying to escape being *muzhiki* and now here he was trawling the forests for mushrooms like a serf. The chauffeur kept his thoughts to himself, which mainly consisted of fear that the boys in the motor pool would not believe a word of this when he told them about it.

After a little more than an hour the buckets were respectably full and Viktor called a halt to the chase. The men retraced their steps, admitting that it had been an enjoyable if slightly damp experience. While Panchev and the driver took up their positions in the car once more and Kopeikin produced a small bottle of cognac to warm them up, Viktor took the brimming buckets onto the porch of the little cottage and placed them quietly by the door, covering them with two tea towels that had been hung out to dry. He looked down at his work, confident that this would give the old woman more pleasure than any bunch of flowers or sticky cake.

With a bear-like growl of satisfaction, he turned and went to the car. The engine purred to life, the car moved backwards and a minute later only birdsong could be heard. By the time the old woman returned, they were already in Russia.

THE END / BEIGAS

Printed in Great Britain
by Amazon

Carte de bucate vegane pentru începători 2023

Rețete incredibil de ușoare pe bază de plante pentru o dietă curată și sănătoasă

Delia Gherban

Cuprins

Supă roșie franceză simplă 12
Supă de ceapă spaniolă vegană Chorizo 14
Supă de fasole marine cu roșii uscate la soare 16
Supă Vegană Chorizo și Cartofi 19
Supă asiatică de spanac și fasole mung 21
Supă de cartofi și fasole albă 23
Supă de fasole albă și roșii uscate la soare 25
Supă italiană de fasole și cartofi 27
Supă de fasole picant Jalapeno Navy 29
Supă de năut și roșii uscate 32
Supă cu mere și morcovi 34
Supă de dovleac și păstârnac 36
Supă chinezească de dovleac 38
Supă de mere și dovleac 40
Supă asiatică de dovleac și piper Cayenne 42
Supă de ciuperci și ceapă roșie 44
Supă franțuzească de dovleac și mere 47
Supă afumată de morcovi și ceapă 49
Supă mexicană de fasole neagră și piper 51

Supă curry thailandeză cu fasole neagră 53

Supă de susan și fasole neagră 55

Supă Jalapeno cu fasole neagră 56

Supa de tortilla Jalapeno 58

Supă de tortilla vegană 61

Supă de tortilla afumată 63

Supă mexicană de fasole neagră afumată 65

Supă de cartofi usturoi 67

Supă de spanac și cartofi 69

Supă Jalapeno de morcovi și cartofi 71

Supă Thai de cartofi 73

Ancho Chili și supă de cartofi 75

Supa de cartofi cu iarba de lamaie 77

Supă maghiară de morcovi 79

Supă picant de morcovi și cartofi 81

Supă Poblano de Chili și Morcovi 83

Supă tailandeză picant de arahide și morcovi 86

Cartofi Poblano Chili și supă de ceapă 89

Supă de curry de linte și dovleac 92

Supă picantă de dovlecei 94

Supă de dovlecei thailandeză cu nuci 96

Supă italiană de dovleac și linte 98

Supă simplă de morcovi 101

Supă chinezească de păstârnac 103

Supă thailandeză de morcovi și ceapă roșie	105
Supă de morcovi picant și picant	107
Supă maghiară de ceapă roșie și morcovi	109
Ciuperci Shitake la cuptor cu roșii cherry	112
Păstârnac copt și ciuperci buton cu nuci de macadamia	114
Ciupercă la cuptor cu roșii cherry și nuci de pin	116
Cartofi curry la cuptor	118
Spanac și păstârnac la cuptor	120
Kale prăjită și cartofi dulci	122
Nasturel și morcovi la cuptor în stil Sichuan	125
Napi și ceapă picante și picante	127
Morcovi cu Curry	129
Spanac și ceapă prăjite picant	131
Cartofi dulci prăjiți și spanac	134
Napi prăjiți, ceapă și spanac	135
Nasturel cu unt vegan prajit si morcovi	136
Broccoli și spanac la cuptor	137
Conopidă și ceapă prăjite cu fum	138
Sfeclă italiană prăjită și varză	139
Nasturel prajit si cartofi	140
Spanac prăjit cu măsline	142
Spanac prăjit cu ardei Jalapeno	144
Spanac curry prăjit	147
Varza de fasole thailandeză picantă la cuptor	149

Spanac si napi picant de Sichuan 151
Nasturel thailandez Morcovi si ceapa 153
Yam prăjit și cartofi dulci 155
Yam alb la cuptor și cartofi 156
Păstârnac și Napi maghiari 158
Spanac simplu la cuptor 160
Spanac și morcovi la cuptor din Asia de Sud-Est 161
Kale prăjită și varză de Bruxelles 163
Spanac cu curry și cartofi 165
Cartofi dulci cu curry și varză 168
Jalapeno Nasturel și păstârnac 170
Nasturel si broccoli in sos de usturoi chili 172
Bok Choy picant și broccoli 174
Spanac și ciuperci Shitake 176
Spanac și cartofi în sos pesto 177
Cartofi dulci cu curry și gură verde 178
Napi și napi în sos pesto 179
Chard și morcovi în sos pesto 180
Bok Choy și morcovi în sos de usturoi chili 181
Napi și păstârnac fierte încet 182
Kale fiert lent și broccoli 183
Andive și morcovi fierte încet în sos pesto 185
Salată Romaine și varză de Bruxelles fierte lent 186
Andive și cartofi fierte lent 187

Napi fierți lent și napi în unt vegan 188
Varză gătită lent și păstârnac în unt vegan 189
Spanac și morcovi în stil chinezesc fiert lent 190
Bok Choy și morcovi fierte lent 191
Micro verdeturi și cartofi fierte lent 193
Verdure și cartofi gătiți lent 195
Varză violetă și cartofi fierte lent 196
Varză și morcovi fierte încet 197
Andive fierte lent în sos pesto 198
Napi fierte lent în sos pesto 199
Bok Choy gătit lent în sos de fasole galbenă 200
Napi fierte lent și cartofi în sos pesto 201
Ciuperci Chanterelle fierte lent 202
Ciuperci stridii și varză gătită lent 203
Ciuperci porcini și napi fierte lent 205
Ciuperci Crimini în stil italian fierte lent 206
Ciuperci Shitake și spanac fierte încet în sos Hoi sin 207
Ciuperci stridii fierte lent și varză în sos de fasole galbenă 208
Bok Choy cu curry gătit lent și ciuperci Button 209
Spanac și ciuperci porcini fierte lent 210
Kale fiert lent și ciuperci Enoki 211
Napi fierte lent și ciuperci 212
Bok Choy și ciuperci Shitake gătite lent 213
Salată romană fierte lent și ciuperci chanterelle 214

Spanac și ciuperci porcini fierte încet 215
Verde de nap fiert lent în sos Chimichurri 216
Bok Choy și ciuperci Enoki fierte încet în sos de fasole galbenă .. 217
Kale și ciuperci de stridii în sos Chimichurri 218
Linte și cartofi în lapte de cocos 219
Dulceata de afine 221
Jambalaya fiert lent 223
Tacos fierte lent cu ardei chipotle 225
Cartofi copți și fasole verde 227
Naut si conopida la cuptor 229
Fasole Garbanzo la cuptor Dovleac și cartofi 231
Morcovi curcubeu la cuptor și varză de Bruxelles 233
Sparanghel copt și cartofi roșii 235
Varza de Bruxelles la cuptor in glazura balsamica 237
Ciuperci Portobello la cuptor și roșii cherry 239
Taco vegan 241
Fajitas cu dovlecei și dovlecei vegani 243
Cartofi curry picante 245
Sparanghel ușor la abur 247
Broccoli la abur 248
Bok Choy la abur în stil chinezesc 250
Conopida la abur 251
Spanac la abur 252
Nasturel la abur 253

Sumă Choy la abur	254
Vegan Pad Thai	255
Se amestecă cartofi și roșii prăjiți	258
Umplutură vegană de sandwich cu fasole Garbanzo	259
Burrito cu fasole simplă și jalapeno	260
Vegan Sloppy Joe	262
Se prăjește Ramen și Tofu	264
Burger cu quinoa și năut	266
Varză curry picant	268
Tofu prăjit în sos de usturoi chili	271
Taitei de dovlecel in pesto	273
Sandwich Vegan Reuben	275
Morcovi Caramelizati Simpli	277
Fructe Jack simple prăjite	278
Se prăjește broccoli și morcovi	280
Dovleac prajit simplu	282
Dovleac prăjit picant	284
Dovleac copt și ardei gras verzi	287
Varza de Bruxelles simplă prăjită	289
Enchilada vegană	291
Fasole Garbanzo și dovleac fierte lent	293
Macaroane gătite lent și brânză vegană	295
Brânză Mozzarella Mac și Vegană	298
Fetuccini și fasole	300

Spaghete în sos Chimichurri 302
Paste Penne şi Măsline 304
Paste Pappardelle şi cremă de brânză vegană 306
Paste Farfalle cu fasole şi chorizo 308
Scoici de paste cu fasole şi mozzarella vegană 310
Paste Farfalle cu rosii 313

Supă roșie franceză simplă

3 linguri ulei de masline extravirgin

1 ceapa rosie mica, tocata

1 morcov mic, decojit și tăiat felii subțiri

1 coastă de țelină, feliată subțire

1/2 linguriță tarhon uscat

2 căni de bulion de legume

2 linguri. otet de vin alb

Încinge uleiul la foc mediu-mare.

Căleți ceapa până se înmoaie timp de aproximativ 5 minute.

Adăugați morcovii, țelina și tarhonul și gătiți încă 5 minute sau până când morcovii devin fragezi.

Adăugați bulion de legume și oțet de vin.

Se fierbe și se reduce la foc mic și se fierbe încă 15 minute.

Supă de ceapă spaniolă vegană Chorizo

3 linguri ulei de masline extravirgin

1 ceapa rosie mica, tocata

1 morcov mic, decojit și tăiat felii subțiri

1 chorizo vegan, tocat grosier (marca Soyrizo)

1 lingura. boia de ardei uscată spaniolă

1 lingura cimbru

2 căni de bulion de legume

2 linguri. otet de vin alb

Pătrunjel pentru ornat

Încinge uleiul la foc mediu-mare.

Căleți ceapa până se înmoaie timp de aproximativ 5 minute.

Adăugați morcovi, chorizo vegan și tarhon și gătiți încă 5 minute sau până când morcovii devin fragezi.

Adăugați bulion de legume, boia de ardei, cimbru și oțet de vin.

Se fierbe și se reduce la foc mic și se fierbe încă 15 minute.

Se orneaza cu patrunjel

Supă de fasole marine cu roșii uscate la soare

Ingrediente

1 kilogram de fasole marine uscată, sortată și clătită

1 1/2 litri de stoc de legume

½ litru de apă

1 ceapă medie, tăiată cubulețe

6 catei de usturoi, curatati si sfaramati

2 linguri sare de mare

1/4 lingurita piper

2 cartofi medii, tăiați cubulețe

1 kilogram de morcovi congelați, tăiați felii

1 cana rosii uscate la soare tocate*

1-2 linguri de mărar uscat

3-4 linguri patrunjel proaspat, tocat

Adaugati fasolea, supa de legume si apa, ceapa, usturoiul, sare si piper intr-o oala si gatiti la foc mic-mediu.

Se fierbe timp de 3-4 ore.

Când fasolea devine moale, adăugați cartofii și fierbeți până când cartofii devin fragezi.

Adăugați morcovii, roșiile și mararul și gătiți până se încălzesc.

Adăugați pătrunjelul.

Asezonați cu mai multă sare și piper.

Supă Vegană Chorizo și Cartofi

Ingrediente

1 kilogram de fasole garbanzo, sortată și clătită

1 1/2 litri de stoc de legume

½ litru de apă

1 ceapă medie, tăiată cubulețe

6 catei de usturoi, curatati si sfaramati

1 chorizo vegan (marca: Soyrizo), tocat grosier

2 linguri sare de mare

1/4 lingurita piper

2 cartofi medii, tăiați cubulețe

1 kilogram de morcovi congelați, tăiați felii

1 cana rosii uscate la soare tocate*

1 lingurita sofran

2 lingurite Paprika spaniolă

3-4 linguri patrunjel proaspat, tocat

Adaugati fasolea, supa de legume si apa, ceapa, usturoiul, sare si piper intr-o oala si gatiti la foc mic-mediu.

Se fierbe timp de 3-4 ore.

Când fasolea devine moale, adăugați cartofii și fierbeți până când cartofii devin fragezi.

Adăugați morcovii, roșiile, chorizo vegan, boia de ardei și șofranul și gătiți până se încălzesc.

Adăugați pătrunjelul.

Asezonați cu mai multă sare și piper.

Supă asiatică de spanac și fasole mung

Ingrediente

3/4 de kilogram de fasole mung, sortată și clătită

1 1/2 litri de stoc de legume

½ litru de lapte de cocos

½ litru de apă

1 ceapă medie, tăiată cubulețe

6 catei de usturoi, curatati si sfaramati

2 linguri sare de mare

1/4 lingurita piper

1 legătură de spanac, tăiat cubulețe

1 kilogram de morcovi congelați, tăiați felii

1-2 linguri de ghimbir tocat

3-4 linguri patrunjel proaspat, tocat

Adaugati fasolea, supa de legume, laptele de cocos si apa, ceapa, usturoiul, sare si piper si gatiti la foc mic-mediu.

Se fierbe timp de 3-4 ore.

Când fasolea devine moale, adăugați spanacul și fierbeți până când cartofii devin fragezi.

Adăugați morcovii, roșiile și ghimbirul și gătiți până se încălzesc.

Adăugați pătrunjelul.

Asezonați cu mai multă sare și piper.

Supă de cartofi și fasole albă

Ingrediente

1 kilogram de fasole albă uscată uscată, sortată și clătită

1 1/2 litri bulion de legume

½ litru de apă

1 ceapă medie, tăiată cubulețe

6 catei de usturoi, curatati si sfaramati

2 linguri sare de mare

1/4 lingurita piper

2 cartofi medii, tăiați cubulețe

1 kilogram de morcovi congelați, tăiați felii

1-2 linguri otet balsamic

3-4 linguri patrunjel proaspat, tocat

Adaugati fasolea, bulionul de legume si apa, ceapa, usturoiul, sare si piper intr-o oala si gatiti la foc mic-mediu.

Se fierbe timp de 3-4 ore.

Când fasolea devine moale, adăugați cartofii și fierbeți până când cartofii devin fragezi.

Adăugați morcovii, roșiile și oțetul balsamic și gătiți până se încălzesc.

Adăugați pătrunjelul.

Asezonați cu mai multă sare și piper.

Supă de fasole albă și roșii uscate la soare

Ingrediente

1 kilogram de fasole albă uscată, sortată și clătită

1 1/2 litri de stoc de legume

½ litru de apă

1 ceapă medie, tăiată cubulețe

6 catei de usturoi, curatati si sfaramati

2 linguri sare de mare

1/4 lingurita piper

2 cartofi medii, tăiați cubulețe

1 kilogram de morcovi congelați, tăiați felii

1 cana rosii uscate la soare tocate*

1-2 linguri de sumac măcinat

1 lingura cimbru

1 lingura mentă

Adaugati fasolea, supa de legume si apa, ceapa, usturoiul, sare si piper intr-o oala si gatiti la foc mic-mediu.

Se fierbe timp de 3-4 ore.

Când fasolea devine moale, adăugați cartofii și fierbeți până când cartofii devin fragezi.

Adăugați morcovii, roșiile, cimbru și menta și gătiți până se încălzesc.

Asezonați cu mai multă sare și piper.

Supă italiană de fasole și cartofi

Ingrediente

1 kilogram de fasole, sortată și clătită

1 1/2 litri bulion de legume

½ litru de apă

1 ceapă roșie medie, tăiată cubulețe

8 catei de usturoi, curatati si sfaramati

2 linguri sare de mare

1/4 lingurita piper

2 cartofi medii, tăiați cubulețe

1 kilogram de morcovi congelați, tăiați felii

1 cană pesto roșu

1-2 linguri de condimente italiene uscate

3-4 linguri patrunjel proaspat, tocat

Adaugati fasolea, supa de legume si apa, ceapa, usturoiul, sare si piper intr-o oala si gatiti la foc mic-mediu.

Se fierbe timp de 3-4 ore.

Când fasolea devine moale, adăugați cartofii și fierbeți până când cartofii devin fragezi.

Adăugați morcovii, pesto roșu și condimentele italiene și gătiți până se încălzesc.

Adăugați pătrunjelul.

Asezonați cu mai multă sare și piper.

Supă de fasole picant Jalapeno Navy

Ingrediente

1 kilogram de fasole marine uscată, sortată și clătită

1 1/2 litri de stoc de legume

½ litru de apă

1 ceapă medie, tăiată cubulețe

6 catei de usturoi, curatati si sfaramati

2 linguri sare de mare

1/2 lingurita chimen

2 ardei iute ancho, tăiați cubulețe

1 kilogram de morcovi congelați, tăiați felii

1 cana rosii uscate la soare tocate*

1-2 lingurite. ardei cayenne uscat

1-2 lingurite. ardei jalapeno, tocat

3-4 linguri patrunjel proaspat, tocat

Adaugati fasolea, supa de legume si apa, ceapa, usturoiul, sarea si chimenul intr-o oala si gatiti la foc mic-mediu.

Se fierbe timp de 3-4 ore.

Când fasolea devine moale, adăugați ardei iute ancho și fierbeți până când cartofii devin fragezi.

Adăugați morcovii, roșiile și mararul și gătiți până se încălzesc.

Adăugați ardeiul cayenne și ardeiul jalapeno.

Asezonați cu mai multă sare și piper.

Supă de năut și roșii uscate

Ingrediente

1 kilogram de fasole garbanzo, sortată și clătită

1 1/2 litri de stoc de legume

½ litru de apă

1 ceapă medie, tăiată cubulețe

9 catei de usturoi, curatati si sfaramati

2 linguri sare de mare

1/4 lingurita piper

2 cartofi medii, tăiați cubulețe

1 kilogram de morcovi congelați, tăiați felii

1 cana rosii uscate la soare tocate*

1-2 lingurite suc de lamaie

3-4 linguri patrunjel proaspat, tocat

Adaugati fasolea, supa de legume si apa, ceapa, usturoiul, sare si piper intr-o oala si gatiti la foc mic-mediu.

Se fierbe timp de 3-4 ore.

Când fasolea devine moale, adăugați cartofii și fierbeți până când cartofii devin fragezi.

Adăugați morcovii, roșiile și sucul de lămâie și gătiți până se încălzesc.

Adăugați pătrunjelul.

Asezonați cu mai multă sare și piper.

Supă cu mere și morcovi

INGREDIENTE

1 dovleac butternut mediu (1 lb de dovleac butternut decojit și tăiat cuburi)

1 ceapă roșie medie, tăiată cubulețe

1/2 lb morcovi, curățați și tăiați în bucăți

1 măr Fuji, decojit și tăiat felii

3 cani de supa de legume

1 cană bulion de legume

1 lingura chimen măcinat

1 lingurita sare

1 lingura coriandru

1/4 linguriță de salvie măcinată uscată

Sare si piper dupa gust

INSTRUCȚIUNI

Combinați dovleceii, ceapa roșie, morcovii, mărul, bulionul, bulionul și foaia de dafin într-un cuptor lent.

Gatiti aproximativ 6 ore la foc mic sau pana cand legumele sunt moi.

Luați frunza de dafin și aruncați-o.

Transferați ingredientele aragazului lent într-un blender

Se amestecă până la omogenizare.

Se toarnă înapoi în aragazul lent și se condimentează cu sare, piper, coriandru și chimen

Gustați și asezonați cu mai multă sare și piper după gust.

Supă de dovleac și păstârnac

INGREDIENTE

1 dovleac butternut mediu (1 lb de dovleac butternut decojit și tăiat cuburi)

1 ceapă roșie medie, tăiată cubulețe

1/2 lb morcovi, curățați și tăiați în bucăți

1 pastarnac, curatat de coaja si feliat

2 cani de supa de legume

1 lingurita sare

1 lingurita piper

2 (13,5 oz) cutii de lapte de migdale

Sare si piper dupa gust

INSTRUCȚIUNI

Combinați dovleceii, ceapa roșie, păstârnacul, morcovii și bulionul într-un cuptor lent.

Gatiti aproximativ 6 ore la foc mic sau pana cand legumele sunt moi.

Transferați ingredientele aragazului lent într-un blender

Se amestecă până la omogenizare.

Se toarnă înapoi în aragazul lent și se condimentează cu sare, piper și salvie

Adăugați laptele de migdale. Se amestecă.

Gustați și asezonați cu mai multă sare și piper după gust.

Supă chinezească de dovleac

INGREDIENTE

1 dovleac butternut mediu (1 lb de dovleac butternut decojit și tăiat cuburi)

1 ceapă roșie medie, tăiată cubulețe

1/2 lb morcovi, curățați și tăiați în bucăți

3 catei de usturoi, tocati

3 cani de supa de legume

4 lingurite Pudră chinezească de cinci condimente

1 lingurita sare

1 lingurita piper

1/4 lingurita ghimbir ras

1 cutie (13,5 oz) de lapte de cocos

3 linguri. ulei din semințe de susan

Sare si piper dupa gust

INSTRUCȚIUNI

Combinați dovleceii, ceapa roșie, morcovii, usturoiul, bulionul, uleiul de susan și frunza de dafin într-un cuptor lent.

Gatiti aproximativ 6 ore la foc mic sau pana cand legumele sunt moi.

Luați frunza de dafin și aruncați-o.

Transferați ingredientele aragazului lent într-un blender

Se amestecă până la omogenizare.

Se toarnă înapoi în aragazul lent și se condimentează cu sare, piper și salvie

Adăugați laptele de cocos. Se amestecă.

Gustați și asezonați cu mai multă sare și piper după gust.

Supă de mere și dovleac

INGREDIENTE

1 dovleac butternut mediu (1 lb de dovleac butternut decojit și tăiat cuburi)

1 ceapă roșie medie, tăiată cubulețe

1/2 lb morcovi, curățați și tăiați în bucăți

1 măr Fuji, decojit și tăiat felii

3 cani de supa de legume

1 frunză de dafin

1 lingurita sare

1 lingurita piper

1/4 linguriță de salvie măcinată uscată

1 cutie (13,5 oz) de lapte de migdale

Sare si piper dupa gust

INSTRUCȚIUNI

Combinați dovleceii, ceapa roșie, morcovii, mărul, bulionul și frunza de dafin într-un cuptor lent.

Gatiti aproximativ 6 ore la foc mic sau pana cand legumele sunt moi.

Luați frunza de dafin și aruncați-o.

Transferați ingredientele aragazului lent într-un blender

Se amestecă până la omogenizare.

Se toarnă înapoi în aragazul lent și se condimentează cu sare, piper și salvie

Adăugați laptele de migdale. Se amestecă.

Gustați și asezonați cu mai multă sare și piper după gust.

Supă asiatică de dovleac și piper Cayenne

INGREDIENTE

1 dovleac butternut mediu (1 lb de dovleac butternut decojit și tăiat cuburi)

1 ceapă roșie medie, tăiată cubulețe

1/2 lb morcovi, curățați și tăiați în bucăți

3 catei de usturoi, tocati

3 cani de supa de legume

1 lingurita sare

1 lingurita piper cayenne

1/4 cană unt de arahide

1 cutie (13,5 oz) de lapte de cocos

Sare si piper dupa gust

INSTRUCȚIUNI

Combinați dovleceii, ceapa roșie, morcovii, untul de arahide, usturoiul, bulionul și foaia de dafin într-un cuptor lent.

Gatiti aproximativ 6 ore la foc mic sau pana cand legumele sunt moi.

Luați frunza de dafin și aruncați-o.

Transferați ingredientele aragazului lent într-un blender

Se amestecă până la omogenizare.

Se toarnă înapoi în aragazul lent și se condimentează cu sare, piper și salvie

Adăugați laptele de cocos. Se amestecă.

Gustați și asezonați cu mai multă sare și piper cayenne după gust.

Supă de ciuperci și ceapă roșie

INGREDIENTE

1 dovleac butternut mediu (1 lb de dovleac butternut decojit și tăiat cuburi)

1 ceapă roșie medie, tăiată cubulețe

1/2 lb morcovi, curățați și tăiați în bucăți

1 conserve (14 oz) de ciuperci, feliate

3 cani de supa de legume

1 frunză de dafin

1 lingurita sare

1 lingurita piper

2 crengute rozmarin

Sare si piper dupa gust

INSTRUCȚIUNI

Combinați dovleceii, ceapa roșie, morcovii, ciupercile, bulionul și rozmarinul într-un cuptor lent.

Gatiti aproximativ 6 ore la foc mic sau pana cand legumele sunt moi.

Luați frunza de dafin și aruncați-o.

Transferați ingredientele aragazului lent într-un blender

Se amestecă până la omogenizare.

Se toarnă înapoi în aragazul lent și se condimentează cu sare și piper

Gustați și asezonați cu mai multă sare și piper după gust.

Supă franțuzească de dovleac și mere

INGREDIENTE

1 dovleac butternut mediu (1 lb de dovleac butternut decojit și tăiat cuburi)

1 ceapă roșie medie, tăiată cubulețe

1/2 lb morcovi, curățați și tăiați în bucăți

1 măr Fuji, decojit și tăiat felii

3 cani de supa de legume

1 tarhon proaspăt

1 lingurita sare

1 lingurita piper

1/4 lingurita ierburi de Provence

Sare si piper dupa gust

INSTRUCȚIUNI

Combinați dovleceii, ceapa roșie, morcovii, mărul, bulionul și tarhonul proaspăt într-un cuptor lent.

Gatiti aproximativ 6 ore la foc mic sau pana cand legumele sunt moi.

Luați tarhonul și aruncați-l.

Transferați ingredientele aragazului lent într-un blender

Se amestecă până la omogenizare.

Se toarnă înapoi în aragazul lent și se condimentează cu sare, piper și ierburi de Provence

Gustați și asezonați cu mai multă sare și piper după gust.

Supă afumată de morcovi și ceapă

INGREDIENTE

1 dovleac butternut mediu (1 lb de dovleac butternut decojit și tăiat cuburi)

1 ceapă roșie medie, tăiată cubulețe

1/2 lb morcovi, curățați și tăiați în bucăți

3 cani de supa de legume

1 lingurita sare

1 lingurita piper

1/4 lingurita chimen

½ conserve (6,5 oz) de roșii

Sare si piper dupa gust

INSTRUCȚIUNI

Combinați dovleceii, ceapa roșie, morcovii și bulionul în aragazul lent.

Gatiti aproximativ 6 ore la foc mic sau pana cand legumele sunt moi.

Transferați ingredientele aragazului lent într-un blender

Se amestecă până la omogenizare.

Se toarnă înapoi în aragazul lent și se condimentează cu sare, piper și chimen

Adăugați roșiile. Se amestecă.

Gustați și asezonați cu mai multă sare și piper după gust.

Supă mexicană de fasole neagră şi piper

Ingrediente:

1 lingurita ulei de masline extravirgin

1/2 cana ceapa rosie tocata

4 catei de usturoi, tocati

2 căni de bulion de legume

1 cană salsa

1 cutie de 14 uncii de fasole neagră

1 ardei gras verde, tocat

1/2 lingurita sare de mare

1 avocado, tocat

1/2 cană de coriandru

Opţional:

1/2 cană chipsuri tortilla de porumb mărunţite

Tăiaţi ceapa şi usturoiul.

Tăiaţi ardeiul gras roşu.

Gatiti si serviti:

Încinge uleiul de măsline la temperatură medie.

Adăugați ceapa roșie și usturoiul în tigaie și amestecați până se înmoaie, 3 până la 5 minute.

Se toarnă bulion, salsa, ardei gras, fasole neagră și sare.

Se fierbe la foc mare.

Reduceți focul la mic și fierbeți până se încălzește timp de aproximativ 5 minute.

Acoperiți cu jumătate din avocado, coriandru și chipsuri tortilla.

Supă curry thailandeză cu fasole neagră

Ingrediente:

1 lingurita ulei de masline

1/2 cana ceapa rosie tocata

4 catei de usturoi, tocati

2 căni de bulion de legume

1 lingura pudra de curry

1 cutie de 14 uncii de fasole neagră

1/2 lingurita sare de mare

1 cană lapte de cocos

1/2 cană coriandru împachetat

Încinge uleiul de măsline la temperatură medie.

Adăugați ceapa roșie și usturoiul în tigaie și amestecați până se înmoaie, 3 până la 5 minute.

Se toarnă bulion, praf de curry, ardei gras, fasole neagră, coriandru lapte de cocos și sare.

Se fierbe la foc mare.

Reduceți focul la mic și fierbeți până se încălzește timp de aproximativ 5 minute.

Supă de susan și fasole neagră

Ingrediente:

1 lingurita ulei de susan

1/2 cana ceapa rosie tocata

4 catei de usturoi, tocati

2 căni de bulion de legume

1 cutie de 14 uncii de fasole neagră

1/2 lingurita sare de mare

Încinge uleiul de susan la temperatură medie.

Adăugați ceapa roșie și usturoiul în tigaie și amestecați până se înmoaie, 3 până la 5 minute.

Se toarnă bulion, fasole neagră și sare.

Se fierbe la foc mare.

Reduceți focul la mic și fierbeți până se încălzește timp de aproximativ 5 minute.

Supă Jalapeno cu fasole neagră

Ingrediente:

1 lingurita ulei de masline extravirgin

1/2 cana ceapa galbena tocata

4 catei de usturoi, tocati

2 căni de bulion de legume

1 cană salsa

1 cutie de 14 uncii de fasole neagră

¼ cană ardei jalapeno, tocat

1/2 lingurita sare de mare

1 cană de porumb

1 lingura pudra de chili

Încinge uleiul de măsline la temperatură medie.

Adăugați ceapa galbenă și usturoiul în tigaie și amestecați până se înmoaie, 3 până la 5 minute.

Se toarnă bulion, salsa, ardei jalapeno, fasole neagră și sare.

Se fierbe la foc mare.

Reduceți focul la mic și fierbeți până se încălzește timp de aproximativ 5 minute.

Acoperiți cu porumb și pudră de chili.

Supa de tortilla Jalapeno

Ingrediente:

1 lingurita ulei de masline extravirgin

1/2 cana ceapa rosie tocata

4 catei de usturoi, tocati

2 căni de bulion de legume

1 cană de supă de legume

1 cutie de 14 uncii de fasole neagră

1 ardei jalapeno, tocat

1/2 lingurita sare de mare

1 lingura. oțet de mere

Opțional:

1/2 cană chipsuri tortilla de porumb mărunțite

Tăiați ceapa și usturoiul.

Tăiați ardeiul gras roșu.

Gatiti si serviti:

Încinge uleiul de măsline la temperatură medie.

Adăugați ceapa roșie și usturoiul în tigaie și amestecați până se înmoaie, 3 până la 5 minute.

Se toarnă bulion, bulion, salsa, ardei jalapeno, fasole neagră, oțet de mere și sare.

Se fierbe la foc mare.

Reduceți focul la mic și fierbeți până se încălzește timp de aproximativ 5 minute.

Supă de tortilla vegană

Ingrediente:

1 lingurita ulei de masline extravirgin

1/2 cana ceapa rosie tocata

4 catei de usturoi, tocati

2 căni de bulion de legume

1 cană salsa

1 lingura Sos iute în stil Louisiana

1 cutie de 14 uncii de fasole neagră

1 jalapeno, tocat

1/2 lingurita sare de mare

1 avocado, tocat

1 lingura chimion

½ linguriță, coriandru

Opțional:

1/2 cană chipsuri tortilla de porumb mărunțite

Tăiați ceapa și usturoiul.

Tăiați ardeiul gras roșu.

Încinge uleiul de măsline la temperatură medie.

Adăugați ceapa roșie și usturoiul în tigaie și amestecați până se înmoaie, 3 până la 5 minute.

Se toarnă bulion, salsa, sos iute, ardei jalapeno, fasole neagră, chimen, coriandru și sare.

Se fierbe la foc mare.

Reduceți focul la mic și fierbeți până se încălzește timp de aproximativ 5 minute.

Acoperiți cu jumătate din avocado, coriandru și chipsuri tortilla.

Supă de tortilla afumată

Ingrediente:

1 lingurita ulei de masline extravirgin

1/2 cana ceapa rosie tocata

4 catei de usturoi, tocati

2 căni de bulion de legume

1 cană chorizo vegan tocat grosier

1 cutie de 14 uncii de fasole neagră

1 ardei gras verde, tocat

1/2 lingurita sare de mare

1 lingura chimion

1 lingura paprika

1/2 cană de coriandru

Opțional:

1/2 cană chipsuri tortilla de porumb mărunțite

Tăiați ceapa și usturoiul.

Tăiați ardeiul gras roșu.

Încinge uleiul de măsline la temperatură medie.

Adăugați ceapa roșie și usturoiul în tigaie și amestecați până se înmoaie, 3 până la 5 minute.

Se toarnă bulion, chorizo, ardei gras, chimen, fasole neagră, boia de ardei și sare.

Se fierbe la foc mare.

Reduceți focul la mic și fierbeți până se încălzește timp de aproximativ 5 minute.

Supă mexicană de fasole neagră afumată

Ingrediente:

1 lingurita ulei de masline extravirgin

1/2 cana ceapa rosie tocata

4 catei de usturoi, tocati

2 căni de bulion de legume

1 lingura chimion

1 cutie de 14 uncii de fasole neagră

1 ardei gras verde, tocat

1/2 lingurita sare de mare

1 lingura. suc de lămâie

1/2 cană de coriandru

1 cană chorizo vegan, tocat grosier

Încinge uleiul de măsline la temperatură medie.

Adăugați ceapa roșie și usturoiul în tigaie și amestecați până se înmoaie, 3 până la 5 minute.

Se toarnă bulion, salsa, chimen, chorizo vegan, ardei gras, fasole neagră, suc de lămâie și sare.

Se fierbe la foc mare.

Reduceți focul la mic și fierbeți până se încălzește timp de aproximativ 5 minute.

Supă de cartofi usturoi

Ingrediente

1 lingura ulei de masline extravirgin

3 lingurite de usturoi zdrobit

1 lingură coriandru proaspăt tocat

1 lingurita pasta de chili

1 ceapa rosie, tocata

3 morcovi mari, decojiti si feliati

1 cartof mare, decojit şi tocat

5 căni de supă de legume

Încinge uleiul într-o oală la foc mediu.

Gatiti usturoiul, coriandru si pasta de chili.

Gatiti ceapa pana se inmoaie.

Adăugaţi morcovii şi cartofii.

Gatiti 5 minute si turnati supa de legume.

Se fierbe timp de 40 de minute sau până când cartofii şi morcovii devin moi.

Se amestecă până la omogenizare.

Supă de spanac și cartofi

Ingrediente

1 lingura ulei de susan

3 lingurite de usturoi zdrobit

1 lingură coriandru proaspăt tocat

2 lingurite sos de usturoi chili

1 ceapa rosie, tocata

3 morcovi mari, decojiti si feliati

1 legatura de spanac, tocat grosier

5 căni de supă de legume

Încinge uleiul într-o oală la foc mediu.

Gătiți usturoi, coriandru și sos de usturoi chili.

Gatiti ceapa pana se inmoaie.

Adăugați morcovii și spanacul.

Gatiti 5 minute si turnati supa de legume.

Se fierbe timp de 40 de minute sau până când spanacul și morcovii devin moi.

Se amestecă până la omogenizare.

Supă Jalapeno de morcovi și cartofi

Ingrediente

1 lingura ulei de masline extravirgin

3 lingurite de usturoi zdrobit

1 lingură coriandru proaspăt tocat

1 lingurita jalapeno, tocat

1 lingura chimion

1 ceapa rosie, tocata

3 morcovi mari, decojiti si feliati

1 cartof mare, decojit și tocat

5 căni de supă de legume

Încinge uleiul într-o oală la foc mediu.

Gatiti usturoiul, coriandru, chimen si jalapenos.

Gatiti ceapa pana se inmoaie.

Adăugați morcovii și cartofii.

Gatiti 5 minute si turnati supa de legume.

Se fierbe timp de 40 de minute sau până când cartofii și morcovii devin moi.

Se amestecă până la omogenizare.

Supă Thai de cartofi

Ingrediente

1 lingură ulei din semințe de susan

3 lingurite de usturoi zdrobit

1 lingură coriandru proaspăt tocat

1 lingurita ardei iute thailandez, tocat

2 linguri. pasta de tamarind

1 lingura Pastă de chili thailandez

1 ceapa rosie, tocata

3 morcovi mari, decojiti si feliati

1 cartof mare, decojit și tocat

5 căni de bulion de legume

Încinge uleiul într-o oală la foc mediu.

Gatiti usturoiul, coriandru, ardei iute thailandez, pasta de tamarind si pasta de ardei iute thailandez.

Gatiti ceapa pana se inmoaie.

Adăugați morcovii și cartofii.

Gatiti 5 minute si turnati supa de legume.

Se fierbe timp de 40 de minute sau până când cartofii și morcovii devin moi.

Se amestecă până la omogenizare.

Ancho Chili și supă de cartofi

Ingrediente

1 lingura ulei de masline extravirgin

3 lingurite de usturoi zdrobit

1 lingură coriandru proaspăt tocat

1 lingurita suc de lamaie

1 linguriță de seminţe de anatto

½ linguriță. piper roșu

1 lingurita ardei iute ancho, tocat marunt

1 ceapa rosie, tocata

3 morcovi mari, decojiti si feliati

1 cartof mare, decojit și tocat

5 căni de supă de legume

Încinge uleiul într-o oală la foc mediu.

Gatiti usturoiul, coriandru, suc de lamaie, seminte de annatto, ardei iute ancho si ardei cayenne.

Gatiti ceapa pana se inmoaie.

Adăugați morcovii și cartofii.

Gatiti 5 minute si turnati supa de legume.

Se fierbe timp de 40 de minute sau până când cartofii și morcovii devin moi.

Se amestecă până la omogenizare.

Supa de cartofi cu iarba de lamaie

Ingrediente

1 lingura ulei de masline extravirgin

3 lingurite de usturoi zdrobit

1 lingură coriandru proaspăt tocat

2 până la 3 tulpini de iarbă de lămâie

1 lingura ghimbir, tocat fin

1 ceapa rosie, tocata

3 morcovi mari, decojiti si feliati

1 cartof mare, decojit și tocat

5 căni de supă de legume

Încinge uleiul într-o oală la foc mediu.

Gătiți usturoi, coriandru, iarbă de lămâie și ghimbir.

Gatiti ceapa pana se inmoaie.

Adăugați morcovii și cartofii.

Gatiti 5 minute si turnati supa de legume.

Se fierbe timp de 40 de minute sau până când cartofii și morcovii devin moi.

Se amestecă până la omogenizare.

Supă maghiară de morcovi

Ingrediente

1 lingura ulei de masline

5 lingurite de usturoi zdrobit

1 lingură coriandru proaspăt tocat

1 lingurita boia maghiara

1 ceapa rosie, tocata

3 morcovi mari, decojiti si feliati

1 cartof mare, decojit și tocat

5 căni de supă de legume

Încinge uleiul într-o oală la foc mediu.

Gatiti usturoiul, coriandru si boia de ardei maghiara.

Gatiti ceapa pana se inmoaie.

Adăugați morcovii și cartofii.

Gatiti 5 minute si turnati supa de legume.

Se fierbe timp de 40 de minute sau până când cartofii și morcovii devin moi.

Se amestecă până la omogenizare.

Supă picant de morcovi și cartofi

Ingrediente

1 lingură ulei din semințe de susan

7 lingurite de usturoi zdrobit

1 lingură coriandru proaspăt tocat

1 linguriță praf de cinci condimente chinezești

1 lingurita pasta de usturoi chili

1 ceapa rosie, tocata

3 morcovi mari, decojiti si feliati

1 cartof mare, decojit și tocat

5 căni de bulion de legume

Încinge uleiul într-o oală la foc mediu.

Gatiti usturoiul, coriandru si pasta de chili.

Gatiti ceapa pana se inmoaie.

Adăugați morcovii și cartofii.

Gatiti 5 minute si turnati supa de legume.

Se fierbe timp de 40 de minute sau până când cartofii și morcovii devin moi.

Se amestecă până la omogenizare.

Supă Poblano de Chili și Morcovi

Ingrediente

Ingrediente pentru supa Poblano:

4 linguri de unt nelactat

1 ceapa rosie mica, tocata grosier

1 praz mare, doar partea albă, feliat

1 ardei gras verde, tocat grosier

1 (sau două dacă vă plac lucrurile picante) chili poblano mic, prăjit uscat, feliat

6 catei de usturoi, taiati cubulete

1 cartof roșu mare, tăiat cuburi (puteți folosi doi dacă vă place supa groasă)

4 căni de bulion de legume

1 cană caju

1-1/4 lapte de migdale

Sare de mare

Piper negru

Garnitura optionala:

Ardei jalapeno felii

Înmuiați caju în lapte de migdale timp de o oră.

Topiți untul fără lapte într-o tigaie.

Adăugați ceapa roșie, prazul, ardeiul iute, ardeiul gras, usturoiul și cartofii.

Gatiti la foc mic si amestecati pana ce ceapa este translucida, 6 1/2 minute.

Adăugați bulionul în tigaie.

Se fierbe până când cartofii sunt fragezi la furculiță timp de aproximativ 25 de minute.

Luați-o de pe foc.

Procesați amestecul într-un blender până la omogenizare.

Întoarceți supa în tigaie.

În blender, amestecați caju cu laptele de migdale până la omogenizare

Adăugați la amestecul de supă.

Se încălzește supa la foc mediu pentru încă câteva minute.

Se ornează cu felii de jalapeno.

Supă tailandeză picant de arahide și morcovi

Ingrediente pentru supa Poblano:

4 linguri de unt nelactat

1 ceapa rosie mica, tocata grosier

1 praz mare, doar partea albă, feliat

1 ardei gras verde, tocat grosier

5 buc. Ardei iute thailandez, feliați

5 frunze de busuioc thailandez

2 linguri. pasta de tamarind

8 catei de usturoi, taiati cubulete

1 cartof roșu mare, tăiat cuburi (puteți folosi doi dacă vă place supa groasă)

4 căni de bulion de legume

1 cană alune

1-1/4 lapte de cocos

Sare de mare

Piper negru

Garnitura optionala:

Ardei jalapeno felii

Înmuiați alunele în lapte de migdale timp de o oră.

Topiți untul fără lapte într-o tigaie.

Adăugați ceapa roșie, prazul, ardeiul iute, busuiocul thailandez, pasta de tamarind, ardeiul gras, usturoiul și cartofii.

Gatiti la foc mic si amestecati pana ce ceapa este translucida, 6 1/2 minute.

Adăugați bulionul în tigaie.

Se fierbe până când cartofii sunt fragezi la furculiță timp de aproximativ 25 de minute.

Luați-o de pe foc.

Procesați amestecul într-un blender până la omogenizare.

Întoarceți supa în tigaie.

În blender, amestecați alunele cu laptele de cocos până la omogenizare

Adăugați la amestecul de supă.

Se încălzește supa la foc mediu pentru încă câteva minute.

Se ornează cu felii de jalapeno.

Cartofi Poblano Chili și supă de ceapă

Ingrediente pentru supa Poblano:

4 linguri de unt nelactat

1 ceapa rosie mica, tocata grosier

1 praz mare, doar partea albă, feliat

1 ardei gras verde, tocat grosier

1 (sau două dacă vă plac lucrurile picante) chili poblano mic, prăjit uscat, feliat

6 catei de usturoi, taiati cubulete

1 lingura. seminte de anatto

1 cartof roșu mare, tăiat cuburi (puteți folosi doi dacă vă place supa groasă)

4 căni de bulion de legume

½ cană unt de arahide

1-1/4 lapte de migdale

Sare de mare

Piper negru

Garnitura optionala:

Ardei jalapeno felii

Topiți untul fără lapte într-o tigaie.

Adăugați ceapa roșie, prazul, ardeiul iute, ardeiul gras, usturoiul și cartofii.

Gatiti la foc mic si amestecati pana ce ceapa este translucida, 6 1/2 minute.

Adăugați bulionul și semințele de anatto în tigaie.

Se fierbe până când cartofii sunt fragezi la furculiță timp de aproximativ 25 de minute.

Luați-o de pe foc.

Procesați amestecul într-un blender până la omogenizare.

Întoarceți supa în tigaie.

În blender, amestecați untul de arahide cu laptele de migdale până la omogenizare

Adăugați la amestecul de supă.

Se încălzește supa la foc mediu pentru încă câteva minute.

Se ornează cu felii de jalapeno.

Supă de curry de linte și dovleac

Ingrediente

1 lingură ulei din semințe de susan

1 ceapa rosie mica, tocata

1 lingura radacina de ghimbir proaspat tocata

3 catei de usturoi, tocati

1 praf de seminte de schinduf

1 cană linte roșie uscată

1 cană de dovleac - curățați, fără semințe și tăiați cuburi

1/3 cana coriandru proaspat tocat marunt

2 căni de apă

1/2 (14 uncii) cutie de lapte de migdale

2 linguri pasta de rosii

1 lingurita pudra de curry rosu

1/4 piper cayenne

1 praf de nucsoara macinata

sare si piper dupa gust

Încinge uleiul într-o oală la foc mediu

Se caleste ceapa, usturoiul si schinduful pana cand ceapa devine frageda.

Adăugați lintea, dovleceii și coriandru în oală.

Adăugați apa, laptele de migdale și pasta de roșii.

Asezonați cu pudră de curry, piper cayenne, nucșoară, sare și piper.

Se fierbe si se reduce focul la mic

Se fierbe până când lintea și dovleceii sunt fragede. Timp de aproximativ 30 min.

Supă picantă de dovlecei

Ingrediente

1 lingura ulei de masline

1 ceapa rosie mica, tocata

3 catei de usturoi, tocati

1 lingura. suc de lămâie

1 cană linte roșie uscată

1 cană de dovleac - curățați, fără semințe și tăiați cuburi

1/3 cana coriandru proaspat tocat marunt

2 căni de apă

1/2 (14 uncii) cutie de lapte de migdale

2 linguri de semințe de anatto

1 lingurita chimen

1/4 piper cayenne

1 praf de nucsoara macinata

sare si piper dupa gust

Încinge uleiul într-o oală la foc mediu

Se caleste ceapa, usturoiul, semintele de annatto si chimenul pana cand ceapa devine frageda.

Adăugați lintea, dovleceii și coriandru în oală.

Adăugați apa, laptele de migdale și sucul de lămâie

Asezonați cu piper cayenne, nucșoară, sare și piper.

Se fierbe si se reduce focul la mic

Se fierbe până când lintea și dovleceii sunt fragede. Timp de aproximativ 30 min.

Supă de dovlecei thailandeză cu nuci

Ingrediente

1 lingură ulei din seminţe de susan

1 ceapa rosie mica, tocata

1 lingura radacina de ghimbir proaspat tocata

3 catei de usturoi, tocati

1 cană linte roşie uscată

1 cană de dovleac - curăţaţi, fără seminţe şi tăiaţi cuburi

1/3 cana coriandru proaspat tocat marunt

2 căni de apă

1/2 (14 uncii) cutie de lapte de cocos

1 lingurita pudra de curry rosu

1 lingura Ardei iute thailandez de păsări

1 praf de nucsoara macinata

sare si piper dupa gust

Încinge uleiul într-o oală la foc mediu

Se caleste ceapa, ghimbirul si usturoiul pana ce ceapa devine frageda.

Adăugați lintea, dovleceii și coriandru în oală.

Adăugați apa și laptele de cocos.

Asezonați cu pudră de curry, ardei iute thailandez, nucșoară, sare și piper.

Se fierbe si se reduce focul la mic

Se fierbe până când lintea și dovleceii sunt fragede. Timp de aproximativ 30 min.

Supă italiană de dovleac și linte

Ingrediente

1 lingura ulei de masline

1 ceapa rosie mica, tocata

3 catei de usturoi, tocati

1 praf de seminte de schinduf

1 cană linte roșie uscată

1 cană de dovleac - curățați, fără semințe și tăiați cuburi

1 cană apă

1 cană de supă de legume

2 linguri pasta de rosii

1 lingurita condimente italiene

1/4 lingurita. piper roșu

sare si piper dupa gust

Încinge uleiul într-o oală la foc mediu

Se caleste ceapa, usturoiul si schinduful pana cand ceapa devine frageda.

Adăugați lintea și dovleacul în oală.

Adăugați apa, supa de legume și pasta de roșii.

Asezonați cu condimente italiene, piper cayenne, sare și piper.

Se fierbe si se reduce focul la mic

Se fierbe până când lintea și dovleceii sunt fragede. Timp de aproximativ 30 min.

Supă simplă de morcovi

2 linguri ulei de masline extravirgin

1 ceapa rosie mica, tocata

1 morcov mic, decojit și tăiat felii subțiri

1 coastă de țelină, feliată subțire

1/2 linguriță tarhon uscat

2 cani de supa de legume

1/4 cană oțet de vin

Încinge uleiul la foc mediu-mare.

Se caleste ceapa rosie pana se inmoaie timp de aproximativ 5 minute.

Adăugați încet morcovii, țelina și tarhonul

Gatiti inca 5 minute sau pana cand morcovii devin fragezi.

Adăugați bulion de legume și oțet

Se fierbe și se fierbe.

Gatiti inca 15 minute.

Supă chinezească de păstârnac

2 linguri ulei din seminte de susan

1 ceapa rosie mica, tocata

1 pastarnac mic, curatat de coaja si feliat subtire

1 coastă de țelină, feliată subțire

1/2 linguriță praf de cinci condimente chinezești

2 căni de bulion de legume

1/4 cană vin de orez

Încinge uleiul la foc mediu-mare.

Se caleste ceapa rosie pana se inmoaie timp de aproximativ 5 minute.

Adăugați încet păstârnac, țelină și praf de cinci condimente

Gatiti inca 5 minute sau pana cand pastarnacul devine fraged.

Adăugați bulion de legume și vin de orez

Se fierbe și se fierbe.

Gatiti inca 15 minute.

Supă thailandeză de morcovi și ceapă roșie

2 linguri ulei din seminte de susan

1 ceapa rosie mica, tocata

1 morcov mic, decojit și tăiat felii subțiri

1/2 lingurita pasta de chili thailandez

2 cani de supa de legume

1/4 cană oțet de vin

1 crenguță de coriandru

Încinge uleiul la foc mediu-mare.

Se caleste ceapa rosie pana se inmoaie timp de aproximativ 5 minute.

Adăugați încet morcovii și pasta de chili

Gatiti inca 5 minute sau pana cand morcovii devin fragezi.

Adăugați supa de legume și oțetul

Se fierbe și se fierbe.

Gatiti inca 15 minute.

Se ornează cu coriandru

Supă de morcovi picant și picant

2 linguri ulei de masline extravirgin

1 ceapa rosie mica, tocata

1 morcov mic, decojit și tăiat felii subțiri

1 coastă de țelină, feliată subțire

1/2 lingurita chimen

½ lingurita piper cayenne

1 lingura seminte de anatto

1 lingura. suc de lămâie

2 cani de supa de legume

Încinge uleiul la foc mediu-mare.

Se caleste ceapa rosie pana se inmoaie timp de aproximativ 5 minute.

Adăugați încet morcovi, țelină, chimen, ardei cayenne, semințe de anatto și sucul de lime

Gatiti inca 5 minute sau pana cand morcovii devin fragezi.

Adăugați bulion de legume și oțet

Se fierbe și se fierbe.

Gatiti inca 15 minute.

Supă maghiară de ceapă roșie și morcovi

2 linguri ulei de masline extravirgin

1 ceapa rosie mica, tocata

1 morcov mic, decojit și tăiat felii subțiri

1 coastă de țelină, feliată subțire

5 catei de usturoi tocati marunt

1/2 lingurita boia maghiara

2 cani de supa de legume

1/4 cană oțet de vin

Încinge uleiul la foc mediu-mare.

Se caleste ceapa rosie pana se inmoaie timp de aproximativ 5 minute.

Adăugați încet morcovii, țelina, cățeii de usturoi și boia de ardei maghiară

Gatiti inca 5 minute sau pana cand morcovii devin fragezi.

Adăugați bulion de legume și oțet

Se fierbe și se fierbe.

Gatiti inca 15 minute.

Ciuperci Shitake la cuptor cu roșii cherry

Ingrediente

1 kilogram de napi, tăiați la jumătate

2 linguri ulei de masline extravirgin

1/2 kilogram de ciuperci shitake

8 catei de usturoi nedecojiti

3 linguri ulei de susan

sare de mare și piper negru măcinat după gust

1/4 kilogram de roșii cherry

3 linguri de nuci caju prajite

1/4 de kilogram de spanac, feliat subțire

Preîncălziți cuptorul la 425 de grade F.

Răspândiți cartofii într-o tigaie

Stropiți cu 2 linguri de ulei și prăjiți timp de 15 minute întorcându-l o dată.

Adăugați ciupercile cu tulpina în sus

Adăugați cățeii de usturoi în tigaie și gătiți până se rumenesc ușor

Stropiți cu 1 lingură ulei de susan și asezonați cu sare de mare și piper negru.

Reveniți la cuptor și coaceți timp de 5 minute.

Adăugați roșiile cherry în tigaie.

Reveniți la cuptor și coaceți până când ciupercile se înmoaie, timp de 5 minute.

Presărați nucile caju peste cartofi și ciuperci.

Serviți cu spanacul.

Păstârnac copt și ciuperci buton cu nuci de macadamia

Ingrediente

1 kg păstârnac, tăiat la jumătate

2 linguri ulei de masline extravirgin

1/2 kilogram de ciuperci

8 catei de usturoi nedecojiti

2 linguri de cimbru proaspăt tocat

1 lingura ulei de masline extravirgin

sare de mare și piper negru măcinat după gust

1/4 kilogram de roșii cherry

3 linguri nuci de macadamia prajite

1/4 de kilogram de spanac, feliat subțire

Preîncălziți cuptorul la 425 de grade F.

Răspândiți păstârnacul într-o tigaie

Stropiți cu 2 linguri de ulei de măsline și prăjiți timp de 15 minute întorcându-l o dată.

Adăugați ciupercile cu tulpina în sus

Adăugați cățeii de usturoi în tigaie și gătiți până se rumenesc ușor

Se presară cu cimbru.

Stropiți cu 1 lingură ulei de măsline și asezonați cu sare de mare și piper negru.

Reveniți la cuptor și coaceți timp de 5 minute.

Adăugați roșiile cherry în tigaie.

Reveniți la cuptor și coaceți până când ciupercile se înmoaie, timp de 5 minute.

Presarati nucile de macadamia peste cartofi si ciuperci.

Serviți cu spanacul.

Ciupercă la cuptor cu roșii cherry și nuci de pin

Ingrediente

1 kg de cartofi, tăiați la jumătate

2 linguri ulei de masline extravirgin

1/2 kilogram de ciuperci

8 catei de usturoi nedecojiti

2 lingurite chimion

1 lingura sămânță de anatto

½ linguriță. piper roșu

1 lingura ulei de masline extravirgin

sare de mare și piper negru măcinat după gust

1/4 kilogram de roșii cherry

3 linguri nuci de pin prajite

1/4 de kilogram de spanac, feliat subțire

Preîncălziți cuptorul la 425 de grade F.

Răspândiți cartofii într-o tigaie

Stropiți cu 2 linguri de ulei de măsline și prăjiți timp de 15 minute întorcându-l o dată.

Adăugați ciupercile cu tulpina în sus

Adăugați cățeii de usturoi în tigaie și gătiți până se rumenesc ușor

Stropiți cu chimen, piper cayenne și semințe de anatto.

Stropiți cu 1 lingură ulei de măsline și asezonați cu sare de mare și piper negru.

Reveniți la cuptor și coaceți timp de 5 minute.

Adăugați roșiile cherry în tigaie.

Reveniți la cuptor și coaceți până când ciupercile se înmoaie, timp de 5 minute.

Presarati nucile de pin peste cartofi si ciuperci.

Serviți cu spanacul.

Cartofi curry la cuptor

INGREDIENTE

1 ½ kg de cartofi, decojiți și tăiați în bucăți de 1 inch

½ ceapă, tăiată subțire

¼ cană apă

½ cub de supa de legume, maruntit

1 lingura. ulei de măsline extra virgin

½ linguriță chimen

½ linguriță coriandru măcinat

½ linguriță garam masala

½ linguriță pudră de chili fierbinte

Piper negru

½ kilogram de spanac proaspăt, tocat grosier

Pune toate ingredientele într-un aragaz lent, cu excepția ultimului.

Acoperiți cu pumni de spanac și umpleți aragazul cu el.

Dacă nu puteți încadra totul deodată, lăsați primul lot să se gătească mai întâi și adăugați mai mult spanac.

Gatiti 3 sau 4 ore la foc mediu pana cartofii devin moi.

Răzuiți părțile laterale și serviți.

Spanac și păstârnac la cuptor

INGREDIENTE

1 ½ kg păstârnac, decojit și tăiat în bucăți de 1 inch

½ ceapă roșie, feliată subțire

¼ cană apă

½ cub de supa de legume, maruntit

1 lingura. ulei de măsline extra virgin

½ linguriță chimen

½ linguriță de semințe de anatto

½ linguriță piper cayenne

½ linguriță pudră de chili fierbinte

Piper negru

½ kilogram de spanac proaspăt, tocat grosier

Pune toate ingredientele într-un aragaz lent, cu excepția ultimului.

Acoperiți cu pumni de spanac și umpleți aragazul cu el.

Dacă nu puteți încadra totul deodată, lăsați primul lot să se gătească mai întâi și adăugați mai mult spanac.

Gatiti 3 sau 4 ore la foc mediu pana cartofii devin moi.

Răzuiți părțile laterale și serviți.

Kale prăjită și cartofi dulci

INGREDIENTE

1 ½ kg de cartofi dulci, curățați și tăiați în bucăți de 1 inch

½ ceapă, tăiată subțire

¼ cană apă

½ cub de supa de legume, maruntit

1 lingura. ulei de măsline extra virgin

½ linguriță chimen

½ linguriță de ardei jalapeno, tocați

½ lingurita boia

½ linguriță pudră de chili fierbinte

Piper negru

½ kg de kale proaspătă, tocată grosier

Pune toate ingredientele într-un aragaz lent, cu excepția ultimului.

Acoperiți cu pumni de kale și umpleți aragazul cu ea.

Dacă nu puteți încadra totul dintr-o dată, lăsați primul lot să se gătească mai întâi și adăugați mai multă kale.

Gatiti 3 sau 4 ore la foc mediu pana cartofii devin moi.

Răzuiți părțile laterale și serviți.

Nasturel și morcovi la cuptor în stil Sichuan

INGREDIENTE

1 ½ kg de morcovi, decojiți și tăiați în bucăți de 1 inch

½ ceapă roșie, feliată subțire

¼ cană apă

½ cub de supa de legume, maruntit

1 lingura. ulei de susan

½ linguriță pudră chinezească cu 5 condimente

½ linguriță boabe de piper Sichuan

½ linguriță pudră de chili fierbinte

Piper negru

½ kg de nasturel proaspăt, tocat grosier

Pune toate ingredientele într-un aragaz lent, cu excepția ultimului.

Acoperiți cu pumni de nasturel și umpleți aragazul cu el.

Dacă nu puteți încadra totul dintr-o dată, lăsați primul lot să se gătească mai întâi și adăugați încă niște nasturel.

Gatiti 3 sau 4 ore la foc mediu pana morcovii devin moale.

Răzuiți părțile laterale și serviți.

Napi și ceapă picante și picante

INGREDIENTE

1 ½ kg de napi, decojiți și tăiați în bucăți de 1 inch

½ ceapă, tăiată subțire

¼ cană apă

½ cub de supa de legume, maruntit

1 lingura. ulei de măsline extra virgin

½ linguriță chimen

½ linguriță de semințe de anatto

½ linguriță piper cayenne

½ linguriță suc de lămâie

Piper negru

½ kilogram de spanac proaspăt, tocat grosier

Pune toate ingredientele într-un aragaz lent, cu excepția ultimului.

Acoperiți cu pumni de spanac și umpleți aragazul cu el.

Dacă nu puteți încadra totul deodată, lăsați primul lot să se gătească mai întâi și adăugați mai mult spanac.

Gatiti 3 sau 4 ore la foc mediu pana cand legumele radacinoase devin moi.

Răzuiți părțile laterale și serviți.

Morcovi cu Curry

INGREDIENTE

1 ½ kilograme de morcovi, curățați și tăiați în bucăți de 1 inch

½ ceapă, tăiată subțire

¼ cană apă

½ cub de supa de legume, maruntit

1 lingura. ulei de măsline extra virgin

½ linguriță chimen

½ linguriță coriandru măcinat

½ linguriță garam masala

½ linguriță pudră de chili fierbinte

Piper negru

½ kg de kale proaspătă, tocată grosier

Pune toate ingredientele într-un aragaz lent, cu excepția ultimului.

Acoperiți cu pumni de kale și umpleți aragazul cu ea.

Dacă nu puteți încadra totul dintr-o dată, lăsați primul lot să se gătească mai întâi și adăugați mai multă kale.

Gatiti 3 sau 4 ore la foc mediu pana cand legumele radacinoase devin moi.

Răzuiți părțile laterale și serviți.

Spanac și ceapă prăjite picant

INGREDIENTE

1 ½ kg de morcovi, decojiți și tăiați în bucăți de 1 inch

½ ceapă, tăiată subțire

¼ cană apă

½ cub de supa de legume, maruntit

1 lingura. ulei de măsline extra virgin

½ linguriță chimen

½ linguriță de semințe de anatto

½ linguriță piper cayenne

½ linguriță suc de lămâie

Piper negru

½ kilogram de spanac proaspăt, tocat grosier

Pune toate ingredientele într-un aragaz lent, cu excepția ultimului.

Acoperiți cu pumni de spanac și umpleți aragazul cu el.

Dacă nu puteți încadra totul deodată, lăsați primul lot să se gătească mai întâi și adăugați mai mult spanac.

Gatiti 3 sau 4 ore la foc mediu pana cand legumele radacinoase devin moi.

Răzuiți părțile laterale și serviți.

Cartofi dulci prăjiți și spanac

INGREDIENTE

1 ½ kg de cartofi dulci, decojiți și tăiați în bucăți de 1 inch

½ ceapă, tăiată subțire

¼ cană apă

½ cub de supa de legume, maruntit

2 linguri. unt vegan sau margarina

½ lingurita ierburi de Provence

½ linguriță de cimbru

½ linguriță pudră de chili fierbinte

Piper negru

½ kilogram de spanac proaspăt, tocat grosier

Pune toate ingredientele într-un aragaz lent, cu excepția ultimului.

Acoperiți cu pumni de spanac și umpleți aragazul cu el.

Dacă nu puteți încadra totul deodată, lăsați primul lot să se gătească mai întâi și adăugați mai mult spanac.

Gatiti 3 sau 4 ore la foc mediu pana cartofii devin moi.

Răzuiți părțile laterale și serviți.

Napi prăjiți, ceapă și spanac

INGREDIENTE

1 ½ kg de napi, decojiți și tăiați în bucăți de 1 inch

½ ceapă, tăiată subțire

¼ cană apă

½ cub de supa de legume, maruntit

1 lingura. ulei de măsline extra virgin

2 lingurite usturoi, tocat

½ linguriță suc de lămâie

½ linguriță pudră de chili fierbinte

Piper negru

½ kilogram de spanac proaspăt, tocat grosier

Pune toate ingredientele într-un aragaz lent, cu excepția ultimului.

Acoperiți cu pumni de spanac și umpleți aragazul cu el.

Dacă nu puteți încadra totul deodată, lăsați primul lot să se gătească mai întâi și adăugați mai mult spanac.

Gatiti 3 sau 4 ore la foc mediu pana cand napii devin moi.

Răzuiți părțile laterale și serviți.

Nasturel cu unt vegan prajit si morcovi

INGREDIENTE

1 ½ kg de morcovi, decojiți și tăiați în bucăți de 1 inch

½ ceapă, tăiată subțire

¼ cană apă

½ cub de supa de legume, maruntit

1 lingura. unt/margarină vegan

1 lingurita usturoi, tocat

½ linguriță suc de lămâie

Piper negru

½ kg de nasturel proaspăt, tocat grosier

Pune toate ingredientele într-un aragaz lent, cu excepția ultimului.

Acoperiți cu pumni de nasturel și umpleți aragazul cu el.

Dacă nu puteți încadra totul dintr-o dată, lăsați primul lot să se gătească mai întâi și adăugați încă niște nasturel.

Gatiti 3 sau 4 ore la foc mediu pana morcovii devin moale.

Răzuiți părțile laterale și serviți.

Broccoli și spanac la cuptor

INGREDIENTE

1 ½ kilograme buchețele de broccoli

½ ceapă, tăiată subțire

¼ cană apă

½ cub de supa de legume, maruntit

1 lingura. ulei de măsline extra virgin

½ linguriță chimen

½ linguriță pudră de chili fierbinte

Piper negru

½ kilogram de spanac proaspăt, tocat grosier

Pune toate ingredientele într-un aragaz lent, cu excepția ultimului.

Acoperiți cu pumni de spanac și umpleți aragazul cu el.

Dacă nu puteți încadra totul deodată, lăsați primul lot să se gătească mai întâi și adăugați mai mult spanac.

Gatiti 3 sau 4 ore la foc mediu pana cand broccoli devine moale.

Răzuiți părțile laterale și serviți.

Conopidă și ceapă prăjite cu fum

INGREDIENTE

1 ½ kg de conopidă, decojită și tăiată în bucăți de 1 inch

½ ceapă roșie, feliată subțire

¼ cană apă

½ cub de supa de legume, maruntit

1 lingura. ulei de măsline extra virgin

½ linguriță chimen

½ linguriță pudră de chili fierbinte

Piper negru

½ kilogram de spanac proaspăt, tocat grosier

Pune toate ingredientele într-un aragaz lent, cu excepția ultimului.

Acoperiți cu pumni de spanac și umpleți aragazul cu el.

Dacă nu puteți încadra totul deodată, lăsați primul lot să se gătească mai întâi și adăugați mai mult spanac.

Gatiti 3 sau 4 ore la foc mediu pana cartofii devin moi.

Răzuiți părțile laterale și serviți.

Sfeclă italiană prăjită și varză

INGREDIENTE

1 ½ kilograme de sfeclă, decojită și tăiată în bucăți de 1 inch

½ ceapă roșie, feliată subțire

¼ cană apă

½ cub de supa de legume, maruntit

1 lingura. ulei de măsline extra virgin

½ linguriță de condimente italiene

Piper negru

½ kg de kale proaspătă, tocată grosier

Pune toate ingredientele într-un aragaz lent, cu excepția ultimului.

Acoperiți cu pumni de kale și umpleți aragazul cu ea.

Dacă nu puteți încadra totul dintr-o dată, lăsați primul lot să se gătească mai întâi și adăugați mai multă kale.

Gatiti 3 sau 4 ore la foc mediu pana cand sfecla devine moale.

Răzuiți părțile laterale și serviți.

Nasturel prajit si cartofi

INGREDIENTE

1 ½ kg de cartofi, decojiți și tăiați în bucăți de 1 inch

½ ceapă, tăiată subțire

¼ cană apă

½ cub de supa de legume, maruntit

1 lingura. ulei de masline

½ linguriță de ghimbir tocat

2 crengute de iarba de lamaie

½ lingurita ceapa verde, tocata

½ linguriță pudră de chili fierbinte

Piper negru

½ kg de nasturel, tocat grosier

Pune toate ingredientele într-un aragaz lent, cu excepția ultimului.

Acoperiți cu pumni de nasturel și umpleți aragazul cu el.

Dacă nu puteți încadra totul dintr-o dată, lăsați primul lot să se gătească mai întâi și adăugați încă niște nasturel.

Gatiti 3 sau 4 ore la foc mediu pana cartofii devin moi.

Răzuiți părțile laterale și serviți.

Spanac prăjit cu măsline

INGREDIENTE

1 ½ kg de cartofi, decojiți și tăiați în bucăți de 1 inch

½ măsline verzi, feliate subțiri

¼ cană apă

½ cub de supa de legume, maruntit

1 lingura. ulei de măsline extra virgin

½ linguriță chimen

½ linguriță pudră de chili fierbinte

Piper negru

½ kilogram de spanac proaspăt, tocat grosier

Pune toate ingredientele într-un aragaz lent, cu excepția ultimului.

Acoperiți cu pumni de spanac și umpleți aragazul cu el.

Dacă nu puteți încadra totul deodată, lăsați primul lot să se gătească mai întâi și adăugați mai mult spanac.

Gatiti 3 sau 4 ore la foc mediu pana cartofii devin moi.

Răzuiți părțile laterale și serviți.

Spanac prăjit cu ardei Jalapeno

INGREDIENTE

1 ½ kilograme buchețele de broccoli

½ ceapă, tăiată subțire

¼ cană apă

½ cub de supa de legume, maruntit

1 lingura. ulei de măsline extra virgin

½ linguriță chimen

8 ardei jalapeno, tocați mărunt

1 chili ancho

½ linguriță pudră de chili fierbinte

Piper negru

½ kilogram de spanac proaspăt, tocat grosier

Pune toate ingredientele într-un aragaz lent, cu excepția ultimului.

Acoperiți cu pumni de spanac și umpleți aragazul cu el.

Dacă nu puteți încadra totul deodată, lăsați primul lot să se gătească mai întâi și adăugați mai mult spanac.

Gatiti 3 sau 4 ore la foc mediu pana cand broccoli devine moale.

Răzuiți părțile laterale și serviți.

Spanac curry prăjit

INGREDIENTE

1 ½ kg de cartofi, decojiți și tăiați în bucăți de 1 inch

½ ceapă, tăiată subțire

¼ cană apă

½ cub de supa de legume, maruntit

1 lingura. ulei de măsline extra virgin

½ linguriță chimen

½ linguriță coriandru măcinat

½ linguriță garam masala

½ linguriță pudră de chili fierbinte

Piper negru

½ kilogram de spanac proaspăt, tocat grosier

Pune toate ingredientele într-un aragaz lent, cu excepția ultimului.

Acoperiți cu pumni de spanac și umpleți aragazul cu el.

Dacă nu puteți încadra totul deodată, lăsați primul lot să se gătească mai întâi și adăugați mai mult spanac.

Gatiti 3 sau 4 ore la foc mediu pana cartofii devin moi.

Răzuiți părțile laterale și serviți.

Varza de fasole thailandeză picantă la cuptor

INGREDIENTE

1 ½ kilograme buchețele de conopidă, albite (muiate în apă clocotită apoi scufundate în apă cu gheață)

½ cană muguri de fasole, clătiți

½ cană apă

½ cub de supa de legume, maruntit

1 lingura. ulei de susan

½ linguriță pasta de chili thailandez

½ linguriță sos Sriracha iute

½ linguriță pudră de chili fierbinte

2 ardei iute thailandez de pasăre, tocați

Piper negru

½ kilogram de spanac proaspăt, tocat grosier

Pune toate ingredientele într-un aragaz lent, cu excepția ultimului.

Acoperiți cu pumni de spanac și umpleți aragazul cu el.

Dacă nu puteți încadra totul deodată, lăsați primul lot să se gătească mai întâi și adăugați mai mult spanac.

Gatiti 3 sau 4 ore la foc mediu pana cartofii devin moi.

Răzuiți părțile laterale și serviți.

Spanac si napi picant de Sichuan

INGREDIENTE

1 ½ kg de napi, decojiți și tăiați în bucăți de 1 inch

½ ceapă, tăiată subțire

¼ cană apă

½ cub de supa de legume, maruntit

1 lingura. ulei de susan

½ linguriță pasta de usturoi chili

½ linguriță boabe de piper Sichuan

1 anason stelat

2 ardei iute thailandez de pasăre, tocați

Piper negru

½ kilogram de spanac proaspăt, tocat grosier

Pune toate ingredientele într-un aragaz lent, cu excepția ultimului.

Acoperiți cu pumni de spanac și umpleți aragazul cu el.

Dacă nu puteți încadra totul deodată, lăsați primul lot să se gătească mai întâi și adăugați mai mult spanac.

Gatiti 3 sau 4 ore la foc mediu pana cand napii devin moi.

Răzuiți părțile laterale și serviți.

Nasturel thailandez Morcovi si ceapa

INGREDIENTE

1 ½ kg de morcovi, decojiți și tăiați în bucăți de 1 inch

½ ceapă, tăiată subțire

¼ cană apă

½ cub de supa de legume, maruntit

1 lingura. ulei de măsline extra virgin

1 lingura. ulei de susan

½ linguriță pasta de chili thailandez

½ linguriță sos Sriracha iute

½ linguriță pudră de chili fierbinte

2 ardei iute thailandez de pasăre, tocați

Piper negru

½ kg de nasturel, tocat grosier

Pune toate ingredientele într-un aragaz lent, cu excepția ultimului.

Acoperiți cu pumni de nasturel și umpleți aragazul cu el.

Dacă nu puteți încadra totul dintr-o dată, lăsați primul lot să se gătească mai întâi și adăugați încă niște nasturel.

Gatiti 3 sau 4 ore la foc mediu pana morcovii devin moale.

Răzuiți părțile laterale și serviți.

Yam prăjit și cartofi dulci

INGREDIENTE

½ kilogram igname violet, decojit și tăiat în bucăți de 1 inch

1 kilogram de cartofi dulci, decojiți și tăiați în bucăți de 1 inch

½ ceapă, tăiată subțire

¼ cană apă

½ cub de supa de legume, maruntit

1 lingura. ulei de măsline extra virgin

Piper negru

½ kilogram de spanac proaspăt, tocat grosier

Pune toate ingredientele într-un aragaz lent, cu excepția ultimului.

Acoperiți cu pumni de spanac și umpleți aragazul cu el.

Dacă nu puteți încadra totul deodată, lăsați primul lot să se gătească mai întâi și adăugați mai mult spanac.

Gatiti 3 sau 4 ore la foc mediu pana cartofii devin moi.

Răzuiți părțile laterale și serviți.

Yam alb la cuptor și cartofi

INGREDIENTE

½ kg de cartofi, curățați și tăiați în bucăți de 1 inch

½ kg igname albă, decojită și tăiată în bucăți de 1 inch

½ kg de morcovi, decojiți și tăiați în bucăți de 1 inch

½ ceapă roșie, feliată subțire

¼ cană apă

½ cub de supa de legume, maruntit

1 lingura. ulei de măsline extra virgin

½ linguriță chimen

½ linguriță coriandru măcinat

½ linguriță garam masala

½ linguriță piper cayenne

Piper negru

½ kilogram de spanac proaspăt, tocat grosier

Pune toate ingredientele într-un aragaz lent, cu excepția ultimului.

Acoperiți cu pumni de spanac și umpleți aragazul cu el.

Dacă nu puteți încadra totul deodată, lăsați primul lot să se gătească mai întâi și adăugați mai mult spanac.

Gatiti 3 sau 4 ore la foc mediu pana cartofii devin moi.

Răzuiți părțile laterale și serviți.

Păstârnac și Napi maghiari

INGREDIENTE

½ kg de napi, curățați și tăiați în bucăți de 1 inch

½ kilogram de morcovi, curățați și tăiați în bucăți de 1 inch

½ kg păstârnac, decojit și tăiat în bucăți de 1 inch

½ ceapă roșie, feliată subțire

¼ cană apă

½ cub de supa de legume, maruntit

1 lingura. ulei de măsline extra virgin

½ linguriță de boia praf

½ linguriță. pudra de chili

Piper negru

½ kilogram de spanac proaspăt, tocat grosier

Pune toate ingredientele într-un aragaz lent, cu excepția ultimului.

Acoperiți cu pumni de spanac și umpleți aragazul cu el.

Dacă nu puteți încadra totul deodată, lăsați primul lot să se gătească mai întâi și adăugați mai mult spanac.

Gatiti 3 sau 4 ore la foc mediu pana cand napii devin moi.

Răzuiți părțile laterale și serviți.

Spanac simplu la cuptor

INGREDIENTE

1 ½ kg de broccoli, decojit și tăiat în bucăți de 1 inch

½ ceapă roșie, feliată subțire

¼ cană bulion de legume

1 lingura. ulei de măsline extra virgin

½ linguriță de condimente italiene

½ linguriță pudră de chili fierbinte

Piper negru

½ kilogram de spanac proaspăt, tocat grosier

Pune toate ingredientele într-un aragaz lent, cu excepția ultimului.

Acoperiți cu pumni de spanac și umpleți aragazul cu el.

Dacă nu puteți încadra totul deodată, lăsați primul lot să se gătească mai întâi și adăugați mai mult spanac.

Gatiti 3 sau 4 ore la foc mediu pana cand broccoli devine moale.

Răzuiți părțile laterale și serviți.

Spanac și morcovi la cuptor din Asia de Sud-Est

INGREDIENTE

½ kg de napi, curățați și tăiați în bucăți de 1 inch

½ kilogram de morcovi, curățați și tăiați în bucăți de 1 inch

½ kg păstârnac, decojit și tăiat în bucăți de 1 inch

½ ceapă roșie, feliată subțire

½ cană bulion de legume

1 lingura. ulei de măsline extra virgin

½ linguriță de ghimbir tocat

2 tulpini de iarba de lamaie

8 catei de usturoi, tocati

Piper negru

½ kilogram de spanac proaspăt, tocat grosier

Pune toate ingredientele într-un aragaz lent, cu excepția ultimului.

Acoperiți cu pumni de spanac și umpleți aragazul cu el.

Dacă nu puteți încadra totul deodată, lăsați primul lot să se gătească mai întâi și adăugați mai mult spanac.

Gatiti 3 sau 4 ore la foc mediu pana cand napii devin moi.

Răzuiți părțile laterale și serviți.

Kale prăjită și varză de Bruxelles

INGREDIENTE

1 ½ kilograme de varză de Bruxelles, decojite și tăiate în bucăți de 1 inch

½ ceapă roșie, feliată subțire

¼ cană apă

½ cub de supa de legume, maruntit

1 lingura. ulei de măsline extra virgin

½ linguriță pudră de chili fierbinte

Piper negru

½ kilogram de varza kale, tocata grosier

Pune toate ingredientele într-un aragaz lent, cu excepția ultimului.

Acoperiți cu pumni de kale și umpleți aragazul cu ea.

Dacă nu puteți încadra totul dintr-o dată, lăsați primul lot să se gătească mai întâi și adăugați mai multă kale.

Gatiti 3 ore la foc mediu pana cand varza de Bruxelles devine moale.

Răzuiți părțile laterale și serviți.

Spanac cu curry și cartofi

INGREDIENTE

1 ½ kg de cartofi, decojiți și tăiați în bucăți de 1 inch

½ ceapă, tăiată subțire

¼ cană apă

½ cub de supa de legume, maruntit

1 lingura. ulei de măsline extra virgin

½ linguriță chimen

½ linguriță coriandru măcinat

½ linguriță garam masala

½ linguriță pudră de chili fierbinte

Piper negru

½ kilogram de spanac proaspăt, tocat grosier

Pune toate ingredientele într-un aragaz lent, cu excepția ultimului.

Acoperiți cu pumni de spanac și umpleți aragazul cu el.

Dacă nu puteți încadra totul deodată, lăsați primul lot să se gătească mai întâi și adăugați mai mult spanac.

Gatiti 3 sau 4 ore la foc mediu pana cartofii devin moi.

Răzuiți părțile laterale și serviți.

Cartofi dulci cu curry și varză

INGREDIENTE

1 ½ kg de cartofi dulci, decojiți și tăiați în bucăți de 1 inch

½ ceapă, tăiată subțire

¼ cană apă

½ cub de supa de legume, maruntit

1 lingura. ulei de măsline extra virgin

½ linguriță chimen

½ linguriță coriandru măcinat

½ linguriță garam masala

½ linguriță pudră de chili fierbinte

Piper negru

½ kilogram de varza kale, tocata grosier

Pune toate ingredientele într-un aragaz lent, cu excepția ultimului.

Acoperiți cu pumni de kale și umpleți aragazul cu ea.

Dacă nu puteți încadra totul dintr-o dată, lăsați primul lot să se gătească mai întâi și adăugați mai multă kale.

Gatiti 3 sau 4 ore la foc mediu pana cartofii dulci devin moale.

Răzuiți părțile laterale și serviți.

Jalapeno Nasturel și păstârnac

INGREDIENTE

1 ½ kg păstârnac, decojit și tăiat în bucăți de 1 inch

½ ceapă roșie, feliată subțire

¼ cană apă

½ cub de supa de legume, maruntit

1 lingura. ulei de măsline extra virgin

½ linguriță chimen

½ linguriță piper jalapeno, tocat

1 chili ancho, tocat

Piper negru

½ kg de nasturel, tocat grosier

Pune toate ingredientele într-un aragaz lent, cu excepția ultimului.

Acoperiți cu pumni de spanac și umpleți aragazul cu el.

Dacă nu puteți încadra totul deodată, lăsați primul lot să se gătească mai întâi și adăugați mai mult spanac.

Gatiti 3 sau 4 ore la foc mediu pana pastarnacul devine moale.

Răzuiți părțile laterale și serviți.

Nasturel si broccoli in sos de usturoi chili

INGREDIENTE

1 ½ kg de morcovi, decojiți și tăiați în bucăți de 1 inch

½ kilogram de broccoli, decojit și tăiat în bucăți de 1 inch

½ ceapă, tăiată subțire

¼ cană apă

½ cub de supa de legume, maruntit

1 lingura. ulei de susan

½ linguriță sos de usturoi chili

½ linguriță. suc de lămâie

½ linguriță. ceapa verde tocata

Piper negru

½ kg de nasturel, tocat grosier

Pune toate ingredientele într-un aragaz lent, cu excepția ultimului.

Acoperiți cu pumni de nasturel și umpleți aragazul cu el.

Dacă nu puteți încadra totul dintr-o dată, lăsați primul lot să se gătească mai întâi și adăugați încă niște nasturel.

Gatiti 3 sau 4 ore la foc mediu pana morcovii devin moale.

Răzuiți părțile laterale și serviți.

Bok Choy picant și broccoli

INGREDIENTE

1 kilogram de broccoli, decojit și tăiat în bucăți de 1 inch

Ciuperci buton de ½ kilogram, feliate

½ ceapă, tăiată subțire

¼ cană apă

½ cub de supa de legume, maruntit

1 lingura. ulei de susan

½ linguriță praf de cinci condimente chinezești

½ linguriță boabe de piper Sichuan

½ linguriță pudră de chili fierbinte

Piper negru

½ kilogram bok choy, tocat grosier

Pune toate ingredientele într-un aragaz lent, cu excepția ultimului.

Acoperiți cu pumni de bok choy și umpleți aragazul lent cu el.

Dacă nu puteți încadra totul dintr-o dată, lăsați primul lot să se gătească mai întâi și adăugați mai mult bok choy.

Gatiti 3 sau 4 ore la foc mediu pana cand broccoli devine moale.

Răzuiți părțile laterale și serviți.

Spanac și ciuperci Shitake

INGREDIENTE

1 ½ kg de conopidă, decojită și tăiată în bucăți de 1 inch

½ kilogram de ciuperci shitake, feliate

½ ceapă roșie, feliată subțire

¼ cană bulion de legume

2 linguri. ulei din semințe de susan

½ linguriță oțet

½ linguriță de usturoi, tocat

Piper negru

½ kilogram de spanac proaspăt, tocat grosier

Pune toate ingredientele într-un aragaz lent, cu excepția ultimului.

Acoperiți cu pumni de spanac și umpleți aragazul cu el.

Dacă nu puteți încadra totul deodată, lăsați primul lot să se gătească mai întâi și adăugați mai mult spanac.

Gatiti 3 sau 4 ore la foc mediu pana conopida devine moale.

Răzuiți părțile laterale și serviți.

Spanac și cartofi în sos pesto

INGREDIENTE

1 ½ kg de cartofi, decojiți și tăiați în bucăți de 1 inch

½ ceapă, tăiată subțire

¼ cană bulion de legume

1 lingura. ulei de măsline extra virgin

2 linguri. sos pesto

Piper negru

½ kilogram de spanac proaspăt, tocat grosier

Pune toate ingredientele într-un aragaz lent, cu excepția ultimului.

Acoperiți cu pumni de spanac și umpleți aragazul cu el.

Dacă nu puteți încadra totul deodată, lăsați primul lot să se gătească mai întâi și adăugați mai mult spanac.

Gatiti 3 sau 4 ore la foc mediu pana cartofii devin moi.

Răzuiți părțile laterale și serviți.

Cartofi dulci cu curry și gură verde

INGREDIENTE

1 ½ kg de cartofi dulci, decojiți și tăiați în bucăți de 1 inch

½ ceapă, tăiată subțire

¼ cană bulion de legume

1 lingura. ulei de măsline extra virgin

2 linguri. pudră de curry roșu

Piper negru

½ kilogram de verdeață proaspătă, tocată grosier

Pune toate ingredientele într-un aragaz lent, cu excepția ultimului.

Acoperiți cu pumni de verdeață și umpleți aragazul cu ea.

Dacă nu puteți încadra totul dintr-o dată, lăsați primul lot să se gătească mai întâi și adăugați mai multe verdeață.

Gatiti 3 sau 4 ore la foc mediu pana cartofii dulci devin moale.

Răzuiți părțile laterale și serviți.

Napi și napi în sos pesto

INGREDIENTE

1 ½ kg de napi, curățați și tăiați în bucăți de 1 inch

½ ceapă, tăiată subțire

¼ cană bulion de legume

1 lingura. ulei de măsline extra virgin

2 linguri. sos pesto

Piper negru

½ kilogram de verdeață de nap proaspătă, tocată grosier

Pune toate ingredientele într-un aragaz lent, cu excepția ultimului.

Acoperiți cu pumni de Napi și umpleți aragazul cu ea.

Dacă nu puteți încadra totul dintr-o dată, lăsați primul lot să se gătească mai întâi și adăugați mai multe verdeață de napi.

Gatiti 3 sau 4 ore la foc mediu pana cand napii devin moi.

Răzuiți părțile laterale și serviți.

Chard și morcovi în sos pesto

INGREDIENTE

1 ½ kg de morcovi, decojiți și tăiați în bucăți de 1 inch

½ ceapă roșie, feliată subțire

¼ cană bulion de legume

2 linguri. ulei de măsline extra virgin

3 linguri. sos pesto

Piper negru

½ kilogram de smog proaspăt, tocat grosier

Pune toate ingredientele într-un aragaz lent, cu excepția ultimului.

Acoperiți cu pumni de smog și umpleți oara lentă cu ea.

Dacă nu puteți încadra totul dintr-o dată, lăsați primul lot să se gătească mai întâi și adăugați mai multă smog.

Gatiti 3 sau 4 ore la foc mediu pana morcovii devin moale.

Răzuiți părțile laterale și serviți.

Bok Choy și morcovi în sos de usturoi chili

INGREDIENTE

1 ½ kg de morcovi, decojiți și tăiați în bucăți de 1 inch

½ ceapă, tăiată subțire

¼ cană bulion de legume

1 lingura. ulei de susan

4 catei de usturoi, tocati

2 linguri. sos de usturoi chili

Piper negru

½ kilogram de bok choy proaspăt, tocat grosier

Pune toate ingredientele într-un aragaz lent, cu excepția ultimului.

Acoperiți cu pumni de Bok Choy și umpleți oara lentă cu el.

Dacă nu puteți încadra totul dintr-o dată, lăsați primul lot să se gătească mai întâi și adăugați mai mult Bok Choy.

Gatiti 3 sau 4 ore la foc mediu pana morcovii devin moale.

Răzuiți părțile laterale și serviți.

Napi şi păstârnac fierte încet

INGREDIENTE

1 ½ kg păstârnac, decojit şi tăiat în bucăţi de 1 inch

½ ceapă, tăiată subţire

¼ cană bulion de legume

1 lingura. ulei de măsline extra virgin

Piper negru

½ kilogram de verdeaţă de nap proaspătă, tocată grosier

Pune toate ingredientele într-un aragaz lent, cu excepţia ultimului.

Acoperiţi cu pumni de spanac şi umpleţi aragazul cu el.

Dacă nu puteţi încadra totul deodată, lăsaţi primul lot să se gătească mai întâi şi adăugaţi mai mult spanac.

Gatiti 3 sau 4 ore la foc mediu pana cartofii devin moi.

Răzuiţi părţile laterale şi serviţi.

Kale fiert lent și broccoli

INGREDIENTE

1 ½ kilograme buchețele de broccoli

½ ceapă, tăiată subțire

¼ cană bulion de legume

1 lingura. ulei de măsline extra virgin

2 linguri. sos pesto

Piper negru

½ kilogram de varza varza proaspata, tocata grosier

Pune toate ingredientele într-un aragaz lent, cu excepția ultimului.

Acoperiți cu pumni de kale și umpleți aragazul cu ea.

Dacă nu puteți încadra totul dintr-o dată, lăsați primul lot să se gătească mai întâi și adăugați mai multă kale.

Gatiti 3 sau 4 ore la foc mediu pana cand buchetele de broccoli devin moi.

Răzuiți părțile laterale și serviți.

Andive și morcovi fierte încet în sos pesto

INGREDIENTE

1 ½ kg de morcovi, decojiți și tăiați în bucăți de 1 inch

½ ceapă, tăiată subțire

¼ cană bulion de legume

1 lingura. ulei de măsline extra virgin

2 linguri. sos pesto

Piper negru

½ kilogram de andive proaspete, tocate grosier

Pune toate ingredientele într-un aragaz lent, cu excepția ultimului.

Acoperiți cu pumni de andive și umpleți slow cooker cu ea.

Dacă nu puteți încadra totul dintr-o dată, lăsați primul lot să se gătească mai întâi și adăugați încă niște andive.

Gatiti 3 sau 4 ore la foc mediu pana morcovii devin moale.

Răzuiți părțile laterale și serviți.

Salată Romaine și varză de Bruxelles fierte lent

INGREDIENTE

1 ½ kilograme de varza de Bruxelles

½ ceapă, tăiată subțire

¼ cană bulion de legume

1 lingura. ulei de măsline extra virgin

Piper negru

½ kilogram de salată verde proaspătă, tocată grosier

Pune toate ingredientele într-un aragaz lent, cu excepția ultimului.

Acoperiți cu pumni de salată verde și umpleți aragazul cu ea.

Dacă nu puteți încadra totul dintr-o dată, lăsați primul lot să se gătească mai întâi și adăugați încă puțină salată romană.

Gatiti 3 ore la foc mediu pana cand varza de Bruxelles devine moale.

Răzuiți părțile laterale și serviți.

Andive și cartofi fierte lent

INGREDIENTE

1 ½ kg de cartofi, decojiți și tăiați în bucăți de 1 inch

½ ceapă, tăiată subțire

¼ cană bulion de legume

1 lingura. ulei de măsline extra virgin

1 lingura condimente italienesti

Piper negru

½ kilogram de andive proaspete, tocate grosier

Pune toate ingredientele într-un aragaz lent, cu excepția ultimului.

Acoperiți cu pumni de spanac și umpleți aragazul cu el.

Dacă nu puteți încadra totul deodată, lăsați primul lot să se gătească mai întâi și adăugați mai mult spanac.

Gatiti 3 sau 4 ore la foc mediu pana cartofii devin moi.

Răzuiți părțile laterale și serviți.

Napi fierți lent și napi în unt vegan

INGREDIENTE

1 ½ kg de napi, decojiți și tăiați în bucăți de 1 inch

½ ceapă, tăiată subțire

¼ cană bulion de legume

4 linguri. unt vegan sau margarina

2 linguri. suc de lămâie

3 catei de usturoi, tocati

Piper negru

½ kilogram de verdeață de nap proaspătă, tocată grosier

Pune toate ingredientele într-un aragaz lent, cu excepția ultimului.

Acoperiți cu pumni de verdeață de napi și umpleți oara lentă cu ea.

Dacă nu puteți încadra totul deodată, lăsați primul lot să se gătească mai întâi și adăugați mai multe verdeață de napi.

Gatiti 3 sau 4 ore la foc mediu pana cand napii devin moi.

Răzuiți părțile laterale și serviți.

Varză gătită lent și păstârnac în unt vegan

INGREDIENTE

1 ½ kg păstârnac, decojit și tăiat în bucăți de 1 inch

½ ceapă, tăiată subțire

¼ cană bulion de legume

4 linguri. unt vegan topit

2 linguri. suc de lămâie

Piper negru

½ kilogram de varza varza proaspata, tocata grosier

Pune toate ingredientele într-un aragaz lent, cu excepția ultimului.

Acoperiți cu pumni de kale și umpleți aragazul cu ea.

Dacă nu puteți încadra totul dintr-o dată, lăsați primul lot să se gătească mai întâi și adăugați mai multă kale.

Gatiti 3 sau 4 ore la foc mediu pana pastarnacul devine moale.

Răzuiți părțile laterale și serviți.

Spanac și morcovi în stil chinezesc fiert lent

INGREDIENTE

1 ½ kg de morcovi, decojiți și tăiați în bucăți de 1 inch

½ ceapă, tăiată subțire

¼ cană bulion de legume

1 lingura. ulei de susan

2 linguri. sos hoi sin

Piper negru

½ kilogram de spanac proaspăt, tocat grosier

Pune toate ingredientele într-un aragaz lent, cu excepția ultimului.

Acoperiți cu pumni de spanac și umpleți aragazul cu el.

Dacă nu puteți încadra totul deodată, lăsați primul lot să se gătească mai întâi și adăugați mai mult spanac.

Gatiti 3 sau 4 ore la foc mediu pana morcovii devin moale.

Răzuiți părțile laterale și serviți.

Bok Choy și morcovi fierte lent

INGREDIENTE

1 ½ kg de morcovi, decojiți și tăiați în bucăți de 1 inch

½ ceapă, tăiată subțire

¼ cană bulion de legume

1 lingura. ulei de susan

1 lingura. ulei de rapita

2 linguri. sos hoi sin

Piper negru

½ kilogram de bok choy proaspăt, tocat grosier

Pune toate ingredientele într-un aragaz lent, cu excepția ultimului.

Acoperiți cu pumni de bok choy și umpleți aragazul lent cu el.

Dacă nu puteți încadra totul dintr-o dată, lăsați primul lot să se gătească mai întâi și adăugați mai mult bok choy.

Gatiti 3 sau 4 ore la foc mediu pana morcovii devin moale.

Răzuiți părțile laterale și serviți.

Micro verdeturi și cartofi fierte lent

INGREDIENTE

1 ½ kg de cartofi, decojiți și tăiați în bucăți de 1 inch

½ ceapă, tăiată subțire

¼ cană bulion de legume

2 linguri. ulei de măsline extra virgin

1 lingura seminte de anatto

1 lingura chimion

1 lingura suc de lămâie

Piper negru

½ kilogram de verdeață micro proaspătă, tocată grosier

Pune toate ingredientele într-un aragaz lent, cu excepția ultimului.

Acoperiți cu pumni de verdețuri micro și umpleți aragazul cu ea.

Dacă nu puteți încadra totul dintr-o dată, lăsați primul lot să se gătească mai întâi și adăugați mai multe micro-verduri.

Gatiti 3 sau 4 ore la foc mediu pana cartofii devin moi.

Răzuiți părțile laterale și serviți.

Verdure și cartofi gătiți lent

INGREDIENTE

1 ½ kg de cartofi dulci, decojiți și tăiați în bucăți de 1 inch

½ ceapă, tăiată subțire

¼ cană bulion de legume

1 lingura. ulei de măsline extra virgin

2 linguri. sos pesto

Piper negru

½ kilogram de verdeață proaspătă, tocată grosier

Pune toate ingredientele într-un aragaz lent, cu excepția ultimului.

Acoperiți cu pumni de verdeață și umpleți aragazul cu ea.

Dacă nu puteți încadra totul dintr-o dată, lăsați primul lot să se gătească mai întâi și adăugați mai multe verdeață.

Gatiti 3 sau 4 ore la foc mediu pana cartofii dulci devin moale.

Răzuiți părțile laterale și serviți.

Varză violetă și cartofi fierte lent

INGREDIENTE

1 ½ kg de cartofi, decojiți și tăiați în bucăți de 1 inch

½ ceapă, tăiată subțire

¼ cană bulion de legume

1 lingura. ulei de măsline extra virgin

Piper negru

½ kilogram de varză mov proaspătă, tocată grosier

Pune toate ingredientele într-un aragaz lent, cu excepția ultimului.

Acoperiți cu pumni de varză violetă și umpleți cu ea aragazul lent.

Dacă nu puteți încadra totul dintr-o dată, lăsați primul lot să se gătească mai întâi și adăugați mai multă varză mov.

Gatiti 3 sau 4 ore la foc mediu pana cartofii devin moi.

Răzuiți părțile laterale și serviți.

Varză și morcovi fierte încet

INGREDIENTE

1 ½ kg de morcovi, decojiți și tăiați în bucăți de 1 inch

½ ceapă, tăiată subțire

¼ cană bulion de legume

1 lingura. ulei de măsline extra virgin

Piper negru

½ kilogram de varză proaspătă, tocată grosier

Pune toate ingredientele într-un aragaz lent, cu excepția ultimului.

Acoperiți cu pumni de varză și umpleți aragazul cu ea.

Dacă nu puteți încadra totul dintr-o dată, lăsați primul lot să se gătească mai întâi și adăugați mai multă varză.

Gatiti 3 sau 4 ore la foc mediu pana morcovii devin moale.

Răzuiți părțile laterale și serviți.

Andive fierte lent în sos pesto

INGREDIENTE

1 ½ kg de cartofi, decojiți și tăiați în bucăți de 1 inch

½ ceapă, tăiată subțire

¼ cană bulion de legume

1 lingura. ulei de măsline extra virgin

2 linguri. sos pesto

Piper negru

½ kilogram de andive proaspete, tocate grosier

Pune toate ingredientele într-un aragaz lent, cu excepția ultimului.

Acoperiți cu pumni de andive și umpleți slow cooker cu ea.

Dacă nu puteți încadra totul dintr-o dată, lăsați primul lot să se gătească mai întâi și adăugați încă niște andive.

Gatiti 3 sau 4 ore la foc mediu pana cartofii devin moi.

Răzuiți părțile laterale și serviți.

Napi fierte lent în sos pesto

INGREDIENTE

1 ½ kg de cartofi, decojiți și tăiați în bucăți de 1 inch

½ ceapă, tăiată subțire

¼ cană bulion de legume

1 lingura. ulei de măsline extra virgin

2 linguri. sos pesto

Piper negru

½ kilogram de verdeață de nap proaspătă, tocată grosier

Pune toate ingredientele într-un aragaz lent, cu excepția ultimului.

Acoperiți cu pumni de verdeață de napi și umpleți oara lentă cu ea.

Dacă nu puteți încadra totul deodată, lăsați primul lot să se gătească mai întâi și adăugați mai multe verdeață de napi.

Gatiti 3 sau 4 ore la foc mediu pana cartofii devin moi.

Răzuiți părțile laterale și serviți.

Bok Choy gătit lent în sos de fasole galbenă

INGREDIENTE

1 ½ kg de napi, decojiți și tăiați în bucăți de 1 inch

½ ceapă, tăiată subțire

¼ cană bulion de legume

1 lingura. ulei din semințe de susan

2 linguri. ceapa verde tocata, tocata

4 linguri. usturoi, tocat fin

2 linguri. Sos chinezesc de fasole galbenă

Piper negru

½ kilogram bok choy proaspăt, tocat grosier

Pune toate ingredientele într-un aragaz lent, cu excepția ultimului.

Acoperiți cu pumni de bok choy și umpleți aragazul lent cu el.

Dacă nu puteți încadra totul dintr-o dată, lăsați primul lot să se gătească mai întâi și adăugați mai mult bok choy.

Gatiti 3 sau 4 ore la foc mediu pana cand napii devin moi.

Răzuiți părțile laterale și serviți.

Napi fierte lent și cartofi în sos pesto

INGREDIENTE

1 ½ kg de cartofi, decojiți și tăiați în bucăți de 1 inch

½ ceapă, tăiată subțire

¼ cană bulion de legume

1 lingura. ulei de măsline extra virgin

2 linguri. sos pesto

Piper negru

½ kilogram de verdeață de nap proaspătă, tocată grosier

Pune toate ingredientele într-un aragaz lent, cu excepția ultimului.

Acoperiți cu pumni de verdeață de napi și umpleți oara lentă cu ea.

Dacă nu puteți încadra totul deodată, lăsați primul lot să se gătească mai întâi și adăugați mai multe verdeață de napi.

Gatiti 3 sau 4 ore la foc mediu pana cartofii devin moale.

Răzuiți părțile laterale și serviți.

Ciuperci Chanterelle fierte lent

INGREDIENTE

1 ½ kg ciuperci chanterelle

½ ceapă, tăiată subțire

¼ cană bulion de legume

1 lingura. ulei de măsline extra virgin

Boabe de piper curcubeu

½ kilogram de spanac proaspăt, tocat grosier

Pune toate ingredientele într-un aragaz lent, cu excepția ultimului.

Acoperiți cu pumni de spanac și umpleți aragazul cu el.

Dacă nu puteți încadra totul deodată, lăsați primul lot să se gătească mai întâi și adăugați mai mult spanac

Gatiti 3 sau 4 ore la foc mediu pana cand ciupercile devin moi.

Răzuiți părțile laterale și serviți.

Ciuperci stridii și varză gătită lent

INGREDIENTE

1 ½ kg ciuperci stridii

½ ceapă, tăiată subțire

¼ cană bulion de legume

2 linguri. unt vegan sau margarina

1 lingura ierburi de Provence

Piper negru

½ kg de kale proaspătă, tocată grosier

Pune toate ingredientele într-un aragaz lent, cu excepția ultimului.

Acoperiți cu pumni de kale și umpleți aragazul cu ea.

Dacă nu puteți încadra totul dintr-o dată, lăsați primul lot să se gătească mai întâi și adăugați mai multă kale.

Gatiti 3 sau 4 ore la foc mediu pana cand ciupercile devin moi.

Răzuiți părțile laterale și serviți.

Ciuperci porcini și napi fierte lent

INGREDIENTE

1 ½ kilograme de ciuperci porcini

½ ceapă, tăiată subțire

¼ cană bulion de legume

1 lingura. ulei de rapita

2 linguri. usturoi tocat

Piper negru

½ kilogram de verdeață de nap proaspătă, tocată grosier

Pune toate ingredientele într-un aragaz lent, cu excepția ultimului.

Acoperiți cu pumni de verdeață de napi și umpleți oara lentă cu ea.

Dacă nu puteți încadra totul deodată, lăsați primul lot să se gătească mai întâi și adăugați mai multe verdeață de napi.

Gatiti 3 sau 4 ore la foc mediu pana cand ciupercile devin moi.

Răzuiți părțile laterale și serviți.

Ciuperci Crimini în stil italian fierte lent

INGREDIENTE

1 ½ kg ciuperci crimini

½ ceapă, tăiată subțire

¼ cană bulion de legume

1 lingura. ulei de măsline extra virgin

2 linguri. usturoi

1 lingura condimente italienesti

Piper negru

½ kilogram de verdeață de nap proaspătă, tocată grosier

Pune toate ingredientele într-un aragaz lent, cu excepția ultimului.

Acoperiți cu pumni de verdeață de napi și umpleți oara lentă cu ea.

Dacă nu puteți încadra totul deodată, lăsați primul lot să se gătească mai întâi și adăugați mai multe verdeață de napi.

Gatiti 3 sau 4 ore la foc mediu pana cand ciupercile devin moi.

Răzuiți părțile laterale și serviți.

Ciuperci Shitake și spanac fierte încet în sos Hoi sin

INGREDIENTE

1 kg de ciuperci shitake, tocate grosier

½ ceapă, tăiată subțire

¼ cană bulion de legume

1 lingura. ulei de susan

2 linguri. sos hoi sin

Piper negru

½ kilogram de spanac proaspăt, tocat grosier

Pune toate ingredientele într-un aragaz lent, cu excepția ultimului.

Acoperiți cu pumni de spanac și umpleți aragazul cu el.

Dacă nu puteți încadra totul deodată, lăsați primul lot să se gătească mai întâi și adăugați mai mult spanac.

Gatiti 3 sau 4 ore la foc mediu pana cand ciupercile devin moi.

Răzuiți părțile laterale și serviți.

Ciuperci stridii fierte lent și varză în sos de fasole galbenă

INGREDIENTE

1 ½ kg ciuperci stridii

½ ceapă, tăiată subțire

¼ cană bulion de legume

1 lingura. ulei de susan

2 linguri. sos de fasole galbenă

Piper negru

½ kg de kale proaspătă, tocată grosier

Pune toate ingredientele într-un aragaz lent, cu excepția ultimului.

Acoperiți cu pumni de kale și umpleți aragazul cu ea.

Dacă nu puteți încadra totul dintr-o dată, lăsați primul lot să se gătească mai întâi și adăugați mai multă kale.

Gatiti 3 sau 4 ore la foc mediu pana cand ciupercile devin moi.

Răzuiți părțile laterale și serviți.

Bok Choy cu curry gătit lent și ciuperci Button

INGREDIENTE

1 ½ kg ciuperci buton

½ ceapă, tăiată subțire

¼ cană bulion de legume

1 lingura. ulei de măsline extra virgin

1 lingura. pudra de curry

Piper negru

½ kilogram bok choy proaspăt, tocat grosier

Pune toate ingredientele într-un aragaz lent, cu excepția ultimului.

Acoperiți cu pumni de bok choy și umpleți aragazul lent cu el.

Dacă nu puteți încadra totul dintr-o dată, lăsați primul lot să se gătească mai întâi și adăugați mai mult bok choy.

Gatiti 3 sau 4 ore la foc mediu pana cand ciupercile devin moi.

Răzuiți părțile laterale și serviți.

Spanac și ciuperci porcini fierte lent

INGREDIENTE

1 ½ kilograme de ciuperci porcini

½ ceapă, tăiată subțire

¼ cană bulion de legume

1 lingura. ulei de măsline extra virgin

2 linguri. sos pesto

1 lingura condimente italienesti

Piper negru

½ kilogram de spanac proaspăt, tocat grosier

Pune toate ingredientele într-un aragaz lent, cu excepția ultimului.

Acoperiți cu pumni de spanac și umpleți aragazul cu el.

Dacă nu puteți încadra totul deodată, lăsați primul lot să se gătească mai întâi și adăugați mai mult spanac.

Gatiti 3 sau 4 ore la foc mediu pana cand ciupercile devin moi.

Răzuiți părțile laterale și serviți.

Kale fiert lent și ciuperci Enoki

INGREDIENTE

1 ½ kilograme de ciuperci enoki

½ ceapă, tăiată subțire

¼ cană bulion de legume

1 lingura. ulei de măsline extra virgin

2 linguri. măsline

2 linguri. capere

Piper negru

½ kg de kale proaspătă, tocată grosier

Pune toate ingredientele într-un aragaz lent, cu excepția ultimului.

Acoperiți cu pumni de kale și umpleți aragazul cu ea.

Dacă nu puteți încadra totul dintr-o dată, lăsați primul lot să se gătească mai întâi și adăugați mai multă kale.

Gatiti 3 sau 4 ore la foc mediu pana cand ciupercile devin moi.

Răzuiți părțile laterale și serviți.

Napi fierte lent și ciuperci

INGREDIENTE

1 ½ kg ciuperci buton

½ ceapă, tăiată subțire

¼ cană bulion de legume

1 lingura. ulei de măsline extra virgin

1 lingura chimion

1 lingura seminte de anatto

1 lingura măsline

Piper negru

½ kilogram de verdeață de nap proaspătă, tocată grosier

Pune toate ingredientele într-un aragaz lent, cu excepția ultimului.

Acoperiți cu pumni de verdeață de napi și umpleți oara lentă cu ea.

Bok Choy și ciuperci Shitake gătite lent

INGREDIENTE

1 ½ kg de ciuperci shitake

½ ceapă, tăiată subțire

¼ cană bulion de legume

2 linguri. ulei din semințe de susan

1 lingura. sos hoi sin

1 lingura. sos hoi sin

Piper negru

½ kilogram bok choy proaspăt, tocat grosier

Pune toate ingredientele într-un aragaz lent, cu excepția ultimului.

Acoperiți cu pumni de bok choy și umpleți aragazul lent cu el.

Dacă nu puteți încadra totul dintr-o dată, lăsați primul lot să se gătească mai întâi și adăugați mai mult bok choy.

Gatiti 3 sau 4 ore la foc mediu pana cand ciupercile devin moi.

Răzuiți părțile laterale și serviți.

Salată romană fierte lent și ciuperci chanterelle

INGREDIENTE

1 ½ kg ciuperci chanterelle

½ ceapă, tăiată subțire

¼ cană bulion de legume

1 lingura. ulei de măsline extra virgin

1 lingura praf de usturoi

1 lingura praf de ceapa

Piper negru

½ kilogram salata romana proaspata, tocata grosier

Pune toate ingredientele într-un aragaz lent, cu excepția ultimului.

Acoperiți cu pumni de salată romană și umpleți aragazul cu ea.

Dacă nu puteți încadra totul dintr-o dată, lăsați primul lot să se gătească mai întâi și adăugați încă puțină salată romană.

Gatiti 3 sau 4 ore la foc mediu pana cand ciupercile devin moi.

Răzuiți părțile laterale și serviți.

Spanac și ciuperci porcini fierte încet

INGREDIENTE

1 ½ kilograme de ciuperci porcini

½ ceapă, tăiată subțire

¼ cană bulion de legume

1 lingura. unt vegan topit

1 lingura. praf de usturoi

1 lingura. lămâie verde

Piper negru

½ kilogram de spanac proaspăt, tocat grosier

Pune toate ingredientele într-un aragaz lent, cu excepția ultimului.

Acoperiți cu pumni de spanac și umpleți aragazul cu el.

Dacă nu puteți încadra totul deodată, lăsați primul lot să se gătească mai întâi și adăugați mai mult spanac.

Gatiti 3 sau 4 ore la foc mediu pana cand ciupercile devin moi.

Răzuiți părțile laterale și serviți.

Verde de nap fiert lent în sos Chimichurri

INGREDIENTE

1 ½ kg de ciuperci shitake, feliate

½ ceapă, tăiată subțire

¼ cană bulion de legume

1 lingura. ulei de măsline extra virgin

2 linguri. sos chimichuri

Piper negru

½ kilogram de verdeață de nap proaspătă, tocată grosier

Pune toate ingredientele într-un aragaz lent, cu excepția ultimului.

Acoperiți cu pumni de verdeață de napi și umpleți oara lentă cu ea.

Dacă nu puteți încadra totul deodată, lăsați primul lot să se gătească mai întâi și adăugați mai multe verdeață de napi.

Gatiti 3 sau 4 ore la foc mediu pana cand ciupercile devin moi.

Răzuiți părțile laterale și serviți.

Bok Choy și ciuperci Enoki fierte încet în sos de fasole galbenă

INGREDIENTE

1 ½ kilograme de ciuperci enoki

½ ceapă, tăiată subțire

¼ cană bulion de legume

1 lingura. ulei de susan

2 linguri. sos de fasole galbenă

Piper negru

½ kilogram bok choy proaspăt, tocat grosier

Pune toate ingredientele într-un aragaz lent, cu excepția ultimului.

Acoperiți cu pumni de verdeață de napi și umpleți oara lentă cu ea.

Dacă nu puteți încadra totul dintr-o dată, lăsați primul lot să se gătească mai întâi și adăugați mai mult bok choy.

Gatiti 3 sau 4 ore la foc mediu pana cand ciupercile devin moi.

Răzuiți părțile laterale și serviți.

Kale și ciuperci de stridii în sos Chimichurri

INGREDIENTE

1 ½ kg ciuperci stridii

½ ceapă, tăiată subțire

¼ cană bulion de legume

2 linguri. ulei de măsline extra virgin

4 linguri. sos chimichurri

Piper negru

½ kg de kale proaspătă, tocată grosier

Pune toate ingredientele într-un aragaz lent, cu excepția ultimului.

Acoperiți cu pumni de kale și umpleți aragazul cu ea.

Dacă nu puteți încadra totul dintr-o dată, lăsați primul lot să se gătească mai întâi și adăugați mai multă kale.

Gatiti 3 sau 4 ore la foc mediu pana cand ciupercile devin moi.

Răzuiți părțile laterale și serviți.

Linte și cartofi în lapte de cocos

INGREDIENTE

3 cartofi dulci mari, tăiați cubulețe (aproximativ 6 căni)

3 cani de supa de legume

1 ceapa rosie, tocata

6 catei de usturoi, tocati

2 lingurițe fiecare coriandru măcinat, garam masala și pudră de chili

1/2 lingurita sare de mare

1 1/2 cani de linte rosie nefiarta (masoor dal)

1 cutie lapte de cocos

1 cană apă

combinați cartofii dulci, bulionul de legume, ceapa, usturoiul și condimentele într-un aragaz lent.

Gatiti la foc mare intr-un aragaz lent timp de 3 ore sau pana cand legumele devin moi.

Adăugați lintea și amestecați.

Gatiti la foc maxim inca o ora si jumatate.

Adăugați laptele de cocos.

Adăugați apă după cum este necesar.

Dulceata de afine

Ingrediente

36 oz. afine, piure (aproximativ 5 căni de piure)

1 cană miere

2 lingurite scortisoara

1/4 lingurita de ghimbir macinat

Zest de 1 lămâie

Gatiti afinele la foc mic timp de o ora.

Se amestecă după o oră și se fierbe încă 4 ore.

Adăugați condimentele, mierea și coaja.

Scoateți capacul și gătiți încă o oră.

Pune toate ingredientele într-un blender și pasează până se omogenizează și depozitează-le într-un borcan de zidărie sau un recipient.

Se pune la frigider.

Jambalaya fiert lent

INGREDIENTE

6 oz chorizo din soia* (opțional)

2 ardei gras verzi, taiati cubulete

¾ cană de bame, rondele de ½ inch

½ ceapă roșie, tăiată cubulețe

3 coaste de țelină (aproximativ 1½ căni)

4 catei de usturoi, tocati

1 conserve de 16 oz de Rotel (roșii tăiate cubulețe și ardei iute verzi)

1½ cani de supa de legume

½ lingurita boia

¼ linguriță sare de mare

¼ lingurita piper negru macinat

½ linguriță piper cayenne

3 căni de orez coriandru fiert

Gatiti chorizo-ul de soia la foc mediu-mare.

Se fierbe și se pune în Crockpot.

Adăugați ardeiul gras, ceapa roșie, țelina și usturoiul în aragazul lent.

Adăugați roșiile tăiate cubulețe și supa de legume.

Adăugați condimentele și amestecați bine legumele.

Gatiti la foc mic timp de 5 ore sau la maxim aproximativ 2 ore si 15 minute.

Adăugați orezul fiert și amestecați cu restul ingredientelor în slow cooker cu 30 de minute înainte de servire.

Tacos fierte lent cu ardei chipotle

Ingrediente principale

30 uncii fasole pinto 2 cutii de 15 uncii fiecare, scurse de apă

1 cană de porumb conservat, congelat sau proaspăt

3 uncii de ardei chipotle în sos adobo, tocat

6 uncii pastă de tomate 1 cutie

3/4 cană sos chili

2 lingurite Pudră de cacao neîndulcită

1 lingurita Chimen macinat

1/4 lingurita de scortisoara macinata

Ingrediente pentru ornat și servire

8 coji de taco porumb alb tare sau preferatul tău, tare sau moale

topping-urile preferate = salata verde, avocado, lime

Sare de mare

Puneți toate ingredientele principale într-un aragaz lent

Gatiti la foc mic 3 1/2 ore sau la foc mare timp de 2 ore.

Întindeți ingredientele pe cojile de taco, tari sau moi.

Acoperiți cu salată verde.

Adăugați roșiile, avocado și lime.

Se serveste cu fasole si orez.

Cartofi copți și fasole verde

Ingrediente

2 cani de cartofi baby

3 linguri ulei de măsline extravirgin, împărțit

2 cani de rosii cherry

2 căni de fasole verde proaspătă tăiată de 1 inch

6 catei de usturoi, tocati

2 lingurite busuioc uscat

1 lingurita sare de mare

1 conserve (15 uncii) de năut, scurs și clătit

2 lingurite ulei de masline extravirgin sau dupa gust (optional)

Sare de mare

Piper negru măcinat după gust

Preîncălziți cuptorul la 425 de grade F.

Acoperiți tava de copt cu folie de aluminiu.

Ungeți cartofii cu 1 lingură ulei de măsline într-un castron.

Se toarnă în tavă și se prăjește la cuptor până se înmoaie, timp de o jumătate de oră.

Adăugați roșiile, fasolea, usturoiul, busuiocul și sarea de mare cu 2 linguri de ulei de măsline.

Scoateți cartofii din cuptor și mutați-i într-o parte a tavii.

Adăugați roșia și fasolea verde.

Se prăjește până când roșiile încep să se ofilească pentru încă 18 minute.

Se scoate din cuptor si se toarna intr-un vas.

Adăugați fasole garbanzo, 2 lingurițe ulei de măsline, sare și piper.

Naut si conopida la cuptor

Ingrediente

spray de gatit

1 lingura ulei de masline

4 catei de usturoi, tocati

1/2 lingurita sare de mare

1/4 lingurita piper alb macinat

3 cani de conopida feliata

2 ½ cani de rosii cherry

1 conserve (15 uncii) de năut, scurs

1 lime mică, tăiată felii

1 lingură coriandru proaspăt tocat

Preîncălziți cuptorul la 450 de grade F.

Tapetați o tavă de copt cu folie de aluminiu și ungeți cu ulei.

Amesteca bine uleiul de masline, usturoiul, sarea si piperul intr-un castron.

Adăugați conopida, roșiile și fasolea garbanzo și amestecați până când sunt bine acoperite.

Se întinde în tava de copt.

Adăugați felii de lime.

Coacem la cuptor pana cand legumele se carameilzeaza, aproximativ 25 de minute.

Scoateți lime și acoperiți cu coriandru.

Fasole Garbanzo la cuptor Dovleac și cartofi

Ingrediente

2 conserve (15 uncii) de fasole garbanzo, clătite și scurse

1/2 dovleac butternut - curăţat, fără seminţe și tăiat în bucăţi de 1 inch

1 ceapa rosie, taiata cubulete

2 morcovi mari, tăiaţi în bucăţi de 1 inch

4 cartofi rușini medii, tăiaţi în bucăţi de 1 inch

3 linguri ulei de masline

1 lingurita sare de mare

1/2 lingurita piper negru macinat

1 lingurita praf de ceapa

1 lingurita praf de usturoi

1 lingurita de seminte de fenicul macinate

1 lingurita de salvie uscata

2 ceai verzi, tocati (optional)

Preîncălziţi cuptorul la 350 de grade F.

Pe o tigaie unsă cu ulei, aşezaţi fasolea, dovleceii, ceapa, cartofii dulci, morcovii și cartofii rumeni.

Stropiți cu ulei de măsline și acoperiți.

Se amestecă într-un castron sarea, piperul negru, praful de ceapă, pudra de usturoi, semințele de fenicul măcinate și salvia frecată bine.

Presărați acest condiment peste legume pe o tigaie.

Se coace la cuptor pentru 25 de minute.

Prăjiți până când legumele sunt moi și ușor rumenite, timp de aproximativ 23 de minute.

Asezonați cu mai multă sare și piper după gust

Se presară cu ceapă verde tocată.

Morcovi curcubeu la cuptor și varză de Bruxelles

Ingrediente

2 căni de varză de Bruxelles, tăiată

1 cană bucăți mari de cartofi dulci

1 cană bucăți mari de morcov curcubeu

1 cană buchetele de conopidă

1 cană de sfeclă roșie cuburi

1/2 cană bucăți de eșalotă

2 linguri ulei de masline extravirgin

Sare de mare

Piper negru măcinat după gust

Preîncălziți cuptorul la 425 de grade F.

Așezați grătarul pe partea de al doilea cel mai jos nivel al cuptorului.

Scufundați varza de Bruxelles în apă cu sare și lăsați-o la macerat timp de 15 minute

Scurgeți varza de Bruxelles.

Combinați cartofii, morcovii, conopida, sfecla, eșapa, uleiul de măsline, sarea și piperul într-un castron.

Așezați legumele într-un singur strat pe o tavă de copt.

Se prăjește la cuptor până se caramelizează aproximativ 45 de minute.

Sparanghel copt și cartofi roșii

Ingrediente

1 1/2 kilograme de cartofi roșii, tăiați în bucăți

2 linguri ulei de masline extravirgin

8 catei de usturoi, feliati subtiri

4 lingurite rozmarin uscat

4 lingurite de cimbru uscat

2 lingurite sare de mare

1 buchet de sparanghel proaspăt, tăiat și tăiat în bucăți de 1 inch

piper negru măcinat după gust

Preîncălziți cuptorul la 425 de grade F

Combinați cartofii cu 1 lingură. de ulei de măsline, usturoi, rozmarin, cimbru și 1 linguriță. sare de mare.

Înfășurați cu folie de aluminiu.

Se coace timp de 20 de minute la cuptor.

Se amestecă sparanghelul, uleiul de măsline rămas și sarea rămasă.

Acoperiți și gătiți încă 15 minute, până când cartofii sunt fragezi.

Creșteți temperatura cuptorului la 450 de grade F.

Scoateți folia și gătiți timp de 8 minute, până când cartofii se rumenesc.

Se presară cu piper.

Varza de Bruxelles la cuptor in glazura balsamica

Ingrediente

1 pachet (16 uncii) varză de Bruxelles proaspătă

1 ceapă albă mică, feliată subțire

5 linguri ulei de măsline, împărțit

1/4 lingurita sare de mare

1/4 lingurita piper negru proaspat macinat

1 şalotă, tocată

1/4 cana otet balsamic

1 lingurita rozmarin uscat tocat

Preîncălziți cuptorul la 425 de grade F.

Amesteca bine varza de Bruxelles si ceapa intr-un castron.

Adăugați 4 linguri de ulei de măsline

Asezonați cu sare și piper

Întindeți mugurii pe o tigaie.

Coaceți la cuptor până când mugurii și ceapa devin fragede timp de aproximativ 28 de minute.

Încinge 2 linguri de ulei de măsline într-o tigaie la foc mediu-mare.

Se caleste saota pana se inmoaie timp de aproximativ 4 minute.

Adăugați oțet balsamic și gătiți până se reduce timp de aproximativ 5 minute.

Adăugați rozmarinul în glazură și turnați peste legume.

Ciuperci Portobello la cuptor și roșii cherry

Ingrediente

1 kg de cartofi, tăiați la jumătate

2 linguri ulei de masline extravirgin

1/2 kilogram de ciuperci Portobello

8 catei de usturoi nedecojiti

2 linguri de cimbru proaspăt tocat

1 lingura ulei de masline

sare de mare

piper negru măcinat după gust

1/4 kilogram de roșii cherry

3 linguri nuci de pin prajite

1/4 de kilogram de spanac, feliat subțire

Preîncălziți cuptorul la 425 de grade F.

Pune cartofii pe o tava de copt si stropim cu 2 linguri de ulei de masline.

Se prăjește timp de 15 minute și se întoarce o dată.

Adaugati ciupercile, cu tulpina in sus, si cateii de usturoi in tigaie.

Stropiți cu cimbru și 1 lingură ulei de măsline

Asezonați cu sare de mare și piper negru.

Aduceți-l înapoi la cuptor; gătiți 5 minute.

Adăugați roșiile în tigaie.

Coaceți până când ciupercile se înmoaie încă aproximativ 5 minute.

Presarati nuci de pin peste cartofi si ciuperci.

Se ornează cu spanac feliat.

Taco vegan

1 lingura ulei de masline extravirgin

1 ceapa rosie, taiata cubulete

2 catei de usturoi, tocati

1 ardei gras verde, tocat

2 cutii (14,5 uncii) de fasole pinto, clătite, scurse de apă și piure

2 linguri de porumb galben

Ingrediente pentru condimente

1 1/2 linguri chimen

1 lingurita boia spaniola

1 lingurita piper cayenne

1 lingurita pudra de chili

1 cană salsa

Încinge ulei de măsline la foc mediu.

Adăugați ceapa, usturoiul și ardeiul gras și căliți până se înmoaie.

Adăugați fasolea piure.

Adăugați făina de porumb.

Adăugați ingrediente de condimente.

Acoperiți și gătiți timp de 5 minute.

Fajitas cu dovlecei și dovlecei vegani

1/4 cană ulei de măsline
1/4 cană oțet de vin roșu
Un praf de oregano uscat
1 lingurita pudra de chili
sare de usturoi după gust
sare si piper dupa gust
1 lingurita miere
2 dovlecei mici, tăiați în juliană
2 dovlecei galbeni medii mici, tăiați în juliană
1 ceapă roșie mare, feliată
2 ardei gras verzi, tăiați în fâșii subțiri
2 linguri ulei de masline extravirgin
1 conserve (8,75 uncii) de porumb sâmbure întreg, scurs
1 cutie (15 uncii) de fasole pinto, scursă

Amestecați bine uleiul de măsline, oțetul, oregano, pudra de chili, sarea de usturoi, sare, piper și mierea.

La această marinată adăugați dovlecelul, dovleceii, ceapa roșie și ardeiul gras.

Marinați la frigider pentru o oră sau peste noapte.

Încinge uleiul de măsline la foc mediu-mare.

Scurgeți legumele și căleți până se înmoaie timp de aproximativ 12 minute.

Adăugați porumbul și fasolea.

Creșteți focul la mare până când rumeniți legumele.

Cartofi curry picante

Ingrediente

4 cartofi, curatati si taiati cubulete

2 linguri ulei de masline

1 ceapa galbena, taiata cubulete

6 catei de usturoi, tocati

1 cutie (14,5 uncii) de roșii tăiate cubulețe

1 conserve (15 uncii) de fasole garbanzo (năut), clătită și scursă

1 conserve (15 uncii) de mazăre, scursă

1 cutie de lapte de cocos (14 uncii).

Ingrediente pentru condimente

2 lingurite chimen macinat

1 1/2 linguriță de piper cayenne

1 lingura. și 1 linguriță pudră de curry

1 lingura. și 1 linguriță garam masala

1 (1 inch) bucată de rădăcină de ghimbir proaspătă, curățată și tocată

2 lingurite sare de mare

Scufundați cartofii în apă cu sare.

Se fierbe la foc mare și se reduce focul la mediu-mic.

Se acopera si se lasa sa fiarba pana se inmoaie, aproximativ 15 minute.

Scurgeți-l lăsați să se usuce un minut și jumătate.

Încinge uleiul de măsline într-o tigaie la foc mediu.

Adăugați ceapa și usturoiul; gătiți și amestecați până când ceapa devine translucidă timp de aproximativ 5 minute.

Adăugați ingredientele de condimente.

Gatiti inca 2 minute.

Se amestecă roșiile, fasolea garbanzo, mazărea și cartofii.

Adăugați laptele de cocos și fierbeți timp de 8 minute.

Sparanghel ușor la abur

Ingrediente

1 buchet de sulițe de sparanghel

1 lingurita ulei de masline extravirgin

1/4 lingurita sare de mare

3 căni de apă

Puneți apă în jumătatea inferioară a unui set de tigaie pentru aburi. Adăugați sare și ulei și aduceți la fiert.

Tăiați capetele uscate de pe sparanghel. Dacă sulițele sunt groase, curățați-le ușor cu un curățător de legume. Așezați-le în jumătatea superioară a setului de tigaie pentru aburi. Se fierbe la abur timp de 5 până la 10 minute, în funcție de grosimea sparanghelului, sau până când sparanghelul este fraged.

Broccoli la abur

Ingrediente

20 buc. buchețele de broccoli, de preferință albite

1 lingurita ulei din seminte de susan

1/4 lingurita sare de mare

3 căni de apă

Puneți apă în jumătatea inferioară a unui set de tigaie pentru aburi. Adăugați sare și ulei și aduceți la fiert.

Puneți legumele în jumătatea superioară a setului de tigaie pentru aburi. Se fierbe la abur timp de 5 până la 10 minute, în funcție de grosimea legumei, sau până când legumele devin fragede.

Bok Choy la abur în stil chinezesc

Ingrediente

1 buchet bok choy

1 lingurita ulei din seminte de susan

1/4 lingurita sare de mare

3 căni de apă

Puneți apă în jumătatea inferioară a unui set de tigaie pentru aburi. Adăugați sare și ulei și aduceți la fiert.

Puneți legumele în jumătatea superioară a setului de tigaie pentru aburi. Se fierbe la abur timp de 5 până la 10 minute, în funcție de grosimea legumei, sau până când legumele devin fragede.

Conopida la abur

Ingrediente

20 buc. buchețele de conopidă, clătite și scurse

1 lingurita ulei de canola

1/4 lingurita sare de mare

3 căni de apă

Puneți apă în jumătatea inferioară a unui set de tigaie pentru aburi. Adăugați sare și ulei și aduceți la fiert.

Puneți legumele în jumătatea superioară a setului de tigaie pentru aburi. Se fierbe la abur timp de 5 până la 10 minute, în funcție de grosimea legumei, sau până când legumele devin fragede.

Spanac la abur

Ingrediente

1 buchet Spanac

1 lingurita ulei de masline extravirgin

1/4 lingurita sare de mare

3 căni de apă

Puneți apă în jumătatea inferioară a unui set de tigaie pentru aburi. Adăugați sare și ulei și aduceți la fiert.

Puneți legumele în jumătatea superioară a setului de tigaie pentru aburi. Se fierbe la abur timp de 5 până la 10 minute, în funcție de grosimea legumei, sau până când legumele devin fragede.

Nasturel la abur

Ingrediente

1 buchet de nasturel

1 lingurita ulei de masline extravirgin

1/4 lingurita sare de mare

3 căni de apă

Puneți apă în jumătatea inferioară a unui set de tigaie pentru aburi. Adăugați sare și ulei și aduceți la fiert.

Puneți legumele în jumătatea superioară a setului de tigaie pentru aburi. Se fierbe la abur timp de 5 până la 10 minute, în funcție de grosimea legumei, sau până când legumele devin fragede.

Sumă Choy la abur

Ingrediente

1 buchet choy sumă

1 lingurita ulei de susan

1/4 lingurita sare de mare

3 căni de apă

Puneți apă în jumătatea inferioară a unui set de tigaie pentru aburi. Adăugați sare și ulei și aduceți la fiert.

Puneți legumele în jumătatea superioară a setului de tigaie pentru aburi. Se fierbe la abur timp de 5 până la 10 minute, în funcție de grosimea legumei, sau până când legumele devin fragede.

Vegan Pad Thai

Ingrediente pentru sos

1/2 cană miere

1/2 cană oțet alb distilat

1/4 cană sos de soia

2 linguri pulpa de tamarind

Ingrediente principale

1 pachet (12 uncii) taitei de orez uscat

1/2 cană ulei din semințe de susan

2 lingurite de usturoi tocat

4 ouă

1 pachet (12 uncii) de tofu ferm, tăiat în fâșii de 1/2 inch

1 lingura si 1 lingura. Miere

1 1/2 linguriță sare de mare

1 1/2 cană alune măcinate

1 1/2 linguriță ridiche orientală măcinată, uscată

1/2 cană de arpagic proaspăt tocat

1 lingura boia

2 căni de muguri de fasole proaspăt

1 lime, tăiată felii

La foc mediu, combinați toate ingredientele pentru sos

Înmuiați tăițeii de orez în apă rece până când se înmoaie și se scurg.

Într-o tigaie mare, încălziți uleiul de măsline, usturoiul și ouăle la foc mediu.

Se amestecă pentru a amesteca ouăle.

Adăugați tofu și amestecați

Adaugati taiteii si amestecati pana sunt fierti.

Adăugați sosul, 1 1/2 linguriță miere și 1 1/2 linguriță sare de mare.

Adăugați alunele și ridichea măcinată.

Se ia de pe foc si se adauga arpagicul si boia.

Se ornează cu lămâie și muguri de fasole.

Se amestecă cartofi și roșii prăjiți

Ingrediente

1 ceapa, tocata

1/4 cană ulei de măsline

1 kilogram de cartofi, decojiți și tăiați cubulețe

1 lingurita sare de mare

Mix de condimente

1/2 lingurita piper cayenne

1/4 linguriță turmeric măcinat

1/4 lingurita chimen macinat

2 rosii, tocate

Se caleste si se rumeneste ceapa in ulei intr-o tigaie.

Adăugați sarea de mare, cayenne, turmeric și chimen.

Amestecați cartofii și gătiți amestecând des timp de 10 minute.

Se amestecă roșiile și se acoperă

Gatiti pana cartofii devin moale, aproximativ 11 minute.

Umplutură vegană de sandwich cu fasole Garbanzo

Ingrediente

1 cutie (19 uncii) de fasole garbanzo, scursă și clătită

1 tulpină de țelină, tocată

1/2 ceapa rosie, tocata

1 lingură maioneză vegană fără ou (Hampton Creek)

1 lingura suc de lamaie

1 linguriță iarbă de mărar uscată

Sare de mare

Piper dupa gust

Clătiți și scurgeți fasolea.

Se toarnă fasolea într-un castron și se zdrobește cu o furculiță.

Se amestecă țelina, ceapa, maioneza vegană, suc de lămâie, mărar, sare de mare și piper după gust.

Burrito cu fasole simplă și jalapeno

Ingrediente

2 (10 inchi) tortilla de făină

2 linguri ulei de masline

1 ceapa rosie mica, tocata

1/2 ardei gras verde, tocat

2 lingurite de usturoi tocat

1 cutie (15 uncii) de fasole neagră, clătită și scursă

1 lingurita ardei jalapeno tocat

3 uncii de brânză cremă fără lactate

1/2 lingurita sare de mare

2 linguri coriandru proaspăt tocat

Înfășurați tortilla într-o folie

Coaceți-le într-un cuptor preîncălzit la 350 de grade timp de 15 minute.

Încinge uleiul într-o tigaie la foc mediu.

Puneți ceapa roșie, ardeiul gras, usturoiul și jalapenos într-o tigaie.

Gatiti 2 minute amestecand din cand in cand.

Se toarnă fasolea în tigaie și se fierbe timp de 3 minute, amestecând constant.

Tăiați cremă de brânză fără lactate în cuburi și adăugați-o în tigaie cu sare.

Gatiti 2 minute in timp ce amestecati.

Adăugați coriandru în acest amestec.

Puneți aceasta uniform pe centrul fiecărei tortille încălzite și rulați tortillale.

Vegan Sloppy Joe

Ingrediente

1 lingura de ulei, sau la nevoie

1/2 ceapa rosie, tocata

1/2 ardei gras rosu, tocat

¼ cană usturoi tocat

1 cană apă

3/4 cană ketchup

3 linguri muștar brun picant

2 linguri sos de soia

2 linguri de sos vegan pentru grătar (de ex. Simple Girl Organic)

1 lingura miere

1 lingură Tabasco sau sos iute Frank

1 lingurita de cimbru

1 lingurita de piper cayenne, sau dupa gust

2 cani de linte fiarta, sau mai multe dupa gust

Încinge uleiul într-o tigaie la foc mediu.

Se caleste ceapa, ardeiul gras rosu si usturoiul pana se inmoaie timp de aproximativ 10 minute.

Adăugați apă, ketchup, muștar, sos de soia, sos grătar, miere, sos iute, cimbru și ardei cayenne la amestec.

Fierbe acest amestec.

Reduceți focul și fierbeți până când sosul se îngroașă, aproximativ 5 minute.

Adăugați fasolea în sos și fierbeți până când fasolea se încălzește.

Se prăjește Ramen și Tofu

Ingrediente

1 pachet (3,5 uncii) taitei ramen (cum ar fi Nissin(R) Top Ramen)

3 linguri ulei din seminte de susan

1 felie tofu ferm, taiat cubulete

1/2 ardei gras verde, tocat

1/4 ceapa rosie mica, tocata

1/3 cană sos de prune

1/3 cană sos dulce-acru

Se fierbe o oală cu apă ușor sărată.

Gătiți tăițeii în apă clocotită și amestecați din când în când, până când tăițeii sunt fragezi, dar încă fermi la mușcătură, 2 până la 3 minute.

Scurgeți tăițeii.

Încinge uleiul într-o tigaie la foc mare.

Pune tofu pe o parte a tigaii.

Puneți ardeiul și ceapa roșie pe cealaltă parte a cratiței.

Gatiti un tofu pana se rumeneste pe toate partile timp de 2 minute.

Gatiti si amestecati ceapa si ardeiul pana se rumenesc, 2 minute.

Amestecați tăițeii în tigaie

Combinați tăițeii, tofu, ceapa și ardeiul.

Peste tăiței se toarnă sosul de prune și sosul dulce-acru.

Se caleste pana se amesteca bine timp de 3 minute.

Burger cu quinoa și năut

Ingrediente

1 1/2 cani de quinoa fiarta

2 linguri muștar de Dijon

1 ou vegan (Brand: Follow Your Heart Egg Vegan), bătut

2 catei de usturoi, tocati

2 piper negru proaspăt măcinat

1/2 cană făină de năut (fasole garbanzo) sau după nevoie

2 lingurițe ulei de măsline, sau la nevoie

2 felii de brânză vegană (Field Roast Chao Vegan Slices)

Combinați quinoa, muștarul, oul vegan, usturoiul și piperul negru împreună într-un castron; adăugați suficientă făină de năut pentru a face 2 chifteluțe.

Încinge uleiul într-o tigaie la foc mediu

Gatiti chiftele in ulei pana se rumenesc aproximativ 4 minute pe fiecare parte.

Adăugați o felie de brânză vegană la fiecare chiflă și încălziți până când brânza se topește, aproximativ 2 minute și jumătate.

Varză curry picant

Ingrediente

3 linguri ulei de masline

2 ardei iute roșu uscat, rupt în bucăți

2 lingurite linte neagră despicată cu piele (urad dal)

1 linguriță de gram bengal (chana dal)

1 linguriță de semințe de muștar

1 crenguță frunze proaspete de curry

1 praf de pudra de asafoetida

4 ardei iute verzi, tocati

1 varză cap, tocată mărunt

1/4 cană mazăre congelată (opțional)

Sarat la gust

1/4 cană nucă de cocos rasă

Încinge uleiul într-o tigaie la foc mediu-înalt

Prăjiți ardeii roșii, lintea, gramul Bengal și semințele de muștar în ulei.

Când lintea începe să se rumenească, adăugați frunzele de curry și pudra de asafoetida și amestecați.

Adăugați ardeii iute verzi și gătiți încă un minut.

Combinați varza și mazărea în acest amestec.

Asezonați cu sare de mare.

Gatiti pana se ofileste varza, aproximativ 10 minute.

Adăugați nuca de cocos în amestec și gătiți încă 2 minute.

Tofu prăjit în sos de usturoi chili

Ingrediente

1 pachet (18 uncii) de tofu extra ferm, feliat de 1/2 inch grosime

1 lingura ulei de masline extravirgin

1 praf sare de mare

1 praf piper negru macinat

2 linguri sos de soia

2 linguri sos Sriracha iute, sau dupa gust

1 1/2 linguriță ulei de susan

1 lingurita sos chili-usturoi

1 lingurita de seminte de susan

1/2 lingurita usturoi tocat

1 ceapă, feliată subțire

Preîncălziți cuptorul la 450 de grade F.

Așezați feliile de tofu pe o tavă de copt.

Unge ulei de măsline pe fiecare felie.

Asezonați sare și piper peste tofu.

Coaceți tofu în cuptor până se rumenește ușor, aproximativ 9 minute.

Adăugați sosul de soia, Sriracha, uleiul de susan, sosul de usturoi chili, semințele de susan, usturoiul și ceapa verde

Presărați deasupra feliilor de tofu.

Prăjiți încă 4 minute.

Taitei de dovlecel in pesto

Ingrediente

1 lingura ulei de masline extravirgin

4 dovlecei mici, tăiați în fire în formă de tăiței

1/2 cană de năut scurs și clătit

3 linguri pesto,

sare si piper negru macinat dupa gust

2 linguri de brânză vegană mărunțită (prăjire de câmp, felii Chao) sau după gust

Încinge ulei de măsline într-o tigaie la foc mediu

Gatiti dovlecelul pana se inmoaie timp de aproximativ 8 minute.

Adăugați năutul și pesto-ul în dovlecei.

Reduceți căldura la mediu-scăzut.

Gătiți până când năutul este cald și dovlecelul este acoperit timp de aproximativ 5 minute

Asezonați cu sare și piper.

Transferați dovlecelul într-un bol și acoperiți cu brânză vegană.

Sandwich Vegan Reuben

Ingrediente

1 kilogram de brânză vegană (prăjire de câmp, felii Chao), mărunțită

1 cană de sos de salată de mii de insulă, sau după gust

1 borcan (16 uncii) de varză murată, scursă

12 felii de pâine neagră de secară

2 linguri ulei de masline

2 roșii, feliate

Combinați bine brânza vegană și varza murată.

Adăugați dressingul și amestecați bine.

Ungeți fiecare felie de pâine cu ulei de măsline pe o parte.

Întindeți un strat gros de amestec de brânză vegană pe partea neunsă a jumătate din fiecare pâine.

Acoperiți cu roșii și încă o felie de pâine.

Încinge o tigaie mare la mediu-mare.

Se prăjește sandvișurile pe ambele părți până se prăjește și brânza se topește.

Morcovi Caramelizati Simpli

Ingrediente

3 linguri de măsline (o marcă vegană, cum ar fi Earth Balance)

4 morcovi (tăiați în felii groase de ¼ inch

2 linguri de miere

Încinge uleiul de măsline la foc mic.

Adăugați morcovii

Se mărește căldura la mediu-mare și se adaugă mierea.

Lasă morcovii să se gătească

Se amestecă des până se înmoaie.

Fructe Jack simple prăjite

Ingrediente

Picătură de miere

Sarat la gust

2 căni de apă

ulei pentru prajit

10 bucăți de fructe de jac scurse

Amestecul de dragare

4 căni de făină universală

1/2 linguriță turmeric măcinat

1/4 lingurita praf de copt

Combinați toate ingredientele amestecului de dragare într-un castron.

Adăugați apă până când aluatul devine gros.

Încinge uleiul într-o friteuză la foc mediu.

Înmuiați fructele de jac în aluat

Gatiti in porturi mici in ulei pana se rumenesc, 2-3 minute pe fiecare parte.

Se prăjește broccoli și morcovi

Ingrediente pentru aluat

1 lingura amidon de porumb

1 1/2 catei de usturoi, zdrobiti

1 lingurita radacina de ghimbir proaspat tocata, impartita

Ingrediente

1/4 cană ulei de măsline, împărțit

1 broccoli cu cap mic, taiat buchetele

1/2 cană mazăre de zăpadă

3/4 cană morcovi tăiați juliană

1/2 cană fasole verde tăiată la jumătate

2 linguri sos de soia

2 1/2 linguri apă

1/4 cana ceapa rosie tocata

1/2 lingură sare de mare

1 lingurita radacina de ghimbir proaspat tocata

Într-un castron, combinați ingredientele pentru aluat și 2 linguri de ulei de măsline până când amidonul de porumb se dizolvă.

Combinați broccoli, mazărea de zăpadă, morcovii și fasolea verde, amestecând pentru a se acoperi ușor.

Se încălzesc restul de 2 linguri de ulei într-o tigaie la foc mediu.

Gatiti legumele timp de 2 minute

Adăugați sosul de soia și apa.

Adăugați ceapa, sarea și 1 linguriță rămasă de ghimbir.

Gatiti pana cand legumele sunt fragede, dar inca crocante.

Dovleac prajit simplu

Ingrediente

1 dovleac - curăţat, fără seminţe şi tăiat în cuburi de 1 inch

2 linguri ulei de masline

2 catei de usturoi, tocati

Sare de mare

Piper negru măcinat după gust

Preîncălziţi cuptorul la 400 de grade F.

Se amestecă dovleceii cu ulei de măsline şi usturoi într-un castron.

Asezonaţi cu sare de mare şi piper.

Puneţi dovleceii pe o foaie de copt.

Se prăjeşte la cuptor până când dovleacul este fraged timp de 28 de minute.

Dovleac prăjit picant

Ingrediente

Un dovleac de 3 kilograme decojit, fără seminţe şi tăiat cubuleţe de 1 inch

2 linguri ulei de masline extravirgin

1 1/2 linguriţă de chimen măcinat

1 lingurita patrunjel macinat

1/4 lingurita piper cayenne

Sare kosher şi piper proaspăt măcinat

Preîncălziţi cuptorul la 425°.

Într-un castron, combinaţi dovleceii cu uleiul de măsline, chimenul, coriandru şi cayenne.

Asezonaţi cu sare şi piper.

Puneţi dovleceii pe o tavă de copt

Se prăjeşte în cuptor pentru aproximativ 40 de minute sau până când se înmoaie

Dovleac simplu proaspăt prăjit cu ierburi

Ingrediente

1 dovleac mare sau 2 mici, tăiați în sferturi pe lungime, cu semințele îndepărtate

ulei de măsline, pentru stropire

2 linguri ulei de masline extravirgin

Sare de mare

Piper negru proaspăt măcinat

câteva crenguțe de cimbru proaspăt, numai frunze, plus câteva crenguțe de cimbru proaspăt, lăsat întreg

Preîncălziți cuptorul la 350 F.

Puneți dovleceii într-o tigaie cu părțile tăiate în sus.

Stropiți cu ulei de măsline.

Asezonați cu sare și piper negru proaspăt măcinat

Se presară frunzele de cimbru

Se prăjește în cuptorul preîncălzit timp de 48 de minute sau până când se înmoaie.

Dovleac copt și ardei gras verzi

1 dovleac butternut mic, taiat cubulete

2 ardei gras verzi, fara samburi si taiati cubulete

1 cartof dulce, curățat și tăiat cubulețe

3 cartofi Yukon Gold, tăiați cubulețe

1 ceapă roșie, tăiată în sferturi

1 lingura de cimbru proaspat tocat

2 linguri rozmarin proaspăt tocat

1/4 cană ulei de măsline extravirgin

2 linguri de otet balsamic

Sare de mare

Piper negru proaspăt măcinat

Preîncălziți cuptorul la 475 de grade F.

Combinați bine dovleceii, ardeii roșii, cartofii dulci și cartofii.

Separați sferturile de ceapă roșie și adăugați-le.

Combinați cimbru, rozmarin, ulei de măsline, oțet, sare și piper.

Se amestecă împreună cu legumele.

Puneti pe o tava mare.

Coaceți timp de 38 de minute la cuptor, amestecând la fiecare 10 minute, sau până când legumele încep să se rumenească.

Varza de Bruxelles simplă prăjită

Ingrediente

1/4 cană ulei de măsline extravirgin (poate avea nevoie de puțin mai mult)

3 morcovi medii, curățați și tăiați în bucăți de 1 - 1-1/2 inch

1/2 liră varză de Bruxelles mari, frunzele exterioare îndepărtate și tăiate la jumătate

1 kilogram de cartofi roșii, tăiați în jumătate sau în sferturi

1 ceapă roșie mare, tăiată în jumătate și tăiată în bucăți groase de 1 inch

1 kilogram (aproximativ 1-1/4 cană) de cartofi dulci, decojiți și tăiați în felii groase de 1 1/2 inch

3/4 lingurita oregano uscat

3/4 lingură rozmarin STRĂMIT uscat

1 lingurita de cimbru uscat

1 lingurita busuioc uscat

Piper proaspăt spart și sare de mare

Opțional: ierburi proaspete (cum ar fi cimbru sau pătrunjel) pentru ornat

Preîncălziți cuptorul la 400 de grade F.

Așezați toate legumele pregătite pe tava pregătită

Amestecați oregano, rozmarin, cimbru și busuioc.

Se condimenteaza cu sare si piper dupa gust

Adăugați uleiul de măsline și amestecați împreună cu tot amestecul de legume.

Se prăjește pe grătarul din mijloc timp de 35 până la 40 de minute, răsturnând la fiecare 20 de minute

Enchilada vegană

Ingrediente

1 lingura ulei de canola

1 1/4 cani ceapa rosie tocata (1 medie)

1 1/4 cani de ardei gras verde tocat (1 mediu)

5 catei de usturoi, tocati

1 1/2 cani de quinoa uscata

2 1/4 cani de supa de legume

1 conserve (14,5 oz) de roșii cu ardei iute verzi, nescurcate

1 conserve de 8 oz sos de roșii

2 linguri. pudra de chili

1 1/2 linguriță chimen măcinat

Sare si piper negru proaspat macinat, dupa gust

1 cutie (14,5 oz) de fasole neagră, scursă și clătită

1 cutie (14,5 oz) de fasole pinto, scursă și clătită

1 1/2 cani de porumb congelat

1 1/2 cană de brânză vegană (prăjire de câmp, felii Chao), tocată

Sare de mare

Piper negru

Topping: avocado tăiat cubulețe, roșii rom cubulețe, coriandru tocat, felii de lime, ceapă verde tocată

Încinge uleiul într-o tigaie la foc mediu.

În această tigaie unsă cu ulei, căliți ceapa și ardeiul gras timp de 3 minute.

Adăugați usturoiul și prăjiți încă 30 de secunde.

Turnați conținutul tigaii într-un aragaz lent.

Acoperiți și gătiți la foc mare timp de 3 ore

Adăugați porumbul și fasolea.

Combinați bine și acoperiți cu brânză vegană.

Acoperiți și gătiți până timp de 13 minute mai mult.

Fasole Garbanzo și dovleac fierte lent

Ingrediente

1 ceapa rosie medie tocata

5 catei de usturoi tocati

1 dovleac mic decojit și tăiat în bucăți mari

1 ardei gras verde tocat

3/4 cană linte roșie

1,15 oz cutie de fasole garbanzo, scursă și clătită

1,15 oz cutie de sos de roșii

1 lingurita de ghimbir proaspat ras

1 lingurita turmeric

1 lingurita chimen

1 lingurita boia spaniola

1/2 lingurita scortisoara

1/2 lingurita sare de mare

Piper negru

3 căni de bulion de legume

a servi:

quinoa fiartă

voinicică

nucă de cocos

iaurt

Combinați bine toate ingredientele într-un aragaz lent.

Gatiti la maxim 3 1/2 ore sau 6 1/2 ore la mic.

Pentru a o face mai groasă, scoateți capacul cu 1 oră înainte de servire.

Se ornează cu quinoa, rucola și iaurt fără lapte.

Macaroane gătite lent și brânză veganǎ

INGREDIENTE

1 ceapa rosie, tocata medie

1 ardei gras verde tocat

Cutie de 15 uncii fasole pinto clătită și scursă

Cutie de 15 uncii de fasole garbanzo clătite și scurse

28 uncii roșii zdrobite

1 ½ linguriță pudră de chili

2 lingurite chimen

½ lingurita sare

1/8 lingurita piper negru

2 cani de supa de legume

8 uncii paste macaroane cu cot din grâu integral nefierte

1 ½ cană de brânză veganǎ (pe baza de tofu)

ceapa verde tocata pentru servire

Pune toate ingredientele, cu excepția pastelor, a brânzei vegane și a ceapei verzi în aragazul tău lent.

Combinați și acoperiți.

Gatiti la foc mare timp de 4 ore sau foc mic timp de 7 ore.

Adăugați pastele și fierbeți la foc mare timp de 18 minute sau până când pastele devin al dente

Adăugați 1 cană de brânză și amestecați.

Se ornează cu brânză vegană rămasă și ceapă verde

Brânză Mozzarella Mac și Vegană

INGREDIENTE

1 ceapa galbena, tocata medie

1 ardei gras rosu, tocat

Cutie de 15 uncii fasole fava, clătită și scursă

Cutie de 15 uncii fasole marine, clătită și scursă

28 uncii roșii zdrobite

3 uncii de mozzarella vegană

1 lingura condimente italienesti

½ lingurita sare

1/8 lingurita piper negru

2 cani de supa de legume

8 uncii paste macaroane cu cot din grâu integral nefierte

1 ½ cană de brânză vegană (pe bază de tofu)

Ingrediente pentru decor:

ceapa verde tocata pentru servire

Pune toate ingredientele, cu excepția pastelor, a brânzei vegane și a ingredientelor pentru garnitură în aragazul tău lent.

Combinați și acoperiți.

Gatiti la foc mare timp de 4 ore sau foc mic timp de 7 ore.

Adăugați pastele și fierbeți la foc mare timp de 18 minute sau până când pastele devin al dente

Adăugați 1 cană de brânză și amestecați.

Stropiți cu restul de brânză vegană și ingredientele de decor

Fetuccini și fasole

INGREDIENTE

Cutie de 15 uncii de fasole

Cutie de 15 uncii fasole de nord

28 uncii roșii zdrobite

4 linguri. pesto

1 lingura condimente italienesti

½ lingurita sare

1/8 lingurita piper negru

2 cani de supa de legume

8 uncii fettuccini nefierte

1 ½ cană de brânză vegană (pe bază de tofu)

Ingrediente pentru decor:

ceapa verde tocata pentru servire

Pune toate ingredientele, cu excepția pastelor, a brânzei vegane și a ingredientelor pentru garnitură în aragazul tău lent.

Combinați și acoperiți.

Gatiti la foc mare timp de 4 ore sau foc mic timp de 7 ore.

Adăugați pastele și fierbeți la foc mare timp de 18 minute sau până când pastele devin al dente

Adăugați 1 cană de brânză și amestecați.

Stropiți cu restul de brânză vegană și ingredientele de decor

Spaghete în sos Chimichurri

INGREDIENTE

5 ardei jalapeno

1 ceapa rosie, tocata

Cutie de 15 uncii fasole pinto clătită și scursă

Cutie de 15 uncii de fasole garbanzo clătite și scurse

4 linguri. sos chimichurri

1/2 linguriță. piper roșu

½ lingurita sare

1/8 lingurita piper negru

2 cani de supa de legume

8 uncii spaghete nefierte

1 ½ cană de brânză vegană (pe bază de tofu)

Ingrediente pentru decor:

ceapa verde tocata pentru servire

Pune toate ingredientele, cu excepția pastelor, a brânzei vegane și a ingredientelor pentru garnitură în aragazul tău lent.

Combinați și acoperiți.

Gatiti la foc mare timp de 4 ore sau foc mic timp de 7 ore.

Adăugați pastele și fierbeți la foc mare timp de 18 minute sau până când pastele devin al dente

Adăugați 1 cană de brânză și amestecați.

Stropiți cu restul de brânză vegană și ingredientele de decor

Paste Penne și Măsline

INGREDIENTE

1 ceapa galbena, tocata medie

1 ardei gras rosu, tocat

Cutie de 15 uncii de fasole, clătită și scursă

Cutie de 15 uncii fasole neagră, clătită și scursă

28 uncii roșii zdrobite

1/4 cană măsline verzi

2 linguri. capere

½ lingurita sare

1/8 lingurita piper negru

2 cani de supa de legume

8 uncii de paste penne nefierte

1 ½ cană de brânză vegană (pe bază de tofu)

Ingrediente pentru decor:

ceapa verde tocata pentru servire

Pune toate ingredientele, cu excepția pastelor, a brânzei vegane și a ingredientelor pentru garnitură în aragazul tău lent.

Combinați și acoperiți.

Gatiti la foc mare timp de 4 ore sau foc mic timp de 7 ore.

Adăugați pastele și fierbeți la foc mare timp de 18 minute sau până când pastele devin al dente

Adăugați 1 cană de brânză și amestecați.

Stropiți cu restul de brânză vegană și ingredientele de decor

Paste Pappardelle și cremă de brânză vegană

INGREDIENTE

1 ceapa rosie, tocata medie

1 ardei gras verde tocat

28 uncii roșii zdrobite

4 linguri. cremă de brânză vegană

1 lingura ierburi de Provence

½ lingurita sare

1/8 lingurita piper negru

2 cani de supa de legume

8 uncii de paste pappardelle nefierte

1 ½ cană de brânză vegană (pe bază de tofu)

Ingrediente pentru decor:

ceapa verde tocata pentru servire

Pune toate ingredientele, cu excepția pastelor, a brânzei vegane și a ingredientelor pentru garnitură în aragazul tău lent.

Combinați și acoperiți.

Gatiti la foc mare timp de 4 ore sau foc mic timp de 7 ore.

Adăugați pastele și fierbeți la foc mare timp de 18 minute sau până când pastele devin al dente

Adăugați 1 cană de brânză și amestecați.

Stropiți cu restul de brânză vegană și ingredientele de decor

Paste Farfalle cu fasole şi chorizo

INGREDIENTE

1 ceapa rosie, tocata medie

1 ardei gras verde tocat

Cutie de 15 uncii de fasole

Cutie de 15 uncii fasole de nord

28 uncii roşii zdrobite

1/4 cana chorizos vegan, tocat grosier

1 lingura cimbru uscat

½ lingurita sare

1/8 lingurita piper negru

2 cani de supa de legume

8 uncii paste farfalle nefierte

1 ½ cană de brânză vegană (pe bază de tofu)

Ingrediente pentru decor:

ceapa verde tocata pentru servire

Pune toate ingredientele, cu excepția pastelor, a brânzei vegane și a ingredientelor pentru garnitură în aragazul tău lent.

Combinați și acoperiți.

Gatiti la foc mare timp de 4 ore sau foc mic timp de 7 ore.

Adăugați pastele și fierbeți la foc mare timp de 18 minute sau până când pastele devin al dente

Adăugați 1 cană de brânză și amestecați.

Stropiți cu restul de brânză vegană și ingredientele de decor

Scoici de paste cu fasole și mozzarella vegană

INGREDIENTE

1 ceapa galbena, tocata medie

1 ardei gras rosu, tocat

Cutie de 15 uncii de fasole, clătită și scursă

Cutie de 15 uncii fasole neagră, clătită și scursă

28 uncii roșii zdrobite

3 uncii de mozzarella vegană

1 lingura condimente italienesti

½ lingurita sare

1/8 lingurita piper negru

2 cani de supa de legume

8 uncii coji de paste nefierte

1 ½ cană de brânză vegană (pe bază de tofu)

Ingrediente pentru decor:

ceapa verde tocata pentru servire

Pune toate ingredientele, cu excepția pastelor, a brânzei vegane și a ingredientelor pentru garnitură în aragazul tău lent.

Combinați și acoperiți.

Gatiti la foc mare timp de 4 ore sau foc mic timp de 7 ore.

Adăugați pastele și fierbeți la foc mare timp de 18 minute sau până când pastele devin al dente

Adăugați 1 cană de brânză și amestecați.

Stropiți cu restul de brânză vegană și ingredientele de decor

Paste Farfalle cu rosii

INGREDIENTE

28 uncii roșii zdrobite

4 linguri. pesto

1 lingura condimente italienesti

½ lingurita sare

1/8 lingurita piper negru

2 cani de supa de legume

8 uncii paste farfalle nefierte

1 ½ cană de brânză vegană (pe bază de tofu)

Ingrediente pentru decor:

ceapa verde tocata pentru servire

Pune toate ingredientele, cu excepția pastelor, a brânzei vegane și a ingredientelor pentru garnitură în aragazul tău lent.

Combinați și acoperiți.

Gatiti la foc mare timp de 4 ore sau foc mic timp de 7 ore.

Adăugați pastele și fierbeți la foc mare timp de 18 minute sau până când pastele devin al dente

Adăugați 1 cană de brânză și amestecați.

Stropiți cu restul de brânză vegană și ingredientele de decor

Ingram Content Group UK Ltd.
Milton Keynes UK
UKHW020652240723
425668UK00013B/573